Upload

Upload

Chris Gladstone

Desktop Publishing by Acrux/Wordright

2018

First edition published: 2018

Gladstone, Chris

ISBN: 978-0-9803841-8-5

<http://christaleyes.com>

Dedication

In memory of my father who died in 2018, aged ninety-seven. I will be forever grateful to him for passing on his passion for nature, science and science fiction to me and my daughter. His legacy will live on in the memory of all those who knew and loved him. He touched so many people's lives with his care and compassion.

Contents

Acknowledgements

Sincere thanks to Ion Newcombe, editor of AntipodeanSF, for his invaluable advice, editing and mentorship over the last seven years.

Acknowledgements to Geralt on Pixabay for the use of the perfect illustration for my book cover.

Thanks also to my family for reading my stories and encouraging me to continue my writing endeavours. Love and gratitude to my husband for his diligent proofreading and helpful suggestions.

Part One: The Past – 2055

Chapter 1

For some reason, the opening lines of an ancient Charles Dickens novel kept running through Kiera's head: something about 'the best of times' and 'the worst of times'. If she'd known her future, she would have realised how prophetic they were.

She sat on the white plastic chair and fiddled with her rucksack; she needed something, anything, to take her mind off the waiting. She dumped her bag on the floor and stared down the right-hand corridor. Bluish light bounced off its surfaces, giving it an icy glow. Kiera shivered, wrinkled her nose and sniffed, catching the faint odour of robot lubricant. There had been no sign of life during the half-hour she had been waiting. Just as she turned away, movement caught her eye. A swisper-bot zipped around the nearest corner and zigzagged from one wall to the other while moving rapidly towards her. God, she'd never seen one travel so fast. She froze as the little cleaning robot swept past, buzzing like a swarm of angry bees and avoiding her legs by millimetres. It vanished around the next corner, and its sound faded leaving her immersed in silence.

She picked up her small rucksack again, rummaged around, and pulled out her V-pad. She started to scroll through her diary to distract herself from an urgent need to go to the toilet.

As the minutes ticked by, Kiera became mesmerised by her watch. Her impatience and edginess crept up a notch with each flick of its second hand. Just as she made the decision to leap up and dash for the toilet, the door sprang open.

The previous candidate, a dark, plump woman in her forties stalked past without a sideways glance and disappeared down the hallway, muttering. Logan Williamson's voice boomed from inside the open door. Kiera sniffed, stood up, and slipped her V-pad back inside her bag. She hoisted the bag onto her shoulder and strode through the door.

"Please sit down, Ms Proud." Logan Williamson smiled warmly as he indicated the chair in front of his desk. Kiera had seen him in numerous newsfeeds. He'd displayed the arrogance of a man who, conscious of his good looks, used them to his advantage at every opportunity. Today, in person, she had to admit, he certainly made an impression. Tall and slim, with jet black hair and eyes almost the colour of coal, he was dressed in an expensive navy suit fitted to perfection. She sat down and watched as he opened her file and displayed it on the embedded desk screen in front of him.

While waiting for Logan, Kiera filled the silence by surveying the room. Logan's desk and their chairs were sitting on a deep blue, flat pile carpet. The rest of the floor, finished in speckled polished cement, flashed with red colours reminiscent of varnished Jarrah. In the right-hand corner behind Logan was a small antique drinks cabinet, and a bookcase occupied the entire wall to her left. She came to the conclusion Logan Williamson must be even more eccentric than she'd thought. Nobody had print books these days unless they were collectors. It hadn't been mentioned in any of the information she'd seen about him. What an archaic way to read. But the worn state of the covers indicated they were well used, so they weren't just for show. She would have loved to have been near enough to see their titles. You could tell a lot about people from what they read.

A quick glance right took in a multitude of photographs of robots and androids that plastered the wall surrounding the door.

Logan Williamson smiled. Kiera shifted in her seat under his unwavering, penetrating gaze. A sudden image of herself sitting there naked flashed into her mind, forcing her to clear her throat. Where on earth had that come from? She sniffed.

"Well, Kiera. May I use your first name?" He placed his elbows on his desk, and steepled his fingers in front of him.

"Yes, absolutely." She'd answered a little too quickly. She had to stay composed.

"Your qualifications and experience are impressive. Tell me why you applied for this position, Kiera."

She pulled herself erect before replying, "I've always been interested in taking AI to the next step, and you are the world's top researcher in the field." She held his gaze, convinced he was one of these people that never blinked. She desperately wanted to work with him, in spite of the unsettling effect he had on her. "I would feel privileged to be able to work with you." Flattery would appeal. She smiled, hoping she had stroked his ego enough to secure the position.

"Are you able to work with minimum direction?" Logan leaned forward and rested his hands on the desk.

Kiera paused. What did he mean? She'd understood she'd be part of a team. She guessed and said, "Yes." God, I hope I've given him the right answer. She held her breath.

"Mmm." He refocused on the desk screen, his face remaining inscrutable. Minutes passed before he looked up.

A vision of herself hanging naked on a meat hook in some Middle Eastern market flooded into her mind. Oh, for God's sake get a grip, Kiera. Get a grip. She could feel her face becoming hot.

After staring at her for a few more seconds, Logan finally said, "Well Kiera, the position is yours."

It took several moments for it to register. This had to be one of the most bizarre interviews she'd ever been to. She couldn't believe there were to be no more questions. He was giving her the job on the spot. Her heart quivered. "That's zinging, absolutely zinging." Recovering and trying to regain some semblance of dignity, she asked, "When would you like me to start?"

"Straight and to the point; I like that. How does next week sound?" He turned off the display and leant back in his chair, fingers steepled and thumbs resting on his chest.

"It would suit me fine. Will I be working exclusively with you, or am I part of a team?" She'd have to learn to deal with his disconcerting stare, so she might as well start now. She held his gaze while waiting for his answer.

"There are three of us altogether, plus the tech team. I've just hired another brilliant recruit named Luke Masters. I'm sure the three of us are going to get along well, extremely well," Logan smiled, before adding, "Meet me here at half past eight sharp on Monday. I'll take you both for a tour of the facilities. We can sort out the paperwork afterwards, and I'll take you down to security to organise your biometric passes. A word of warning, please don't stray from your designated work areas. It's a rabbit warren in here and easy to get lost. I don't want to be spending time extricating you from other parts of the complex. There are many independent research groups working here, and they don't take too kindly to people wandering into their areas. I'll see you Monday."

Williamson sat back clasping his hands behind his head. With the discussion obviously over, Kiera stood and walked to the door. When she turned, Logan sat unmoving, with his eyes still fixed on her. "I'll see you on Monday." She stepped into the hallway and eased the door closed. Buoyed by exhilaration and relief, she turned left and headed for the exit and, the toilet. When she emerged, she waved at the Greetbot by the entrance and it obliged by opening the exit doors. The building's security had to be high because of the nature of the research carried out there. To enter the facility she'd had to buzz from the outside and be cleared by the Greetbot in reception before being allowed admittance into the main complex via another set of security doors.

Kiera stepped out into dazzling sunlight and her spirits soared. Welcoming warmth flooded into her, a dramatic contrast after the cold interior inside the complex. She hurried on past the trees and shrubs hiding the trans-terminal. Once there, she startled several onlookers by jumping up and down and dancing a little jig. She called out to the nearest person, "I've just landed my dream job."

The older man, dressed in a grey suit and carrying a briefcase, nodded in acknowledgement before boarding the autonomous, electric trans-bus that had stopped in front of him. The door closed, and the bus slid silently away. The other onlooker, an elderly woman in a floral suit, chose to ignore her completely. Kiera didn't care. Nothing could dampen her excitement and elation. She'd celebrate by travelling home in style, so she pressed the call button for a single person e-car. After she had keyed in her destination and swiped her embedded wrist credit chip, she sat down on one of the seats lining the platform and waited. The car soon arrived. She lived in the Wembley sector, only fifteen minutes away. When she'd settled in for the trip home to her apartment, she thought about Monday. And this time, her heart jigged in her chest. It couldn't come soon enough.

Chapter 2

On Monday morning Kiera arrived ten minutes early. She tapped on Logan Williamson's door, only to be greeted by silence. The two white plastic chairs were still in place, so she sat down to wait.

Kiera heard a squeaking sound. Faint at first, it grew louder as whoever, or whatever, approached. She visualised an army of mice marching towards her. Presently, a tall, slim, young man with dark red hair strode around the corner. Blue must be his favourite colour. All his clothes were various shades of it. He wore a light blue top, a light blue denim jacket, dark blue jeans and a pair of light blue, fluorescent sneakers. A blue bag, slung over one shoulder, made him look slightly lopsided. She couldn't help giggling as he strode up to her.

"Well, at least I'm not going to sneak up on anyone." He flashed her a wide, mischievous grin as he flung his bag onto the floor next to the vacant chair and sat down.

"It sounded like…" Kiera dissolved into laughter.

"Mice!" He laughed as he flicked a stray strand of hair out of his eyes with one finger.

"Are you the other team member?" Kiera said, suppressing another giggle.

"Sorry—yes. I'm Luke." He held out his hand.

Time momentarily ceased as she gazed into eyes iridescent with the colour of the Esperance Ocean on a summer's day. For a nanosecond her breath caught in her throat, and something inside her clenched. She realised she'd been staring. She recovered and extended her hand. "I'm Kiera."

He smiled and gave it a firm, but gentle shake. "Enchanted, Kiera."

"Pleased to meet you too, Luke—and the mice."

Luke laughed.

Kiera found it soft, open, and somehow endearing—the kind of laugh you didn't encounter often. She watched, amused, as he bent down and took off his shoes.

Logan Williamson materialised around the corner from the opposite direction and purposefully strode up to them. Kiera and Luke stood up simultaneously, looked at one another, and burst out laughing.

"What's the joke?" Logan Williamson asked with an expression of faint annoyance.

Luke cleared his throat. "It's just my shoes, they squeak dreadfully on this floor and it sounds like…"

"Mice. An army of mice," Kiera said, giggling.

"Mmm, I should have warned you about our floor," Williamson said, sourly. "You'll have to put your shoes back on Luke; you can't go into the lab in socks. We'll just have to put up with the noise. You will be putting on booties to go into the clean room areas, so it won't be a problem in there. Please make sure you get some non-marking soled shoes as soon as possible. Frankly, I don't find it amusing. Now follow me."

Kiera and Luke dropped in line behind Williamson as, setting a cracking pace, he navigated them through a maze of passages. Kiera wondered how she'd ever remember the route. Almost breathless, she struggled to keep up without breaking into a jog. She turned to look at Luke; he wiped his hand across his brow as if clearing sweat out of his eyes and winked. She smiled. She and Luke were going to get on just fine.

Chapter 3

After what seemed like an eternity they finally reached the AI laboratory. The sign on the door, read: Warning! Class 1 Clean Room. Full Gowns Required - Airlock Inside. Williamson opened the door and impatiently motioned for them to enter. They filed into a small anteroom.

"Jackets and bags go in here." Williamson indicated the lockers.

After stowing their things, Kiera and Luke followed him through the double doors into a small, brightly lit room. On the right were shelves holding packs of white coveralls sealed in plastic, whilst the left held a disposal chute for used garments. There was another door at the end of the room.

"I'm surprised you need a class one clean room. That's higher than hospital operating theatre standards," Kiera said, as she unwrapped a coverall and shook it out.

"It's entirely necessary Kiera." Williamson sounded irritated. "It's vital to keep contaminants out of our rapid prototype manufacturing areas."

"I didn't realise you manufactured on-site," Kiera said, feeling stupid.

"Our prototypes are manufactured by robots on-site in sealed areas, but our R&D laboratories have to be sterile. Otherwise we wouldn't know if any glitches in the machines are internal or from dust contamination."

"You won't be involved with the research there; it's managed by my tech team. I'll introduce you at morning tea. They mostly keep to themselves, but you should at least know what they look like."

Sounds like one big happy family, Kiera thought as she stepped into the coverall and glanced at Luke.

He looked up. "I enjoy dressing up, but white isn't exactly my colour."

"White isn't my colour either," Kiera said, as she zipped up. "I like the hood and the booties, though."

"They suit you." Luke pulled on his gloves.

"You look like a white rabbit, or maybe a white mouse." Kiera threw him an impish smile.

"Don't," he leaned over and whispered, "You'll start me laughing again, and we can't have that, can we?"

Williamson, already suited up, stood by the door scowling. "Go through the door, step on to the turntable, and when it's finished go through into the airlock."

After being blasted by sterile air in turn, they stood in silence in the airlock until the pressure equalised. The door slid open, and a gust of icy air flowed over them. Kiera shivered as they stepped into a cold, sterile world of gleaming, stainless steel benches and white walls. Imprisoned workers floated around like white ghosts. Nearby, in stark contrast, a tall, beautiful, Asian woman, dressed in a long, flowing, blood red robe, stood immobile. As they approached, the woman turned her head towards them. She targeted Luke by smiling seductively. She held out her hand and greeted him in a foreign language.

Luke reached out and took her hand. "Charmed, I'm sure."

A nearby worker whirled, and his expression turned to horror when he spotted Luke letting go of her hand. He hurried over. "Oh God, I'm so sorry." He anxiously focused alternately from Williamson to Luke. "I didn't see you come in. I'm in the middle of checking the pheromone program. It's administering too strong a dose, and I'm afraid your gloves don't offer any protection." The flustered man reached into his pocket and pulled out a packet of what appeared to be chewing gum. He took out a piece. "You're going to need this. You need to chew it for several minutes, and you need to begin right now."

Luke stared at the proffered gum.

Kiera watched, mesmerised, as Luke's eyes glazed, and an imbecilic smile slid across his face.

"That's all right," he said, dreamily, his gaze fixed on the Asian woman's face.

"No, it's not all right Luke." Williamson snatched the gum and tore off the wrapper. "You need to chew it now." He shoved it directly into Luke's mouth. As Luke chewed placidly, his smile vanished, replaced with a look of zombie-like idiocy.

Kiera observed a noticeable bulge appearing in his coveralls. She turned away and put her hand over her mouth, trying unsuccessfully to stifle laughter.

Williamson, looking thunderous, turned to Kiera. "We are testing a new type of artificial pheromone. It's delivered via touch. The gum contains an antidote. This new prototype is one of our more…umm…exotic models."

"I gathered that, so are they purely for sex? I…I wouldn't have thought you were into that sort of thing. Aren't they illegal?"

"They are extremely popular. The simple fact of life is, Kiera, if I don't make them you can be sure someone else will."

God, just what was she getting into here? This guy was turning out to be a total sleaze.

"Don't worry, Kiera. You won't be involved in anything to do with this particular line."

"So because I'm not involved, I'm just supposed to ignore it am I?" Kiera frowned.

"As I said, sex androids are already being made, but ours are far more sophisticated. We cater for the upper end of the market. They fulfil a need. I'm sure you would agree that it's better than real women having to work as prostitutes. It's certainly healthier. I'm sorry if I've shocked you." He turned to Luke. "Have you recovered now?"

Luke's face took on a sheepish expression, but his eyes were alert and he had lost the stupid grin. He glanced at Kiera. "I'm fine, but it was a bit of an experience. Whatever you are using—it's super strong, I mean I felt like…umm…perhaps I'd better not go into details." He brushed a strand of red hair out of his eyes and concentrated on the floor as his face flushed bright red.

"All right," Williamson said, "Let's move on."

"Do you make other androids here as well as prototypes?" Kiera asked, changing the subject completely, aware he had evaded answering her question.

"Only prototypes, we buy in the basic chassis for the majority of our work unless we're doing a complete redesign. Once we have perfected the entire unit, assembly is contracted out to companies like Androids-R-Us and Classicbots."

"I thought you had your own company." Kiera raised her eyebrows.

"Sentioids Inc. is ours, but we supply prototype models to the other two companies as well. The market is highly competitive, and it is imperative that we maintain our leading edge. Our androids are top of the range and our standards are high. I work my people hard, but I'm sure you are aware the salary reflects that. Fooling around and time wasting will not be tolerated. Excuse me one moment."

With the lecture finished, he strode over to the flustered worker still hovering around the Asian android. "I will deal with you later, Carlson," he hissed, before marching off.

Luke raised his eyebrows, but Kiera ignored him. She turned and hastened to catch Williamson, who was now standing by the air-lock motioning impatiently.

They finished the tour by going into VR in a dedicated presentation lounge. It reminded Kiera of the VR tour into the innards of the Large Hadron Collider Mark Four that she'd seen during her course at UWA.

She and Luke virtualed through 3-D printers and arrays of robots performing tasks at impossible speeds. The presentation included a VR journey into the sealed plants housing nano-bots manufacturing Quantum chips.

The tour complete, Luke and Kiera were ushered into Williamson's office where they were presented with their contracts and confidentiality agreements. Kiera sat and read hers before signing.

Luke gave the documents a cursory glance before scrawling a flamboyant signature at the bottom of each.

Once Kiera had finished signing hers, Williamson escorted them to security for their iris scans and voice code templates. After the formalities were taken care of, he showed them to their offices. Thankfully, they were some distance down the passage from Williamson's and next door to one another.

"Here are the electronic keys." He handed them to Luke. "They're only temporary; your security passes will be ready in a few days. You will need to swipe them over the entry pad and say your name to open your door. The same goes for the building's entrance, except once you're inside you'll need to do an iris scan to be admitted to the building proper. The keys must be returned to the Greetbot, it retains them in case of an emergency." Williamson stepped back. "I'll leave you to settle in. I think you'll find that your needs have been adequately provided for, but if there's anything else you require please let me know. I'll be back in half an hour to take you to morning tea."

"See you in half an hour," Luke said.

Once Williamson had disappeared into his office, Luke, dangled a key from each hand. "Which hand would you like Kiera?"

She stared into his blue eyes. "Tell me, what did it feel like?"

Luke's face flushed. He focused on the floor and mumbled, "I'd rather not talk about it if you don't mind."

"Okay, I'll take the left one." She could see she'd made him uncomfortable.

As an expression of relief tracked across his face, he sighed and handed her the key. "Let's see what we've got to play with." He inspected the tag, stepped over to the appropriate door, and pressed the button on the remote key. With a faint click the door unlocked. Luke turned the handle and pushed it open. His expression transformed into awe. "Great Universe! I'm impressed."

Kiera peered inside. "My God, this is absolutely zinging! I never expected anything as sophisticated as this. It's state-of-the-art." She stood transfixed. She imagined someone as high profile as Williamson would never tolerate substandard equipment; he probably updated it every other month.

Luke, like her, stood gaping at the array of technology spread out in front of him. The desk held an embedded touch screen. As Luke ventured in, a gallery of motion sensing screens, located on the wall opposite the desk, illuminated. He dumped his bag onto the luxurious beige carpet and gazed around.

Kiera smiled to herself as she watched him. He radiated wild enthusiasm like a child let loose in a toyshop just before Christmas. She found it intoxicating.

"Great Universe!" Luke sat down and began swinging the chair from side to side with his legs. "It's like—" he hesitated, groping for words, "It's like everything I've ever wanted." He jumped up. "Let's have a look at your room, Kiera." In his rush he almost bumped into her as she turned to go out the door.

Kiera's office appeared identical to Luke's, apart from her chair. It glowed a bright cherry red. "I didn't have anything nearly as flash as this at any of my previous jobs," Kiera said, enjoying the sensation of running her hands over the plush velvet chair.

"I didn't either." Luke slipped out her door adding, "The red chair suits you."

"Your chair matches your shirt," Kiera called after him.

"So it does," Luke called back before she heard him shut his door.

Half an hour later, they were seated at an oval, stainless steel table in the tea room along with Williamson and several other staff members. Superficially, the tech staff seemed friendly enough. But Kiera noticed they all had a kind of reserved defensiveness about them.

She regarded the bare white walls and suppressed a shiver. Everywhere, apart from her room, felt cold, and the place had a colourless, clinical atmosphere. Even in here, no effort had been made to make the place friendly. Perhaps that was the idea so people wouldn't linger too long. Maybe it reflected Williamson's attitude; the staff appeared to be frightened of him for some reason. Well, he's not going to frighten me.

Luke, draped comfortably in a chair, appeared to be engaged in an intense discussion with a blonde thirty-something who had chosen to sit next to him before Kiera had had the chance.

Williamson, seated immediately opposite, looked up from his coffee. He fixed his dark, mysterious stare on her, and to her surprise reached across and placed his hand over hers.

"I hope you'll be happy here. If there's anything you need please don't hesitate to ask."

His hand lingered, so Kiera extracted hers and placed it on her lap. She glanced at Luke. He gave her a quizzical look before he turned back to the blonde, who was clearly engaged in a monologue. Kiera picked up her cup and gulped down the remains of her tea. She excused herself, stood up and bolted.

Chapter 4

"Sorry Melanie, I've got to go. Nice to meet you." Luke ignored the disappointed look and hurried out of the tea room. He jogged to catch up with Kiera. They walked side by side back towards their offices. The tea room, handily located, lay around the corner and a little way down another long hallway. Because it was staffed by androids, they could eat or drink at any hour of the day or night.

"Was Williamson coming on to you?" Luke became aware of his clenched fists. A familiar feeling began to rise from the pit of his stomach. He wouldn't, no, he couldn't just ignore it. He couldn't let it happen again.

"I'm not sure." Kiera screwed up her face. "But I'll let it go for now. If it happens again, I'll deal with it."

He reached out and put his hand on her shoulder. "Is that wise? I mean shouldn't you…"

Kiera cut in before he could finish. "It could have been innocent. I'm prepared to give him the benefit of the doubt, for the time being." They came to a halt and Kiera stepped back, out of his reach.

Luke let his hand fall, uncertain of what to do next.

Kiera glared at him. "Look, I'm quite capable of dealing with it. You don't need to wade in for me, Luke. I can look after myself, and I don't want to get you into trouble."

"I can handle it." Luke flipped a strand of hair out of his eyes. "I just wanted you to know that you have backup. Okay?" And he added silently, sometimes you need other people to take a stand. His heart thumped in his ears, and his chest had tightened making it difficult to breathe. They walked on in silence until they came to a standstill outside her door.

"I just wanted..." Luke tried again.

"I will deal with it if, and when I need to," Kiera's voice rose. "I don't need you to be a bloody White Knight." She took out her key and opened her door. Once inside, she slammed it hard, leaving him standing alone in the hallway. Shocked, he just stood there trying to collect his thoughts. With a mental effort, he unclenched his fists and took a series of deep breaths, the way he'd been taught. After several minutes his breathing became relatively normal. He went over to his door.

What had made Kiera so angry? He unlocked his door and stepped inside. Well, I'm off to a great start on all counts. I've made a bad impression on the boss, almost abandoned myself to an android in front of everyone, and now I appear to have trodden on Kiera's toes. Zark! Oh well, let's see if I can stuff up my toys for good measure.

Late in the afternoon he heard Kiera's door close. Zark! He had wanted to catch her before she went home. He'd worked well past knockoff time. He'd gone into a time-warp and lost himself in programs and manuals. Oh well, it was his first day in a new job after all.

He'd try and make good with Kiera tomorrow, he promised himself, as he closed down and logged off. He stood up and stretched stiffness out of his arms and legs. Too much time spent poring over screens. He needed to take better care of himself—to take more breaks.

#

The next morning, when he came around the corner, Luke spotted Kiera turning away from his door. She must have decided to come in early as well. He waved and quickened his pace. To his relief, she waved back and smiled.

"Hi Kiera." He flashed her a smile. "I was hoping to catch you before you started work. I'm sorry if I upset you yesterday." I hope I look suitably remorseful. He held his breath momentarily.

"That's okay." Kiera's expression became apologetic. "I overreacted. Sometimes anger just gets the better of me, but I wasn't angry at *you*."

"That's a relief. I was beginning to think I'd pissed off everybody on my first day."

"It would take more than that to piss me off." She touched his arm.

"I'll see you at teatime, then?" Luke opened his door.

"Are you sure you wouldn't prefer to talk with the blonde?"

"Melanie? Great Universe! Please spare me from that again." He held his hands up to his chest, feigned distress and pretended to pray.

"See you later," Kiera said, laughing.

Chapter 5

Three weeks later, Luke and Kiera were sitting together in the tea room.

Oh God, Melanie was ogling Luke again, in spite of the fact he had ignored her since that first day. Mind you, she enjoyed watching him too. Kiera focused back on Luke. He was hoeing into a sugared doughnut.

"You look like you're really enjoying that."

"Doughnuts are one of my weaknesses." Luke wiped the sugar from around his mouth. "They're really good, why don't you have one?

Kiera smiled to herself. "I never eat between meals."

"Is that discipline, or don't you get hungry?" Luke loaded three teaspoons of sugar into his coffee.

"Discipline, otherwise I'd be the size of a house." She giggled.

"I'm not coming to your place, I'd probably starve to death." Luke stirred his coffee vigorously, managing to slop it onto the table.

Kiera grabbed a serviette and began mopping up the spill. "Who says I'm going to invite you?" Their daily tea room banter had become an established ritual between the two of them. She enjoyed it immensely and looked forward to it.

"I'm working on it, but maybe I'll BYO my own food." He pushed his chair out and stood up.

She watched, as he helped himself to another doughnut. She caught his eye and shook her head, but Luke simply shrugged. He scanned the doughnut's barcode, tagged his wrist chip and started back to her. But before he could sit down again, Williamson slid into Luke's seat and pushed his cup aside.

Kiera bristled as Williamson leaned over.

"Kiera, I'm glad I caught you. I want you to come to my office after you've finished your tea. There's something I need to discuss with you."

As she moved her chair away from him, Luke sat down on the other side of Williamson. Judging by the angry expression on his face, she knew he'd overheard what Williamson had said. Oh God, I hope he's not going to create a scene.

"I've just organised a discussion with Kiera, after tea," Luke said, as he brushed hair out of his eyes and fixed Williamson with a solemn look.

"No, you haven't. Your discussion can wait, Luke. I need to talk to Kiera, now." Williamson's tone dripped with malice.

Williamson had his back to her, so Kiera gave Luke a warning shake of her head and said, "It's okay, Luke. We can talk later."

Luke stuffed the remains of the doughnut into his mouth, guzzled down the rest of his coffee and stood up so abruptly his chair nearly toppled. Without a word he stalked off.

"How rude," Williamson commented.

Kiera gulped the rest of her tea and got up.

Williamson jumped to his feet and rushed to usher her to the door. She tensed when he placed his hand on her back to guide her through.

When they reached his office, he held the door open for her and indicated the chair in front of his desk. "Please, sit down, Kiera."

"I prefer to stand, thank you."

Williamson sat down and locked eyes with her.

She stepped forward and placed both hands on his desk. "Please don't treat me like a child." A flicker of fury flashed across Williamson's face—one blink and she'd have missed it. A nanosecond later, his face transformed into a mask of contrition. "I think we should treat one another with mutual respect. I found it humiliating to be ordered around in front of other staff, and there was no need to be rude to Luke. She deliberately put her hands on her hips.

Williamson's mouth opened, but Kiera put her hands up to head him off. "Please let me finish. I think it's in both our interests to keep our relationship professional." She paused, and dropped her hands. "Otherwise, I'll be forced to resign." She became aware of her own heavy breathing, and she could feel herself trembling.

Williamson stood up and opened his arms wide. With a shocked look, he said, "Kiera, Kiera. I can assure you I have nothing but respect for you. I'm sorry if you thought otherwise. I was just trying to create a friendly atmosphere. You are a brilliant young lady and a joy to work with." His face radiated contriteness. "Please accept my sincere apologies." He placed his hands, palms together, in the centre of his chest and gave a slight bow. "Please, let's sit down and chat about your future."

Kiera sucked in a deep breath. Why did she get the feeling this was all a ruse? Calm down, Kiera. Calm down. With effort, she managed to slow her breathing.

"All right, I accept your apology, but please, don't touch me again."

"You have my word. Now, can we get down to business? I have something important to discuss with you. Please," he said, indicating the chair again.

Kiera sat. She clasped her hands and attempted to look composed. Her breathing had almost returned to normal.

"I've had a chance to observe your work and I'm impressed. I'd like to offer you your own project. I feel you would do a superior job to Luke." Williamson held up his hands with his palms out. "Now, because I don't want any feeling of competition or jealousy to arise between you two, our discussion has to remain secret. We wouldn't want Luke to know your work is of a higher standard than his, would we?" He put his hands on the desk and surveyed her with gleaming eyes.

Kiera worked hard to remain stony-faced. Inside, her mind whirled like a dust storm on Mars, as she wondered what he was going to say next. She waited in silence.

"So, what I'm going to share with you now remains our secret. I need your assurance you won't discuss it with anyone."

"Absolutely," Kiera said, holding her face in a mask of seriousness.

"My current focus, Kiera, centres on developing a program to enable the uploading of the human consciousness into a computer. The ultimate goal, of course, is to upload consciousness into an android."

Kiera sat stunned. It was so unexpected, revolutionary and exciting. Oh my God, and he was going to ask her to be involved? "Wow, I had no idea."

Williamson smiled. "Now you know my secret, your discretion is of the upmost importance."

"I understand."

"Good." He leant back in his chair. "My engineers and tech people are well advanced with the design of a specialised machine to carry out the physical task. Basically, it incorporates a designed-for-purpose computer along with the physical apparatus necessary."

"So, how would I be involved?" She only barely managed to contain herself. Any minute now, she'd float to the ceiling and bob around like a helium balloon.

"We are having some difficulty with the algorithms, and I think involving you in the project would perhaps give us some fresh insight and new ideas." He paused. "So, Kiera, are you interested?"

Interested? Good God. He was talking about accomplishing the Holy Grail. She was just about bouncing to the moon and back. She cleared her throat. "Yes, I would consider it a privilege."

"Excellent! This particular project is only the beginning. The next step, in the not too distant future, will be to upload the human consciousness into human clones."

Clones, Kiera thought, human clones, but... "What's the reason for the development of your program?" she asked Williamson.

"There are still many people, Kiera, for whom stem cell therapy is, for many reasons, of little or no benefit. For these particular people, being uploaded into an android is far preferable to being little more than a vegetable or being locked in a non-functional body—or being in continual pain. Believe me, I already have people who have volunteered to undergo the process."

He locked his eyes onto hers, and she shifted uncomfortably in her seat. "Okay, I understand that, but I thought human cloning had been banned years ago." She stared straight back at him.

He gave her an irritated look and sighed. "Things have moved on since then, Kiera. I'll send some recent papers across to you to bring you up-to-date. Uploading to a human clone is only theory today, but you know what they say—today's theory is tomorrow's future."

When they'd finished their discussion, Kiera left his office filled with excitement and elation. She didn't want it ruined by a confrontation with Luke. He could wait until tomorrow. She knew he'd grill her about her conversation with Williamson. It was liable to cause trouble and it could be a bit curly. She'd think about it overnight, get it straight in her own head, and invent something plausible. Could she get away with telling him she'd been told to keep the project secret and couldn't discuss it? Unlikely—even though she'd only known Luke three weeks, she knew him well enough to know he wouldn't buy it. He would start needling her. She sighed. It would be just another thing she'd have to learn to deal with.

Chapter 6

Luke received a memo from Williamson just before he left work, requesting him to come in early the next morning for a meeting. *What's it about, I wonder? I hope it doesn't have anything to do with the thing in the tea room.*

He'd become so involved in his work he'd forgotten Kiera and he were supposed to talk. She'd probably realised their meeting had been a ruse, but he'd been a bit surprised when she hadn't poked her head in after she had seen Williamson. He'd overplayed the tea room scene. Maybe she was angry and was punishing him.

Parts of Kiera were still a complete enigma. She could be so prickly. He knew he'd have to rein in this protective thing. She was fiercely independent. It was one of the things he really liked about her. He envied her strength. He sighed, at least he'd figured out one of the things that set her off. But most of the time it was like being in a partially programmed robot. He needed more information for things to fall into place, to make sense. Part of him longed to get close enough to her to find out what went on inside her head.

In some ways, he was like Kiera. He had secret parts he never showed, parts he kept locked away deep inside of him. He longed to be more open, more trusting. But fear always tightened around his mind like a nano-net, and the more he struggled the tighter it held him. Sometimes he couldn't breathe.

Memories of Jenna would bubble up into his consciousness, usually just when he thought he'd finally put it to rest. It had spoiled work relationships and some of his personal ones. He'd get angry, and his paranoid protective instinct would kick in, causing a problem.

Stupid, stupid, stupid, he told himself. He couldn't bring his sister back. She'd died five years ago. He should be well and truly over it, but for some reason, he just couldn't seem to move on—to let go.

He sighed, and as he slowly packed up, a sudden disappointment flooded over him. Why hadn't Kiera come to talk to him? He stood immobilised, ambushed by the realisation that he was beginning to like her, *really* like her. They were well matched and had so many things in common. They both loved science-fiction, Indian food and the same style of music. Although neither of them practised a religion, they both classified themselves as spiritual. Oh well, he'd just have to see how things turned out.

Luke trudged down the hallway, weighed down by a lead cloak of sadness. He missed Jenna so much. They had been really close. They had always told one another everything, so why didn't she tell him about the one thing that had mattered the most? It was a question he'd asked himself hundreds of times but still didn't know the answer. He ached for the companionship and the warmth their friendship had brought. Filled with empty loneliness, he walked out through the exit into the cold twilight.

#

Luke approached Williamson's office, his stomach churning. He hadn't slept much. The little sleep he'd managed had been disturbed by graphic nightmares about Jenna. One bloody image had seared itself into his brain. Jenna, with her arms outstretched had stood pleading with him while rivulets of blood streamed from her hands. In the next instant, she had morphed into Kiera. He'd stood paralysed while she'd bled to death and crumpled to the floor in a bloodied heap. The image had lasered itself into his brain and kept rewinding and repeating in an endless loop.

Luke shook his head, took a deep breath, and knocked on Williamson's door.

"Enter," boomed Williamson from inside. "Good morning Luke, right on time I see. Always makes a good impression. Please sit down." He indicated the chair.

Luke placed his bag on the floor and sat. He brushed a strand of hair out of his eyes and met Williamson's gaze. "What's this about?"

"It's about a little project I want you to be involved in. I've had a chance to see your work in progress. I'm impressed. You seem to have a far better grasp of the various concepts compared to Kiera. I'm going to involve you in some research, along with myself, in a brand-new project. Because I don't want any feelings of jealousy or competition to arise between the two of you, you will need to keep this secret. I don't want you to talk to anyone about it, let alone Kiera. Can you manage that, Luke?"

"I...guess so." Great Universe, this guy was bizarre, one minute curt and snarly and the next pouring on the charm. He needn't have worried about the tea room thing. Williamson appeared to have forgotten all about it, and now he was offering him his own project. A cursor began flashing at the back of his brain. Something didn't add up. He didn't trust the guy. He was up to something, but what? With an effort, Luke pulled his face into a nonchalant expression. "What's the project about?"

"Basically, I've been working on algorithms for a program to upload the human consciousness. Initially, the upload will be into a computer, but subsequently, when the glitches have been ironed out, into an android and ultimately into a human clone." He fixed Luke with a steady stare.

Luke, all ears now, couldn't believe what he was hearing. "I thought that particular line of work had been banned ten years ago."

"A lot can happen in ten years, Luke. Things have moved on, and there's been some success with mice."

"How on earth could you ever prove the accurate uploading of consciousness from one mouse to another?" Luke said, wide-eyed.

"Quite simply; you teach one mouse to navigate a complicated maze. That mouse's consciousness is uploaded into an untrained mouse who is placed in the same maze. It's been shown that the untrained mouse can navigate the maze on the first try and with greater speed than the original mouse. The experimental results have been duplicated by many researchers now. I'll send a couple of the papers to you, so you can verify the results for yourself."

"I'm impressed. I had no idea things had progressed so far. Are there any serious side-effects?"

"Initially yes, but they've been all ironed out." He leant back in his chair and put both hands behind his head. "So, are you interested?"

"I am interested," he frowned, "but what about the ethics of testing this on humans?"

"Many people have volunteered for the process. They are of sound mind and have signed all the relevant papers. These are people trapped in paralysed bodies and unable to be helped by stem cell technology. I'm just hoping it doesn't take too long, otherwise some will die, and we'll just have to go through the selection process all over again. That would be most inconvenient."

Luke held his face in a solemn expression, but his thoughts raged. Unbelievable! Inconvenient for Zark's sake, these were people, not bloody mice.

"We will be doing them all a huge favour," continued Williamson. "So, do you want the project or not?"

"Will Kiera be involved in this?" Something wasn't right here.

"I thought I'd already explained to you." He gave Luke an exasperated look. "To put it bluntly, she simply isn't bright enough to be involved."

What a blatant lie. He thought Kiera far brighter than himself. They had had some interesting discussions about their work. Some of her approaches were unique and quite different from his. They would make a brilliant team. "I don't agree with you and I think we would make more progress if we worked together as a team."

"She is not to be involved. Is that quite clear?"

Luke stared back at him in silence. All pleasantness had vanished from Williamson's face.

"Now, answer my question. Do you want the project or not?"

Luke thought quickly. Whatever Williamson's game, he should play. He would talk to Kiera later about it, despite Williamson's warning. Nobody shut him down like that and got away with it.

"Okay, I do want the project, but I'm not happy with the secrecy aspect."

"Duly noted. I'll send all of the appropriate files to you later today, and they are for your eyes only. Is that clear?" His eyes narrowed.

"Yes."

"All right, off you go." He made a shooing motion with his hands for Luke to leave. Luke did.

He returned to his office. He sat down, almost overwhelmed by the sound of his heart thundering in his ears. He needed to think. How could he approach Kiera with this? His stomach churned and he broke out into a sweat as he realised his feelings extended beyond just like. They were beginning to crystallise into something far more serious. She's become important to me. How could that have happened in such a short time? Prickly or not, he loved her bubbly nature, her intellect and her positive outlook on life. She could be my last chance. He had a dismal track record for the few relationships he'd had in the past. He'd put his life on hold when his parents had died to look after Jenna. When she'd died, he'd retreated into a cocoon of guilt. He couldn't afford to lose Kiera.

He wouldn't, no matter what. He'd even quit this job if it stood between them. Great Universe! Perhaps he shouldn't tell her about his conversation with Williamson. What if he told her and she reacted unpredictably? She might become jealous or resentful. It could mean the end of any possibility of a relationship between them. Could he afford to take the risk? Why did things have to be so Zarking difficult?

He stared at the screens on the opposite wall, as a battle of indecision raged inside him. The sound of Kiera's door jerked him back into awareness. He took a deep breath. He'd made up his mind.

He went out his door, walked over to Kiera's and gave a light tap.

"Come in," she said, in a friendly tone.

He opened her door and leant on the door frame. "Hi Kiera. I need to talk to you. Is now okay?" He struggled to hear himself over his juddering heart.

Kiera's face softened. "Sure." She paused, before asking, "Are you okay? You look really pale, and…" she trailed off and sat studying him.

"I hardly got any sleep last night." He planted himself in the chair opposite her. "I've got something important to tell you...and it's difficult." His speech faltered, and he concentrated on his clenched hands.

"Luke, what's wrong?" Her expression had transformed into concern.

He took a deep breath. "It's...complicated, so Zarking complicated."

"Is it something to do with me, or work, or Williamson?"

"All of it." Luke fought to stay in control and tried to blink away his tears.

Kiera sprang from her chair and rushed over to him. She crouched down and took both of his hands in hers. "It's okay. Just take your time, Luke."

He gripped her hands, as tears began streaming down his face.

"Oh Kiera, Kiera...I'm so lonely. I don't want to lose you. I'm afraid what I'm going to tell you..." As the words stalled in his throat, he pulled his hand from hers, and wiped his face with his sleeve. "I'm afraid it will rip us apart forever."

"I'm sure nothing you tell me would do that, Luke." Kiera stood up, grabbed a tissue from the box on her desk, and patted his face. "Why are you lonely? Don't you have a sister?"

"She committed suicide five years ago." He began to sob. The domino wall he'd so carefully constructed broke in an avalanche of tears.

"Oh God...Luke, I'm so sorry." Kiera put her arm around him and began stroking his head.

Minutes passed before he could stop crying.

Kiera sat back down on the floor in front of him. "What happened Luke?"

"She'd been sexually abused at work for six months—six months, Kiera, and she didn't tell me. I noticed the change in her, her withdrawal and the dull look in her eyes. I asked her so many times what was wrong, but she said it was nothing. I only found out what had happened after she'd died. She'd been raped, Kiera, and the day she killed herself, she'd found out she was pregnant."

"Oh God."

He could see the horror in Kiera's eyes and on her face. "I'd gone to the gym. When I came home and found all the lights on I should have realised something was wrong. I should have checked on her." He reached across, grabbed another tissue, and dabbed at his face.

Kiera stood up. She went around the other side of the desk and trundled her chair around to him and sat down. "Would it have made any difference?"

"No, her watch stopped at 8:27 p.m.—I didn't get home until 10:30." He met her eyes.

Kiera frowned. "Why did her watch stop, Luke?"

"It wasn't waterproof—she got it wet—in the bath. She lay dead in the freezing bathwater all night; all night, Kiera, while I was asleep."

Luke saw Kiera's expression change, saw her brace herself.

"How did she die? Pills or…?"

Before he could stop himself, he blurted it out. "She cut her wrists with a kitchen knife. She was lying there under the bloodied water and…and there were all these obscene pink tinged bubbles floating around. Zarking bloody pink bubbles, Kiera. Even her hair was tinged pink."

Kiera put her hand to her mouth. "Oh Luke."

She wrapped her arms around him and squeezed him tight. He could feel her trembling.

"What did you do?"

He ran his hand through his hair. "I managed to drag her out. I laid her on the bath mat and covered her with a towel then I sort of went numb. I sat there for a while, plucking strands of her hair off her face. When I finally decided to ring the police, I found her suicide note propped up against the salt and pepper shakers on our table. I've read it every night since. It said, *'Dearest Luke, you're the best brother anyone could ever have. You cared for me so well after Mum and Dad died. I will love you forever. I'm so sorry to leave you like this, but the pain has become too much. I've been such a burden to you, Luke—now you and I are free. Live and love to the max bro. May the universe guard, guide and protect you, wherever you are. Kiss kiss kiss Jenna.'"*

Kiera's eyes were brimming with tears. "You must have been devastated."

"We were supposed to stick together. We made a pact after Mum and Dad died to always be there for one another. I let her down, Kiera. I let her down."

"From the note Jenna left you Luke, she didn't think you had let her down."

"Then why did she leave me, Kiera? Why did she abandon me?" The words almost choked in his throat.

He could see Kiera struggling to find the right words, finally she said, "She was ill, Luke. Her thought processes were all Zarked up—she didn't abandon you."

"Now I'm terrified, Keira, terrified that every time I get close to someone something's going to happen to them." Kiera's eyes flooded with sympathy, warmth and...? Was it love he could see in them?

Kiera frowned and asked, "What happened to the person who had assaulted her?"

"Other staff at her workplace blew the whistle on a senior partner in the firm. He was brought to trial, and they proved he was the

36

father from DNA evidence obtained from the foetus. He got five years. I wanted to kill him." His stomach had gone tight and he had curled his fists into balls.

"Were you able to grieve?"

"This is the first time I've been able to cry. I still feel I could have done so much better. The guilt is always gnawing away at my insides, Kiera. Jenna's dead face haunts me, I can't let it go."

"It's been five years, Luke. You did the best you could for Jenna. Judging by her note, she thought you'd done an incredible job caring for her. She would have wanted you to move on and to be happy." She cocked her head to one side and stared into his eyes. "But that wasn't what you came to tell me was it?"

"No, I came to tell you about my meeting with Williamson." He told her what had transpired in Williamson's office. To his surprise, anger flashed over her face. He fished a handkerchief out of his pocket, dried his face and blew his nose.

Kiera got up, wheeled her chair back to the other side of the desk and sat down. "I feel like telling him just where to shove his job. God! I've been so stupid. He pulled the exact same thing with me, and," she paused, her face holding a mixture of guilt and contrition, "I fell for it." She picked up a pencil and began to doodle.

"I think we've got a few choices," Luke said. "For a start he doesn't know we're on to him. We could play his game. We could each work on a different section of the program and collaborate. We both have different approaches, so I think that could work. What's your feeling?"

"Yes, we could do that, or we could both resign." She pressed so hard the pencil point broke.

"Do you really want to resign, Kiera?"

"No." She threw her pencil down and met his eyes. "Does that sound awful?"

"No. I don't want to resign either. This has to be one of the most revolutionary projects ever contemplated. It's too Zarking important to walk away from. The implications are almost incomprehensible. We're talking about humans becoming machines. Remember that slogan that used to be bandied around way back in the twenties?"

"*Live long enough to live forever.* That was Ray Kurzweil; the Singularity guy wasn't it?" Kiera said, looking thoughtful. "God it's hard to believe that was way before we were born. Didn't he predict uploading of the human consciousness by twenty fifty?"

"Yes, and if what Williamson told us is true, he was only five years out. Pity he didn't live long enough to see it. Anyway, let's get back to the subject in hand, shall we?" Kiera watched him intently as he flicked a strand of hair out of his eyes.

"What?" he said, suddenly feeling uncomfortable.

"I'm just glad to see you back to your normal self and pulling me back in line." Her smile widened.

"Okay, so where are we? Are we going with staying and playing him at his own game? Williamson is no fool. His work borders on genius, but for some reason he obviously needs other people. Maybe he gets bogged down and needs a new point of view, fresh blood as it were," Luke said.

"He certainly fits the vampire image. God, I hate that smile of his and his stare." She shivered involuntarily. "It's almost like he can see into your soul." She picked up her pencil again and sharpened it furiously. She began to add bits to her original doodle and shaded in little areas as she spoke. "I think he's scary stuff, capable of almost anything. So we need to be exceptionally careful."

"I agree, but I think we can pull it off. We can progress things so much faster if we work together. What I don't understand is that he originally said we would be working as a team. So, what's changed his mind, I wonder?"

"I can't help feeling it's got something to do with me." Kiera screwed up her drawing and flung it into the bin.

"Okay. Now we're agreed, we'd better get on with it." Luke stood up. When he reached the door, he turned back to face her. "I'm sorry I loaded all that stuff about Jenna on to you. It all just sort of slipped out."

Kiera tilted her head to one side. "You obviously needed to talk about it, Luke. I'm glad you chose me, and I hope I've helped."

"You did. Thanks so much, Kiera. Thanks for your time…and your understanding."

Kiera hesitated before asking, "Do you feel like sharing some Indian tonight?"

"Sounds like a great idea, will we go straight from work?"

"Yes, absolutely."

"See you at knockoff time." He slipped out the door.

He sat down at his desk and stared vacantly into the distance, as the realisation struck him that he had finally been able to cry. After Jenna's suicide, he'd been too terrified to allow his grief to surface. So afraid of what might have been unleashed, he'd smothered it deep inside and overlaid it with guilt. He sighed as a profound relief flooded through him. All the tension drained away, and he became filled with an intense sense of lightness and—almost happiness— almost.

Chapter 7

Later that evening, Luke and Kiera were comfortably ensconced at a table in the corner of a small Indian restaurant in Wembley. The air, redolent with curry with hints of coriander, ginger and garlic, made their mouths water in anticipation.

"I love the cosy intimacy here. It's a place where you can have a real conversation," Kiera said.

"It certainly has a relaxed ambience, and the Indian tapestries are stunning—I like the *ye-old* colonial furniture," Luke said.

He looked relaxed. With his face lit with a broad smile, it was the happiest she'd ever seen him.

A young, dark haired Indian girl dressed in an emerald sari approached. She gave them a shy smile as she handed them the menu.

She and Luke decided they would share dishes because their tastes were so similar. At the end of the meal, they left only empty plates. She and Luke had chatted comfortably whilst they were eating, and after splitting the bill, left the restaurant.

Kiera shivered in the cold air. "It's only 8:30; would you like to come back to my place for a while? It's not far away. We could al-

most walk, but it's a bit chilly. It's only five minutes by trans-bus."
She took his hand in hers and looked up into his face, smiling. "I
can't offer you anything to eat other than fruit though, but I do have
decent coffee and tea."

"I'm a bit tired so…" Luke stared at his feet.

She reached over and gently touched his face. "You could stay
over. I mean…we could just go home and go to bed. I'm pretty tired
too." She held her breath, hoping. Her heart sank as Luke shifted
uneasily.

He stepped back, let go her hand, and ran his hand through his
hair as he continued to stare at his feet.

"I'm not sure."

His face was plastered with uncertainty; like a space cadet about
to jump into a zero gravity chamber for the first time without a safety harness. His expression became determined. "Look Kiera, I think
I would just prefer to go home to my place. I'm just not…"

"Sure." Flooded with disappointment, she started heading for
the trans-station. Well, that's that. She glanced over her shoulder and
called, "See you tomorrow, Luke."

She watched as Luke suddenly galvanised himself into action
and came hurrying over to her, "Kiera. Kiera, wait."

Kiera stood, and put her hands on her hips, "Changed your
mind?" Well, what a turn up!

"I…" He hesitated.

"Oh, for Zark's sake, yes or no?" She scowled. Her patience, not
one of her strong points, was beginning to run a bit thin. Besides,
she was getting cold.

"Yes," he held her gaze.

"Are you sure—really sure?"

"Sorry, I'm not very good at this sort of thing." Kiera watched
as Luke's mouth twitched upwards, threatening a smile.

"Well, we'll have to make sure you get in plenty of practice." She giggled. "Come on, before we both freeze to death." She grabbed Luke's hand and set off at a breakneck pace for the trans-station.

Neither of them said much during the short journey home. Kiera observed Luke's head nodding as the bus glided along. She took his hand again after they got off. After a two-minute walk, they reached her apartment.

It was situated on the tenth floor of a barely cream, cement-rendered building that towered forty storeys over Lake Herdsman. Her cleverly designed one-bedroom apartment consisted of a kitchen at one end that opened out into a spacious lounge-dining area. Two doors led off the lounge, one into a bedroom, the other into the semi-ensuite bathroom. Kiera had made it her own snug, comfortable little nest. Decorated in bright golds and reds, she regarded it as *'her sanctuary'*. She wondered what Luke would think of her photographs. Her cream walls were adorned with scenes of rugged coastlines and green rainforests. Her favourite, an amazing picture of dolphins surfing a blue-green wave, had been taken when she'd just happened to be in the right place at the right time—one of those rare *'magic moments'* she'd been lucky enough to capture with the camera.

Luke took it all in. "This is zinging, and I love your photographs. They're so relaxing…tranquil. Did you take them?"

She could see he'd started to relax again.

"Yes, backpacking around Australia during my younger days. Now, what would you like to drink tea, coffee, or wine?"

"Do you have any green tea?"

"What do you think?" She smiled and went into the kitchen to put the kettle on. An intensive search of her cupboard produced a box of green-tea bags and her jar of coffee. While she waited for the kettle to boil, Kiera watched Luke as he sank into the deep red cushions on her two-seater lounge. She made the tea and coffee and set the two mugs down on the pine coffee table in front of Luke.

"Thanks, Kiera."

She turned on the gas log fire, nestled in its small fireplace, before joining him on the lounge. He sipped his tea and studied the room.

For a while she became lost in her own thoughts, and stared off into the distance, until a question from Luke pulled her back to the moment.

He'd spotted her collection sitting on the mantelpiece above the fireplace.

"It looks like you're really into nature, Kiera. Where did you collect your driftwood and shells?" He took several gulps of his tea.

"My dad collected them down the coast at a place called Preston Beach. Do you know it?" She took another sip of coffee before cradling the mug between her hands.

"That's down near Bunbury, isn't it?" He set his empty mug down.

God, he must have positively gulped his tea down—obviously not into savouring things, she thought. "Used to be, but it's almost deserted now because it wasn't economical to build a trans-service there, so people were forced to move away."

Luke yawned. "Sorry, I'm so tired. I feel I could sleep for a week."

"Okay let's go to bed," Kiera said, trying to sound matter-of-factly as she put her still half full mug down.

"I think I should just head home."

"Oh, for God's sake, if you don't want to have sex or you're just too tired, say so."

"I'm too tired." Luke's expression became unreadable.

Kiera stood up in front of him and placed her hands on her hips. "Okay, fine. Let's just go to bed and cuddle." A sudden wave of emotion washed over her. "I just need someone to hold," she heard herself say in a plaintive tone. Where the hell had that come from?

Luke's expression changed.

My God, who cares where it came from, it's worked.

"Well, if you put it like that how can I refuse?" Luke gave her a weak smile.

She took his hand and led him into the bedroom. She grabbed her pyjamas, went into the bathroom and changed. When she emerged, several minutes later, Luke was already in the queen-sized bed with the covers pulled up to his neck. He had taken the left side and looked up drowsily.

"Am I on the right side?"

"You're fine." She slid in beside him. "Let's spoon." As she shuffled over towards him, she noticed he had stripped down to his underpants.

"What do you mean?" Luke mumbled, half asleep.

"Just rollover onto your left side, facing away from me, and I'll put my arms around you."

Luke obediently rolled over on to his side, and Kiera snuggled up to his back as she wrapped her arms around him. She gave a contented sigh. I can't believe he's never heard of spooning. She cuddled into him. Poor guy. God, I hope he's not a virgin.

Luke fell asleep in minutes. Kiera withdrew her arms, leant over and kissed the back of his neck. He stirred but didn't wake. She turned over and slipped gently into oblivion.

#

Luke slowly opened his eyes. He looked across the empty queen-sized bed. For a few frantic seconds he couldn't remember where he was. He rolled over.

Kiera, still clad in her giant red poppy pyjamas, sat in a chair only a metre away, contemplating him. She half smiled and commented, "You have a really nice body." She leant forward, put her elbows on her knees and rested her chin on her hands.

Luke, embarrassed now, pulled up the sheet to cover his mostly naked form. "You're so…" he trailed off.

"Direct? Yes, so I've been told. There's no need to hide; I saw all of you this morning when the sheet sort of slipped."

"Not all of me."

"No, but I'm working on it." Kiera gave a little giggle. "Would you like to have a shower before breakfast?"

"What time is it?" He was beginning to feel like a trapped butterfly.

Kiera reached over and picked up his watch from the bedside table. "It's just gone six o'clock, so we've got plenty of time."

Luke sat up, pulling the sheet up around him. He studied Kiera. Even with her dark hair in a tangled mess, her face still held an exquisite beauty. She seemed different somehow—more relaxed.

"I think I'd just better get up and go home to have a shower, if you don't mind."

"Now how did I guess you were going to say that?" She frowned, stood up abruptly, picked up his clothes from the dresser, and shoved them into his arms. "You can change in the bathroom." Her face had become sullen.

Luke took his clothes, went into the bathroom and closed the door. Why do I feel so guilty? It's not as though anything really happened last night. He dressed quickly, ran his fingers through his hair, and went through the door out into the lounge. Kiera, already busy in the kitchen, didn't look up. She must've heard him. Luke sighed, picked up his bag, and slung it over his shoulder. When he reached the front door, he turned. She still had her back to him. "See you at work," he called, as he opened the door. She looked at him, but did-n't answer, her face still cloaked in a sullen mask. He left. After he'd closed the door quietly, he trotted down the hallway to the lift. Once on the ground floor, he strode out into the icy morning air. Now what? he wondered. Where do I go from here?'

Chapter 8

Kiera had decided to let Luke stew until morning tea time, and then to behave as though nothing had happened. She kept her eye on the tea room door. When he came in, she gave him a bright smile and patted the seat next to her. "You look better this morning. You must have had a good night's sleep." She deliberately flashed him a wicked little smile.

Luke cleared his throat. "Yes." He sat down and gave her a worried look.

She leant over and said, in a low voice, "Don't worry, your secret's safe with me."

He sighed, and his face flooded with relief. "It's just that, I wouldn't want Williamson to find out about us. We have to behave like nothing's changed," he whispered.

"Nothing has changed." She struggled to keep her expression unfathomable. "Nothing at all." She winked.

She watched Luke let out his breath in slow motion. He was right though, they had to be careful about Williamson. Outwardly, they needed to maintain the relationship at the same level it had been. Even though Williamson didn't frequent the tea room often, one or two of his staff were usually there. She had no idea where their real loyalties lay, so it would be best to play it cool in front of them. Just in case.

#

The week flew by uneventfully. Late on Friday afternoon, Kiera heard Luke's familiar knock on her door. "Come in, Luke."

During the week, they had confined themselves to discussing work issues but always when Williamson was absent. Because they were sharing information, they had already made some significant inroads into the various problems facing the upload program.

Luke had made no mention of the meal they had shared together, or what had happened afterwards. *'Slowly, slowly, catch-um monkey'*, Kiera thought. I came on too strong for him. I need to back off just a little and give him time to get used to the idea. God—am I really thinking there could be a stable relationship here? He stuck his head around the door, and her heart leapt like a gazelle. He opened the door a little wider and leant on the frame. My God, I really am.

"Do you fancy trying some Italian food tonight? I have a favourite restaurant just around the corner from my place. They serve great garlic prawns."

Mmm, so my strategy is working. Should I hold off a little longer, I wonder? She toyed with her pencil, as she held his gaze.

"Please, I could do with some company." His face took on a slightly pleading look.

Her resolve melted and evaporated. "Garlic prawns are my favourite food." She deliberately put on a serious expression. "I thought food was supposed to be the way to a man's heart but in this case, well…I can't turn down garlic prawns. Just give me a few minutes to close down and pack up."

"I haven't closed down myself yet, so I'll see you shortly." He disappeared out the door.

#

Kiera discovered Luke's apartment lay only a five-minute walk from the trans-station. He'd decided that since the restaurant was just around the corner, it would be more convenient for them to drop their bags at his apartment first.

Perched on a hill, the upmarket block had panoramic views of Scarborough Beach and the ocean beyond, still just visible in the fading light. Luke lived on the top floor of the fifteen-storey building. The crashing roar of the winter ocean assaulted her ears, and the familiar tang of fresh seaweed and salt reminded her of her hometown, Esperance. The sound reduced to a muffled roar once inside the luxurious, elegantly furnished, three-bedroom unit. A plush, deep blue carpet enveloped the open-plan living area. A door near the kitchen lay ajar and led off to a small powder room. The kitchen floor, polished Jarrah, glowed a deep red under a glossy varnish. She had been wrapped in warmth as soon as they had entered—obviously fully air-conditioned. As Kiera wriggled out of her jacket, she noticed a spectacular, brilliant red and yellow dot aboriginal painting hanging off the longest wall.

"Wow, what a zinging painting, it's really stunning." She turned back to Luke, "I didn't realise you were so well off."

Luke concentrated on the floor and mumbled, "My parents made a fortune in real estate, so I sort of inherited this place…" he trailed off.

Inherited! Oh God, they must be dead. "I'm so sorry Luke, I had no idea," she said, softly, deeply concerned she had put her foot in it.

"How could you? It's not something I talk about." His eyes were filled with a deep sadness.

"What happened to them?"

"They died in a car accident when I was twenty-two. Jenna was only sixteen. That's why we became inseparable, we only had one another." He held her gaze.

How could so many bad things happen to one person? God, this is awful. She felt like shrivelling up and disappearing into the carpet. Sometimes, I need to think before I open my big mouth. "How did you cope? God, it must've been terrible."

"We had no choice but to cope." He ran his hands through his hair and focused on his feet.

He appeared on the verge of tears, so she went over to him and enfolded him in her arms. To her surprise and without hesitation, Luke wrapped his arms firmly around her. They stood there in a comfortable silence until Luke's stomach rumbled, breaking the spell.

"I think we had better go and get something to eat, don't you?" Luke said, giving her a weak smile.

"Good idea." Kiera shrugged her jacket back on.

#

Half an hour later, they were both hoeing into huge plates of sizzling garlic prawns.

"These have to be the best garlic prawns I've ever eaten," Kiera said, as she helped herself to some tossed Italian salad from the bowl in the centre of the table.

"They are pretty good, aren't they? I usually come here once a week. Giovanni is an excellent cook and the prices are so reasonable. I've never had a lousy meal here yet." Luke wiped a trickle of garlic oil from his chin. "Tell me about your parents, Kiera."

"It's pretty boring. They've been divorced for about twelve years now. Mum still lives in Esperance and Dad lives in Albany. He moved away not long after they first separated. I don't get to see either of them much because it's such a long trip. There are so many damn stops along the way. Dad comes up to Perth about once a year." She hesitated. She didn't want to go into details about what had happened with her dad at this stage. It would be a case of too much too soon. "He calls me every couple of months to see how I'm going. We're... not close. Let's leave it at that." She focused on her plate.

Luke took the hint. "What about your mum?"

"She's happy enough; she does various cleaning jobs around town to supplement the payments from Dad. She's passionate about the local history, and she writes short stories. They're quite brilliant, and she's had a few published in various anthologies from time to time. She paints too. I vidcall her once a week and we usually chat for about half an hour. I think you'd like her, she's warm, laid back and nothing fazes her. There's a long weekend coming up in a couple of months, we could take a trip down there although at that time of year it's bloody cold." She immediately regretted suggesting it. God, I hope I'm not moving too fast again. A quick glance at Luke reassured her—he still seemed relaxed.

After a few moments, he said, "Yes, why not. I've not been anywhere much since Jenna died. Do you know some good places to stay?"

"We can stay with Mum. She's still in our family home, and there's plenty of room. It's a four-bedroom, two-bathroom house, and there is even a queen size bed. I mean, assuming you will want to sleep with me."

Luke stared at his feet. "We'll see." He smiled broadly as he looked up.

By the time she and Luke had finished their meal they were too full to have sweets, so they decided to have tea back at Luke's apartment. After thanking Giovanni profusely for the wonderful meal, they waddled slowly back, hand in hand. They took the lift to the fifteenth floor, and Kiera was soon happily ensconced on Luke's lounge.

"Would you like tea or coffee?"

"Do you have green tea?" Kiera grinned. "No, just joking. Ordinary tea will be fine."

Several minutes later, they were sitting comfortably enjoying their tea.

"Since I've told you a bit about my parents, how about you tell me about yours—if you're okay talking about them," Kiera said.

"Yes, I am okay talking about them. Jenna and I had a happy childhood. My dad was an entomologist. He was a strong, fun loving person. I went out camping with him during the school holidays and some weekends, when he did some of his collection runs. It was great fun, especially the butterflies. To anyone else, we must've looked like lunatics because we were jumping around all over the place waving our butterfly nets. Dad's main interest was jewel beetles, they're exquisitely beautiful but not easy to find."

"Jewel beetles. I don't think I've ever seen one," Kiera said.

"I kept a box of specimens." Luke leapt up and disappeared into a room off the lounge. He soon emerged, carrying a small wooden box. He sat down next to her, opened it with reverence and handed it to her.

"Wow!" The box held around half a dozen specimens. They were mounted on small pieces of cardboard, skewered through and pinned to the bottom of the box. There were males and females of each species. The insects had been glued to the cardboard and there were tiny, neat labels on each piece. The beetles glowed in iridescent colours of blue, green and gold. "I had no idea there were beetles out there with colours like these, Luke. These are beautiful. Thanks so much for sharing one of your precious treasures with me." She closed the lid carefully and handed him the box.

Luke set it down the table.

"What did your mum do, Luke?"

"Mum loved animals, so she became a vet. She came with us on some of our camps, when she could. Sometimes work rosters got in the way."

"What was she like, Luke?"

"She was a quiet, thoughtful person, probably a bit introverted. I think I take after her more than Dad. They loved one another so much, Kiera. They were such intelligent, moral, ethical people. They didn't deserve to die when they did, it was so unfair."

"Life's just life, Luke. It's never fair." Kiera could see Luke was becoming upset so she changed the subject. "Do you think Williamson's noticed anything?" Kiera set her mug down carefully on the glass topped table. Williamson, thankfully, had been away at a conference in Sydney, and wouldn't be back until the middle of the next week.

"I don't think so. Although he did comment at my rapid progress, so I hope he thinks he has underestimated my intellect and expertise in the area." Luke grinned. He got up and took the two empty mugs back to the kitchen. When he returned, he sat a little closer to Kiera on the lounge.

Kiera reached up and stroked his face.

Luke closed his eyes.

"You look like a contented cat," she said, as she ran her fingers through his hair.

His eyes flicked open, and as his gaze held hers she went back to stroking his face.

"You make me purr," he said, fondling her ear. "Can I kiss you?"

"You don't need to ask," she giggled before adding, "Yes please." She drew his face towards her until their lips met.

He kissed her briefly at first, but soon, his kisses became long, intense and passionate.

Kiera, breathless now, murmured, "I really want you, Luke."

"Let's go to bed." He pulled her up and led her into his bedroom. He pulled down the bed covers.

Kiera sat on the smooth, soft sheets.

"I bought some condoms."

"No need, Luke. I have it covered."

"Are you sure?"

"Are all your shots up-to-date?"

"Yes, of course."

"Then I'm sure." She inwardly smiled at his sweet naiveté.

Luke knelt in front of her and began to undo her blouse buttons.

God, this was getting too much. He was taking too long. She fumbled with the next button, but Luke grabbed her hand.

"Slow down, Kiera. Let me do it, I want to look at your body. I don't want our first time to be a blurred rush. I want us to remember this forever."

She took a deep breath as Luke finished unbuttoning her blouse. He slipped the blouse off and began to stroke her breasts. "You are so beautiful, Kiera."

She undid his shirt and ran her hands down his chest. When she gazed into his eyes, they held such a loving intensity that something inside her gave way. Her eyes blurred with tears.

"Kiera, what's wrong?" Luke brushed the tears away with his fingers.

"I love you, Luke." She wrapped her arms around him and pulled him close.

"Oh, Kiera. I love you too."

He kissed her eyelids, her mouth, her neck and her breasts. Ripples of pleasure ran through her as he moved his lips down her body.

She trailed her fingers in circles, up and down his spine, around his buttocks, up his abdomen and around his chest. She surrendered to his slow rhythm; she let go and relaxed. She trusted him and felt so safe in his arms; safe enough to relinquish control, to let him set the pace.

With his help, her jeans and pants came off and were flung aside. She tugged at his belt buckle and it finally gave way. She giggled, when his bulging zip refused to budge and Luke had to come to her aid. Even he had trouble. Once he'd wriggled out of his jeans, she peeled off his underpants. She pulled him down onto the bed, and drank in his scent, his taste, and the electric sensation of his skin on hers. When Luke finally slid into her, she was swept away into a universe of sensation and movement. As they climaxed, time melted.

When it was over they collapsed onto the bed, laughing and crying simultaneously. Afterwards, they just lay there, quiet in one another's arms.

Kiera experienced a sense of completeness, and she was still brimming with an exquisite ecstasy of joy and love. Now she knew the difference between sex and real love-making. What she'd just experienced with Luke was so profoundly intense it transcended anything that had gone before. She propped herself up on one elbow. One look at Luke's face was enough to tell her that she didn't need to ask how it had been for him.

#

Kiera woke up and checked the bedside clock. It showed almost two a.m. Luke breathed gently beside her. She lay there, quiet and content, listening to the susurration of the ocean and drinking in the starlight glittering through the open curtain. A deep relaxed calm enveloped her, and she felt happy, deliriously happy. I'm in love. My

God, I'm really in love with this guy. He's so sweet and gentle. She chuckled inwardly. He'd have to be the most considerate guy she had ever made love to but passionate even so. Right now, I feel like I could spend the rest of my life with him. He had whispered 'I love you' in her ear just before she had dropped off to sleep. She had believed him.

Chapter 9

Logan Williamson sat pondering Kiera's work. Her algorithms were exquisite. He marvelled at her ability to spot and effortlessly remedy flaws that he'd been blind to. Interestingly though, Luke appeared to be equally skilled. He'd also managed to fix faults in the various program sections that he'd been allocated but in a totally different way.

I certainly have a gift for ferreting out brilliant people. Logan smiled to himself, and they'd made so much progress. He couldn't in his wildest dreams have anticipated the speed at which things were advancing. Seemingly unsolvable problems were being dealt with at such an incredible rate that he could probably start testing on live subjects early next year.

He flicked his desk screen into hibernation and sat back in his chair. This is too good to be true. I think there is more going on here than meets the eye. He frowned. I'm going to have to take measures to check my suspicions. He had been sure that his strategy of divide and conquer would work, but it appeared to be going awry. In spite of his plans, Luke and Kiera had already got too friendly, far too friendly for his liking. I think these two have been collaborating.

Well, he would soon wipe the smiles off their faces. He would have Kiera in the end. It was only a matter of time. She would come around to his way of thinking, eventually. *I think I need to reactivate one of my little spies.* He reached up and pressed inside his right ear to turn on his phone connection.

"Melanie Carter," he enunciated, carefully.

After a few short rings she picked up.

Time to turn on the charm. "Melanie," he said, in his long-lost friend voice, "Logan Williamson here, can you come down to my office? Yes, now." He pressed inside his ear, breaking the connection, and allowed a satisfied smirk to slide across his face.

Presently, he heard her knock at his door. "Come," he boomed.

The door opened, and a breathless Melanie Carter darted in and stood in front of his desk. She still had her lab coat on. Pity, it hid her voluptuous figure. He always enjoyed getting a view of that. Melanie appeared rather fond of displaying her ample cleavage, not that he would ever complain.

"It's been quite a while since we caught up, hasn't it?" He sat back, put his hands behind his head and stretched without taking his eyes off her.

Melanie hovered near the chair opposite him like a robot with a short circuit.

"Do sit down. I have a little mission for you, similar to the last time."

Melanie perched on the edge of the chair and pushed her long blonde hair back behind her ears.

Williamson paused, savouring the moment. "I've noticed that you seem to have a thing for Luke, is that the case?" He watched as her face coloured, and she focused on the floor.

"Yes," she squeaked, as she clasped her hands tightly in her lap.

"Have you noticed anything in the tea room between Luke and Kiera that would suggest they have a relationship other than friendship?" He noticed her immediate relaxation, punctuated by an audible sigh. He'd counted on the fact that being smitten by Luke, Melanie would certainly have no great love for Kiera. She would probably jump at the chance to break up the relationship. He knew that in her eyes, Kiera had come between her and Luke. He had not missed the promising start she and Luke had got off to on that first day. Her reaction illustrated that she still had the hots for Luke. Aah, the joys of intense emotions. They always provided such strong tools for manipulation.

"There hasn't been anything definite." Her lab coat gaped open as she leant forward in her chair, giving him an eyeful, "But the way they look at one another seems to have changed. They look kind of…involved, if you know what I mean." She batted her eyelids.

"I want you to watch them for me. I suggest that you follow them discreetly on Friday evening. There'll be a substantial bonus for you next month if you should come up with some results. But, be sure of your facts, Melanie. I don't want any false accusations. Is that clear?"

"Of course, I wouldn't dream of making anything up"

Her expression held so much sincerity he struggled to stifle laughter. He smiled as Melanie sat waiting for his permission to leave. Excellent! So compliant—as always. He paused for effect before he gave her a dismissive wave. "Off you go." He smirked as she popped up from the chair and hurried out. He chuckled. He did *so* enjoy watching his people squirm.

Chapter 10

On Saturday morning Kiera gripped Luke's hand playfully and pulled him out the front door and down the steps. The day, although icy cold, was awash with sunlight. As was their custom, they had slept late and decided to go out for breakfast. A small café, just around the corner, had become their regular favourite.

Kiera spotted Melanie on the other side of the street. "Don't look now, but Melanie's over the road from us trying to look inconspicuous."

"Oh Zark!" Luke's grip on her hand tightened.

"Precisely, let's just pretend we haven't seen her and act accordingly. She's not going to follow us into the café. I doubt it's a coincidence though, I've seen her summoning the trans-bus, and she doesn't live anywhere near here. I'm sure there are no shops of interest to her nearby."

Once inside the café, after placing their orders, they sat at their usual table near the window where they could view all the passers-by. Kiera loved the cosy quiet of the small café . It had comfortable seats, and its cream walls featured original watercolours of narrow, sloping, cobbled streets and tiny fishing harbours.

"Is she still there?" Luke asked, looking worried.

"I can't see her, but I've got no doubt she's spying on us for Williamson. I think it's time we developed a backup plan, and I've got some ideas."

"Enlighten me."

"I've come across an organisation called RFA, which stands for Rights for Androids. They've posted some interesting comments regarding AI and the various research streams. Logan Williamson's name often crops up and the site's comments aren't complimentary. I've subscribed to their website, and I'm going to do some digging." She unfolded the paper serviette and smoothed it onto her lap.

"So, what's your idea?"

"I want to see if there's anything we can use as leverage if Williamson starts to get heavy-handed." Kiera sat back as their usual waitress deposited bowls of muesli, a fresh fruit platter, a bowl of Greek yoghurt and a jug of milk in front of them. "Thanks," Kiera said.

"No problem. I'll bring your toast and preserves when you've eaten your cereal. Tea as usual?"

"Yes thanks, Sarah," Kiera smiled up at her.

Luke spooned strawberries, sliced banana pieces and some chunks of apple onto his muesli as he waited for the waitress to disappear back into the kitchen. "So you're hoping to dig some dirt on Williamson?" he said between mouthfuls of the fruit laden muesli.

"That's the general idea." Kiera poured milk onto her muesli followed by a dollop of Greek yoghurt. "As I said before, he gives me the creeps. I have a sense for these things, and I'm not usually wrong. There's something dark there."

"He certainly likes power. I can see that. But we need to be careful, Kiera. If he cottons on to the fact we're doing some digging, who knows how he will react." Luke sloshed more milk onto his muesli.

"Well we have to do something! I've got no doubt Melanie will run straight back to him on Monday morning. Anyway, enough of that for now, let's just relax and enjoy our breakfast, shall we?"

"Good idea," Luke said with a widening grin.

#

First thing on Monday morning Melanie knocked on Logan Williamson's door. Thoughts about reporting to him had been an unpleasant reminder of the last time. She'd had jitters all weekend and wanted to get the meeting over so she could enjoy the rest of her day.

Williamson had a file on her and knew all about her history. She'd attained first class honours in a robotic design degree from the University of Melbourne but had been convicted of shoplifting and later had become a drug addict. Under extreme pressure at the time, it had been her way of dealing with her mother's chronic health problems. Although arrested, she'd managed to get her sentence converted into time in a rehabilitation facility. It was the best thing that had ever happened to her. She managed to turn her life around and find herself a good job.

She'd been working in the main robotic lab, a job she'd loved. Someone had been stealing equipment from her lab, so Williamson had recruited her as his spy—no, not recruited—blackmailed her by threatening to tell everyone about her past. Unfortunately, she'd bungled the job, and everyone had known what she was up to. Subsequently ostracised, she'd had to be transferred into another section. Now, she designed and constructed robotic eyes, with some forays into hair and nails. They never did find out the identity of the culprit, but apparently, according to Williamson, the thieving stopped. Everybody probably thought it was her.

Not averse to some manipulation herself, she had dressed in a tight outfit with a low cleavage. Excusable under the circumstances; she knew what Williamson liked. She would do anything, well almost anything, to keep him happy. She'd seen many staff come and go due to his whims. She wasn't going to be one of them. She liked her job, and it paid well. She aimed to keep it that way.

"Well, Melanie," Williamson steepled his fingers, "do you have something for me?"

"I did as you suggested. I followed them home on Friday." She paused for effect, watching satisfied as he drank in her cleavage.

"And…"

"They are an item. They went back to his place. I watched them go in and afterwards ran inside to see what floor the lift stopped at."

"Smart girl."

"He lives on the top floor. I ran back outside, and watched the lights go on." She paused for effect again.

"Get on with it, girl."

"I also watched the lights go out, and Kiera didn't leave. I went back early the next morning just in time to see them emerge together. They went off and had breakfast at a nearby café." A brief flash of rage swept across Williamson's face only to disappear again. Its intensity frightened Melanie, and she wondered just what Williamson might be capable of. She didn't want to think about it. She hoped he'd finished with her and that she could leave.

"So, I was right. Thank you, Melanie, your bonus will appear in your first pay packet next month. So off you go now." He waved his hands in a shooing motion.

She leapt up and darted out the door, sighing with relief as she pulled it closed. The things I do for my job. She didn't care about the extra money, but at least it hadn't turned out like last time.

#

The smile Williamson gave Melanie instantly vanished the moment she shut the door. He picked up a glass paperweight from his desk and hurled it into the corner. It made a satisfying sound as its broken pieces scattered along the tiles. He got up and carefully crunched all the pieces underfoot, imagining it was Luke. It would give him great satisfaction to break him into a thousand pieces and grind him underfoot to dust. He took a deep breath. He needed to think. A stiff drink might lubricate his thought processes. He went to the drinks cabinet, took out his expensive, well-aged, malt whiskey, and poured himself half a tumbler full. He sat down at his desk and sipped thoughtfully. The amber liquid warmed his throat and cooled his temper.

He had a complicated dilemma here. He needed to separate Luke and Kiera, because he wanted Kiera all to himself. But the two of them were making such rapid progress, and he knew it was because they were collaborating. What should he do?

He leant back and downed the remaining whiskey. Over the past week it had dawned on him that Kiera could be even brighter than he and possibly Luke, too. He wanted to get Luke out of the picture, but there were advantages in keeping him engaged in the project. His priority should be to advance the project as quickly as possible and with minimum cost. Luke and Kiera were doing just that, he realised. He was just tweaking their work, and it wasn't requiring a great deal of effort on his part.

He leant forward and pressed a button on his console to summon the swisper-bot. It would take care of the floor. As he relaxed back in the chair again, an idea occurred to him. He smiled.

Chapter 11

Kiera arrived at work on Monday with some trepidation. She knew Melanie would report what she'd witnessed. They'd now have to play a waiting game to see how Williamson reacted. Luke and she had spent most of the weekend on their computers, and they were as prepared as they possibly could be given the circumstances.

She made her way to the research lab after making several wrong turns and having to backtrack. She paused at the door. This is risky, she thought, but I think it will be worth it. She went in and proceeded straight into the gowning room. All kitted up, and after navigating the airlock, she marched into the main laboratory and looked around. God, it's difficult to recognise anybody when they're all dressed in white. She approached the nearest worker and tapped him on the shoulder. Startled, he jumped and spun around. Good choice, Carlson first up.

She smiled, "Sorry if I frightened you. You're just the person I wanted to speak to."

"I'm…busy, can't it wait until teatime?"

Kiera noticed the fear in his eyes. She stepped in close. "I've never actually seen you at teatime, and besides I don't want this to be overheard by anyone."

He glared at her. "What exactly do you want, Miss...I'm sorry I've forgotten your name?" He shifted uneasily.

"It's Kiera. I'll get straight to the point. I saw the way Williamson treated you on my first day. He seemed pretty angry. I've come to the conclusion we were never meant to see what we did."

"What exactly is this about?" Carlson asked, irritably, moving slightly away from her.

"During the time I've been here, I've had the chance to observe Williamson's interactions with his employees. It's clear everyone is afraid of him. I won't mince words, he's a bully and he rules by fear and manipulation. If I'd known what he was really like I would never have taken this position, but since I am here I now have to deal with the same behaviour myself. I won't stand for it, and I'm about to do something about it—something that will probably benefit everyone in the long run. I've come to you because I, and my friend Luke, need some help. Will you help us?"

"Absolutely not! Now please leave, or I'll have to call security." His frightened eyes darted around the room.

Kiera sighed. "In that case I'm afraid I'm going to have to implicate you in the illegal activity going on in this laboratory."

Carlson took another step back and eyed her suspiciously. "I don't know what you're talking about. Now please leave."

Kiera stepped in close to him again. "I'm talking about the illegal use of sexual stimulants, the pheromones you're somehow incorporating into your sex androids."

Carson gasped, and the colour drained from his face.

"I want you to help me blow the whistle on Williamson. No, let me clarify that. I want you to help me *threaten* to blow the whistle on him. I won't implicate you directly, I will simply say I have evidence that this is occurring and am prepared to give it to the appropriate authorities. I assume you're not getting kickbacks to do the work. Am I correct?"

"Yes. We all work under the threat of dismissal if we don't toe the line. Everyone knows what goes on here, but nobody is willing to do anything about it."

"Until now," Kiera said.

"Yes, until now."

"Will you help us?"

"What's in it for us? Can you guarantee our jobs? Can you guarantee that he won't blacklist us?"

"No, I can't, but what I can do is take away some of the fear, so everyone feels more comfortable because they're no longer working on illegal stuff. This is not the only matter I'm going to raise with him. I'm going to use my full armoury, and believe me I have a lot on him and I have proof. I've just spoken to my father. He's a retired detective and well connected. I have clout. So, how about it?"

"Let me talk to the others."

"As long as Melanie doesn't get wind of it. She's his spy."

"We already knew that, there have been incidences in the past. She doesn't work in this lab anymore, so she'll be kept well and truly out of the picture. How soon do you have to act?"

"We thought there would be a showdown today, so I have to be ready," Kiera said.

"Okay, I'll talk to everyone now."

"I'll give you my mobi number, don't call me on the internal system."

Kiera wrote down her number for him before she hurried out. I hope to hell this doesn't come to a head before I've heard back from him. She was prepared to go ahead without Carlson's support, but the more ammunition she had the better.

#

Williamson ambushed Luke on Tuesday morning. Luke was summoned to his office about an hour after he arrived at work. He took a deep breath and stood tall before knocking on the door.

Williamson boomed a response.

Luke went in and sat down. He was not reassured by Williamson's wide smile. Neither of them spoke.

Finally, Luke broke the silence, "What did you want to see me about?" He fought the urge to flick a strand of hair out of his eyes and tried to stay calm.

"Well, Luke, I'm sorry to say that things aren't working out too well. I've thought long and hard about it over the weekend and have come to a decision."

Zark! He's going to fire me. Luke wriggled in his seat and clenched his fists. Oh, for Zarks sake, get it over with.

Williamson, his smile still plastered on his face, said, "I feel that you would be more useful in our Sydney office. There is a problem there that your...limited expertise would be more useful in solving. I think you're well and truly out of your league here."

Luke felt his mouth go dry. "You can't make me go to Sydney."

Williamson's smile deepened as he steepled his fingers. "Oh yes I can, it's in your contract, your five-year contract. It's always wise to read the fine print, Luke. Oh, and before you go, may I remind you that you cannot default on the contract. That's in the fine print too. So, if you should think about resigning, I will take you to court. I also have powerful connections and I'll make sure that you never work in AI again, ever. I'd think very carefully before you make any rash decisions that you may later regret." He sat looking smug.

Luke wanted to wipe that look of Williamson's face. He wanted to…easy Luke…think…think. My best option before I say something I really will regret, or I actually thump this guy, is to get up and leave.

It took all his willpower to swallow his anger. He got up from the chair and said, "I'll have to take some time to consider what you've said. I'll come back later in the week to let you know my decision." He strode out of the office slamming the door satisfyingly behind him. He headed straight for Kiera's room with his mind swirling. Kiera. Great Universe, I will have to leave her, he thought. I can't…I won't. He knocked on her door and without waiting for her reply opened it and went in.

"What's happened?" Kiera stood up, came around her desk, and put her arms around him. "You're as white as a sheet, and you're trembling."

"He's…he's…"

"He's what, for God's sake? Tell me."

Luke could feel the tears brimming in his eyes. "Williamson's transferring me to Sydney."

"Surely he can't do that." She held him tighter, burying her face in his chest.

"He says it's in the fine print in my contract." He paused for breath before continuing, "I can't break the contract either. He said, if I resign, he will sue me."

"I read my contract. It says nothing of the sort." Kiera stood back from him. "Luke, Luke…he's bluffing. Come on, you're stronger than this, remember we have our own leverage now, and I'm quite prepared to use it. Come and sit down."

Luke allowed her to lead him to the chair. He sat down feeling defeated.

"I rang my father before I came to work this morning. He is going to contact an old colleague, a detective in the Special Crimes Unit who will be able to help us. We've already got some solid proof of Williamson's criminal activities; this will just add an extra bow to our armoury. I've already placed a call to Detective Sergeant Harrington, and I'm waiting for him to ring me back when he gets out of a meeting."

She reached up and patted his face. "What did you do with your contract?"

"It's in a drawer in my office," Luke said, in a low voice.

"Okay, go and get it and we'll have a look just to make sure so we know exactly what we are dealing with."

Luke got up slowly and without saying anything further headed out the door.

#

Luke slumped in his chair and pulled out his drawer, rifling through its contents until he found his contract; all ten pages of it. He pulled out his confidentiality agreement as well.

He kept running his fingers through his hair as he read through the document. And there it was, on the final page. *The company may, at its discretion, relocate an employee at any time during his employment to another office in Australia, or overseas, if it determines it necessary, for the employee to perform at his optimum level. A relocation allowance will be paid if it is warranted.*

Half way down the page he read, *This contract is legal and binding for a period of five years and may not be broken under any circumstances other than terminal illness. The employer, in the event of the employee resigning, has the right to take legal action to recover costs.*

Luke felt sick. Zark. Why the hell didn't I read this before signing it? But Kiera said she had read hers and that it contained nothing of the sort. Surely her contract was the same as his? His hands shook as he picked up the confidentiality agreement and read it carefully. No surprises there, thank the Universe. Although it couldn't get any worse than it already was could it?

He picked up his contract and headed back to Kiera's office. She was on her mobi when he knocked so he came in and sat down. She locked eyes with him momentarily to acknowledge his presence before continuing to write furiously in the notebook in front of her. He continued to watch her as his thoughts ran wild. Great Universe! She's so vibrant, positive, assertive, intelligent and loving. Just about everything I'm not. I won't survive without her. She's the love of my life, my soul mate. I'll curl up and die…

Kiera put her mobi down and smiled broadly. "We've got the bastard, by the short and curlies."

Luke leaned forward. "We've still got a major problem. The contract says exactly what he told me."

"Show me." Kiera opened her drawer and pulled out her own contract.

They were both right. The reference to relocation appeared to be missing from Kiera's contract, but it did contain the clause about resignation. Kiera's face wrinkled in disgust. "The sneaky bastard, so he's had this safety valve in place all the time. Well, it's time for some well thought out blackmail. Now, let's talk strategy."

Chapter 12

Kiera knocked on Luke's door, opened it, and stepped just inside.

"Is it time to go home already?" Luke said.

"Almost, I just wanted to let you know I won't be coming home with you tonight."

"Oh?" A look of disappointment flashed across Luke's face.

"I've got some urgent business to attend to, so I'm heading off a little early." She turned and slipped out the door before he had time to reply. She knew it was mean. But he would want to know why, and at this point she didn't want to tell him. He wouldn't approve. What he didn't know couldn't hurt him. As she went out the building's doors her stomach clenched. God, I hope I'm doing the right thing. She checked her watch. Plenty of time, no need to rush.

Kiera detoured on the way home to do some last-minute shopping. She added a salad platter for one, some feta cheese, a container of orange juice and a small carton of skim milk to her purchases. Since she'd been going home with Luke, almost living with him in fact, little food remained in her apartment.

She sat and mulled over the evening's plans while slowly eating her meal. She wished she'd included some bread. She was ravenous, must be stress.

After she finished, she cleaned up and threw the empty containers in the bin. She took the bag out and tossed it in the garbage disposal chute opposite her door. When she came back she took a leisurely shower to help her relax.

For camouflage purposes Kiera had ferreted out all her black clothes and had laid them out on the bed before showering. She donned a polo necked skivvy, tracksuit pants, black socks and matching sneakers. She took the balaclava she had bought that afternoon from its wrap and stuffed it, along with a pair of black gloves, into the back pockets of her tracksuit pants. She pulled her old jacket off the hangar and laid it on her bed next to a polar fleece jumper.

Kiera sat at the desk holding her computer and printer. She systematically worked through all the evidence she'd accumulated in the past couple of days. After finishing the summary, she copied the file onto the half dozen memory sticks she'd purchased for the task. With shaking hands, she packed these carefully into containers for postage. She'd been given access to the Police Airgap Server's evidence locker by Detective Inspector Harrington and would take a copy with her to save there when she saw him tomorrow.

She emailed copies to the people she had spoken to, including her father. They had all agreed to publish in the event of her death or disappearance. With her insurance taken care of, she sat back and tried to calm herself, but anxiety erupted inside her and gnawed away like a plague of mice in a grain silo. God, I hope I know what I'm doing.

She printed off the material she intended to present to Williamson the next morning. It had been gathered via various websites, although the majority of it came from the RFA group. The most important thing would be the uplink memory stick that Detective Inspector Harrington would give her, but the printed material would give her something to make and impact with, something substantial to wave in that bastard's face. She took a deep breath and unclenched her fists. She turned her palms over. Deep imprints showed where her nails had dug into them. I've got to relax. This is only the beginning. If I keep going like this, I'll have a nervous breakdown by tomorrow. She took several deep breaths and managed to calm her thoughts.

When she'd finished all her tasks, she glanced at her watch; still another hour to go. She went downstairs and posted the packages. That's that, she thought. She shivered in the cold night air and stared up at the moonless, starlit sky; at least it wasn't raining.

She took the stairs instead of the lift. The exercise will help me calm down. It did. By the time she got to the top she felt strong and determined. This would work.

Right on eleven o'clock, her door buzzer rang. She ran to the door and flicked the talk button.

Jack's familiar voice said, "Kiera, are you ready?"

Images of him flooded into her mind; his dark-brown, close-cropped, military style haircut and his short, slightly tubby form. Dear Jack, why had she lost contact with him? They'd been like brother and sister during uni days.

"Yes Jack, I'll be right down." He sounded no different. She couldn't believe seven or eight years had gone by since she'd last seen him. A pang of guilt surfaced. They'd never fallen out; they'd just gone their separate ways.

"I need to come up, so you can put your contacts in."

"Oh, I'd forgotten that." She pressed the door open button. "Come on up."

She'd already put on her fleecy jumper. She picked up her jacket and her black bag and set them down by the door. She jumped when the buzzer rang.

"How the hell are you Kiera?" Jack said, stepping inside and embracing her warmly. "You look like Cat Woman."

Kiera gave a nervous giggle. "Wait till you see me in the mask. God, it's great to see you after all this time, and you haven't changed one bit."

"You haven't either." He grinned and held her at arm's length, inspecting her. After releasing her, he said, "Let's get to work." He went over to the kitchen table and carefully placed his bag on its glass surface.

Kiera watched him take out his various bits and pieces and place them in a neat line. No, he hasn't changed one little bit. She'd often thought he had characteristics bordering on obsessive-compulsive and, as a perfectionist, everything had to be just so. She smiled to herself.

Jack, without taking his eyes off the screen asked, "Nervous?"

"A bit, well…I felt nervous earlier, but I've managed to calm down since." She unclenched her fists again, feeling self-conscious.

Jack grinned. He rummaged in a pocket and handed her a small plastic container. "Here are your HUD contacts. Slip into the bath-room and put them in so I can check they're working properly. I've got a backup pair just in case."

He had his computer up and running by the time she came back out.

"Okay?" Jack asked.

"Yes, they're really soft, in fact I hardly know they're in there."

"Right." His fingers flashed over the keyboard, "You should be seeing something, now." He stabbed the enter key.

"Wow!" Various displays lit up, seemingly inside her head. "The clarity is brilliant."

"Is this the first time you've used them?" Jack asked, raising his eyebrows.

"No. I don't like them, and I don't really have any need for them. I think the last time I used them was at uni, but they weren't anywhere near as good as these."

"Technology marches endlessly onward." Jack's focus remained on the screen as his fingers continued to fly over the keyboard. "When we get there, I'll switch you over to night vision once you're inside the building. The lenses also act as cameras, so I'll be seeing what you see and recording when appropriate."

"Saves me taking a camera, but why will I need night vision? Doesn't the plant operate twenty-four seven?"

"No. According to my informant, because they rely solely on solar energy, and the plant operates with such efficiency and speed, they only operate 9-to-5. Here's your earpiece." He watched while she placed it into her ear. "Okay, let's do a sound check. Kiera had a little lamb, how's that?"

"Loud and clear." She hesitated before adding, "It's great to know that you're going to be with me during this, Jack. I couldn't have coped by myself."

Jack gave her a brief smile before re-focusing back on his screen.

The enormity of what she was about to do hit her like an oncoming mag-rail train. Her stomach tightened and her mouth suddenly went dry. She sniffed and took a deep breath.

"Are you sure about this? You seem pretty nervous," Jack's face creased into an expression of concern.

"It's not a matter of wanting. It's a matter of having to do it. I tried to get the people in the lab to back me up, but they're simply too frightened. Are you sure you want to get involved?" She locked eyes with him.

"And miss all the fun? I go where you go when there's trouble. You should know that, Kiera."

She did. A feeling of deep affection swept over her, along with a profound gratitude that, after all this time, he was still willing to put himself out on a limb to help her. "I hope I might be able to return the favour someday." She smiled warmly, stepped forward and gave him a brief hug. She felt his body stiffen.

"I'm not counting." He sounded slightly embarrassed. His hands had not left the keyboard and he remained facing away from her. He coughed, cleared his throat and said, "Everything seems in order, so let's go. The sooner we get there, the sooner this is over."

After Jack packed his things neatly away, they headed downstairs to his electric motorbike parked at the back entrance. He insisted she wear the helmet so the police wouldn't have any reason to pull them over.

They set off just before midnight. Jack took a circuitous route to avoid the bulk of the surveillance cameras. They couldn't avoid them all, but the substantial gaps in between surveillance would make it hard for anyone looking to piece their journey together. Once they turned into the now deserted industrial area in Balcatta, he switched off the lights. They circled around and pulled up at a small bush reserve at the rear of the Sentioids Inc. manufacturing plant. They got off and he wheeled his bike a little way into the bush and parked it behind a tree out of view of the road.

"Give me a few minutes to set up," he said in a hushed voice.

Kiera shivered in the cold night air in spite of her layers of clothing and the balaclava. She sniffed; her nose filled with the smell of damp earth and eucalypt leaves. She watched Jack unpack his gear from the box at the rear of the bike. He set his small computer on the saddle and unfolded a tentlike black cover. To Kiera's amazement, he draped it over himself and settled back on to the bike. It stood securely braced upright, in no danger of it toppling over. She suppressed a giggle when a muffled voice came from inside.

"This is so we can't be snooped on by satellite. No cameras zooming in on me typing. It's an extra safety precaution. Has the HUD come on?"

"Yes, it's up and running."

"Okay." Jack's hand, holding a small pair of wire cutters, appeared from under his canopy. "You'll need these. I've hacked the security programs and looped all the cameras along your route, outside and inside the facility. I'll guide you via the HUD. All set?"

"Yes." Kiera took the wire cutters from him. His hand disappeared again underneath the cover.

"Okay Kiera, off you go. It's straight ahead. Good luck."

Kiera smiled, as Jack's hand reappeared and gave her the thumbs up signal.

Chapter 13

Kiera sniffed. Armed with the cutters, she turned and padded off towards the cyclone fence some thirty metres away. Cutting a hole proved easy and took no time at all. She noted the razor wire along the top of the fence. Not logical from her point of view, although she supposed it would keep children out. Once inside, she leant the cut-out piece on one side of the opening leaving only a small gap. She propped it up with the wire cutters to hold it in place. She'd pick the cutters up on the way back, no point in carrying them with her. Kiera scuttled across the starlit bitumen yard guided by green arrows from the HUD and the reassuring sound of Jack's voice from her earpiece. She stopped in front of the two steel double doors that opened out into the yard, but the green arrow on the HUD clearly indicated that she should go further right.

"Press the button when you reach the single door." The sound had such clarity it seemed like Jack was right behind her.

She followed Jack's instructions when she reached the single door, and it swung soundlessly outward revealing a black-hole interior.

"Close the door once you're inside, and I'll switch on your night vision."

Only a few seconds passed in the black stillness before a greenish hue lit up a long hallway with multiple doors exiting off it. The directional arrows on her HUD, now glowing yellow, indicated she should go straight ahead. Enveloped in an eerie fog of silence, she padded silently down the passage past several doors.

She jumped as Jack's voice chimed in her ear. "Next door on your right."

Kiera's heart started to thump as she stopped, reached out, and put her hand on the doorknob. The yellow arrow turned scarlet and flashed rapidly. "Jack?" No answer. "Jack?" she said, more loudly as her heart skittered, "Are you seeing this?"

"Wait, Kiera."

Kiera's heart beat rocketed. In spite of the icy cold, her hands were becoming clammy.

Jack's voice came again, "Okay. Sorted. In you go."

Kiera turned the handle and stepped through the door. She screamed as a super-nova of light engulfed her.

"That shouldn't have happened. Stand still, I'm switching off your night vision. It will take a while for your eyes to readjust."

"Jack, I'm totally blind. All I can see is black and white flashing patches."

"After images, Kiera. Don't panic. You must have activated a motion sensitive light system my informant didn't know about; otherwise I would have switched off your night vision. Slow your breathing Kiera, you'll hyperventilate. Your eyes will be fine. "

Kiera heard a faint clunk.

"Jack?"

She realised she had her eyes squeezed shut. The sound came again.

"Jack?"

"Busy, Kiera. Stay calm."

Her breathing became more rapid and ragged. She opened her eyes, and with some effort, took deep measured breaths. Her vision slowly cleared and she found herself in the centre of the manufacturing floor.

"That's better," came Jack's voice, "okay now?"

"Yes, but I wouldn't want to go through that again. God it's creepy in here, there are hibernating manufacturing bots everywhere." She whirled as the sound came again. A couple of androids, plugged into chargers, were standing by the wall. One of the male androids turned its head. It slowly detached itself from the wall and began tap-tapping towards her.

She froze. Her pulse skyrocketed. "Jack! The android…Jack, what the hell do I do?"

"Get out fast."

"What?"

"Door—now."

Kiera pivoted and darted back through the open door. She slammed it behind her, the sound echoing down the hallway.

"Stay still."

Seconds passed. Kiera stood shaking. She slid to the floor, struggling to breathe as her legs turned to jelly. Seconds drifted into minutes in the smothering silence. The door remained closed.

"Zark, Jack! What the hell now?"

"If nothing's come out you're safe. The android was responding to your presence. It will have gone back into hibernation now you've disappeared. We're safe to proceed. I'll need to find another route to the prototype vault. It will take a few minutes to work that out and deal with the cameras. I'll have to erase the android's login of your intrusion. Okay? "

"Are you sure it's safe?"

He sighed. "Yes, Kiera."

For the first time in her life doubt about Jack's expertise flooded into her mind. She took a deep breath and pushed the thought away as she stood up in the darkness. Jack's brilliant. He'll find a way around this. He has to; I can't fail Luke...dear Luke. She imagined him here now with his arms firmly around her. She had to do this for him. She loved him too much to give up now. He had become the core of her existence. God, I can't believe...

Her thoughts were interrupted as the night vision flashed on. She jumped when Jack spoke again.

"Right. Follow the arrows."

She turned, calmer now, and padded slowly down the glowing green hallway. After what seemed like half a kilometre through labyrinthine passages, the yellow arrow indicated the next door on her right. She hesitated.

"Are you sure there are no nasty surprises behind this one, Jack?"

"Trust me, Kiera. The door goes through to reception."

"I feel like *Alice in Wonderland*. I hope there is no mad hatter waiting for me on the other side."

"Probably not, maybe a white rabbit."

"Very funny."

She held her breath, twisted the handle and went in. Jack was right. She whooshed the air from her lungs. A sudden flood of panic hit as the door clicked shut behind her. She swivelled left and right, overwhelmed by an uncanny feeling that another android was about to materialise from somewhere.

"Relax Kiera," Jack's voice said, in her ear. "You're nearly there. Follow the arrow."

The yellow arrow indicated left. She went to the left-hand door and turned the handle. It opened into a small room, similar to the gowning room at her work place.

"Stand still while I switch off your night vision and turn on the lights."

Kiera waited as a momentary darkness followed. A nanosecond later, the overheads flicked on and the room lit up like a spaceport. She screwed up her eyes against the glare. An airlock door lay directly in front of her.

"There's an airlock, Jack. Why would they need that?"

"In case of fire, to protect all their prototypes. The area is sealed off and gassed with carbon dioxide. It's also an extra security measure."

Kiera shivered involuntarily at the thought of being trapped inside the vault. She walked over and pressed the admittance button but nothing happened.

"The button's not working, Jack."

"I have to unlock it from night mode. There we go, press again."

"It's opening." Kiera stepped inside and the door slid silently closed. She walked over and pressed a button on the wall outside the other door. The indicator light flashed green. Air hissed past her as the door opened.

She stepped through into a large, long room filled with glass cases holding a plethora of robots of all shapes and sizes. Each case had a display screen. When pressed, she discovered, it gave the specifications of the robot inside. The cases were clearly labelled with the type and function of the machines they contained. She went past multipurpose, standard male and female domestic models, typically used as housekeepers, maids, waiters and waitresses. There were also heavy labour models as well as a large assortment of manufacturing assemblers. She inspected all the glass cases lining one wall, followed by those housed in the central column. Finally, she traipsed past the cases lining the far wall.

"Well Jack, you're seeing what I'm seeing. There's nothing unusual here. There's no sign of the sex android I saw in Williamson's laboratory on my first day. It looks like this is a Higgs boson chase."

"My plan shows a smaller room off the one you're in. You should be able to see another door down the other end."

"I can only see a blank wall." Kiera jogged to the end of the room. "There's nothing here. I can't see a Zarking thing, Jack!"

"There's definitely another room. Just bringing up the details now. Aah."

"Aah what?"

"Patience, Kiera, I'm not a miracle worker."

"Jack, what the…" The wall turned opaque and a bright display materialised in front of her. "It's requesting a password," she said in a defeated tone.

"Working on it. Here we go. It's long and complex, I'll read it to you slowly so you can enter it as we go."

She tapped out the numbers, symbols and letters using the virtual keyboard on the wall. Finally, she pressed enter. The display disappeared and a heavy door cranked open.

"Don't freak, there's an android guide. Act like a tourist."

"Zark, Jack!"

Bright lights flicked on as soon as she entered. A hand touched her shoulder. She yelped, spun around and came face-to-face with a smiling female Asiatic android.

"Sorry if I startled you," it said in a sexy, flowing voice. "My name is Lianna. Welcome to my playground. I am your guide. What is your particular interest?" With the smile still plastered on its face, it stood waiting for her response.

Jack's voice said, "Say you would like to see everything."

"Show me everything you've got." Kiera surveyed the room's display cases. There were no display screens. They'd been replaced with a few static labels and Lianna.

"You are a woman of wide tastes. Let us start at the first case." She moved to the nearest display case. It held a handsome, naked, exceptionally well endowed, dark haired male android. She explained all his functions in lucid details, including the fact that he could be programmed for bisexual, homosexual and heterosexual acts. At this rate, we'll be here all night, Kiera thought. I'll have to be a bit more specific.

"Sorry to interrupt, but I'm a bit short on time. How about we do a quick walk-around and I'll stop you if I want details of a particular model."

"As you wish," Lianna said, and proceeded to the next case. There were thirty models in the room including the one she'd seen in the laboratory. She asked about the pheromones. Lianna gave her a vivid and detailed explanation of the different types available. Kiera was gripped by wave of disgust when Lianna outlined the special types specifically designed to cause excruciating pain.

After viewing all the models in the room, Lianna walked over to a partitioned off section. She turned and beckoned.

"This is our top of the range, very special selection, very expensive." She smiled as she opened the door, "Perhaps there will be something to engage your interest in here."

As the door swung open Kiera's legs went weak. So this was it. This was what Jack's female informant couldn't talk about.

"Jack?" she hissed.

"Filming, Kiera. Be brave."

"Who is Jack?" Lianna asked, with a puzzled look.

Kiera swallowed. "Oh…sorry, just thinking out loud."

Lianna's smile returned, "So, is there anything here that interests you?"

Kiera realised she needed to give an Academy Award winning performance. It was going to be one of the hardest things she'd ever done in her life. Smothering her anger, she took a deep breath and smiled wickedly. "This is exactly what I've been looking for, tell me about all of them."

"Well done," Jack's voice said.

The room was filled with children, both boys and girls; android children ranging from babies to preteens. Numerous models lined the walls and were dressed in a variety of different costumes. They ranged from girls in fairy outfits, sleazy jumpsuits and tiny bikinis to boys in Tarzan outfits, sailor suits and skimpy bathers.

"These are the base models." Lianna pointed to twelve children, featured in display cases, in the centre of the room. They were all naked.

"I'm not interested in babies." Kiera struggled to keep the horror out of her voice as she walked to the next case. It held a blonde-haired girl aged about eight or nine.

Lianna touched a button on the display case.

The child fixed Kiera with her blue eyes as she began to speak.

"Would you like to take me home? We could play together. I know some great games. I like to be naughty. Do you like to be naughty?"

"Let's move on," Kiera said, almost choking. There were four other girls, and the conversations became progressively more sexual. Kiera dug her fingernails into her palms. She wanted to turn around and run, but she had to keep going. She had to get this recorded. Next, they studied the six boys. As she walked around with Lianna, Kiera made what she hoped were appropriate comments, but inside she struggled to maintain her smile and enthusiasm. When they came to the last one she came close to losing it. This boy appeared different somehow. She suddenly realised why. God, he looked so much like Luke—the deep auburn hair, the impossibly blue eyes. She stood, transfixed with shock, as Lianna touched the button.

"Are you my mother? I'm so lonely. Please take me home," the little boy said as his face took on a pleading look, "Please. I don't like it here. It's dark and cold, and I'm frightened." He stretched out his arms. "Please take me home and be my mother." Kiera stood mesmerised, as tears began streaming down his face.

"Kiera," came Jack's voice. "Your breathing and heart rate have slowed, you're being drugged."

"Convincing, isn't it?" Lianna said as she silenced the demonstration. The boy froze, arms outstretched, with tears still glistening on his cheeks.

What was wrong with her? She actually wanted to take this one home. She wanted to be his mother, she wanted to hold him in her arms, to tell him not to be afraid, to…

"Kiera. Move!"

Jack's voice reverberated through her head, jerking her back to awareness.

"We've got enough footage. Go—go now! "

She shook her head, took a deep breath, and turned to Lianna. "Thank you so much. There's so much choice. I'll have to go away and think about it. I need to leave now, but I'll be in touch."

"Come with me and I will let you out."

Kiera followed the android back to the blank wall.

Lianna waved her hand and the door slid open. "I hope you enjoyed the tour and you don't find choosing a model too taxing. Prices can be negotiable depending on the volume of the order. We hope to hear from you soon. Goodbye."

Kiera stepped back into the main display area. The door glided shut behind her. The image of the little boy still filled her mind. She felt guilty about leaving him behind.

"Jack, what the hell was that? I'm still feeling it."

"My guess—oxytocin, or a derivative of it. It's the bonding hormone, the hormone of love."

"Get me out of here, Jack." She felt the effects of the chemical slipping away, as a furious revulsion welled up inside her, and she flooded with anger. She'd expected some of it but not the children. She hadn't been prepared for that. What a disgusting animal Williamson was.

"Go back out the way you came. Once you're through the airlock, I'll turn your night vision back on. Follow the arrows and stay calm, Kiera. We have all the evidence we need." He sounded so matter-of-fact, almost tranquil. She could have strangled him.

Kiera retraced her steps back through the airlock. Once Jack had turned off the lights and activated the night vision, she only had to follow the arrows. She pounded down the seemingly endless passageways until finally she reached the exit door. When Jack had opened it, she dashed through and hurtled towards the cyclone fence. She skidded to a stop in front of it and screamed.

"Kiera?" came Jack's worried voice. "I'm on my way."

#

Jack had already begun to pack everything away, but after hearing Kiera's scream he turned and ran to the fence. Kiera stood immobile and dazed on the other side.

"Kiera, are you okay?"

"The bloody cutters are stuck to the fence and the hole's vanished," she snarled. "It's Zarking gone." She thumped down on to the ground. Bracing herself with both feet, she gripped the fence with her hands and began to yank it hard backwards and forwards like a trapped wild animal.

"Calm down, Kiera, and stop shouting. It must be a nanolone fence. It automatically repairs itself. If the cutters were leaning on it, they will have been absorbed. I'm sorry, I should have thought of that. Stand back. I'll see if I can kick it in. It takes a while to harden up."

Kiera stood up and moved to one side.

In the moonlight, he could see her shaking silhouette. God, I hope she's not going into shock, Jack thought. He sat down and bent both knees up to his chest. He lent forward and gripped the fence with both hands either side of where the hole should have been. Launching his legs, he kicked as hard as he could. A metallic crash echoed through the silence, and he felt the fence give a little in one corner.

"A second go should do it. Can you get hold of the centre and pull while I push? "

Still silent, Kiera sat down opposite him. She braced her feet on the fence on either side and threaded her fingers through the wire.

"Okay, on the count of three. One, two, three."

Jack kicked as hard as he could while Kiera hauled. She fell over backwards as his feet punched the hole through, narrowly missing her. He pulled himself upright and stood up. Kiera scrambled up, hurled the piece of fence aside and came at him; a screaming, punching, ball of fury. He staggered back under the reign of her blows. He put his arms up to ward her off but tripped over and went sprawling onto his back. Blood streamed from his forehead and into his right eye from where he'd caught himself on an overhanging branch on the way down. Kiera went over with him and continued to pummel his chest.

"For God sake Kiera, calm down." He managed to grab her wrists, but she still struggled furiously, trying to get free.

"Kiera! Stop it!" He gave up, let go her wrists, put his arms around her waist and rolled over on top of her. He grabbed both her wrists again and pinned her legs underneath his.

"Kiera! Kiera for God's sake. Remember Lisa. Remember what happened the last time your anger got out of control?" he shouted.

She stopped struggling.

Jack sat up and wiped the blood from his eye with the back of his hand, "What the bloody hell was all that about?"

Kiera, quiet now, cried silently, her tears barely visible in the moonlight. Jack climbed off her and pulled her upright. He wrapped both arms around her and held her as she sobbed. Minutes passed, and part of him wished he could stay that way forever.

The sobs subsided, and Kiera looked up at him. Her face, lit by moonlight, softened with contrition as she noticed the blood trickling down his face.

"Oh Jack, did I do that?"

"No, but you did everything else. I'm going to be covered with bruises. What on earth bought that on? You were like a wild animal."

"I...just lost it. You should have known about the fence and warned me so I wouldn't have left the cutters where I did."

"A little out of proportion don't you think?"

"It wasn't just that. It was what I'd seen inside as well as everything that happened. It was all just..."

"I saw the same thing, Kiera," Jack said, quietly.

Kiera took a clean handkerchief out of her pocket and reached up to gently dab the cut above Jack's right eyebrow. "I'm sorry," she said almost imperceptibly.

"Remind me never to really piss you off in the future. I'll forgive you this time, but if you ever do that again, Kiera, that will be the end of our friendship. Is that clear?"

Kiera nodded.

"Go back to the bike and put your helmet on, I'll put the piece of fence back so nobody will know we were here."

After he had reinstated the fence as much as possible, he limped back to the bike. He saw Kiera don her helmet like an automaton. When he reached her, she reanimated.

"Jack, are you okay to drive?" Her tone held concern.

"I'm okay. Are you civilised now?" He put his arm around her and gave her a little squeeze.

"Yes." She wrapped her arms around him and buried her face in his chest. "I'm really sorry Jack. I promise it won't happen again…ever. Now let's get out of here."

"Okay, let's go."

Kiera helped him pull the bike off its supports and wheel it back to the road. They got on and rode away.

\#

When they reached Kiera's apartment, they pulled around the back. Kiera got off the bike and stood up stiffly. When Jack made no attempt to dismount she said, "Come up with me and I'll clean up that cut for you."

"I'm too bloody tired. I'm liable to flake out," he said in a tired voice.

"Stay the night. The lounge is comfortable, and I don't snore." When he still didn't move, she took off her helmet and fastened it to the back of his bike. "I'll make you a hot chocolate. Come on." She tugged at his elbow.

He relented, climbed off the bike and followed her inside. Up in her apartment, Jack limped to the lounge and sat down.

Kiera put the kettle on and went into the bathroom. She rummaged in her bathroom cabinet for cotton wool, disinfectant and plasters. The kettle had just begun to boil when she re-emerged. After she made them both hot chocolates, she tipped some of the hot water into a bowl. She added a little cold water before setting it down on the coffee table near Jack. After bringing over the cups of hot chocolate she knelt down in front of him and gently dabbed at the cut above his eyebrow. When she'd finished she cleaned the blood off the rest of his face. She patted his face dry with some tissues before she dabbed antiseptic on the cut and placed a plaster over it. By the time she'd finished Jack's eyes were drooping closed.

She got the spare pillow and blanket from her bedroom and brought them into the lounge. Jack had taken off his jacket and his shoes and had already stretched out. She placed the pillow under his head and draped the blanket over him. Within seconds he fell asleep. As she watched his peaceful, relaxed face, she found herself filled with tenderness followed by a wave of guilt. Dear Jack, how could she have attacked him like that? She'd let anger overwhelm her. She'd lost control. He'd done the right thing by reminding her of the last time—of Lisa. When memories of Lisa had flooded back grief had washed away her anger. Kiera sighed. She couldn't afford to let her anger run riot. I need to learn how to cope with stress a lot better than this, she realised.

Exhausted by the night's events she went into her bedroom. She stripped down to her underwear, slipped into bed and soon fell into a deep sleep.

She awoke to the sound of her mobi. Surely, she'd only been asleep for minutes? She sat up groggily and picked up her mobi from her bedside table.

"Hi Kiera," Luke's cheery voice said, "I bought a surprise breakfast. Can you buzz me in?"

"Oh. I hope there's enough for three, I've got company." Bloody hell, Kiera thought, I shouldn't have said that. She hung up before Luke could reply. She rolled out of bed, wriggled into her jeans and pulled her jumper on. When she came out into the lounge, Jack was just putting his shoes on. The buzzer now sounded impatiently. She went to the door and pressed the button.

Jack grinned at her. "Just as well your mobi rang, otherwise, I'd still be out cold." He glanced up and frowned. "What's wrong?"

"It's going to be…" At that moment her door bell sounded. "It's Luke. Follow my lead." Kiera opened the door.

Chapter 14

Jack zipped up his boots and looked up when Kiera opened the door. So, this was Luke.

Luke said, "I know it's early, so I hope…"

Luke's voice trailed off as his laser blue eyes locked on to him. They were filled with a burning intensity, and his smile transitioned from hurt to anger.

He turned on Kiera and hissed, "Who the hell is this?"

Oh God, Jack thought. He's got the wrong idea. He had to act fast before the situation escalated. He winced as he pushed himself up from the lounge.

Kiera's expression hovered between embarrassment and sheepishness as she attempted to introduce him. "This is my friend, Jack. Jack, this is Luke. Jack's been helping me navigate through the evidence on Williamson."

Clever choice of words, Kiera, Jack thought. "So this is Luke," he said, limping over to him and smiling. "Kiera and I go way back. Here, let me take some of those for you." He reached out and caught hold of one of the bags Luke held.

Luke tugged the bag free from his grip. "I can manage, thank you."

Another angry person. He'd had enough of anger over the past twelve hours, and now this. He'd have to call on all his old psychology skills, and fast. He stepped back and held up his hands, "Okay, I surrender, I wasn't about to pinch your favourite."

Kiera gave a nervous giggle.

Luke walked over to the dining table and dropped the bags with a thump.

Jack shrugged, this wasn't going to be easy. "Takes me back to kindergarten days, Kiera."

Kiera chuckled. "Just what I was thinking."

But he wasn't going to be deterred that easily. He knew how important Luke was to Kiera, and he needed to make sure they got off to a good start. He limped over to the table, smiled, and holding out his hand tried again, "Pleased to meet you, Luke. I've heard a lot about you."

Luke, frozen to the spot, glared at him without speaking, his right hand still locked by his side.

Jack pulled a face. "Parties at your place must be fun." His humour wasn't working, so perhaps a strategic withdrawal might be the best option. "Should I go, Kiera?"

"Absolutely not!" She rounded on Luke, "For Zark's sake, Luke, Jack is an old friend. He helped me through an extremely difficult time in my teens. You're behaving like a child."

Luke stood immobile.

Jack saw his expression soften when he spotted the neatly folded blanket topped by the pillow he'd used last night on the lounge. Perhaps now they'd get somewhere.

Luke seemed to come to a decision of some sort and asked, "What happened to your face Jack, and why are you limping?"

Before he could reply, Kiera jumped in, "He slipped on the pavement last night, rolled his ankle and cut his forehead. The job took hours, and he wasn't in good shape by the time we finished, so I persuaded him to sleep on the lounge."

She could hardly say she had come at him like a screaming banshee, and had knocked him over causing his injuries, could she, Jack thought? He couldn't do anything other than play along with her, so he simply nodded.

"Oh. I'm…sorry." Luke finally held out his hand. "I'm Luke. I obviously don't need to say any more, since you've heard all about me."

He reached out and took Luke's hand.

Luke held it in a vice-like grip and gave it a single shake. With an expression of uncertainty tinged with anger, he held it captive as he locked eyes with him.

At least I've made some progress, Jack thought as he watched Luke's face mellow and felt his imprisoned hand released.

Luke walked over to Kiera and kissed her on the lips.

He's laying claim to her, Jack thought. He had the sudden urge to laugh but coughed instead.

Kiera raised her eyebrows as Luke went back to the table and stood facing him.

In an attempt to lighten the atmosphere, Jack said, "I don't know about you, but I'm starving. It looks like you've bought enough for a small army, Luke. Let's eat." He grinned. How long could he keep this up? His face was beginning to ache from the effort.

Luke sat down at the table, and Jack sat opposite him.

Kiera fetched plates from the kitchen and dished out Danish pastries from one of the bags.

Just as well Luke had bought a choice of items, Jack thought.

After she'd given them each a plate, she sat down at the end of the table. "Help yourself, you two."

After they'd dished out a pastry each, Luke said, in between a mouthful, "So Jack, what exactly was it that you helped Kiera with when she was a teenager?"

Bloody hell. Jack looked at Kiera.

She frowned and gave an almost imperceptible shake of her head. She glared at Luke. "Jack was my youth counsellor." She sniffed and began to carefully brush invisible crumbs off her jumper. "I got myself into trouble and Jack helped me work through it. I'll tell you all about it sometime."

"Oh?" Luke fixed him with an unwavering stare.

Jack squirmed in his seat and examined his plate, "Those were the days weren't they, Kiera?" Kiera remained silent so he prattled on, "Those pastries were great, Luke. Has anybody besides me got room for some fresh bread and jam?" he said, eyeing the crusty loaf in the centre of the table.

"I'll get the bread knife." Kiera escaped to the kitchen where they heard her delving in the knife drawer.

He'd felt like saying 'is that wise, under the circumstances', but decided he'd better not.

"So, Jack." Luke skewered him with his gaze, "You've been helping Kiera sort through our evidence against Williamson?"

"Something like that." Luke's eyes held him captive and Jack felt as though he was about to drown.

The moment shattered when Kiera returned to the table. "There you go." She sat down and put the bread knife on the breadboard. "Tuck in, I'm going to."

An awkward silence followed. Luke grabbed the knife, and pointedly cut slices for Kiera and himself. He smothered his with apricot jam before looking up. "Are you still a youth counsellor,

Jack?" Luke picked up his slice of bread and took a mouthful before he fixed him with a steady gaze, waiting for his answer.

Jack picked up the bread knife and cut himself a slice before replying. Two could play that game, "No, I'm a bit too old now. They like youth workers to be not too much older than the people they're working with. It helps you to relate to one another."

"You look a lot older than Kiera."

Jack winced. "Ouch. I'm only eight years older than Kiera, but it *was* a tough night."

Luke smiled this time, before asking, "So what do you do now?"

"I'm a computer and IT consultant." He wiped jam off the corner of his mouth and helped himself to another slice.

"Oh," Luke said, "what area in particular?"

"Predominantly computer security, I set up systems, and ferret out problems."

"He's also a hacker extraordinaire," Kiera said, in between licking jam off her fingers. "And he has a network of informants scattered around heaps of organisations he's able to call on for help, if he needs to. He's been absolutely invaluable in sourcing information to help us out with our campaign against Williamson. Would anybody like a cup of tea?" Kiera leapt up from the table.

Jack heard her sigh as she darted towards the kitchen; probably with relief.

"Yes thanks," Jack said.

Luke echoed his reply.

Jack felt himself relax at last or was it exhaustion? At least his struggle with Luke appeared to be over; he seemed calmer.

"I'll be back in a minute," Kiera said, ducking into the bedroom.

He made a sudden decision. Luke registered surprise when he leant forward and whispered, "She loves *you*, Luke. I've never seen her look so happy." When he heard the toilet flush, he put his finger to his lips as he sat back again.

Relief flooded Luke's face, and he gave a slight nod of acknowledgement.

Finally, he had understood.

Kiera fixed them all tea. She continued to distract them by encouraging them to talk about their uni days. Surprisingly, he and Luke in many ways had a lot of things in common. Once Luke had thawed, he found him to be an intelligent, warm, and likeable young man. He thought Kiera had found herself a perfect match.

#

After breakfast, Kiera walked Jack down to his bike. The sky had turned leaden, and a light drizzle misted the air.

"Thanks for playing along," Kiera said, "I didn't tell him what I was going to do last night, because I knew he'd try and stop me, or worse still, he'd have wanted to come."

Jack paused and turned to her. "I understand. I'll edit the files and send you copies by this evening. How are you going to explain the footage to Luke?"

"He's not going to see it until Williamson is confronted with it."

"Kiera, confronting Williamson will be stressful enough without adding to it. Show the footage to Luke tonight, otherwise he'll feel ambushed." He wanted to say more, but he could tell by the look on her face he didn't need to labour the point. He turned his back on her as he unfastened his helmet from his bike. He didn't want Kiera to see how angry he was. He wanted to shake her, to shout, 'don't you know what you've got here you stupid girl.' He'd seen how much Luke loved her. It had shone from his eyes. He would hate to see that light go out.

Kiera sighed. "I hadn't thought about it, Jack, but you're probably right. I'll show him tonight. Yesterday, I just couldn't think of any other way to deal with it. I had too many other things on my mind."

"Good." Jack went to get on his bike.

Kiera touched his shoulder. "Don't I get a hug before you go?"

He turned, and after he gave her a brief hug, he got on his bike and rode away. He didn't look back.

Chapter 15

Flashback to 2041

"Are you busy, Jack?"

He looked up from his desk. "Brian. How the hell are you?" A wave of shock ran through him. Brian's face appeared thin and drawn, his clothes were dishevelled and he'd aged considerably. Was he ill? Guilt spiked into his consciousness when he realised he hadn't seen him for around six months. Brian was still standing by the door. "Come in Brian, and sit down."

Brian walked over to the chair opposite and flopped into it.

"Are you okay, Brian? You look..." He snapped the case file he'd been reading closed and pushed it out of the way.

"I have a bit of a situation, Jack. I need to ask you a huge favour."

"Oh?" In the past it was usually him asking the favours.

"This is...awkward, Jack, but I better fill you in on the details, so you know all the facts." He leaned forward in his chair.

"I'll assume you haven't heard any of the rumours about me." He gave him a questioning look.

"No."

Brian laid both hands on the desk. He seemed to be struggling to put whatever *it* was into words.

Jack waited. Brian's expression held a strange mixture of embarrassment and something else he couldn't fathom.

"I've done something incredibly stupid, Jack. It's cost me my marriage, and it's sent my daughter, Kiera, off the rails."

"Bloody hell, Brian. What's happened?"

"I had a short affair with a junior officer. It's over now, but the damage has been done, and now I have to face the consequences." He paused and stared at him.

Jack, shocked to the core, managed to keep his expression neutral. He couldn't believe what he'd just heard. He knew Brian to be an honourable, honest man of integrity. He was the last person he would have expected to have had an affair.

Brian Proud had stepped into his life when he'd been in trouble. He'd been fifteen, and without Brian's help, he probably would have ended up in gaol. At a time when he'd needed a male role model, Brian had been there for him. Although he hadn't seen him for a while, they were still close.

Brian had steered him into the Youth Counselling Program. It had proved invaluable and had given him a totally new perspective on life.

After finishing school he'd needed a part-time job to support himself—and to take some of the load off his mum—while he was doing his digital science course at the University of Western Australia. Brian had persuaded him to do the six months training program necessary to qualify as a youth counsellor. The pay, once he'd qualified, wasn't spectacular, but it fitted his needs as the hours were flexible and allowed him to enrol as a part-time student at uni.

Initially, he'd found it difficult to be emotionally detached but over the years had mastered the art; most of the time. He could now pull on a convincing poker face, even under dire circumstances.

"How can I help?"

"It's Kiera. To cut a long story short, she's not been able to handle the breakup. She's been binge drinking, and last night she and a friend wrote off my car in Kings Park."

"Bloody hell! Is she alright?"

"Yes, but her friend wasn't wearing a seatbelt and got thrown out. She's in a critical condition and is currently on life support in Royal Perth Hospital."

"Bloody hell! How did they get hold of your car?"

"She stole it from out the front of my place."

Brian, anguish etched into his face, looked as though he hadn't slept for weeks.

"She's up before the magistrate tomorrow. Because of my position I've been able to pull a few strings. She's got no priors, and she's a minor, so the lawyer thinks he can get her off. He's going to make a plea of mitigating circumstances and ask that she be placed in counselling to undergo an anger management course."

"Ah, so that's where I come in."

"I know it's a big ask, Jack, but frankly you're the only person that I think might be able to reach her."

"I'll do my best, Brian." He felt privileged Brian trusted him enough to ask him. Although shocked by his disclosures, he owed Brian so much that he certainly wasn't going to judge him. Brian had often talked about Kiera. He doted on his daughter—and his wife for that matter. What could have…?

"I warn you, Jack, she's incredibly angry, and she's struggling with the fact her friend is probably going to die. Kiera was driving."

"Oh God. How soon do you want me to see her, Brian?" Kiera wasn't the only person struggling.

"It all revolves around tomorrow's hearing. If we get a judgement in Kiera's favour, the next day—if you're able."

He consulted his appointment book. "I've got lectures at uni all day Thursday, but I could do a late appointment at five. Would that suit?"

A wave of relief spilled over Brian's face. "That would be great, Jack. Thanks, I owe you."

"We're friends, Brian, you don't owe me anything."

Brian got up to leave, but when he reached the door he paused and turned around. "For Christ's sake don't let on it was me that organised this, Jack. She's in payback mode, if she knows I've been involved she'll refuse to co-operate. She's refusing to speak to me at the moment."

"Sure. No problem, Brian."

He could see the pain behind Brian's eyes as he turned away and went out the door. Stunned, he sat and allowed his thoughts to trickle around until they finally congealed. He was going to have his work cut out with this one.

Chapter 16

Flashback to 2041

God, she looks like a real piece of work, Jack thought, eyeing Kiera Proud as she plonked down opposite him. She'd sauntered in late and unapologetic. Dressed entirely in black apart from her jacket, accessorised with matching jack boots and a satchel, she'd not uttered one single word since she'd come through the door, and now she sat contemplating her hands.

Jack pretended to be looking through her file. He'd had his approach all mapped out, but it went out of the window as soon as she had walked in.

One side of her head was completely shaved while the other was covered with long, bright pink hair. She'd topped that off with a tight-fitting purple jacket, which, after settling in the chair, she'd proceeded to slowly unzip in a slow and provocative manner. He'd found it slightly unnerving. She was exquisite, in spite of the hair. A strong attraction pulled on him like a magnetic field. For all her punk bravado, she exhibited a delicate, sensitive, calm poise.

He cleared his throat, and she looked up. She locked eyes filled with pain and anger on him.

"Would you like a cup of tea or coffee, Kiera?"

"No, thank you."

He inwardly breathed a sigh of relief. At least she was going to be polite. He'd half expected a language filled rant followed by her storming out.

Without taking his eyes off her, he said, "This is just an information gathering session, Kiera, so we can get to know one another."

Her sullen expression didn't change, but at least she hadn't looked away.

"We need to figure out a program that will suit you. How about we start with you telling me what your expectations are and how I can best help you?"

She gathered herself up before answering him. "Isn't that your job?"

"We endeavour to work closely with our clients so we can effectively fulfil their needs."

"That's just bullshit jargon."

At last, a reaction. "Okay, to put it more simply, I can't help you if I don't know what you need or want."

"I don't want to be here, and this isn't what I need." She stood up.

"Sit down. You're here by order of the Magistrate's Court. You might not want to be here, but from what I've read on your file you certainly need to be. Now please, sit down." He sighed, got up from his desk, walked around and stood in front of her chair.

She gave him a look filled with venom. "Don't try and push me around by standing over me."

"Okay." He crouched down in front of her. "Is that better?"

A brief flutter of surprise flitted across her face before she pulled it back into a sullen mask.

"Kiera, I've seen your charge sheet. By some miracle, your lawyer managed to get your charges suspended, but it's conditional on you working with me to try and sort out some of your problems. If you refuse, they'll charge you with stealing a vehicle, driving without a license, dangerous driving and possibly manslaughter. Do you understand?"

"I'm not stupid." Her eyes lasered into him as though she was hoping he'd vanish in a puff of light.

He held both palms out. "Okay, let's take this down a notch. I noticed you're on an advanced scholarship and you're just six months into a degree in digital science. I'm only six months short of completing mine and I've won a scholarship to start a PhD next year." He caught another flicker of interest before a defiant mask reinstalled itself on her face.

She began a slow clap. "I'm supposed to be impressed, am I?"

He stayed put and ignored her comment. "How are you finding the course?"

This time, the surprise stayed on her face. "It's zing… It's okay."

Progress. "What are you hoping to specialise in, Kiera?" He already knew, it was mentioned in her file. It was clear she was exceptionally intelligent, had an excellent grasp of the subject, and a unique and intuitive way of looking at things. He intended to make sure she didn't throw her chance at a brilliant career away. Bloody hell, he'd do somersaults and backflips if that's what it took.

She hesitated. "I'm not sure."

Jack knew she was fudging. According to her file she was dead set on specialising in AI, which was also his passion. His legs were beginning to cramp, so he stood up and went back to his chair.

"The AI lecturers are bloody brilliant." He spied the beginnings of a smile on Kiera's mouth. "Dr Peter Bronstein is doing a six months stint as a lecturer next year."

Instantly, Kiera's face lit with enthusiasm. "Wow! He's brilliant."

Gotcha. Progress at last. Jack grinned inwardly.

"I noted your attendance at lectures and submission of assignments has fallen right off in the last month. I suggest you defer the rest of this year's course until next year, Kiera. Then, when we've sorted your problems out, you can recommence. That way, you won't lose your scholarship." He paused and waited for a response.

Kiera smiled. "You're a persistent little bastard, aren't you?"

"Look, you obviously have an exceptional intellect." A lot like mine, actually, he thought to himself. "I'd hate to see you throw away the chance of a brilliant, exciting career. So, how about we work together, to get you back on track. Do you mind me calling you Kiera?" He raised his eyebrows.

"It's a bit late now—*Jack*," she chortled. "In answer to your questions, yes, and no."

#

Jack groaned inwardly. Kiera had arrived late again and had lapsed back to the sullen silence she'd fronted him with yesterday. He noticed the red eyes and the puffy face. Perhaps, direct confrontation might work—what did he have to lose by trying it?

"Tell me what's wrong, Kiera?"

As her eyes met his, he could see her lips trembling.

"I can't do this." She screwed up her eyes, but it didn't stop the tears from leaking out.

"Can't do what, Kiera?" His stomach tightened into a knot. He had to figure out a way to help her.

She lost it and started to sob. "This! I can't sit here and pretend everything is normal. I just can't."

Jack took a deep breath, struggling to maintain neutrality. Perhaps it was because she was Brian's daughter. It was all he could do not to leap up and put his arms around her—to hold her until she stopped crying. Totally inappropriate, but he had to do something. He got up and went to crouch in front of her. He reached out and took her hand in both of his.

"Kiera, whatever we talk about here is between us, so please, tell me what's wrong. Tell me how I can help."

There was an unexpected flash of anger in her eyes. She pulled her hand free and shouted, "You can bring people back from the dead, can you?"

Realisation struck him. Her friend, the one on life support—oh God. "Has your friend died, Kiera?" He experienced a surge of anger. Why hadn't anybody told him?

"They turned off her life support, this morning. They—they wouldn't let me see her. They wouldn't let me say goodbye." Her whole body shook as her sobs turned into howls.

He pushed himself up off the floor and went to stand behind her chair. He reached out and rubbed her arm with one hand. "I'm so sorry, Kiera." He continued to comfort her until her sobbing subsided. He crouched in front of her again, and her tear-filled eyes locked onto his.

"Do you want to talk about it, or would you like to me to run you home? I've got time."

"Talk."

"Okay, how about I fix us both a cup of tea?" He stood up.

"Thanks, Jack, that would be good." Kiera grabbed a tissue from the box on his desk and began to wipe her eyes.

#

He spent an hour and a half with her. She talked about her friend, Lisa; how they'd met; how she'd been seduced into the binge drinking; and their numerous drunken exploits; and how they just seemed to egg one another on. She'd managed to keep a lid on it until her father's affair. It was only then it had got totally out of hand. She talked a lot about guilt, the fact she'd been driving and felt ultimately responsible for her friend's death.

Jack tried to get her to talk about her father—without success. He decided it would have to wait until another time. She wouldn't let him take her home but did allow him to drop her off at the trans-station. He squeezed her in for another appointment for the following Monday.

She got off his bike and popped the helmet in the storage compartment. "Thanks, Jack." She hesitated. "You've been really helpful. You're—easy to talk to—kind, and so open."

Jack merely nodded, but inside his helmet he could feel himself grinning from ear to ear. Careful Jack, his inner voice began, and what exactly did she mean by open?

"See you, Monday. I'll make sure I'm on time." She gave him a wave and was gone.

He sat for a moment while he gathered his thoughts. Here he was at twenty-four years old, on the cusp of his chosen career in advanced digital science, worrying about his client. In six months' time, his difficulty with remaining emotionally detached was hardly going to be an issue, was it?

But although the session had been emotionally draining, it had also left him with a sense of elation. He and Kiera had finally connected.

Chapter 17

Flashback to 2041

True to her word, Kiera had arrived right on time. They had quite a lot to discuss, but first he had to get her to talk about her father in order to determine which programs best suited her needs.

"Right Kiera, I've got a lot of things to discuss with you, but—" He hesitated.

She smiled at him. "But what, Jack?"

"To enable you to move on, it's essential we talk about your father."

Her smile vanished, displaced by a look of annoyance. "Not that again, Jack. I don't want to go there."

They sat eyeing one another.

"It's necessary, Kiera for two reasons." He held up a finger. "Reason one, I need to know what, and the extent of your problem with your dad is in order to determine which program to put you into."

Kiera shook her head and went to speak, but he held up two fingers this time and said, "Reason two, the fact you're avoiding talking about it means it's a significant issue for you. It has to be dealt with, Kiera."

She crossed her arms.

He'd have to go to his Plan B. It was a risk, and he'd never done it before, but he had to do it.

"Okay, Kiera." He took a deep breath before beginning. "You're not alone in having father issues. What I'm about to tell you is strictly between you and me. I've never discussed this with anyone other than my mother and my aunt."

That got her attention, she leaned forward and fixed her eyes on him.

"I'm taking a big risk trusting you, Kiera. Do I have your word that it doesn't leave this room?"

"Yes, Jack." She unfolded her arms and placed her hands in her lap.

"Okay." He let his mind time travel backwards to when he was seven.

Flashback to 2024

He heard a thump, followed by the drawn-out scrabbling of his dad trying to get his key into the front door lock.

Jack was helping his mum by doing the drying up. His mother sighed, dumped the frying pan into the sink, and snapped off her gloves. He heard the sound of the front door opening and his dad's footsteps thump—thumping, down the hall.

"You'd better get to bed, Jack, before…" His mum muttered something under her breath, just as his father lurched through the door.

"Where's my tea, woman?" His dad growled, staggering over to the table and wobbling into the chair.

"It's coming, Malcolm, I'll just get it out of the oven. I won't be a tick."

She always sounded so nice. He'd never heard her be nasty or shout at his dad.

"What's he still doing up?" His dad jerked his head in his direction. He looked really annoyed. He wondered what he'd done wrong now. His dad always seem to be angry with him for some reason.

"I was helping Mum by doing the drying up."

"I was helping Mum," he mimicked, glaring at his mum. "Boys don't help their mums with domestic stuff, Jack. Drying up is a woman's job, not yours."

"Why, Dad?" Jack heard his mum suck in her breath, like she had something too hot in her mouth.

She'd just opened the oven and had pulled out the plate of tea she'd dished up for his dad, earlier. As she turned, his dad thumped the table and it made his knife and fork jump up and down. Almost in slow motion, Jack watched as the hot plate of food leapt from his startled mum's hands. The plate clattered onto the tiled floor and smashed into pieces. Broken pieces of plate and his dad's food went flying all over the kitchen.

With a roar, his dad lurched up from the table and launched himself at his mum.

His fist connected with thin air because his mother had skipped out of his reach. It would have been funny, except Jack saw the familiar frightened look in his mum's eyes. His dad swayed towards her, but Jack darted in front of him.

"No, Jack. Go to bed." His mum's voice had that funny tight sound she often got when his dad was around.

He didn't move. A sob caught in his throat but he stood his ground.

"How dare you, you little shit," his dad spat at him. His father's large, hairy hands grabbed both shoulders, whirled him around, and threw him towards the oven. There was a crack as his head connected with the oven door, followed by darkness.

When he opened his eyes, his mum's troubled face was hovering over him. He could see she'd been crying. His head hurt; a lot. She was holding something on top of his forehead. He shivered with the cold of it. To one side of her he could see his dad's legs. He shifted his head and saw his dad, flat on his face, partly under the table.

"Are you alright, Mum?"

"Yeah, I'm okay. How about you, my little hero?"

He grinned up at her. "What happened to Dad?"

"I clobbered him with the frying pan, Jack."

"Wow!" He'd never seen his mum fight back before. His dad hadn't stirred. "You haven't killed him, have you?"

"Nah, more's the pity. He'll have a big headache when he wakes up, though." She lifted the tea towel full of ice away from his forehead. "You'll have a bit of a bump there Jack, but at least it's not bleeding. Right!" She got up off her knees and stood up. "You just keep holding the ice against your head, Jack. I'm going to go and pack us a few things, and then we'll get out of here. I'm not going to wait around for him to wake up. I'm going to make damn sure, he never touches either of us again."

From the doorway, she said, "If he starts to wake up, Jack, give me a yell."

His head started to throb. He could hear his mum rummaging around at the back of the house. A little while later, he saw her trundle two small suitcases past the kitchen door. Then he heard her talking on the phone.

She came back into the kitchen and gave his dad the once over.

"Well, the bastard's still breathing. Right, let's go."

114

She stepped over to him and pulled him up. After she dumped the ice blocks onto the floor, she led him into the hall. When the taxi arrived, she threw the keys down the hall, pulled him outside and slammed the door.

Jack never forgot the expression on his mum's face as they drove away that night. Her face had glowed like she'd just won lotto. It was in the taxi he decided he would never drink. He was the man of the family now, and he was going to make sure no one ever hurt his mum ever again. It was the last time he saw his dad, and he didn't care one little bit.

Year 2041

"So, you never saw him again, ever?" Kiera asked.

"No. He never contacted my mum either. You're probably wondering what this has got to do with you. I've asked around about your dad, Kiera," he lied. "My sources tell me he's an outstanding policeman who goes out on a limb to help young people who've got into trouble—to turn their lives around. He's well-respected and regarded as an honest, and decent person who always treats people fairly." At least that part wasn't a lie. "According to Constable Harrington, he moved heaven and earth to get your charges suspended. He's really cut up by the whole situation. The constable told me your dad loves you dearly, Kiera. He's devastated you won't speak to him."

Kiera exploded. He'd expected it sooner.

"He had an affair, Jack, with someone twenty years younger than him. My mum was shattered. Every time I ring her she bawls her eyes out," she yelled, balling her fists up. She thumped her fist on the desk. "Is that a decent, honest man? Is it, Jack? Is it?"

"Did he beat your mum up, Kiera? Did you dread him coming home? Did he fail to provide for you and your mum? Did you live in fear every second he was in your house?

"He made a terrible mistake, Kiera, which according to Constable Harrington, he deeply regrets. At least you have a dad." The last part sort of slipped out, and he realised he'd raised his voice.

Kiera stared at him for a moment before a single tear trickled down her face, followed by another, and another. "I'm so sorry, Jack. It must've been horrible having a dad like yours." She grabbed a tissue and wiped her eyes.

Jack swallowed. He couldn't think of anything to say. His last comment had even surprised him.

"I'm ready to talk now, Jack."

"Good girl." He opened his notebook and picked up his pen.

Chapter 18

Year 2055

Luke paced up and down until he heard Kiera at the door, then stood ready to confront her.

"What the Zark is going on between you two, and what were you and Jack really doing last night?" He stood in front of her with his hands on his hips.

Kiera pushed past him as she stepped inside and closed the door. She brushed water from her sleeves and the front of her jumper, before turning to face him. "I've already told you. We were collating the information I've gathered about Williamson. I'll discuss it with you when I get the edited material back from Jack. He's sending it through tonight. Now that's it Luke. I don't want to hear anything more about it."

He wasn't going to be fobbed off. "Why did you lie about what happened to Jack?" he shouted. "I want the truth Kiera, and I want it now." He felt himself shaking.

"All right," Kiera yelled. "I lied because I felt ashamed, Luke. We discovered something last night that pushed me over the edge. I lost it and took it out on Jack—that's how he fell over and got hurt."

"Did he hurt you? I'll kill him if he hurt you." He clenched his fists.

"No Luke, Jack would never hurt me." There were tears in her eyes.

"I saw the way he looked at you, Kiera."

"Don't be ridiculous, Luke. We're friends. That's all. I know you're angry, and I'm sorry if I've hurt you. I'm still trying to process what we discovered. I'll show you tonight. I think you'll understand after you've seen it." Kiera gave a deep sigh.

"Now, we need to get a move on or we'll be late for work. I'm going to go and have a quick shower, I presume you've already had yours?" She regarded him, her face sullen.

He was being dismissed. "You've gone behind my back, Kiera. It makes me feel that you don't trust me. Why would you do that?" He blinked away tears.

"Oh, Luke." She wrapped her arms around him. "Of course, I trust you. It was just something Jack and I had to do on our own. It was risky, and I wanted to keep you safe." She reached up and took his face in her hands. "I love you so much, and I didn't want anything to happen to you."

"Kiera, how do you think I would have felt if something had happened to you? We're a team, Kiera. I don't need protecting. Please, please don't ever do anything like that again without telling me." He wrapped his arms around her and hugged her tight, and for a moment, they stood together in silence. As she let go of him, he held her at arm's length and said, "No more secrets—promise?"

She wiped the tears from her face. "Promise. Now I need to go have my shower."

118

She disappeared into the bedroom, and after a few minutes, Luke heard running water. His breathing had become ragged and his fists were still clenched. He sat down at the kitchen table and took some deep breaths to reclaim his racing brain.

He'd managed to calm himself by the time Kiera reappeared, dressed and ready to go. He still needed answers about where Kiera and Jack had been last night. They certainly hadn't been sifting through papers in Kiera's apartment.

Kiera grabbed her bag, hoisted it over her shoulder and moved to the door, one hand on her hip. "Okay, are we going?" she said, smiling at him.

He picked up his bag and followed her out. He'd ask more questions tonight. Jack had allowed his guard to drop a few times this morning. The way he'd looked at Kiera was unsettling. It wasn't that he didn't trust Kiera. Perhaps it was more that he didn't trust Jack. And what did he mean by what he'd said to him when Kiera had gone to the toilet? He hadn't been quite sure how to take that. Because Kiera obviously thought the sun, moon and stars shone from him, the less he said about it the better, so he'd sit on it for the time being.

#

At lunchtime, he knocked on Kiera's door. Without waiting for an answer, he opened it and peered in, relieved when Kiera greeted him with a smile.

"Shall we go and get some lunch in the cafeteria?" Luke asked.

"How can you be hungry after such an enormous breakfast?" Kiera raised her eyebrows.

"I've been working on a difficult problem all morning. I've used kilojoules of brainpower, and I've got hollow legs." He laughed.

"Okay, I'm feeling a bit peckish myself, it must be all the energy I expended last night. You go ahead. I'll be with you in a minute." She smiled up at him.

Thank the Universe, she was back to her usual self. He'd become accustomed to the fact that Kiera's anger, although fiery and intense, dissipated rapidly. In the cafeteria, he joined the short queue, not realising Melanie was directly in front of him. She turned before he could escape.

"Luke, how nice to bump into you, would you like to join me for lunch?" She batted her eyelids and flicked her hand through her blonde hair.

"No thanks, Kiera is joining me shortly." He hoped like hell Kiera didn't suddenly materialise and misconstrue this exchange. He didn't think he could cope with another flare up. He moved away from Melanie slightly and shifted uncomfortably from foot to foot.

"We could share a table," Melanie persisted.

"Kiera and I have got some things to discuss, so no thanks." Kiera where the hell are you?

"Oh Luke, all work and no play makes Luke a dull boy. I like to live a little dangerously myself." She closed the distance between them and gazed into his eyes.

At that moment he saw Kiera come through the door, so he peeled off the queue and went to join her. She gave him a quizzical look.

"Don't ask," he said, "You've just rescued me."

To his surprise, Kiera leaned across and kissed him on the lips. Standing back and taking his hand she flashed Melanie a smile.

Melanie blushed before looking away.

He and Kiera re-joined the queue and were soon devouring ham and salad rolls at their usual table in the corner.

"Okay Luke, here's my plan. But first, do you trust me?" She gazed at him with an open earnest expression.

"Yes, of course. Surely you don't doubt that?" He focused on his plate and used his fingers to pick up some tomato that had fallen out of his roll. He slipped the piece into his mouth.

"I wasn't too sure after this morning and the thing with Jack." Kiera frowned.

"As long as tonight you tell me exactly what you and Jack were doing and where you were last night."

"I've already said I'll explain everything, okay?"

"Okay, Kiera."

Kiera took a quick look around the tea room before she leant over and whispered, "We are going to have to leave the company."

"Why? What the hell's happened?" Luke whispered back. A wave of shock hit him, followed by anger. He pushed his plate away.

"It is complicated. I'll explain tonight. I've brought my laptop so when we get home, we can look at the edited files, Jack's sending through to me." Kiera sniffed.

"I assume you mean at my place?" Luke shifted uncomfortably in his seat.

"Absolutely, I'm going to feign a migraine. I'll go home now to get the process started, but you'll need to go back to work, otherwise Williamson will get suspicious. When is he expecting an answer about your move to Sydney?"

"By the end of the week, which I had intended to be Friday. He probably won't be expecting me to front up tomorrow morning. Why do we have to leave?" he asked, in a low voice.

"Later." Kiera got up, put her hand on her forehead and grimaced as though in pain. Luke watched as she deliberately staggered to the door, opened it and disappeared.

#

121

Kiera maintained her act as she went into her office and packed up. Once she'd left the building, out of sight of cameras, she picked up the pace. She took a trans-car to the Perth Central Police Hub to meet with Detective Inspector John Harrington, head of the Special Crimes Unit. While there, the police would take a statement from her about the pheromone lab incident. Up until now she'd only spoken to Detective Harrington on the phone, after being put into contact with him by her father. Detective Harrington, in charge of coordinating tomorrow's raids on Sentioids Inc., Williamson's apartment and her work place, had already organised the appropriate warrants. The tall, thin man in his forties had a thick unruly mop of grey-flecked, black hair—and a friendly, vaguely familiar face.

"Hello Kiera, it's been a while."

She shook his hand, convinced she knew his face from somewhere. "Have we met before?" As soon as the words were out of her mouth, she remembered. "Oh my God, you were the young constable that arrested me when I was sixteen, weren't you?"

"That's right." He smiled. "You look a bit different to the way you presented then, Kiera. You've turned into a fine young lady."

Kiera blushed. "I didn't know you knew my father so well, Detective Harrington."

"Please, call me John, Kiera. Your dad was my mentor. Just about everything I know, I learned from him. In fact, he's held in high esteem by everybody that knew or worked with him."

Kiera nodded, taken by surprise by his warmth and candour.

"Right, Kiera, let's get down to business. I'll take you down to one of our interview rooms and a constable will take a statement. Follow me."

Once her statement had been taken, John took her up to his office and outlined the plans for the following day. When he'd finished, he escorted her down to the equipment section.

"I'll leave you with Constable Johnson. She'll fix you up with a TD."

Kiera stared at him. "Sorry, what's a TD?"

"Police jargon for transmission device." He headed to the door, but before he left he said, "Come up to my office when you've finished here, Kiera. There's something I need to tell you."

Constable Johnson demonstrated the various places she could hide the TD. She opted to put it inside her bra. Constable Johnson also gave her the memory stick containing the link that would upload to Williamson's computer when she plugged it in. After being shown how to operate the TD, she headed up to John Harrington's office. She wondered what he wanted to tell her. She tapped on his door and went in.

"All set?" John indicated the chair in front of his desk.

"Yes, as much as I can be." She sniffed. "What did you want to tell me, John?"

"I wanted to tell you about Jack, because I didn't want you to find out somewhere down the track." He pushed the file he'd been looking at to one side.

"Oh?"

"What I'm about to tell you, Kiera, is strictly confidential. Jack has been on our payroll for around six years now." He sat back and paused.

For a moment she was speechless. "Jack? Jack works for you? I had no idea."

"It's not something he would broadcast, Kiera. He raised it with me because he was concerned for you. He wanted to make sure that what you did last night wasn't going to compromise you, or his contract with us. Jack wanted to tell you himself, but I thought it was better coming from me. He's employed as a consultant, but in this particular instance, he's acting as an undercover operative. He's going to facilitate us entering Sentioids Inc. and the hidden prototype vault. He is one of our most valued and trustworthy operatives. He's helped us gain many convictions in cybercrime and other computer related matters."

"Wow!"

"Now, I guess I don't need to tell you not to repeat what I've just told you to anyone else."

"No, of course not, but can I tell Luke?"

"I'm afraid not, Kiera."

Oh God, she'd just promised Luke there wouldn't be any more secrets. She bit her lip. It couldn't be helped.

"Right. Now I need your reassurance that you and Luke are able to perform your tasks tomorrow. If you're in anyway doubtful, now is the time to say so." He locked eyes with her.

"I can guarantee Luke and I are up to tomorrow's assignment. We won't go all wobbly on you."

"I'd still like to ring and speak to Luke tonight, just to reassure myself, Kiera."

"Okay. We'll be at his place; do you have his mobi number?"

"Yes thanks. I'll ring at 9 p.m. to confirm the operation. Right, that's everything, Kiera. I'll see you tomorrow." He got up and ushered her to the door. "Good luck."

\#

During the trip home, she worried about Luke. The element of surprise was everything. It was essential that he stayed calm. After this morning's argument, she hoped like hell he'd support the actions she'd taken. If Williamson got wind of anything, the whole thing could fall apart. Fingers of fear wrapped around her insides and squeezed. For a moment she couldn't breathe, and a wave of nausea swept over her.

When she got home, she called her dad. She realised how lucky she was that he'd maintained all his contacts and had been able to give her credibility with his associates, John Harrington in particular.

"Hi, Dad."

"Hi, sweetheart. From what I hear, it's all falling nicely into place."

Kiera found his steady voice comforting. "Yes, mostly thanks to your influence. I couldn't have done this without you, Dad."

"You realise you're probably about to go down in legal history. When this comes to trial, it will establish new precedents. I think it will be a landmark case. I'm so proud of you, Kiera. What you've done has taken real guts."

Kiera heard the slight choke in her father's voice. Perhaps she had finally redeemed herself. A couple of years ago, at her mum's insistence, she'd forgiven her dad for his affair and the marriage breakup. The relationship had remained cool, distant and restrained. But over the past couple of weeks, they'd grown closer. Like a nan-neuro circuit, threads had reconnected to make their love whole again.

"Thanks, Dad." Her own throat tightened. "But it wasn't just down to me. Jack's been incredible, and Luke's my inspiration. I just hope we can pull it off."

"Everything will go like clockwork, you'll see. Good luck sweetheart, and be careful. If anything goes wrong, don't put yourself in danger, just pull out."

"Okay, Dad."

"I'm dying to meet this fellow of yours when this is over. He must be something really special."

"He is. I can honestly say that I've found the love of my life, Dad. Speak to you soon, bye." She hung up, and brushed tears from the corners of her eyes. She couldn't afford to get all sentimental.

She needed to be rational and focused, and more to the point, she needed Luke to be rational and focused. Her stomach tightened at the thought of another confrontation. Seashells came to mind, and it reminded her of crunching through shell grit along a deserted beach.

Chapter 19

Luke left work earlier than normal but not enough to arouse suspicion. When he arrived home, the mouth-watering aroma of steak and onions was wafting from his door. As soon as he opened it, Kiera darted out of the kitchen. She skipped across the room and threw her arms around him.

"Hi sweetie, how was your day?"

"Have you been drinking?" Luke dropped his bag and gave her a gentle hug.

"Just a little. I needed some red wine to add to the steak and onions, so I raided your cellar. I had to try it, of course, to make sure it was okay. I've only had half a glass, and I've poured you one."

"My cellar? All six bottles? Luke groaned, "You haven't used the forty-five, have you? Please tell me you haven't used it for cooking." He grabbed the wine bottle and turned it around. "Thank the Universe for that." He gave a relieved sigh before chuckling.

"I'm not a total idiot when it comes to wine, I'll have you know. Oh God! My onions are beginning to burn." She dashed back into the kitchen. Luke followed her and surveyed the carnage. In Kiera's usual style, cutting boards, vegetable scraps, and various utensils littered the kitchen benches. He struggled to keep his expression neutral.

"I think it's cooked, I just have to make some toast. I promise I won't burn it." Kiera opened the freezer and got out the bread.

He could already smell the burnt toast—time to escape. "I'll just go and wash my hands and change." When he re-emerged, Kiera was setting two plates down at the table.

"There you go; steak and onion sandwiches with salad, accompanied by a glass of wine." She sat down opposite him and began hoeing into her toasted sandwich. Brown juice began running down her chin and dripping off her fingers.

His mouth watered, as he realised how hungry he'd become—again. He wolfed down his own sandwich. They sat there in comfortable silence licking juice from their fingers. "You make a pretty mean steak sandwich, Kiera."

Kiera beamed at him. "I do, don't I. I bought some cake for sweets. Just a little indulgence before tomorrow."

"Are we comfort eating?" Luke asked.

"Absolutely." Kiera vanished into the kitchen.

Luke cringed when he heard his plates, crash into the sink. Fortunately, his crockery was sturdy enough to be Kiera proof.

After they'd cleared the table, Kiera set up her laptop.

"Worktime," Kiera said, "Time to reveal exactly what Jack and I were up to last night."

"I was beginning to think it was a taboo subject."

"I wasn't going to show you, but Jack changed my mind."

Luke frowned. Jack again! He imagined Jack's ghost poised behind him about to tap his shoulder.

"Luke!"

He started. He needed to stay focused. "Sorry."

"I warn you, Luke, you're going to find this shocking." Kiera grimaced. "It's an experience I don't ever want to go through again."

Luke wondered what on earth was coming. Kiera brought up the file and pressed enter. They sat in silence as its contents played on the screen in front of them. His thoughts drifted from mild amusement to revulsion. He sucked in his breath when Lianna, the Asian guide, described in detail the use of the various illegal pheromones, including those that induced pain.

"Zarking hell, the bloody bastard. The Zarking, bloody bastard." Kiera pressed the pause button.

"No wonder you were so upset. I understand now why you didn't want to talk about it, but why didn't you tell me what you were going to do? I could have gone instead."

Kiera scowled. "No, you couldn't have! You wouldn't have been able to trust someone you'd only just met."

Luke avoided her gaze, and mumbled, "No, probably not."

"Jack and I know one another well." She hesitated. "We have a certain connection."

Luke raised his eyebrows. "Is that what you call it?"

Kiera ignored his comment and continued on, "You couldn't have helped. Only Jack's skills and knowledge enabled me to get in and out without being detected. It was strictly a job for two people."

"But it was so Zarking dangerous. Great Universe, Kiera, what if you'd been caught?" He shook his head. "I can't believe you did this without telling me." He sat rigid in his seat, struggling with his anger.

Kiera remained quiet and stared at the screen. "You need to see the rest. If you think what you've seen is bad, the next bit will make you feel positively sick." She avoided meeting his eyes and pressed play.

Luke sucked in his breath and sat forward, "Oh Zark...please, Holy Universe, tell me this isn't real." He began rocking backwards and forwards, "Oh Zark! Oh Kiera...this is Zarking unbelievable." On the screen, the camera panned around a small room—full of children. He listened intently to the exchange between Lianna and Kiera.

The camera zoomed in on the main label in front of the central section holding the android children. Luke's breath caught in his throat when he read the words, 'each orifice stretches comfortably ...' His stomach lurched. He leapt up, raced to the bathroom, and heaved into the toilet.

Kiera, appeared in the doorway, her face full of concern. "Luke! Are you okay?"

"I'm okay." He flushed the toilet and splashed cold water on his face. He caught his image in the mirror. A deathly white apparition stared back at him. After he patted his face dry, he walked back into the lounge.

Kiera had sat back down at the computer.

"I don't think I want to see any more," he said, weakly, as he sat next to her.

"I need to show you the last one," Kiera fast forwarded through the rest of the children. She pressed pause when it reached the final boy. "This was the one that made me lose it, Luke, because he looked so much like you." She pressed play.

Luke sat transfixed—the uncanny resemblance to himself as a boy made the hairs on the back of his neck stand up. He listened to the commentary and reached out and took Kiera's hand when he heard the boy say, 'Please take me home and be my mother.' Kiera started to sniffle, so he stabbed the pause button. The scene froze in front of them. Luke swallowed hard and sat forward to read the close-up of the label on the screen, 'All available options from the previous room are available with these models. Pain is one of our specialties. Ask the guide to elaborate and remember we can tailor your order to your specific needs.'

"Oh Kiera." Luke turned away. His throat went tight, as tears prickled in the corner of his eyes. "I'm sorry…I can't…that's enough. Shut it down"

Kiera wiped her face with her hands before shutting down the laptop.

Luke stood up. "I need a drink, how about you?"

"No, I think I've had enough for tonight. I need a clear head for tomorrow morning."

Luke went into the kitchen and opened the fridge but after a few seconds slammed it shut.

Kiera called after him, "I'm sorry, Luke, but you had to see it. We're springing a slightly different version of this on Williamson tomorrow."

"I know, but I wish I hadn't. I'm going to find it hard to get those images out of my mind." He stuck his head out of the kitchen door. "Let's sit on the lounge, and you can fill me in on the details for tomorrow. I'll make us some tea."

When he came out with the tea, Kiera, lost in thought, sat staring blankly into space.

She focused on him as he set the cups down.

He sat next to her, leant over and wrapped his arms around her.

She began to cry.

He held her and stroked her hair while she sobbed.

"I…wanted…to rescue him, Luke," she said, in between gulps of air. "It took all of my strength not to pick him up and run out of that dreadful place."

Luke took her face in his hands. "It will end for them tomorrow, Keira, when Williamson is arrested, and, it will be down to you."

"And Jack."

"And Jack," Luke reluctantly agreed.

"But what about the thousands of other androids that must be out there? Williamson's can't be the only ones. How does this help them?"

"It will focus the public's attention, Kiera, and bring it out into the open. Most people are probably unaware it's going on. Hopefully, it will result in changes in the laws. It will certainly make things more difficult for people involved in this sort of thing."

Kiera's expression brightened. "Yes, you're right. I guess we have to believe in the basic goodness of most of us." She drew in a deep breath. "Okay. Enough of that. Let's get on with our plans for tomorrow. We are going to pull the SAD routine."

"What?" Luke gave her an incredulous look.

Kiera laughed. "It's an acronym for shock, anger and distract. We're actually providing the police with a diversion. It's to keep Williamson busy, so he doesn't become aware of the three raids, the police are going to carry out."

"Oh, I see."

"It's to prevent him from activating any of his fail-safes. I mean, he's certain to have procedures in place to dispose of incriminating evidence in an emergency. So, I've been told to shock Williamson as much as possible."

"How are you going to do that?"

"I've been given a memory stick that, when plugged into Williamson's computer, will upload a link to a live feed. A policewoman is going to be filming the same tour I did last night."

"So, he won't see the footage you took, Kiera?"

"No. That way, my involvement is kept secret."

Luke rested his chin on his hand. "I'm not sure Williamson will just let you plug in a memory stick to his computer."

"I have a strategy for that." Kiera sighed.

"Enlighten me."

"That would spoil it. It's on a need-to-know basis, and currently, only I need to know. But whatever I say or do, Luke, don't intervene, okay?"

"Kiera, I thought we'd agreed there would be no more secrets." He ran his fingers through his hair.

"This is different, Luke. John thought it would be best."

"John? Who's John?" His stomach clenched, and his fists became tight.

"Oh, for God's sake, Luke. John Harrington—Detective Inspector John Harrington." She glared at him. "I thought you said you trusted me, Luke."

He took a deep breath and relaxed his hands. "Sorry, Kiera. I do trust you."

"I'll show you the transmission device I'm going to wear tomorrow." She fished around in her pocket and pulled out a clear bag containing a spherical object about the size of a small button.

"Great Universe! You wouldn't want to drop it. How does it stay on?"

"It's coated with Gek-skin, it will stick to anything. You can't pull it off, it slides off." She dropped the bag into his outstretched hand.

Luke examined its contents closely before handing it back to her. "So that's going to record everything we say and transmit it back to the police?"

"Yes." She glanced at her watch. "It's almost 9 o'clock. Detective Harrington insisted on speaking to you tonight, Luke, because he wants to reassure himself you're okay with all this. He'll pull the operation, in its current form, unless we can guarantee that neither of us will lose our tempers."

"Look, I know the importance of staying cool, Kiera. I promise I won't lose it," he paused, "under any circumstances."

"Okay. The other thing I need to tell you is that the police need you to give a statement about the pheromone lab incident."

"Oh." He locked eyes with her.

Her expression was so serious.

"I'm sure I can get through that, it won't be the end of the world." He swallowed down his acute embarrassment.

At that moment, his mobi rang.

"That will be Detective Harrington."

Luke pulled his mobi out and answered it. It was Detective Harrington. He set the detective's mind to rest by convincing him that he could execute the plan *and* stay in control. The detective, after a brief conversation with Kiera, confirmed that the operation would go ahead.

Kiera handed him back his mobi. She appeared calm.

"It's reassuring, knowing five minutes after confronting Williamson, the police will be coming through the door."

"Absolutely." Her face became sombre. "Do you think this is worth the risk, Luke?

"After what you've shown me tonight Kiera—yes."

Kiera's eyes brightened, and she smiled up at him.

"What did Detective Harrington say to you, Kiera?"

"I was hoping you wouldn't ask. He said Williamson is unpredictable, and we need to be extremely careful. But he was adamant he didn't want either of us to place ourselves in any danger. So, if things get too hot—we scarper." Kiera took a deep breath. "Okay. Let's have a bit of a run through."

Once they'd rehearsed their performances as much as they were able, he and Kiera went to bed at around ten. Sleep proved elusive, his brain inundated with thoughts about the next morning.

Chapter 20

"Ready?" Kiera whispered, squeezing Luke's hand.

"Ready." Luke gave her a quick kiss on the cheek.

Kiera tapped on Williamson's door.

"Enter," boomed Williamson's voice.

She opened the door and strode in, followed by Luke.

Williamson looked up. Holding his face in an unreadable expression, he stood, walked around and leant on the front of his desk. His eyes flicked from her to Luke.

"Well, this is a surprise." He smiled his empty smile. In an instant it vanished, replaced by an expression of controlled fury. "What do you want? I'm busy." He stood glaring at them, his hands gripping the desk behind him. "Ah, let me guess. You wish to discuss Luke's relocation. I am afraid the decision's been made, and it's nonnegotiable. I won't be persuaded otherwise. Quite frankly, Luke, I'm a little disappointed that you thought involving Kiera would convince me to change my mind. Quite to the contrary, it only reinforces my resolve." He leant back on his hands.

"We've something you need to see," Kiera said, unfazed by his smug expression. She placed the folder containing all the information she had gathered on the desk.

"Oh, I very much doubt that, Kiera. Anything that you say, do, or show me now, would be a total waste of time. Now get back to work, both of you." He stood up from the desk as if to reinforce his superiority." Actually, before you go, I have something to show you." He moved back around his desk and sat down. "Luke's going to be interested, Kiera. Very interested indeed." He swished his hands past his desk screen. "Turnaround, Kiera, Luke."

She and Luke turned.

A second later, to Kiera's horror, the three screens on the wall facing Williamson's desk displayed multiple images of a bleary eyed, dishevelled young girl, complete with long, bright pink hair on one side, a shaved scalp on the other, and wearing an angry expression. It was her mug shot taken after her arrest when she was sixteen.

She glanced at Luke. His mouth had fallen open in shock. Her hands tightened into fists. "You Zarking bastard! That information is confidential. It's way in the past." A little voice in her head was saying—careful Kiera, don't lose your cool. She smothered her anger and eyed Williamson, keeping her expression calm. "I have no criminal record. How did you get hold of it?" she hissed.

"Oh, I have connections everywhere," Williamson smiled. "I always make sure that I have a little insurance for all my employees, just in case they get out of hand. It makes for a peaceful workplace."

Kiera watched as Luke swallowed shock and pulled his face back into a mask of calmness.

"This is irrelevant," he said, indicating the screens.

"You mean she didn't tell you about how she killed her friend?" Williamson feigned an expression of shocked surprise.

"Kiera is my partner. I don't care what she did in the past," Luke said, defiantly. "Show him what *we've* got, Kiera."

"How dare you defy me." Williamson, his face twisting, half rose from his chair.

Dear Luke, Kiera thought. Time for Plan B. In her mind, she conjured up the image of the android child that looked like Luke. She let the emotion swell inside her. She transformed the image into Luke and imagined him holding his arms out and pleading with her to take him home. She let the tears well, let them spill out, let herself dissolve into sobs. As she wallowed in the sadness, she said, "I'm…not sure…I want to…show you. It's going to make you so… angry. But it affects, it affects…all of us, so I have to. Please." She plumbed to the depth of her emotions and made it sound like she was pleading for her life. "Please…you have to look at it." She put the memory stick on the desk in front of him.

Williamson sat down again. "Why?" His expression had changed to mild surprise.

Luke jumped in. "Because somebody has published an upload program. You've been beaten to the post."

Kiera felt her jaw drop.

With a look of shock, Williamson snatched the stick and stuck it in the appropriate slot.

She and Luke watched in silence as the file opened and the link uploaded.

As well as playing on the desk in front of him, its images flooded onto the room's screens, displacing her mug shot.

At first Williamson sat unmoving. The transmitted footage showed Lianna conducting *the tour*, and it had reached the section detailing the various pheromones. He sat frozen as the footage progressed through to the twelve android children. His face turned ashen. "How did you get this footage?" he snarled, rising to his feet,

"I'm the only one that can authorise access to that section of my facility." His knuckles turned white as he clenched the edge of his desk.

"It's live footage, being filmed as we speak by a plainclothes policewoman," Kiera said.

Silence followed, punctuated only by the sound of Luke's heavy breathing. He met her eyes, and she gave him a reassuring half smile. To her relief, he took a deep breath and managed to compose himself.

Kiera's attention snapped back to the policewoman's voice and the unmistakable lilt of Lianna, the android guide.

Williamson, galvanised into action by fury, surged around the side of his desk and lunged at Kiera.

"You little bitch! I'll teach you to play games with me."

As his arm came up to strike her, Luke leapt towards him. At light speed, his hand shot forward, blocking Williamson's upraised arm, while the other hand slid under his armpit. He twisted around behind the man, taking the arm with him. Williamson whimpered in pain as Luke twisted his arm up behind his back and held it there effortlessly.

"Settle down, and I'll let your arm go." Williamson tried to kick backwards, but Luke nimbly sidestepped and twisted the arm up further. "Stop! Just stop. Now, I'm going to walk you back to your chair, and I want you to sit down. Is that clear?"

Williamson nodded.

Luke turned him around and pushed him forward. Before he sat him down, Luke said, "Can you grab that piece of twine from the shelf over there please, Kiera? I don't trust him. He might bolt or try and have another go at you."

Kiera, stunned by the unfolding spectacle said, "Wow! That was unexpected." She grabbed the piece of thick twine from the shelf.

"Where did you learn to do that?" She grinned as she handed it to him.

"Didn't I tell you I have a black belt in karate?" Luke pulled Williamson's other hand behind his back and bound them together. He pushed Williamson on to the chair.

"Would have been nice to know, Luke." She stared down at Williamson.

"Need-to-know, Kiera." Luke tapped his finger on his nose.

Kiera snorted.

Williamson looked up at them, red-faced. "You'll regret this as long as you live. I'll make sure you never work anywhere in AI again. I'll make your lives a misery. You'll be sorry that you were ever born. I'll…"

His tirade ceased as the door to the office burst open, and three uniformed officers surged into the room, followed by Detective Harrington.

"Thank God," Williamson said, "these two attacked me. They tied me up. I don't…"

"Don't bother, Mr Williamson," Detective Harrington said, interrupting him. "We've been listening in on what's transpired here so I suggest you keep quiet."

Kiera stepped out of the way and went and stood next to Luke.

Detective Harrington faced the fuming man. "Logan Williamson, you are under arrest for possession of objectionable goods, namely, the instruments for engagement in obscene activities. You are also charged with illegal tampering with android circuitry to circumvent the normal safeguards to allow *them* to engage in illegal activity. You are also charged with the manufacture and supply of illegal substances. Further charges are pending and will be determined on the basis of the evidence gathered. Cuff him and caution him, please officers." He turned to Kiera and Luke. "Let's step outside, you two, while my men proceed." He headed out the door.

Kiera and Luke followed him into the passage. After they'd gone a short distance, the detective turned and held out his hand to Luke. "I'm Detective Inspector John Harrington, head of the Special Crimes Unit. Nice to put a face to the voice."

Luke shook his hand. "Nice to meet you too, detective."

"I need you to come down to the hub and make a statement tomorrow, if that's okay, Luke."

"Sure, I'd be happy to."

"How did it all go, Detective Harrington?" Kiera asked.

"The timing worked perfectly. Our operative's computer wizardry proved invaluable in getting us into Sentioids Inc. unobstructed. We seized all the various androids, including the guide, and they're being loaded into trucks as we speak. We've also confiscated his computers and all of his records. There were several computers and storage drives in Williamson's apartment—and they've been seized as well. There also appears to be some interesting material in cloud storage. All in all, thanks to you two, the operation has been a total success. I don't need to detain you any further, so you can pack up and leave. We'll be in touch later." He walked back to Williamson's door.

Kiera took off up the passage. She needed to get away before Luke started to ask questions. But he caught up to her, grabbed her elbow, and pulled her to a halt.

"What the Bloody Zark was it that Williamson just showed us, Kiera?"

"I don't want to talk about it. Not here, and definitely not now, okay?" She scowled and folded her arms.

"No. It's not okay. You need to tell me about it. For the second day in a row, I've been emotionally ambushed. You promised there wouldn't be any more secrets between us." Luke's voice rose in anger. "It's not good enough Kiera. Williamson said you'd killed someone."

"Keep your voice down, Luke," Kiera hissed, "I was ambushed as well." She sighed. "I'll explain, when I'm good and ready. Now let's just pack up and go home. I just want to get out of here."

As they were about to enter their respective offices, two policemen, holding Williamson securely, emerged from his room and proceeded to frogmarch him down the passageway.

Detective Harrington and another officer followed them out. The detective closed Williamson's door, and headed down the hallway. Suddenly, he turned and strode back to Kiera and Luke. He held his hand out to Kiera.

When Kiera took it, he said, "Thanks for finally being your father's daughter Kiera, I think you have well and truly redeemed yourself."

When Kiera let go his hand he turned to Luke. "See you tomorrow, Luke. I'll be in touch later." He smiled, saluted, trotted off down the passage and disappeared around the corner.

"Was that about what Williamson just showed us?" Luke glared at her.

"Yes." Her anger had mellowed. "And I will tell you everything when we get home, okay?"

"Okay." He started towards his door. Before he opened it, he turned to look at Kiera. "I love you Kiera."

"I love you too, Luke." She slipped inside her room.

Chapter 21

Kiera didn't feel like talking, so they rode home in the trans-car in silence. Luke had a solemn expression and refused to meet her eyes. By the time they reached the apartment, it was around 11 o'clock. They dumped their bags next to the lounge chair.

"Do you have anything to eat? I'm starving," Kiera asked.

"We could have some toast."

Kiera wrinkled her nose.

"Or we could nip down the local coffee shop for something more exotic," Luke said.

"I don't feel like going out again. You go and get something. Surprise me." She flopped onto the lounge.

"Okay, I won't be long. Perhaps you could make us a cup of tea while I'm gone." He slipped out the door, closing it quietly.

By the time he got back, he found two cups of tea waiting on the coffee table in front of the lounge chair.

"So, what did you get?" Kiera looked up at him, smiling.

"I got a couple of jam doughnuts for myself, and I got this for you." He placed a second bag on the table in front of her. "I'll grab us a couple of plates." He disappeared into the kitchen.

Kiera opened the bag. Inside were two chocolate éclairs filled with cream.

Luke came back with two small plates and some paper towels. He sat down, and they both sat eating in silence.

Kiera sipped her tea. She had already demolished the first éclair. She put her cup down, wiped her hands on the paper towel and turned to him.

He'd just bitten into the second doughnut.

She smiled; he had sugar all over his chin.

"What?"

"I love you." She leaned over and kissed his sugary lips. "Now, let's talk." She sighed, where to start? Perhaps the mug shot. No, she'd start from the beginning. "So," she began, "I'd just turned sixteen when I first started uni. I'd been classified as exceptionally intelligent so they accelerated me through school. Towards the end of my final school year Dad had an affair with one of his work colleagues and decided to leave my mother after twenty years of marriage."

Luke's face softened. "Great Universe! That must have been hard on you both."

"It left Mum devastated. The affair had gone on for over a year and she'd had absolutely no idea. Neither had I." Kiera inspected her hands. "So they decided on divorce and Dad agreed to move out and leave Mum with the house. I had to move up to Perth to start my course at UWA, which made it worse for both of us. I stayed at St Catherine's College. In hindsight, I would have been better off in an apartment by myself, but Dad wouldn't pay for it, and Mum certainly couldn't have afforded it." She picked up her cup and took a few

144

more sips of tea before continuing. "I just got angrier and angrier about the whole thing, and I started drinking heavily. I became friendly with another girl at St Catherine's College. She was also into heavy drinking, so we sort of egged one another on. Anyway, I started skipping classes, mostly because Lisa and I were up until the early hours partying. Study took a back seat to having a good time and getting blind drunk every night." Kiera paused, picked up the second éclair and took a bite.

What would Luke make of all this? Would he be able to handle what she was going to tell him? He appeared calm at the moment. But he gave himself away by running his hand through his hair. He grabbed the paper towel after realising he'd put sugar everywhere. After he'd wiped his hands, he looked up at her expectantly.

"What happened next?"

"I found out Dad had bought a jazzy new sports car. So one night we got plastered and went to his place at about three in the morning. Lisa was experienced in hotwiring cars, so she got it started in no time. We took it up to Kings Park and tore around the roads inside the park. It was a rainy night with poor visibility; we came hurtling around a bend and I lost control. We ended up hitting a tree and rolling. I'm not sure how many times we rolled. It was all pretty much a blur." Kiera lapsed into silence and stared off into the distance.

Luke reached over and grasped her hand, giving it a reassuring squeeze.

She gave him a sad smile.

"So…what happened next?" Luke prompted.

"Lisa didn't like seatbelts. She was thrown out onto the verge and ended up horribly injured. Oh, Luke. It should have been me, it was my fault." Kiera sniffed and wiped a tear from her eye with her finger.

Luke put his arms around her, "Why did you feel it should have been you?"

"If I hadn't been so angry at Dad, we wouldn't have pinched his car. None of it would have happened. Lisa would still be alive. I'm directly to blame because I was driving. It haunts me, Luke, and I can't forgive myself." Kiera wiped away more tears.

"From what you've told me, it sounds like you were both on a path to self-destruction. *You* were hurting badly and didn't have the maturity to deal with it. Kiera, you were just a teenager, away from home for the first time and trying to make sense of a difficult situation. It sounds like you didn't have a lot of support." He smoothed her hair and patted her face.

"She didn't die outright, Luke." Kiera sniffed. "She ended up on life support, but in the end her parents made the decision to allow the doctors to switch it off and let her go. They wouldn't let me see her, Luke, so I never got to say goodbye." Tears began to run down her face and she fished in her pocket for a handkerchief to wipe her eyes.

Luke put his arm around her shoulders. "Were you hurt in the rollover, Kiera?"

Dear Luke, his face held such love and concern. Kiera kissed him gently, before answering. "No, I ended up suspended in my seatbelt. I managed to release it and crawl out of the car."

"You may have been driving Kiera, but if you weren't hurt you need to ask yourself if Lisa would have survived if she'd been wearing a seatbelt. If the answer is yes, you weren't responsible for her death. You didn't force her not to put a seatbelt on, did you?"

Kiera stared at him. She'd never thought about it. A coronial enquiry had given a finding of accidental death.

"What happened after that?" Luke asked.

"The police arrested me. That's where the mug shot came from. But because I was a juvenile and had no previous record, Dad managed to pull strings. He was a senior detective at the time. The police made allowances because of the road conditions and the mitigating circumstances. They were persuaded not to pursue a charge of dangerous driving on the condition that I participate in an anger management course, so I was assigned a youth worker for counselling."

"So that's how you met Jack."

She caught the slight sneer in Luke's voice. She sighed. "Yes. We grew close—like brother and sister." She hoped he could relate to a brother and sister love, but his expression still conveyed a lack of conviction. "He helped me so much, Luke. He gave me the support I needed."

Luke frowned.

"We remained staunch friends after I left the program, until he went off to a new job in Melbourne. We exchanged emails for a while but it gradually got less and less, and we eventually lost touch with one another. Fortunately for us, I was able to track him down by contacting his previous employer. I didn't know he'd moved back to Perth." She picked up Luke's hand, holding it in between both of hers. "We were never involved in a relationship, Luke. There's absolutely nothing to worry about."

Luke sat and regarded her with a serious expression.

"Perhaps not from your point of view, but it's the way he looks at you, Kiera. He's in love with you." He gazed at her intently.

"What? Jack? Absolutely not. I told you we are just like brother and sister."

"That's not what I saw, Kiera. You need to open your eyes. Why do you think he's always so eager to help you?"

"Because he's a really nice guy, and we're good friends," Kiera insisted, looking down at her plate.

"I can only tell you what I see," Luke said, standing and picking up the empty plates.

"Well, I don't agree. Are you sure it's not just jealousy on your part?"

Luke took the plates into the kitchen without speaking. When he came back he said, "I think we are just going to have to agree to disagree. I don't want us to argue about it. Okay?" He stood with his hands on his hips.

Kiera swallowed her anger and said simply, "Okay."

Luke embraced her. "We are both a bit tense, but I think I can think of a remedy for that." He grinned.

"Mmm, you still taste of sugar. At least we agree on something." She pulled him towards the bedroom door. "Let's get naked."

Chapter 22

It took the police six months to sort through all the evidence. In spite of fast tracking, nine months went by before the trial commenced. One of the difficulties had been determining the offences and criminal charges, some would set precedents for the future.

It had been a complex, gruelling period for Luke and Kiera. The trial itself had lasted for months. Their careers were in a hiatus and their futures uncertain. They were only required to be at the trial for one day to give their testimonies. Detective Harrington made sure they were protected from the media scrum. On his advice, they stayed away from the rest of the proceedings. Detective Harrington emailed through a summary of the trial's proceedings every evening.

Luke had taken a part-time job on an AI helpdesk, and Kiera had found temporary work tutoring at the University of Western Australia while waiting for the trial to commence and for its duration. It had at least helped to pass the time and generate a little income.

Detective Harrington rang with the news of a verdict. After nine days, during which the jury had been summoned back and spoken to by the presiding judge twice, they had come to a decision. Logan Williamson and his company Sentioids Inc. were found guilty of all charges. The judge reserved his decision on sentencing due to the number and seriousness of the offences. It took another three months before sentence was passed.

Luke and Kiera took the day off to enable them to catch the live coverage of Williamson's sentencing and the judge's summation. They sat on the lounge in Luke's apartment to watch on the big screen.

Kiera sat bolt upright as the footage began. Aware of the tension building inside himself, Luke reached over, took Kiera's hand in his, and gave it a gentle squeeze. He took a deep breath and let it out slowly.

"Well, this will be interesting." Kiera said, as she gave his hand a couple of quick squeezes back. Luke knew she was trying to sound nonchalant.

The judge, seated at the bench, began to speak, "I'm going to announce my sentencing decision before I give my reasons. I will not give details pertaining to the various charges Williamson and Sentioids Inc. have been convicted of, as there are well over two thousand in total. They will be listed in an appendix attached to the complete reasons which will be available online. I intend to give an abbreviated version at this time.

"I have sentenced Logan Williamson to ten years in prison with no parole which is currently the maximum allowable sentence. He is banned from holding a directorship of any company for life, and I am imposing a personal fine of two million dollars. I am also fining Sentioids Inc. one billion dollars."

Luke heard Kiera gasp just as he exclaimed, "Great Universe!"

"If it were up to me," Kiera said, "I would have put him away forever."

"Reading between the lines, I think the judge would have liked to have made it longer."

As though on cue, Luke heard the judge say, "…necessary that the maximum sentence be substantially increased," the judge continued. "There are many elements of this case that have been profoundly disturbing. The ethics involved bring to light the inadequacies in many of the laws relating to these matters. I will be making several recommendations about increases in penalties in an attempt to address this.

"As human beings, and the creators of androids in our image, we have an obligation to safeguard their dignity and to make sure they are treated with respect. Certain protections have been built into their programming and circuitry to ensure that the aforementioned is enacted. There is no doubt that the interference that Williamson enacted would have caused much mental anguish, and in some cases, pain to the androids involved. It is our responsibility to send a clear and strong message that interference of this type will not be tolerated under any circumstances.

"Current day androids are not toys. They must not be used for sexual gratification. There are firm laws regarding their treatment, and abuse of any sort cannot be condoned. The advancement of AI has proceeded to the point where androids can be programmed with human emotions, feelings and understanding. If, as Williamson implied, the uploading of the human mind into androids is soon to become a reality, new laws need to be drafted now so that they are enacted before uploading comes into fruition.

"To maintain our society's morals and values at the highest possible level, certain standards have to be maintained. The fact that there were child sex androids is repugnant, horrifying and unconscionable. We must continue to enshrine the protection of our children in our legal and moral system. In a decent and moral society there can never be any justification for using children or child androids as sexual objects.

"To conclude, we as a society must consider decency, dignity, morality, and the future of both human and android society in our future laws."

"Wow! What an elegant summation," Kiera said.

Luke picked up the remote and turned off the screen.

Kiera's phone beeped. "Detective Harrington has sent us a message," she said. She scrolled through the text. "Apparently there's a panel on tonight, discussing the trial and sentencing, and he thinks we would find it interesting."

"Oh." Luke couldn't keep the disappointment out of his voice. "I thought we might celebrate now it's over, so I booked a table at our Italian restaurant."

"Well, if Detective Harrington thought it worthwhile, we probably should watch. It's only an hour, and we can celebrate afterwards."

"Okay, I'll change the booking to later." Luke pushed himself off the lounge. "I need to go for a walk to clear my head. Do you want to come?"

"No thanks. I think I'll just sit for a while and think. I don't know about you, but I feel sort of flat."

"Me too." He walked to the door. "See you later, Kiera."

#

"Let's see if Detective Inspector Harrington is right." Kiera flopped onto the lounge. Luke sat next to her and activated the wall screen.

They still had a few minutes before the program started. Luke asked, "Do you feel like a cup of tea, or perhaps something stronger?" He got up and looked down at Kiera. She had let her hair grow a little longer and it now hung in dark curls around her neck. Great

Universe, she was so beautiful. A wave of emotion washed over him, and he bent and kissed her forehead.

"What was that for?" She gave him a quizzical look.

"I love you." His eyes started to brim with tears, and he quickly wiped them away.

"Oh, Luke." Kiera stood up and put her arms around him. "You are the best thing that has ever happened to me. I'm so glad we found one another. I couldn't live without you. You form part of my soul now, and if you ever left I would lose a part of myself forever." She kissed him deeply.

Luke heard the introductory music for *Talking Point*, and Kiera pulled him down onto the lounge with her. "Let's forget the tea, for now," she said, as they both focused on the screen and the program's presenter, Charlotte Peterson.

"Good evening everyone, and welcome to Talking Point. Tonight's panel is about to discuss the recent outcome of the landmark case against Sentioids Inc. and its owner and director, Logan Williamson. I'm Charlotte Peterson, your host for this evening." Charlotte introduced the panel guests and they acknowledged the introduction with a simple nod. They included Peter McKenzie, spokesperson for the Rights for Androids Association, accompanied by an android called Jerome; Patrick White, a legislative lawyer specialising in androids and robots; Senator Stuart Cromer, Greens representative, currently in opposition; Stephanie Granger, Catholic Archbishop for Perth; and Sophia Fanelli, President of the Rights for Humans Organisation, appearing via vid-link from Rome."

"We can all guess what she's going to talk about," Kiera said, as the screen filled with the image of a petite, raven haired woman of around forty. Fluorescent, orange framed glasses, perched on her long nose, highlighted her narrow face. She made no attempt to smile.

"Let's just see shall we." Luke took Kiera's hand as the camera flashed back to Charlotte.

"To summarise the case, last week Logan Williamson and his company Sentioids Inc. were convicted of a total of 2,041 charges relating to the misuse and abuse of androids over a number of years, and the possession of objectionable goods. I would like to ask each of you for comments. We'll start with you Patrick."

Patrick, a tall, pale man in his thirties, ran his hand through his black hair before answering. "This is certainly a landmark case. I think we will see additional legislation to protect, in particular, the new generation of androids in deference to their ability to feel emotions as well as pain—and to make moral judgements according to their programming. I..."

Charlotte cut him off. "Thank you, Patrick." She turned to her left and addressed the tall, thin, grey-haired elderly woman who looked up from jotting something down on the tablet in front of her. "Stephanie?"

"Looks like he's not going to get much of a say—typical Charlotte!" Kiera snorted.

"Shuuush." Luke gave her hand a squeeze but kept his eyes fixed on the screen as Stephanie began to speak.

"...of the main issues is the question of soul. Does a being that has not been created by God have the right to be treated with the same respect as their human counterparts?" Her blue eyes stared fixedly into the camera.

"Oh, here we go." Kiera leant forward in concentration.

Peter McKenzie, a tall, handsome man of around forty with deep auburn hair and slightly greying sideburns, drew himself up to his full height and jumped in with, "If we've created beings to be like us, given them emotions, along with the ability to feel pain and suffering, isn't there an obligation to treat them the same way we would treat any other fellow human?" He leaned forward and skewered Stephanie with his gaze.

"Thanks Stephanie—Peter." Charlotte turned to acknowledge them both, "Now let's go to the Shadow Minister for Technology and Innovation, Stuart Cromer."

Stuart, a squat man of considerable girth, sat forward and beamed at the audience. With a roguish expression he said, "I agree with Patrick, Charlotte. The current laws don't go far enough. It's a common problem. Legislation often lags behind technological developments. It seems to be the only thing that the current Liberal government excels in."

A smattering of applause came from the audience.

"Oh—well said!" Kiera clapped her hands together.

Luke smiled, typical Kiera—never hesitant about expressing an opinion.

"Let's cross to Sophia," Charlotte said. "Could you briefly explain, for the benefit of our audience and viewers, the ethos behind the RFH organisation, Sophia, before commenting on the Sentioids Inc. judgement?"

Sophia's image filled the screen. "*Certamente* Charlotte. The RFH totally opposes giving any rights to what are, simply, machines." She raised both hands, palms out, level with her shoulders and moved them up and down as she spoke. "They are not human beings, they are merely sim…how do you say it?"

"Simulations," Charlotte proffered.

"*Sì*—simulations. Last century, we would not have dreamt of giving any sort of rights to vacuum cleaners, washing machines, or cars. Androids are no different, they are machines programmed by humans for humans."

The camera flashed to Charlotte. "If I recall, autonomous vehicles were initially regarded in some states as entities, and accordingly legislation regarding their operation was put in place. I ..."

Peter jumped in with, "We've been advocating for stronger, and more encompassing legislation for the current generation of androids since they first emerged on the market some years ago. This generation could almost be said to be pseudo-human. Mistreatment of them is abhorrent. It is an abomination that child androids can be used as sexual objects. What does that say about the human race? It's a total paradox that humankind can produce such exquisite and complex works of art and music, but at the same time certain elements can descend into such barbarous depravity. I think..."

The camera shot back to Sophia. Her face held an expression of barely contained anger. She gave an exaggerated shrug and hissed, "How can autonomous vehicle be regarded as person?"

"I think this would be a good time to hear from Jerome," Peter said.

"Go ahead, Peter," Charlotte said.

Jerome, a typical general worker model of medium height, had the standard black hair swept back from his face. His eyes, however, were an iridescent blue. His clothes were far from standard, and he wore a red sweater emblazoned with 'I ROBOT' in large gold letters.

"Jerome, I would like you to tell everyone what happened when you had hot oil thrown in your face by a human co-worker several months ago while you were working as a chef's assistant," Peter said.

Jerome stared directly into the camera and answered in a voice typical of an English butler, "It happened when I slipped on some grease that had been spilled on the floor. I accidentally knocked a human. He was carrying a pot of boiling oil. He became angry, and he turned around and threw it in my face."

The audience gasped.

"I thought my head had exploded. The sensations were so extreme I fell to the floor, and I could not stop screaming. My face melted, and I couldn't see. I thought I was going to terminate."

"So, you thought that you were going to die, Jerome?" Charlotte said.

"Yes."

"Jerome, can you tell us, how it made you feel?" Charlotte asked.

"Helpless. I felt helpless. All the circuits in my head were burning. It didn't stop until someone turned me off."

"Jerome, would you describe it as pain?" Charlotte's face held a sympathetic expression.

"Yes, I never want that to happen again." Jerome's face twisted in anguish. He stared at his hands and whispered, "Ever."

"I wonder what Sophia is going to say about that?" Kiera said.

"Mmmm," Luke responded, as Charlotte addressed Sophia.

"…comment on Jerome's account." Sophia's image once again filled the screen.

"He has been programmed to say these things," Sophia spat back.

"Bloody hell!" Kiera said.

Simultaneously, Luke muttered, "Great Universe!"

The camera panned back to Peter. In a calm, civil voice, he said, "Androids cannot lie, and I resent the implication that I have committed illegal acts similar to those Logan Williamson has just been convicted of."

"*Scusa*, I meant that Jerome has been told what to say," Sophia blustered. "I did not mean to offend." She tried, unsuccessfully, to look contrite.

Charlotte jumped in. "Let's ask Jerome. Jerome, has Peter told you what to say?"

157

"No. I have told you exactly what happened." He glanced at Peter.

"Thanks, Jerome. I repeat, androids cannot lie. Please retract your statement, Ms Fanelli, or I will be forced to take legal action," Peter said, in a voice now full of menace.

"*Scusarsi*, Peter, I did not sleep well last night. I apologise if I have offended you."

"I think it should be Jerome you apologise to," Peter said, evenly.

"*Certamente*, I am sorry, Jerome."

Jerome nodded at the screen.

Charlotte jumped in to rescue the situation. "Sophia, I'm sure you didn't mean to offend, but we're getting off track here and time is limited. Could I have your comments on the Sentioids Inc. judgement?"

"In the context of RFH, we found the whole thing ridiculous. While we don't condone Logan Williamson's behaviour, our organisation feels that the trial and the outcome was a waste of time and money." She sat back and folded her arms.

"Thanks, Sophia. Let's move on." Charlotte's expression became serious. "Do any of you think there is a legitimate place in our society for the use of sex androids—one could argue, as did Logan Williamson, that it saves human women from prostitution?"

Stephanie drew herself up and snorted. "In my opinion it merely condones prostitution. If androids are made in our own image and programmed by us, doesn't that reinforce the stereotype of the female sex slave?"

Patrick cleared his throat. "Can I interrupt here?"

"Yes, go ahead, Patrick."

"Can I make the point that there were also male androids involved that were being used by women and men, in heterosexual, bisexual and homosexual acts. It is unfair to simply ignore the facts to suit one's own particular hobby horse."

"Oh," roared Kiera, sitting bolt upright again.

"Good point, Patrick." Charlotte beamed at the camera while flicking a strand of blond hair aside. "So, is the issue here one of sexual morality or human morality in general? Let's hear from you, Peter."

"I think both, Charlotte. If we're going to build machines like us, that may ultimately be us, it is imperative that they be treated as humans. We can't have one set of standards for a subset of humanity and another for us. It creates an attitude of abuse. For example, how many times have we heard people say, *'it's just a stupid machine'*? The truth of the matter is that this is no longer the case—as Jerome has clearly illustrated. These are intelligent, thinking and feeling beings. If we are to integrate them into society as equals, we need the appropriate legislation to bring that about."

"Thank you, Peter." Charlotte turned and swept her gaze around the panel members before speaking. "Do you think we should be making AIs equal to us? Isn't that dangerous?"

Stuart jumped in with, "In a democratic society, I don't think there is any room for *'an us and them'* mentality. Ideas like those are just divisive and don't get us anywhere. It's time the law stepped up to its responsibility to all humans, including androids."

"Thanks for your comment, Stuart. We're coming to the end of our time, so I'd like a brief wrap-up comment from all of you. Peter."

"Logan Williamson clearly broke the law and twisted the interpretation to suit his own ideals. I think the sentence he received and the magnitude of his fines, both personal and company, are justified. One point no one has mentioned is the possibility that in the near future, we may be able to load the human consciousness into a machine. Ask yourself the question—what then?"

"Interesting point, Peter, we may discuss that in a future panel. Stuart."

"I agree. Logan Williamson's behaviour was unconscionable. In my view the sentences weren't severe enough."

"Stephanie."

"I think everybody has sidestepped the issue, and that issue is— should we give these soulless creatures the same rights and privileges as humans?" Charlotte opened her mouth to speak, but Stephanie waved her hand dismissively, "Please let me finish. Sex is not a commodity to be traded and manipulated by anyone that has the power to do so. Women should not be thought of as merely sexual objects. The current laws are inadequate. Thank you," she added, turning to Charlotte as though giving her permission to speak.

Charlotte, with a slightly peeved expression, turned to Patrick, "Patrick?"

Patrick, unfazed, drew himself up. "There clearly needs to be reform that reflects the current norms of society. By that, I mean laws that allow both humans and androids to be treated as equals and with respect." He leant forward and addressed his conclusion directly at Stephanie, "And I mean everyone, not just women."

"Oh, well said," Kiera said.

Luke squeezed her hand.

"I hope this discussion has provided food for thought for all our viewers tonight. Thanks to Peter, Jerome, Stuart, Stephanie, Patrick and Sophia. Good night everyone, and until next time stay happy and stay safe."

Kiera grabbed the remote and punched the off switch. She turned to Luke and grinned. "Well, that *was* interesting. I'm glad we decided to watch it."

Luke sighed. "I really felt sorry for Jerome. Clever strategy by Peter to bring home to the general public just what androids are capable of, as far as feeling pain and emotions."

"Yes," agreed Kiera. "It must've been a dreadful experience for him. Let's hope it changes the public's perceptions of androids."

Luke stood up. "Well, it's finally over, Kiera. Now we can get on with the rest of our lives. I bought some champagne on the way home yesterday. I thought we might have a celebratory glass before we go to the restaurant, and we can take the rest with us."

Kiera, ignoring him, frowned and asked, "What do you think will happen to the company?"

He frowned and put his hand on his chin. "It sounds like Williamson may have been playing it too close to the wind. I doubt he's got the funds to pay the fine. The company will be sold up, probably along with any of the existing patents. Come on, Kiera, lighten up. Let's forget about it for now. It's over."

But she wasn't going to be silenced that easily. "I would love to see where the discussion will go when you and I perfect the upload program." She grinned. "What do you think everyone will think about us evolving beyond bodies to become human machines?" She didn't wait for him to answer. "I mean, don't you think it's a given that we'll need to become machines? How else are we going to be able to negotiate the incredible distances and time spans to travel to other galaxies?"

"You may be right, Kiera, although cryo is well advanced." He didn't want to dampen her enthusiasm. "But we've got quite a way to go yet."

Excitement surged through him as the realisation finally struck him. "Great Universe!" He enfolded her in his arms. "That will change humanity forever, but I wonder what it will mean for you and me? Will *we* get to live forever?"

Kiera kissed him and gave him a broad smile. "Who knows what the future holds? What's most important is that we're on the journey together. Let's have that glass of champagne now, shall we?"

"At last!" Luke dashed off into the kitchen. He took the bottle from the fridge and withdrew the cork with a satisfying pop. He carefully poured two glasses, picked them up, and took them out to Kiera. He handed her one before sitting down next to her.

As Kiera stared at the effervescent liquid, Luke contemplated the bubbles rising in his own glass. Humans were a little like those bubbles—their lives were brief, ephemeral and mostly insignificant. But his and Kiera's lives were going to make a significant difference. The bubbles also reminded him of all the worlds out there just waiting to be explored. He leaned over and gently clinked his glass with Kiera. "To us," he said, smiling at her.

"Yes, to us," she said, taking a sip. "To us and the rest of our lives."

Upload Part 2

The Future-Year 2221

Chapter 23

Awareness dawned...cold became warmth...darkness became light.

I heard sounds...the sounds, faint at first, became louder...speech...it was speech...I began to comprehend. A voice told me to relax...it explained that although my mind was awake, my body still slept. In soothing tones, it said that it would take time for my body to catch up...to stay calm...stay relaxed.

Tingling...tingling, as I began to feel feet, hands, arms and legs. The tingling became pain, but the soothing voice said it would only be momentary. The voice was right.

It told me to wriggle my fingers and toes, and to open my eyes. I tried, but I still couldn't move...I stayed calm, and the light that seeped through my closed lids reassured me. I grew warmer...my eyes flickered open...Blurred images everywhere...Slowly...Slowly things came into focus. I lay cocooned in a pod of some kind. There were lights and buttons to the right of me. The voice told me to press the first button when I was able. It told me that after I pressed the button, I would feel a series of light sensations run down my body but not to worry. It would only be the leads disconnecting from my sleep suit. Seconds ticked by. I tried to move my hand, but it still wouldn't respond. I relaxed and counted to ten.

I reached out and pressed the button. A wave of dragging sensations cascaded down my body. As promised, the pod leads had disconnected.

With a hiss and a pop, the canopy covering my pod slid silently sideways and disappeared. Cool, fresh air caressed my face, and the soothing voice told me to remain still. My pod began to slide out, and tilt up, as a prelude to moving me into an upright position. Straps around my legs and chest tightened and held me secure.

After a few moments, the reassuring voice returned. It told me that once fully upright, I should wait until my body acclimatised before I released the restraints. It told me to expect to feel a little lightheaded but that it would only be temporary. It instructed me to press the green button once the sensation had passed and to carefully step out onto the floor.

I took a deep breath and pushed the button. The restraints slid away. I stepped out gingerly with my right foot. It wobbled a little, but it didn't collapse, so I followed with the left. I paused and took in my surroundings. The memories all tumbled back as I recognised deck twenty-six of the *Serenity*, our behemoth ship bound for the Kalgarin star system. I took a few more uncertain steps towards the glowing control panel in the centre of the deck, where a single red light flashed insistently. As I moved I had a strange feeling. An odd sensation niggled at the back of my mind. I felt…unbalanced somehow. I looked down. I screamed. It wasn't my scream.

Chapter 24

I sank, my mind spinning, as my knees thumped onto cold metal. I jumped, and my pulse accelerated as a hand gripped my shoulder. I stared up at the tubby man wearing a red sleep suit and my brain flooded with recognition; Jack? Great Universe, it *was* Jack.

"Kiera? I heard a scream, are you alright?" Jack grabbed hold of my hands and pulled me up. "What the hell is going on? You're not supposed to be awake."

Immobilised by shock, I could only stand and stare.

Jack gripped my shoulders. "Are you alright? Kiera? Kiera, answer me for God's sake."

As I gazed into Jack's familiar brown eyes, the appalling truth finally penetrated. Somehow my consciousness had been uploaded into Kiera's body. My mouth went dry, and I tried to speak, but no sounds would come.

Jack wrapped his arms around me, patted my back, and made soothing noises.

It must've been the shock, because without thinking I squirmed out of his grip and pushed him away. I heard myself say in Kiera's voice, "I'm not Kiera, Jack. I'm Luke." I watched as disbelief flashed across his face, only to be displaced by anger.

"I don't have time for this, Kiera. We've been woken up because there's an emergency. We need to link, now!"

He started to turn, but I grabbed his arm. "I—am—Luke—Jack. Someone has fouled up on the uploading."

Jack stood motionless. "Not possible. Either you've suddenly developed a split personality or you've gone insane."

"Neither, but let's get moving." I ran my fingers through my hair, swallowed down fear and confusion, and tried to concentrate. I headed to the nearest console, slipped into its chair, and pressed the link button. As I leant back into the soft headrest, Jack hurried around me and followed suit. My headband array deployed and wrapped itself comfortably around my forehead. The chair cocooned me in softness, moulded to my form, as the array arms linked and the process completed. A familiar surge of energy hit me as the system booted up. My training kicked in. I relaxed, closed my eyes, and slowed my breathing. The familiar giddy sensation enveloped me, as I was sucked down into a void of darkness. Next, I was hurled into a universe of dazzling light. I fought off nausea as I swirled down into a dancing, psychedelic rainbow streaming out to infinity.

I concentrated to form the question clearly in my mind.

—State the nature of the emergency.

I opened my eyes, and my vision cleared as the screen in front of me began blinking a message. My heart sank.

—*Error—brain bio-electric parameters do not match body parameters.*

—*Upload error—try again.*

I sighed in exasperation. Of course, I wasn't in my body. I should have guessed that this would happen. I carefully formed the thought response.

—Emergency override authority, capital L, capital A, capital M, six, one, zero, two five. Bypass all bio-parameters. Confirm with bio-electric password.

The screen cleared, and I waited. I glanced at Jack. His slack, blank face indicated he'd already engaged the information download process. My screen blazed into life.

—*Password located—please verify.*

The cursor flashed, waiting for my response. I formed the thought.

—Army of mice.

—*Confirmed match—please wait—rebooting in progress for Luke John Masters.*

I waited, shivering in spite of my thick, blue sleep suit.

—*Reboot complete.*

Flooded with relief, I concentrated and repeated my question. The response leapt from the screen in blinking red letters.

—*Imminent failure of module three.*

—Bring up schematics, show location.

The plan of our location; section seven, deck twenty-six P, flashed onto the screen. The problem area was highlighted in red.

—Zoom in and immerse.

I closed my eyes and allowed Virtual space to envelop me. My pint-sized avatar materialised in the midst of an immense maze of electrical circuitry. Abruptly, I snapped back into reality. Take it easy, Luke. Slowly does it. Take nice slow breaths. I'd always had a problem with the immersion process. Some people took to it naturally, unfortunately I wasn't one of them.

It took about a minute to calm myself back into a sufficiently relaxed state to think clearly. As I jolted back into Virtual, a gigantic electrical discharge reverberated through me. I whirled as the sound assaulted my ears again.

—Damp sounds—damp sounds.

Instantly, the noise of the sparking, tree-sized cable dropped to a bearable level. But I still started as the eroding cable flashed again, sending white hot sparks flying outwards in all directions. I moved in as close as I dared; aware my mind couldn't tell the difference between a Virtual injury and a real one. There was always the risk of going into shock. Bloody Zark! Being in Kiera's body was enough of a shock for one day.

I remembered in the developmental stage of Virtual immersion, there had been instances of people becoming catatonic. Fortunately, in most cases it had been reversible, but I had no intention of testing it out.

One side of the cable remained intact, but with each discharge more wires melted out of existence. Time I linked up with Jack.

—Link to other user, Jack Summers.

A giant cursor blinked, and a billboard sized message superimposed itself on the screen in front of me.

—*Link complete—engaging now.*

"Jack, are you getting this?"

"Bloody hell! You really are Luke," Jack's voice answered from immediately behind me.

"Zark, Jack!" Startled, I whirled and came face-to-face with Jack's avatar.

"Gotcha! Nice to see you back to your old self." Jack's avatar grinned.

"Very funny. What do you think? Can we fix the problem?"

Jack's avatar screwed up its face. "No, it's cactus. This circuit is the end of the line in a system of redundancies."

"What about a crawler?"

"Take too long. Even if we had a Robo-critter handy, and we don't, they're in maintenance on deck forty-six. There's no time. It's too late, Luke. We'll have to use the emergency shutdown, while we still can."

My mind reeled. I didn't want to think about it. My brain flooded with images of Kiera. Where the Zark are you, Kiera? I had to think about something else.

"Where's the fault relative to our module?" I asked.

"It's a couple of modules down, on the other side. Come out and I'll show you. No point in staying here. See you up top." He winked out.

I concentrated.

—Zoom out and disengage immersion.

I opened my eyes and found myself back in my body. I sat and stared at the screen for a few moments before giving the next command.

—Disengage link.

The screen cleared before the blinking cursor reappeared with the message

—*Please repeat bio-electric password to disengage.*

—Army of mice.

—*Disengaging.*

Chapter 26

The screen blanked, and the headband slid away as the chair slackened its grip on me. When the process completed, I stood up. In hindsight, not a good idea as I nearly fell over, and I only saved myself by grabbing the back of the chair. As I stood and waited for wooziness to pass, I gazed at the banks of gleaming syn-spex pods that lined each side of the deck. It all seemed so clinical; the darkened pods, so devoid of life. There were 100 people in our section—each with their own unique dreams and hopes for the future. I remembered Kiera's comment on our prelaunch tour. She'd said: 'We'll all wait in our pods like fairy-tale sleeping princes and princesses for the kiss of technology to wake us in a strange, new, exciting future.'

I shook my head and inhaled deeply. The ship still smelt of new metal and plastic. "So, which module is it, Jack?"

He hurried around from his side of the dual screen and reached out to me. I flapped him away. "I'm alright," I growled.

"Okay, okay. Don't get shirty." He held up his palms and backed away from me. "We came from module one. The fault's in module two six P seven three." He turned and pointed. "It's the last across the other side, on our left."

At least, having seen me in Virtual, Jack now accepted me as Luke. No more cuddles, thank the Universe. If things weren't so serious, we could have both had a good laugh about that one. I pulled myself back to the current moment.

"Are you sure you're okay?" Jack's expression radiated concern.

"I'm fine, Jack. All the dizziness is gone now. Let's go and see what we are dealing with."

"No, wait here, Luke. I'll go and initiate the shutdown process. There's no need for both of us to be involved." He walked off.

Just the way he'd said it, and the lack of emotion on his face, made it sound like he was going to tighten a loose screw somewhere. I gritted my teeth with the effort of keeping my mouth shut.

I leant on the console and watched as he padded diagonally, some fifteen metres across the grey, metal deck, past banks of horizontal sleep pods, to the middle of module three. He tapped the small touch screen to access the names, photos and bio-data of the occupants.

"Why do you need to do that, Jack?" I called. They were all going to die. I didn't want to know who they were.

"I need to check something."

"What?" I put my hands on my hips.

"Don't distract me," he said, in a terse tone.

Jack excelled at shutting people out when it suited him. It's funny how things occur to you at the oddest moments. I found myself thinking; of the few girlfriends he'd been with over his lifetimes, none of them had stayed long enough to chip away at his stony exterior to see what lay underneath. I sat down on the deck with my back resting against the console and closed my eyes. I must've fallen asleep, because I was woken by Jack tapping my arm. When I opened my eyes, Jack's white, anxious face leant over me. He was trembling.

"You need to come and look, Ki—Luke. I…Just come and look." He extended both hands and this time, I took them. Without another word, he turned and walked off to module three. I trotted after him, fighting down nausea and the overwhelming sense of my world about to shatter into shards of infinity.

Jack pointed to the display with a shaky hand. "They're not where they're supposed to be."

Julian, my twenty-year-old son, grinned at me from the screen. He and his eighteen-year-old sister, Tiani, should have been in module one. We'd all decided to stay together—Jack, Kiera, Julian, Tiani and myself, so in the event of anything happening to our module, we would all go at the same time. None of us wanted to be left behind to grieve.

My turn to start shaking. Jack had said ' they're'. Great Universe, surely he didn't mean…I watched as Jack, muttering, turned back to the screen and swished to the next photograph.

"Unbelievable," he whispered, almost to himself.

Tears began to stream down my cheeks. Tiani's young face, her eyes bright with excitement, slid into view. My knees buckled, and I began to see stars. I reached out and put my hand on Jack's shoulder to steady myself. I could feel him trembling.

This couldn't be real. This couldn't be happening. Not my children. Great Universe—not my children. My mind whirled. Perhaps they weren't my children. What if everybody had been mixed up? If my consciousness had been downloaded to Kiera's body, whose consciousness occupied mine? But Jack's in the right body, and he'd come from the same module I had; module one.

Bloody Zark! Julian and Tiani weren't clones; they were gen one humans. They hadn't gone through the upload process the rest of us had. Somebody had to have engineered this. This couldn't have happened randomly. It just couldn't. Great Zarking Universe! Who could have done this and why? Why? My mind screamed.

Jack hesitated. He forced himself to take a deep breath before he swiped to the next photo with a shaky hand. A shudder ran down my entire body.

Zark! Bloody Zark. From the screen a smiling photograph of myself, or at least my bodily self, stared out at me, occupant unknown. My legs sagged. I let go of Jack and slid to the deck. My head spun, as the Universe pressed in and sucked all the life from me. My breath came in ragged gulps.

"There's something else, Luke," Jack said, as he bent down, slipped his arms under my shoulders, and helped me to my feet. "It's a message for you."

I stood paralysed in front of the screen. I stared and stared. Underneath the photograph lay a message where my bio-data should have been. It read: 'Luke, now you will know what it's like to lose everything. It's taken three lifetimes, but I'm a patient man. My only regret is that I can't be there to see the look on your face when you read this, Logan. PS Kiera is with me now. You won't find us.'

Logan Williamson? After all this time? I couldn't believe it, and what did he mean? How could Kiera be with him when I occupied her body? I wilted, in spite of Jack's support.

"Bloody hell, Luke." Jack sucked in his breath and turned towards me, white faced. His voice cracked, "I have no choice. I have to euthanise the whole of module three."

It had been part of our conditions of acceptance. Everyone on the ship had to agree to humanely shut down pods or modules that failed.

"We can't."

Jack let go of me. He stood and stared at me, momentarily help-less, emotional agony etched on his face

"We have to, Luke. Otherwise everyone is going to die a slow, painful death. I'm sure you don't want that."

A murderous, irrational and powerful, Zarking rage surged up-wards inside of me. I heard myself scream, high-pitched and female; Kiera's scream. I dropped and began pounding the deck with my fists. I screamed and screamed and pounded and pounded.

Jack's strong arms wrapped around me from behind. He wrenched me over backwards, snapping me back into sanity. Ex-hausted, I struggled up to a sitting position. Jack sat down in front of me, the only sounds our heavy breathing. I inspected my knuckles, they were a bloody mess. Kiera would kill me, Kiera…Great Uni-verse…Kiera, my beautiful, vibrant, loving Kiera. Where the Zark are you?

Jack eyed me warily. "The nanocytes will take care of your inju-ries, but we need to wash the blood off and put some bandages on."

Nanocytes; I'd forgotten about them. Before we'd left Earth, Tiani and Julian had been given infusions of the most technologically advanced brew. The rest of us had been infused post being uploaded into our un-imprinted clones.

Jack pushed himself to his feet and held out his hand.

I waved him away. "You'll get blood all over you." With some effort, I managed to stand up without his help. "I'm alright. I'm…sorry, for what just happened."

"That's okay." Jack's expression remained neutral. "The first aid supplies are in the bathroom."

As I followed him across the deck, I began to feel stronger. I became enveloped by a strange tranquillity. Perhaps everyone should have a good scream now and then. Kiera would probably say some-thing along those lines. I shook my head…oh Kiera.

Jack opened the door to the bathroom. The muted pastel pink room held a shower, a separate toilet and a sink. The floor, in contrast to the deck outside, had a spongy texture that made it pleasant to walk on. Shelves set into the left-hand wall contained emergency medical supplies, whilst the wall opposite held a large full-length mirror. Kiera's cherub face, framed with her short brunette hair, stared back at me with her dark-brown eyes. I had to turn away.

"Sit," Jack commanded, as he pulled a seat out from the opposite wall. "On second thoughts, come over to the sink and wash your hands." He went to the basin and turned on the tap.

I placed my hands under the warm running water and watched it run red into the sink. I ran my hands over one another until the water cleared. Jack patted them dry with a paper towel. He inspected both palms, followed by my knuckles.

"They're not too bad, are they hurting?"

"Not yet." Hit by an unexpected wave of embarrassment, I had to look away.

Jack unwound the end of a bandage and expertly wrapped each hand in turn. He pinned the ends in place with a small clip. His face held an expression so tender, and his touch had been so gentle, I became almost overwhelmed by a desire to burst into tears and put my arms around him. Great Universe! Kiera would probably do something like that, under the circumstances. I had a weird thought. Perhaps some sort of residual effect remained present in Kiera's body. Would I gradually become Kiera after being flooded by her hormones? How ridiculous! I had to pull myself together. Thoughts like those were the path to madness.

"Probably no need to bandage them, but better safe than sorry." Jack stowed the kit neatly back on the shelf where it had come from. "I've an idea. If it's to work, we have to act bloody fast. I need you to check the other modules in case Logan has organised any other nasty surprises."

"What's your idea? Two brains are better than one."

We walked back out to the deck.

"I need to check it out. There's no time to explain, so do as I asked, Luke." He strode to the nearest console and sat down. He pressed the link button, and the headband began to engage.

Shut out again. I sighed and went over to module one, our module, and quickly flicked through its other occupants. My thoughts were distracted. I wondered which lucky three had been moved to our module from module three. With the search completed, I repeated the procedure with the remaining modules, apart from the damaged one. Everything seemed normal and operating as it should.

The deck, made up of ten sections, held five modules with twenty people in each. Redundancies were inbuilt for safety, but a small percentage of failures over the lifetime of the voyage were expected. Why the Zark did it have to be one of ours?

Just as I finished checking the last module, I saw Jack disengage from the console and stand up. He grinned and gave the thumbs up signal. I trotted over to him.

Chapter 27

When I reached him, he said, "Sorry, Luke. I needed to check out some things before I got your hopes up."

"So you sent me off as a distraction so I wouldn't bother you?" My mind reeled, spinning downwards into a spiral of anger and despair. I struggled not to direct it at Jack.

"It was necessary. I've checked my idea, and it's viable. I've already set up the protocols." Jack's expression conveyed calm and confidence.

His calmness fuelled my anger. "This better be good, Jack. I don't like being sent off on a fool's errand." I glared and clenched my fists.

"I thought it would stop you from thinking about things too much." His expression softened.

That surprised me. At times Jack showed remarkable insight, probably a throwback to his stint as a youth counsellor during his first lifetime, before his nano-gen extensions. I kept quiet, waiting for him to continue.

"I want you to go into Virtual and link directly to Julian and Tiani. I need to know they are in their own bodies. I also need you to check who's in your body. It's risky. Direct linking hasn't been done before, but I've gone through the data and it should be possible. Will you do it?" He paused, waiting for me to react, his face cool and composed.

"Yes, but what happens if their bodies are occupied by other people?" I frowned. The thought of other people in my children's bodies chilled me to the core.

"We don't have time to check the other seventeen occupants. I'll initiate shutdown. The pods will flood with carbon dioxide, inducing anoxia, resulting in a quick, painless death," Jack said, matter-of-factly.

"And if they *are* in their own bodies?" I couldn't believe we were having this conversation; to anyone listening it would have sounded absurd.

"I'll isolate them from the module's other occupants before initiating the process. When that's complete, it will conserve enough energy to proceed to the next step."

Great Universe, how could Jack look so bloody serene? These weren't inanimate objects. They were human beings, they were my children. I struggled to control my breathing as I tried to keep my anger at bay.

"If we can't find them, couldn't we save three other people? If we've…"

"It's bloody dangerous, Luke. I wouldn't be taking the risk if you and your children weren't involved," Jack snapped. "Just get on with it. Now!"

I reflected back on our pre-flight training. It had included graphic details of what would happen in the event of pod failure; pain, fitting and slow suffocation. Each module had its own independent power supply. Individual pods could be shut down in the event of an irreparable fault. However, a fault occurring in the whole module, our current scenario, necessitated a total systems shutdown.

The pods held their occupants in a low temperature, hiber-sleep. Although the metabolic rate was markedly reduced, breathing still occurred at a low level. Cold, oxygen-enriched air saturated the pods. This, along with nanocytes and various bio-conditioning agents, enabled the brain to remain alive and functioning at a minimal level. The heart pumped around twice a minute. Intravenous lines supplied nutrition and fluids. We became something akin to hibernating bears or naked mole rats; barely alive but still completely viable. The state could be maintained, according to experimental results, almost indefinitely, an absolute necessity for long space voyages to distant systems in our own Milky Way Galaxy.

"Luke!" Jack's shout jolted me back into reality. "We're running out of time."

"How long do we have?" I glared at him.

"Three hours, more if I initiate the shutdown promptly." Jack's expression remained cool.

Bloody Zark, how does he do it? Focus...focus. I took a deep breath, "Okay, I'll go and link now." Halfway to the console's chair I turned back to him. "What happens after that?"

"I upload their consciousnesses into the ship's main computer."

"What? Bloody Zark, Jack. I thought you were going to wake them up."

"The energy is too low, Luke. Uploading them is the only way I can save them."

"That means they become sapioids. It's the end of them as biological entities." My voice broke, "They will never have their own children. Kiera will be devastated." Shock, anguish and a sense of

180

utter helplessness exploded like a min-shrap grenade into my brain. "Is uploading them even possible, Jack?"

"Yes, not without risk, but considering the alternative there's no choice."

"So, they'll stay there until we reach our destination?"

"Not exactly."

"What exactly, Jack?" I folded my arms and stared at him, wondering what was coming next.

"We'll need to bring some blank androids up from storage and upload them into those."

Why can't they be held in the computer?" I shouted.

"Have you forgotten, Luke, that it's illegal to copy and save a person's consciousness to a computer?" Jack's expression remained calm.

I had forgotten.

"After sixteen hours, the computer will regard them as viruses and delete them. It's a safety measure I designed to prevent illegal activity plus any external tampering while we're asleep. You never know what we may encounter during the voyage, aliens for example."

"If you designed and programmed it surely you can disable it?"

"No. I specifically designed it so it couldn't easily be meddled with, even by me."

"Zark Jack! What a Zarking stupid thing to do."

Jack flinched.

"Zark! Zark!" I exploded. Right at that moment, I could have killed him.

"Time." Jack pointed at the wall clock. "Link now, otherwise we'll lose everyone. I've set a timer. You'll have ten seconds once you see the 'out of time' start to flash."

I stormed to the nearest chair and slammed myself down into it. This time, after the headband had engaged, the computer immediately requested my bio-electric password. It took a full minute for me to calm myself sufficiently to be able to form the thoughts necessary to establish the link.

—Army of mice.

—*Password verified—proceed.*

—Link to module two, six, P, seven three.

—*Linking—state name or position in pod.*

—Link to Julian John Masters and display position.

—*Position two.*

—Direct link.

—*Direct linking inadvisable due to high risk of fatal error or instability. Do you wish to proceed?*

—Yes—direct link.

—*Linking.*

Seconds passed until, momentarily, I became enveloped in a suffocating blackness. I fought to control panic. A small green message began blinking reassuringly in the right-hand top corner of the blackness. It read 'time okay'. My anger evaporated and dissolved into relief. Jack. Just knowing I wasn't alone gave me the courage to try to reach Julian.

—Julian—it's Dad.

I paused and listened as the darkness smothered me. I heard... Something.

—Julian, Julian—it's Dad. Answer me, it's important.

Seconds passed...I caught a faint thought whisper.

—Hey...can't see anything...Dad?

Relief washed over me. It was Julian's voice. The 'hey' confirmed it, but I still had to check, to satisfy Jack.

—I've linked to you in your pod. That's why you can't see anything. Don't worry, just listen. Tell me what your password is.

After a pause, a faint thought whisper came.

—Hey…Easy…Hitchhiker.

Now came the hard part.

—Listen carefully, your module has failed. Jack's going to upload you to the ship's computer. Because of the ship's security systems, he can't leave you there. You'll have to be transferred into an android.

I waited.

—Ship's computer…That's…forever…it? Julian's thought replies drifted into my mind like pieces of flotsam on a beach. They were jumbled and indistinguishable. What was he asking me? I couldn't spend any more time, so I guessed.

—No. We will upload you into your identical android, later. You'll be a sapioid.

—Become me…

More fragments. I struggled to decipher what he meant. I could only hope he was hearing my thoughts clearly.

—Will we go ahead? It's either that, or you die with the rest of them.

Silence.

—Julian, I need an answer.

—Mum…Tiani?

—Tiani is with you. I don't know where your mother is.

—How?

His response was fading.

—Can't explain now. Yes or no?

Again silence.

—Julian?

—Yes.

—I love you. See you soon.

—Love....

—Break link.

—*Terminating link.*

I repeated the process to link with Tiani.

—Tiani, it's Dad.

A clear response came immediately.

—Dad, what the hell is going on? Why can't I see anything?

—You're in your pod. Listen carefully.

I quickly explained the problem and what her choices were. She, unlike Julian responded immediately.

—Yes.

—I love you Tiani. See you up top.

—Love you.

—Break link.

—*Terminating link.*

A running argument raged inside my brain. One part of me didn't want to know, but I had to find out who occupied my body. Jack's message, 'time okay', still flashed green in the corner of my vision. I took a deep breath and swallowed fear.

—Link to Luke John Masters, and display position.

—*Linking—Linking—Linking.*

I held my breath, as I waited for the response. Seconds passed––still nothing. My heart exploded in my ears as a message finally materialised.

—*Error—brain bio-parameters do not match body parameters—upload error—try again.*

—Ignore all bio-parameters, give position.

—*Error—cannot give position—access unauthorised without parameter match—check with administrator.*

Something niggled at the back of my brain. We'd been given a critical code to bypass the administrator, to be used in a dire emergency. I struggled to recall it, so I deliberately slowed my breathing. The code popped into my mind.

—Critical code override capital letter c, numeral two, capital letter x, numeral one, zero, eight, one, lower case o, lowercase p, numeral six, five, one, lower case x.

—*Critical code accepted—state request.*

—Give position of Luke John Masters using body parameters.

—*Position four—module 2673 P.*

—Search brain bio-electric parameters of occupant.

—*Searching.*

I waited. Precious seconds ticked by. Jack's message flashed green in a sea of blackness. I remembered to breathe.

—*Occupant Kiera Susannah Proud.*

My heart leapt. So, Kiera *was* in my body. Logan Williamson had lied, but I still needed to make sure. Knowing Logan, it could be some sort of trap. My pulse jumped and my stomach clenched, as I fought to stay focused.

—Link to occupant Kiera Susannah Proud.

—*Linking.*

—Kiera?

My heart juddered. My breath caught in my throat. I could hear only the thump, thump, of blood pounding through my ears.

—Luke?

Faint, but it sounded like Kiera. Could thought sound the same as a person's voice?

—Yes. I need you to give the computer your password for verification.

I just hoped she didn't argue.

—Why?

Bloody Zark. I tried again.

—We have an emergency, Kiera. Give your password now.

—How do I know it's you?

—My password is 'army of mice'. Tell me where that comes from.

A faint sound—a thought giggle? Was that possible? Again, Kiera's voice, a little louder now.

—It happened on the first day we met; you wore those shoes that squeaked all the way down the hallway. And I won't remind you of what happened with the android on the lab tour.

I remembered. It was like it had happened yesterday, and it still made me cringe.

—Okay, I still need you to confirm your password for the computer.

I waited.

—Locate password for Kiera Susannah Proud. I heard Kiera think. After a short pause the standard response appeared.

——*Password located—please verify.*

—White mouse.

I checked the screen.

—*Password verified.*

Halfway through my sigh of relief, Jack's message became a beacon of red exploding out of the darkness.

'Out of time' Flash. Flash.

—Kiera, you become a sapioid, or you die. Your choice—now.

—I…Oh God Luke…The children?

—I'm out of time—answer me, Kiera.

I heard an unintelligible whisper. Suddenly, the screen went dark; Jack's message had disappeared.

—*Terminating link.*

The link had automatically terminated. I hadn't even had time to tell her I loved her.

Chapter 28

I stared at the blank screen. Kiera's last thoughts echoed through my brain like bullets ricocheting off metal. Anger surged through me, but I swallowed it down. No point in raging at Jack. I had taken too long.

I willed my legs to move and tottered over to where Jack stood working with the damaged module's screen. He heard me approach and turned. Worry transformed his face. He spoke in a quiet whisper.

"What did you find K...Luke?"

I told him.

"Did they agree to be uploaded?" He said, quietly. His hands were shaking, and his face had turned pale.

"Julian and Tiani did, but I ran out of time with Kiera."

"So?" Seemed all he could manage.

"I..." I studied my feet, trying to come to a decision.

"Wait any longer and you won't have a choice." Jack's face took on a solemn expression.

"Upload her."

"That would have been my choice."

I stood, rooted to the spot, watching him. Light fingers flew over the screen, and after a few minutes he turned and said, "Well that's it, I've isolated them from the rest, and I'm ready to proceed with the termination."

"We both know it has to be done." I put my hand on his shoulder. He turned back to the screen and pressed enter.

"Thanks, Luke." He took a deep breath. I watched in awe as the placid mask re-established itself on his pale face.

"Right, let's get on with the uploading, there's not much juice left in the backup battery. I hope it will be enough."

"Is there anything I can do?" I relaxed my hands and tried to mirror Jack.

"No… Well, you could try praying." He turned back to the screen, and after making a few adjustments, sat down at the console.

"I'm going to be busy inside, but there is one question I need to know the answer to."

"Yes?" I think I knew what was coming.

"What order do you want me to upload them in?" As I was standing behind him, I couldn't see his face, and his headband array had already engaged.

"Does it matter, Jack?"

"It might," he said, without a hint of emotion.

That meant…Great Zarking Universe. I couldn't choose. My stomach clenched, and my shoulders ached with tension. I don't think I could ever remember being in such mental agony.

"You choose, Jack." I slunk off to the sanctuary of the bathroom. I shut the door, pulled out the seat, and sat down. Would Kiera think I'd been a coward? What would she have done? I wanted to blank it all out. I stood up, poured myself a cup of water from the sink, and sat down again. I forced myself to drink it slowly. I concentrated on the sensation of the liquid in my mouth, and on the feel of it sliding down my throat, in an attempt to drown my thoughts. It worked to some extent.

Time passed. Minutes dragged like hours, and my breathing seemed to come in slow motion. I couldn't stand it any longer. I stood up and went to see if I could determine how far Jack had got in the upload process. Perhaps I could link and go inside and watch. No, not a good idea. I might distract him at some vital point.

When I reached his chair, I went to stand by his side. His blank, white face glistened with sweat. I rushed back to the bathroom and poured a cup of water. I grabbed some paper towels and dashed back out in time to see his headband disengaging. When I reached him, he struggled to push himself out of the chair. I took his arm to help him up, but his legs buckled. Being in Kiera's body, I didn't have enough strength to hold him, so he slid to the deck and ended up leaning against the side of the chair. His whole body was shaking.

"Jack, Jack. What's happened?" A wave of nausea washed over me. As his eyes met mine, tears spilled over and trickled down his face. I knelt down in front of him, and waited, terrified, as I watched him struggling to speak.

"There was only enough power left to save two of them, Luke." My world splintered. "Which two?"

He sat staring blankly. I raised my voice. "Which two, Jack, which two?"

"Oh God, Luke, I'm so sorry. I'm so sorry."

He said it over and over, until finally, in desperation, I slapped his face and repeated my question, "Which two?" A cold sweat started trickling down the back of my neck. This time he answered.

"Julian and Tiani. I couldn't save Kiera, Luke. I tried, I tried so bloody hard, but I couldn't save her. The power...the power...was just too low." His eyes were full of anguish. As a shroud of silence enveloped us, he reached out with both arms. I wrapped him in mine, and we held one another and cried and cried.

Chapter 29

"Luke," Jack said, "how are we going to handle you being in Kiera's body, with your kids?"

I'd kept pushing the thought away. I didn't want to have to deal with it, but I'd have to at some stage.

Eight hours had passed since Jack had completed the uploading. After crying ourselves into exhaustion, we'd managed around six hours sleep. We'd used the pull-out bunks housed in the small living quarter module adjacent to the bathroom. After waking, we'd made a meal using the food synthesiser. I don't think either of us had tasted any of it, but it lifted our mood and energy levels. Although still numb with grief, we were spurred on by the urgency of transferring my children's consciousnesses before the ship's computer activated its anti-virus program and eliminated them.

I brushed hair out of my eyes and cleared my throat. "What would you suggest?"

"I don't know. I'm having trouble dealing with the fact that Kiera is right in front of me, even though I know she's dead." He stared back at me. A sudden, overwhelming guilt forced me to look away.

After a moment, I steeled myself and met his eyes. "I've thought about getting you to upload me into the computer as well. Kiera and I had numerous heated discussions about uploading. You were there for some of them, do you remember?"

Jack nodded.

"We agreed we'd both do it at the same time. I might as well become a sapioid now she's gone." I picked up my cup and drained the remains of cold coffee.

"Wrong time for you to be making that decision, Luke. Once you become a machine, it's forever." He got up and tipped the remains of his coffee into the sink housed in one corner of the kitchen alcove.

"With Kiera gone, I don't care. She was everything that gave my life meaning." I focused on my hands; my human hands.

"Your kids will care. Don't you think they've got enough to deal with already?" he said in an angry tone.

He had a point. I'd allowed grief to cloud my judgement.

"You'll feel differently later when the grief wears off. At least you *have* a biological body, even if it's not yours. Remember, we've all got spare embryonic clones in storage. You'll be able to transfer back into your own body when we get to our destination, once the ship wakes up."

"I'll give it more thought on the way down. I'd better get into that suit." I scrambled up and tossed my empty cup into the recycler.

"Are you sure you're up to this?" Jack's face was full of concern. "I can go if you want."

"No, I'll do it. You are much better at giving directions than I am, and you're faster in Virtual, if I need it."

I went out the door and down the deck, to the bulkhead adjacent to the airlock. Eight suits hung on the wall like corpses. I unhooked the nearest one. "I think I'm going to need some help to get into this," I yelled.

Jack stuck his head round the door. "It's self-fastening. Don't you remember?"

I had forgotten. He strode over to me and quickly showed me the process. Once I'd put the suit on, it was a simple matter of putting the seals in contact with one another. They immediately self-adhered, making the suit airtight. Within half a minute, I was ready to go apart from the helmet. I held it in my hand, reluctant to put it on until necessary. I hated suits. Although, flexible and light, the bulk and weight of the air tanks made them cumbersome. I still found them claustrophobic in spite of their efficient ventilation systems.

Currently, only our section had been pressurised prior to Jack and I waking up. As an added safety precaution, each deck section remained sealed for the duration of the voyage. They would only be unsealed and joined once we reached our destination. I had to go through to the next section to access the lift, and I would travel down from there.

"Time to put your helmet on," Jack said, standing by the airlock door. "Good luck and be careful. Okay?"

"Don't worry, I'll be careful." I reached out and patted his shoulder reassuringly. "We'd better do a sound check once I've got my helmet on."

I slipped the helmet over my head and the seal connected with a hiss. The air stirred, and a cool breeze began wafting around my face. Jack had already gone to the nearest terminal. He turned and gave me the thumbs up signal prior to sitting down. I watched as he went through the link process. I jumped when his voice spoke, seemingly, from inside my head.

"How's the sound level, Luke?"

"Loud and clear."

"Okay, off you go."

I pressed the button, and the door slid open in silence. The two airlocks in our section had pressurised the moment our awakening had been initiated. I hesitated, and turned around for one last look, before I stepped inside. I closed the door and pressed the button to start depressurisation.

When the air had been vented, the far side door opened. Light from the airlock spilled out into a cave of darkness. I activated my headlamp and stepped out onto the deck. The lift lay outside another airlock at the far end, and to reach it I had to walk past unlit modules filled with sleeping humans. Shadows leapt out at me, as I moved in an eerie silence. I walked through the unpressurised airlock into the lift-well. When I pressed the call button, my face was instantly bathed in the soft glow of a wall screen. The display indicated the lift had to travel down from deck five. Time until arrival counted down in front of me. Around ten minutes—time to think.

I thought about Jack, Kiera and myself. We'd been together for so long and had become inseparable. We called ourselves 'The Three Sapes', and we did everything—well almost everything—together.

I recalled my first lifetime. After the trial had ended, we'd received a substantial reward and had decided to use it to set up our own company in Canada. The authorities had been concerned about our safety because of Logan Williamson's powerful connections in Australia—even though he had been jailed for ten years.

We had been able to duplicate Williamson's upload program using alternative algorithms, so there had been no infringement of his intellectual property rights. Due to our strict ethical and moral codes, unlike Williamson, it had taken three years to develop and test a foolproof upload program. We'd called our company Sapioid Inc., and androids with humans uploaded into them were known as sapi-oids. This distinguished them from sentioids—self-aware, intelligent, autonomous robots who had been granted the same rights as humans.

Some twenty years later, nano-gen technology had been perfected. We had all chosen to have the infusions.

By 2088 human cloning had been legalised, the result of the discovery that the nano-gen process could only be used once and so could only extend lives by around thirty years.

Subsequent rapid advances in cloning technology had led to the development of un-imprinted clones. We, at Sapioid Inc., had been directly responsible for developing the programs and technology involved in the uploading of the human consciousness to these clones.

In 2098 we'd all had our consciousness uploaded to our own un-imprinted clones. These clones, known as gen zero, had many of the major genetic faults either eliminated or repaired. I'd chosen to damp the genes responsible for my anxious personality just a little; too much would have altered my creativity. I didn't regret it.

The three of us—Jack, Kiera and myself, had been uploaded to our gen two clones immediately before the voyage. We'd been granted an extra gen for participating in the voyage, as well as a spare set of embryos in storage. The law dictated that all final clones had to be sterile. Somewhere down the track, we would have to make the choice to either die or be uploaded into a machine.

My thoughts swung back to Kiera. What the hell were we going to do about me being in Kiera's body? Perhaps the best way forward would be for me to remain out of sight until Jack had explained the situation to Julian and Tiani. They were in for a terrible shock, but it would at least give them time to process the information. Julian would probably be staunch, but I knew Tiani would dissolve into an emotional mess. Jack would have to try and pick up the pieces. I couldn't avoid confronting them forever. It had to be done, sooner or later.

On the other hand, perhaps it would be better if they didn't see me. If Jack didn't tell them anything. That might work. In fact, why bother switching them on at all? I sighed. No, not practical; we needed to check that the uploads had been successful and were functioning properly. We had to turn them on.

The best thing would be if Jack told them about Kiera's death and not give them the gory details. I could simply be… Missing or back in hiber-sleep.

I jumped as the fire doors slid slowly open in front of me—revealing the lift doors. When they parted, the interior lit up with a soft, warm light. I stepped inside and found myself wishing I could take my helmet off.

"Any chance of pressurising this thing?" I inspected the control panel in front of me.

"Sorry, no can do." Good old Jack, always brief and to the point.

"You're not going stir crazy already are you?"

"No, I'm okay." I flicked off my headlamp and pressed the button for deck forty-six where the spare, blank androids were stored. There were two-hundred spares for use in emergencies. The ship had the facility to manufacture them, but that would only be activated when we reached the Kalgarin system.

My thoughts circled around and around, as I argued with myself about the situation. I watched seconds tick away on the screen in front of me. Jack's voice startled me back into awareness. "Any more thoughts on how we deal with Julian and Tiani, Luke?"

"Try one thousand and one." I let out a sigh.

"They will be foggy when they wake up so it may not register, but we need to leave them turned on until they stabilise. That takes a couple of hours. I think we've got two options. My option one; just leave them in the dark and you pretend you're Kiera. I could tell them I've already put *you* back to sleep. That would explain your absence," Jack paused.

"No. That's not fair; I wouldn't want you to lie for me. What's option two?"

"Well…" I heard the hesitancy in his voice, "we could tell them we don't know where Kiera is. Which wouldn't quite be a lie, she could be anywhere in spirit couldn't she?" His voice held a slight catch.

"I suppose, but if we create hope the truth will be even more traumatic, *and* what about me?"

"We tell them. Then you can at least come out and give them a hug to reassure them. Once you've done that, we'll put them back to sleep."

Jack had always preferred 'back to sleep' to 'switching off'.

"Okay, that sounds reasonable." I glanced at the screen, two minutes to go. Another minute passed, and I found myself being flooded with images of Kiera. Kiera laughing, Kiera with that particular mischievous expression she was famous for, Kiera looking up at me, her eyes glistening with tears, holding Tiani just after she had been born, saying, 'She is so beautiful, Luke'.

I wanted to just let go—to bawl like a baby. I repeated over and over—take it easy, Luke. I can't cry in a helmet. Take it easy—just breathe. In through the nose, and out through the mouth. I began to relax.

The lift bumped to a halt, and the door slid open. I had never got used to the shock and awe of this deck. On this occasion, its vast cavern, filled with machines and stackers—row after row of stackers—glowed with the illumination of hundreds of brilliant white lights. Jack had switched on the entire deck for me.

Jack's voice crackled to life in my ear. "Okay. Step out of the lift and turn right. The stacker with the blank androids is immediately in front of you."

"I see them." Sensible, to put them right next to a lift. Each of ten levels held ten inanimate androids. They were all dressed in the designated yellow jumpsuits of the basic model.

"Touch the screen, Luke; it will give you a selection. Each level has five identical males and females. There's not much variation, but at least you can pick one with the same hair colour and sex as your kids."

"What a relief." I touched the screen. "I think one male in a female body is enough don't you?"

"Definitely."

"Okay, I'm scrolling through now. This one looks alright." I pressed enter to choose an auburn female android with a slim build, similar to Tiani, from level one. Only in the last level did I find a male that bore any resemblance to Julian. He had his blonde hair but a chunkier build. I pressed enter followed by the load button. A message scrolled onto the screen in front of me.

—Move back and stand behind the yellow line—Stacker is unloading— Please wait.

I looked around, the line lay behind me, and so I did as instructed. The stacker began to move. A platform holding the male android slid out from the top of the stacker. It moved sideways to the end of the row and into the lift which lowered it to ground level. As soon as it had reached the ground, a second platform slid out from the first level and repeated the manoeuvre.

Just as I was about to step out beyond the yellow line, a new message popped on to the screen.

—Danger—Keep back—Initialising trolley loading—Please wait for process to complete.

I stood, impatient now, as a trolley slid out from beneath the stacker, and the two androids were manoeuvred onto it. The empty platforms elevated one at a time and returned to their original positions.

—*Process complete—You may approach and remove the trolley.*

The screen became lifeless.

"Okay, Jack, what do I do now?" I stepped forward and inspected the two motionless forms.

"There's a small screen on the handle, just tap it."

I did. A small display lit. "What now?" I gazed down.

"There's an icon showing a man walking. Tap that, and the trolley will automatically follow you, Luke."

"Oh, right. Ah, here we go." I turned to the lift. I suddenly realised why the doors were so big. Initially, when I had got out, the opening had been small, but now a wide gap between the two doors would easily allow the passage of the trolley into the lift. I stepped inside, and after the trolley followed me in, the doors closed.

"Jack."

"Yes, Luke." He sounded tired.

"I've had second thoughts. I think your option one is the way to go." I sighed.

"Okay. You had better start practising Kiera. You need to try and speak the way she did, even think like she did."

"Right. That will certainly occupy my time on the way up."

I just hoped I could pull it off for Julian and Tiani's sake. I began to choke up when I realised that I wasn't just grieving for Kiera, I was also grieving for myself, for the loss of my own body.

I realised that that raised another dilemma. Sometime in the future when I uploaded to my own un-imprinted clone, Kiera's body would become vacant. In one sense she would be alive, Kiera's body but with no mind. I wondered if there were any protocols in place to deal with that situation. Would she be euthanised, or would she have to be kept alive until she died naturally?

Focus, Luke. Let's just think about how Kiera would react to Julian's and Tiani's situation. Focus.

Chapter 30

I sat on the floor staring at the sapioid that held Julian's consciousness. After the upload, Jack and I had moved him on to one of the bunks in the living module. Every now and then he would twitch, but according to Jack, it would be ten minutes before he opened his eyes.

The upload had gone without incident. I wriggled around in an effort to make myself more comfortable, turning a little towards the opposite wall. I found myself gazing through a large picture window, crafted using 3-D holography. It featured a tranquil scene of a deep, blue lake, surrounded by trees gently swaying in the breeze. A sailboat, with its scarlet sail billowing, skimmed the water, creating a rippling wake. I could almost hear the waves lapping the shoreline. The scene soothed and comforted me. Jack's voice broke my reverie, just as the boat disappeared around the headland.

"Tiani is on her way now. It's looking good." He paused in the doorway. "I've been thinking about Kiera."

"Oh?" What now? I unwillingly tore my eyes from the holographic window, stood up, and stretched my cramped limbs.

"Once you're transferred back to your own body, Kiera's body will still be alive, and it will still contain her identity spherule."

"What difference does that make?" My right hand instantly strayed to my neck, and I could feel a small hard lump there.

"Technically and legally, she is still Kiera. Even though the spherule only contains her genome, records of genetic modifications, and her bio-electric password, somewhere in the future it might be possible to re-programme her. If we could get it to work, we could fill her in on the details of her life."

"That's insane, besides being impossible, Jack. Without her own memories and experiences, she would be a totally different person. She wouldn't be Kiera." Great Universe, is he becoming irrational? Is he finally cracking under the stress of everything that has happened? What will I do if he is?

Jack rattled on, "All the basics would be there. You could probably make her fall in love with you all over again." He leaned on the door frame looking decidedly cheerful.

Something snapped inside, and I exploded, "You can't *make* someone fall in love with you. *You* of all people should know that, Jack!"

Jack straightened, and without a word, turned and walked away.

I had spoken the unspeakable, kept locked away inside for three lifetimes. Invisible threads dissolved. The Universe broke apart around me, and an unspeakable grief overwhelmed me. "Jack! Jack!" Only Julian's eyes fluttering open prevented me from going after him.

"Where…Feel strange…Hey, Mum?"

I swallowed hard. "Yes, sweetheart?" Further words stuck in my throat. He made to get up, but I put my hand on his chest. "No Julian, don't get up, it's too soon." I tried to smile.

"Why? Something's not..." He held up his hand and examined it. His expression transformed into horror. "But...this...not me."

I reached out and touched his frightened face just like Kiera used to when he was sick as a child. I tried to think of something soothing to say. "It's only temporary, Julian. We'll be able to transfer you into a sapioid that will look just like you, later on." I smoothed his blonde hair back. He gazed back at me and smiled.

"Good old, Mum. Hey, where's Dad? I think he spoke to me. I can't...think...can't remember what he told me." He looked so lost. I had to be careful. "Yes, he did, sweetheart, but he's gone back into hiber-sleep." I tried to give him a reassuring smile.

"Why?" His eyes fluttered closed and he went still. I panicked.

"Jack! Jack—I need help. Something is wrong with Julian." I heard running feet, and Jack pelted through the door. Just as he reached us, Julian's eyes opened.

"Hey, Uncle Jack, what are you doing here?" He made another attempt to sit up.

I reached out to stop him, but Jack grabbed my hand.

"He's okay to sit up, Kiera," he said, without looking at me. He slipped his hand underneath Julian's left shoulder. "Just sit up slowly, Julian."

As my son sat up, Jack, still refusing to meet my eyes, said, "He's alright, Kiera, don't mollycoddle him." His tone was terse and admonishing.

I watched him help Julian to his feet.

"Let's see if you can stand up by yourself. Take my arm if you need to." He let go of Julian and stepped back.

"Still...a bit...wobbly." Julian stood and looked around. "This is the ship. I remember now. Is there...a mirror?...want to see what I look like now." He giggled, "It feels...strange." He took a few shaky steps.

Jack took his arm. "There's a mirror next door." He guided Julian towards the door.

"Jack! Is that wise?"

"It's fine. He has to know some time." He and Julian disappeared. I followed them into the bathroom.

Julian studied himself in the mirror. He turned around and flashed me a wicked grin. "Is that the best you could do, Mum? It doesn't look anything like me."

"It's the best your dad could do. Don't blame me."

"Oh well, I guess it's only temporary. So, have I got the process right, Uncle Jack? I'll be uploaded when my body's ready?"

My stomach clenched, and I glanced at Jack. His face remained passive.

"Not exactly, Julian, but don't worry about it now. Come back next door, and I'll check you out to make sure everything's okay." He took Julian's arm and guided him back to the living module. Jack didn't meet my gaze once. I had become invisible.

I sat and watched Jack run through a series of tests to make sure everything was functioning normally. Julian and Jack chatted on as though they were sitting in our kitchen back on Earth.

Jack, over the years, had become part of our family. Julian and Tiani, from a very early age, had called him Uncle Jack. Kiera had insisted he be present at the births of both of them. I'd been put out about it, but the expression on his face when we'd given him Julian to hold dissolved it all away. Jack's face had radiated an ecstatic joy suffused with tenderness and love. I didn't object a second time. He'd watched them grow from babies into young adults.

A horrible thought struck me; everything had changed. In some ways, they were no longer my children. What a ridiculous thought, but I couldn't shake the emotions the idea generated. They began to spill to the surface. As I sat watching them laughing and talking, my eyes began to water up. Perhaps I *was* becoming Kiera. As the tears spilled down my cheeks, I wiped them away—but not quickly enough.

"Hey, Mum, don't cry. Everything will turn out okay," Julian turned to Jack, "Won't it, Uncle Jack?"

Jack, keeping his expression neutral, said, "Sure, Julian. Will you two be okay while I go and check on Tiani?" He was still refusing to look at me.

Julian frowned. "Are you guys okay?"

Jack smiled. "Yes, Julian, we're okay." He met my eyes for the first time since I'd shouted at him. But his smile had a falseness about it, a lack of depth. I stared back, drained by his emptiness and simply nodded.

"No, something is wrong. I mean hey, I might be in a different body, but my mind is still the same. What's going on?" He folded his arms and kept looking at each of us, alternately.

No one could ever fool Julian. He'd always been exceptionally perceptive, and he often picked up underlying emotional currents his sister frequently missed. I swallowed. Great Universe, what explanation could I safely give?

"We had a slight disagreement, but it's all settled now isn't it, Kiera?" Jack unfolded his arms and smiled his empty smile.

"Absolutely! You'd better go and check on Tiani in case she wakes up and wanders off."

Without another word, Jack vanished through the door. I breathed a sigh of relief—too soon.

"I can see it's not." Julian folded his arms. "What's happened, Mum? What's going on?" He stood, came over and put one arm round my shoulder, and gave me a squeeze.

I shrivelled inside. "I'll tell you some other time, but not now, sweetheart. Jack might need help with Tiani, so I'd better go and check. Help—" I trailed off. 'Great Universe!' I nearly said help yourself to some food, or tea and coffee. I turned away; the basic units Julian and Tiani had been uploaded into weren't equipped to eat and drink. They were only meant to be used in emergencies. True sentioid and sapioid bodies were more sophisticated, and we would be able to manufacture them after landing using the ship's equipment. I had to turn away momentarily to prevent myself from breaking down.

I covered it by heading towards the door. When I reached it, I turned and said, "Sit and relax, or walk around if you like, but stay here. I'll come and get you when Tiani is awake." I made a quick exit before he could reply. Too close, Luke. Far too close.

I hurried over to Jack, busily unplugging a myriad of leads. "Jack, please stop. You're upsetting Julian. If you keep this up, you'll upset Tiani as well. If you can't do it for me, at least do it for my children." His cold gaze pierced my insides with icy crystals. "Please… Please Jack. I'm sorry. I'm really sorry."

Jack's face softened a little, and just at that moment Tiani gave a sigh and opened her eyes. I went over to her side and stroked her face.

"Just lay still, Ti. We'll move you to somewhere more comfortable in a few minutes." I watched as her expression changed from passive to one of pure panic. I'd been afraid this would happen. "Jack?" He'd always been better at calming Tiani down than either I or her mother.

"Hey Ti. Don't worry, Uncle Jack's here." He patted her shoulder.

Her expression transformed into recognition. "Uncle…Jack…Jack…really you?" She raised a shaky hand and took hold of his arm.

"Yes, it's really me, or it was the last time I checked." He grinned down at her. She managed a weak smile.

I realised I'd been holding my breath. I let out a gush of air and followed it up with a couple of deep gulps while I continued to stroke her face. I let out a long sigh of relief, but it turned out to be premature. When Tiani met my eyes, her face flooded with fear and she began to scream—long, high-pitched animal screams.

Julian shot through the door and raced over. Before either of us could stop him, he shoved me out of the way and scooped up Tiani. Cradling her in his arms, he began rocking her backwards and forwards while making soothing sounds. She continued to scream.

"Zark, Jack, do something," I yelled.

Jack reached into his pocket and pulled out a small black box. He pressed the top button. Tiani's screams ceased. Her face became a passive mask as she went limp in Julian's arms.

"What the hell's with the box, Uncle Jack?" Julian laid her inert form down and stood staring at us, his hands characteristically on his hips. "Tell me what's just happened." His voice was full of a quiet fury.

Jack slipped the box back into his pocket before replying, "I switched her to sleep mode. Her adjustment to the download will continue normally. She'll be okay when it's complete. Calm down, Julian, or you'll upset your own integration."

Julian contemplated his sister's still form. "That's not Tiani." His voice was full of conviction. "It doesn't look anything like her. It's not her. It can't be. She doesn't scream like that. She wouldn't scream like that." He began to shake.

I reached across to give him a hug, but he batted me away. His face twisted with horror.

"You're not Mum, either. You're all imposters." He started to back away from us.

I didn't know what to do.

Jack did. He reached into the other pocket and whipped out a duplicate box. Julian went limp. Jack rushed forward and caught him before he fell—and eased him to the floor.

"Bloody Zark, Jack." I rushed forward and bent down over the prone form. "What have you done?"

"What was necessary." His face remained impassive.

"I thought you said we couldn't turn them off until they'd stabilised." I grabbed his arm, but he shrugged me off.

"They're not off, they're in sleep mode." He turned away from me and went over to Tiani. He started plugging leads back in. Refusing to meet my eyes, he said, "Give me some bloody credit, I know what I'm doing."

I stood with my hands on my hips. "Explain to me what you're doing."

"Sleep mode won't hurt them; it will simply slow down the integration process. Julian's is almost complete anyway. Tiani's will take a bit longer. Just leave me alone and let me get on with it." His face was flushed with anger.

Great Universe, doubts crawled into my brain like cockroaches. Perhaps we were all deluded; perhaps none of us were who we thought we were. A wave of queasiness saturated me, as Tiani's screams echoed through my mind, accompanied by the image of Julian's horrified face.

I wanted it to end. I wanted to just close my eyes and not be here. I had never seen Jack so unemotional; he could have been an automaton. I didn't know how to deal with it. Overwhelmed with exhaustion, I went back to the living unit. I laid down on the bunk Julian had vacated. I would just close my eyes for a few minutes...just a few minutes...just...

I jerked back into awareness. Somebody was shaking my shoulder. "Dad, you need to wake up." I opened my eyes. Tiani's face, lit with a brilliant smile, came into focus.

"Tiani, you're alright! Thank the great..." I trailed off. She sat down next to me as I sat up and swung my legs to the floor. I wrapped my arms around her. Relief and joy surged through me as she flung her arms around me. We held one another in a long, tight hug. Finally, we untangled ourselves and stood up. "How's your brother?"

"I'm fine," Julian said, from the doorway.

Jack's head appeared around the door frame. "We're all fine." He followed Julian into the room. "You've been asleep for around two hours. Do you feel better now, Luke?" He smiled; a genuine smile—one filled with warmth and feeling. I smiled back as threads reconnected and stabilised. We were whole once more. Finally, it registered. He'd called me Luke. Great Universe! They knew.

Chapter 31

Everyone began talking at once. Jack held his hands up in front of himself to quieten us. We stood facing one another, breathless, bright eyed and smiling.

"How did you two find out?" I faced Jack. "Did you tell them?"

"No." He folded his arms and became serious. "Tiani knew. That's why she started screaming." Jack dropped his arms to his side. "You explain, Tiani."

Tiani's expression became thoughtful and she drew in a deep breath. "I'm not sure I can." She reached up and began twirling a lock of hair around her finger. "I just knew it was you, Dad, and that something had happened to Mum." She screwed up her face in an attempt to stop herself from crying. "Oh, Dad, this wasn't supposed to happen. If something went wrong, we were all supposed to go together, weren't we?" She began to cry. I cradled her in my arms and held her while she sobbed. I spotted Jack trying to surreptitiously wipe his face. A staunch Julian stemmed his emotions by biting his lip.

"What *did* you tell them, Jack?"

Tiani's sobs were beginning to subside. She let go of me and turned to Jack, wiping her face with her sleeve.

"The truth, Luke, as gently as I could. Tiani had stabilised by the time I woke her, but she still insisted you were her dad."

"I don't know why, Dad, but I felt certain it was you. It was so weird; almost like I had x-ray vision and could see through to you, inside Mum's body." She gave me a sad little smile.

"I have a theory," Julian said, in a quiet voice. "I think it has something to do with linking. I mean..." He paused to gather his thoughts. "Directly linking with someone while they're in suspension is pretty unusual, isn't it? I don't know of any documented accounts of it being done. Has it been done before, Uncle Jack?" He went and put his arm around his sister's shoulder.

"Not that I'm aware of. It's possible we've created an entirely unique process. Your dad and I might be famous in the future." Jack put his hand on his chin. His face took on a thoughtful expression. "There may be a residual effect, post linking that creates some sort of psychic connection." He went to the water dispenser, pulled a cup from the chute, filled it, and took a deep swig.

"It's strange, but I feel certain Mum hasn't gone, that she is still here somewhere." Tiani met my eyes, twirling her hair again. "You feel that too, don't you Dad?"

What should I say to her? I'd had a steadily growing niggle I couldn't shake. Williamson's cryptic message kept coming back to haunt me, ' Kiera is with me now.' Like Tiani, I too had an overwhelming feeling she wasn't gone. I knew, if I searched, I would find her. I'd kept trying to dismiss the thoughts, putting them down to grief, denial and wishful thinking. They'd persisted in spite of my efforts to put them to rest and strengthened as time had passed.

"Yes, that's exactly what I feel."

Jack frowned. "I know it's what you want to believe, but she *is* dead. You can't bring her back." He leapt up, strode to the door, and stood with his hand out—waiting to usher us through. "Okay, it's time to get everyone back to sleep."

Nobody moved.

"No, Uncle Jack." Tiani turned to me. "I'm going to help Dad to look for Mum."

"So am I." Julian walked over to join us.

We were now a conspiracy of three.

"You can't be serious." Jack shook his head as his expression became one of incredulity. "Bloody hell, you're all deluded. I'm going back to sleep."

"Please help us, Uncle Jack. You're the only one that can." Tiani gave him one of her best classic pleading looks. An amazing feat, considering she inhabited an android barely resembling her. I could see Jack beginning to waver. Tiani always had had him wrapped around her little finger.

He sighed.

"Hey, even if we're wrong, Uncle Jack, what have we got to lose?" Julian said.

"Uncle Jack?" I smiled at him. "It's three against one."

"All right, but..." He held up both hands to stop us interrupting. "There has to be a time limit." He dropped his hands.

"But..." Julian tried.

"No. No buts. My terms and conditions are; I will give you forty-eight hours, after which, regardless of the outcome, we will all go back to sleep. It's simple. No agreement—no help. In my opinion, it's a waste of time. As designated section leader in the event of an emergency, I'm in charge, so you're all bound to obey my orders for the duration. Okay?" His expression remained, determined and officious.

We could see it would be pointless to argue with him. Three heads nodded simultaneously.

#

We sat around the table and discussed how we were going to tackle the problem. Jack ducked out and tried the easy option of searching for Logan Williamson and Kiera by name, just on the off chance he and Kiera were hiding in plain sight. He had also searched for Kiera, using facial recognition and normal bio-parameters. It had come up negative. Jack failed to find any information in the ship's computer about Williamson. Neither Jack nor I could remember his face that well, but we did think we would recognise him if we saw him.

"He mightn't be on the ship," Jack said, taking a sip of his coffee.

"I have a strong feeling he's here somewhere, but he may have changed his appearance. I doubt he's transitioned to a sapioid form, yet. He enjoyed his humanness too much, or should I say lack thereof. As a control freak, he'd be worried about being forced to undergo GM. Remember, everybody's genome was screened as part of the selection process. They wouldn't have selected Williamson, unless he'd agreed to, or had already had genetic modifications. He wouldn't have got on board carrying the same glaring psychological traits that we all knew so well. He'll only become a sapioid when he's out of viable alternatives," I said.

Jack nodded his head in agreement.

"So, are we looking for his clone?" Julian asked.

"Absolutely. The question is, did he opt for an identical copy, or has he done all sorts of physical modifications, in which case, it will be difficult to recognise him." I finished eating my energy bar and mopped up the crumbs with my fingers.

"I have an idea." Tiani leaned back in her chair and looked thoughtful.

"Let's have it," Jack said, before he drained his cup.

"If there is some sort of psychic link between Julian, myself and Mum and Dad, what if we all linked up in Virtual and went deeper into the matrix to search?"

I watched as she began, absentmindedly, twisting her hair again. In some ways it was reassuring to see her performing one of her normal, everyday habits. Normal—nothing would ever be normal again. A wave of sadness broke over me, and I struggled to contain it. I pulled my mind back to the current conversation.

"It can't be done, Tiani. The human mind can't cope with the whole matrix. It's too powerful. It wouldn't be possible to do that using Virtual, anyway. When we link to Virtual, it's peripheral. We're using our minds to issue commands instead of speaking to the computer or keying them in. When we go into Immersive Virtual, which is a lot deeper, it's via an avatar. It's totally different from the direct link your dad established with you, Julian and your mum. The depth of that is probably somewhere in between.

Anybody that has attempted to link with the matrix has ended up dead or a vegetable." Jack's face took on a sombre expression. "I lost a good friend that way a couple of years ago. He ended up dead, with bits of his memory embedded all over the matrix."

Tiani wasn't about to be put off that easily. "But they were all single people efforts, Uncle Jack. We would be a group of three, and two of us have android brains. If we joined together, it might make us strong enough to be able to cope."

"No, it's too risky, Tiani, and I can't see how that would help to find Williamson."

"But we wouldn't be looking for Williamson."

"Oh?" I raised my eyebrows.

"We would be looking for Mum. Tell me the exact words of the message again, Dad."

"'Kiera is with me now, you won't find us.'" I shivered with the memory of it.

Tiani leant across and gave my hand a gentle squeeze. "What if he copied her onto a chip or some other storage device and hid it somewhere on his own body?"

Could it be that simple? Far from it. It would mean we would be back to uploading Kiera (if possible) into an android. It still left the issue of Kiera's body—my body now—dangling.

Jack thought for a moment before saying, "Probably a Higgs boson chase. Chips complex enough to hold the whole human consciousness haven't been perfected yet, besides, copying a human's consciousness is illegal. That law was designed to stop any further research, but it's a possibility, considering Logan Williamson's past history.

You wouldn't need to go into the matrix, Tiani. If it's been secreted in Williamson's body, a search through human and clone bodies for one containing a foreign body, other than the identity spherule, would suffice. You could use the password test to identify Kiera, Luke, just as you've done previously."

"Except, we can't check it against her bio-parameters."

"No, but who else would know the password? Williamson wouldn't." Jack straightened in his chair and grinned.

"He might, if he's been able to get into her mind somehow, Jack." I met his eyes.

"It's unlikely. If we find something, I'm prepared to take the risk, Luke. Are you?"

I nodded.

Jack sat silent for a moment. "Technically, I've committed an offence by uploading and saving you two kids to the ship's computer. It could be considered making copies, although it was only tempo-

rary. I deleted them once I was sure your uploads had been successful."

"Under the circumstances, Jack, I think we could say it was justified. My understanding is, it refers to permanent copies on
computers and storage devices, doesn't it?"

Jack shrugged. "Let's hope so, Luke." He turned to Tiani and
patted her arm. "Bloody hell Tiani you're a genius. I don't know why
I didn't think of a chip or device search. Okay, let's get to it." He
leapt up and darted towards the door.

We filed out after him. Tiani was almost bubbling over with enthusiasm and Julian's smile lit his face from ear to ear. I just hoped. I
knew we were grasping for a remote possibility, but at least it gave us
something to focus on. I followed them out, my own spirits buoyed
up by theirs.

Chapter 32

Jack linked in and set up the search. Now, it was just a matter of waiting. He'd set up an alarm that would alert us to a positive result. Since only one of us needed to stay awake, Jack decided the rest of us could grab some sleep. Tiani volunteered for the first shift.

When people were first uploaded into sapioids, we'd thought they wouldn't need sleep. To everyone's surprise, even though sapioids didn't get physically tired, their human minds still required it. A further revelation was that they were able to dream.

Interfering with their sleep caused them to exhibit the same symptoms as sleep deprived humans; loss of concentration, memory problems and personality changes. Sleep for humans was an essential part of the functioning brain. It allowed the processing, sorting and consolidation of information gained during waking hours. Unwanted material was discarded and the brain was flushed clean of clogging amyloid, tau and other proteins.

Since there were only two bunks in the living module, Julian volunteered to sleep on the floor. He settled himself comfortably by lying on a blanket with another one rolled up under his head. He fell asleep in minutes. So did Jack. I laid there listening to his slow, relaxed breathing. My mind still raced with thoughts of Kiera; of my children trapped in machines. The finality of it, Julian, and possibly Tiani, didn't yet realise. The sentence of forever, of never being able to have children. I would have to tell them, and I dreaded it.

Roused by a loud buzzing, I opened my eyes, and shook away the muzzy feeling of sleep. Julian's excited face hovered over me. "Hey, Dad. We've found her."

I sat up and rubbed my eyes.

The buzzing ceased abruptly, and presently, Jack stuck his head around the door. "We found a body with an FB on deck twenty-eight P."

"FB?" I queried.

"Foreign body, Dad," Julian's eyes radiated hope, excitement and expectation.

"It's a male clone, recorded as Peter Cales," Jack said.

I swung my legs to the floor and stood up. "Is it Williamson?"

"I can't tell. The photographs are probably not reliable, Williamson could easily have inserted a fake. It appears hopeful, the biological parameters fit—dark hair, brown eyes, right height as far as I can remember."

"Do you want me to go down and look?" I focused on him, and just for an instant could see pain in his eyes, but in a flash it vanished.

"I think we should both go. We need to wake Mr Cales to scan the FB. Perhaps he could be persuaded to tell us about it." Jack frowned and tightened his fists. "I wouldn't be beyond using force."

My mouth dropped open. Jack's last comment was totally out of character. "I don't think that would be wise. You might damage the chip, or whatever it is."

"It depends on what I do, doesn't it?" He flashed me an evil grin. "There are so many options, I really don't know which to choose."

Shock reverberated through me, and my skin crawled. I had never seen Jack resort to violence.

"Hey, I'll be in that," Julian said.

I put my hand on his arm. "No you won't." It was one thing for Jack, or me, to entertain using violence, but I wasn't going to let Julian go down that track.

"Dad." His face took on a pained expression.

"It's not necessary! If he doesn't talk, we'll access the chip. I have no objection to restraining him, if he refuses, but I do have an issue with you or Jack using violence."

"You sound just like Kiera." Jack frowned and gave me a sour look.

"Not funny." I was in no mood for his humour.

"Can I come too?" Tiani asked.

An insistent buzzer sounded again. Jack cocked his head to one side, puzzled. "I turned that off, unless..." He shot out the door. Filled with a sinking feeling, I filed out behind Tiani and Julian. We hurried over to the console. "We have another body with an FB. It's on deck twenty-nine P," Jack said, as he silenced the buzzer.

"Why would anybody have inclusions? What could they possibly be?" I asked Jack.

"I don't know. I'm just searching this person's parameters. "This one is a woman whose parameters fit Kiera's but..." He fiddled with the keyboard. "It's not Kiera.

We peered at the photograph displayed on screen. It bore no resemblance to Kiera.

"That's not her." Tiani crinkled up her face in disappointment.

"I agree." Julian bit his lip.

"Definitely not, but how can we be certain? Williamson is capable of anything. What do we do now, Jack?" I wrapped my arms around myself, suddenly feeling cold. Jack appeared calm, almost detached.

"We can't assume the first one is her. We're going to have to scan all the FBs we find, to rule them out. You know how I feel, but you've raised a remote possibility, so because we're family I'm prepared to see this through."

Tiani burst into tears. Julian put his arm around her shoulders. "Hey, Ti, the first one might be her." He tried, unsuccessfully, to look hopeful.

"Great Universe, Jack. How far through the search are we?"

"The computer's conducting the search deck by deck. It's just started on twenty-nine." He consulted the screen. "According to this it will take another four hours and twenty-six minutes. I suggest we start looking at the ones that have already come up. Tiani and Julian should stay here. It will be easier to coordinate pressurising the sections where these people are located. I'll need to show you two how to do it."

"Are they stable enough?"...I trailed off, embarrassed at discussing my children's stability in front of them.

"Dad?" Although Tiani's face registered annoyance, I sensed fear in her voice.

"Hey, we're okay, aren't we Tiani?" Julian leant over and gave her a quick, one arm hug.

Tiani turned to Jack. "Are we, Uncle Jack?" She screwed up her face, fighting back tears.

Jack put his arms around her. "Yes, Tiani." He turned to me and said, "They'll be fine, they're well and truly stabilised now, Luke. There won't be any dramas. Okay, kids, come over to the console, and I'll show you how everything works and what programs you'll need to access."

Julian sat down in the chair, and Tiani sat opposite him at the console on the other side. I stood by and watched as Jack filled Tiani and Julian in on what the various buttons did and how to set up the necessary protocols for pressurising a section and reviving people.

After allowing enough time for the pressurisation of our first section to be almost complete by the time we got there, Jack said, "Let's suit up and get going, Luke. I'm starting us off with deck twenty-eight P, and we'll work up from there if we need to."

Julian and Tiani waved as we set off. I followed Jack down to the bulkhead where the suits were hanging.

My emotions were in limbo.

Chapter 33

After making our way through numerous airlocks, we finally reached the lift closest to our destination. Jack summoned it, and we waited for it to come down from its default position on deck five. We could hear Julian and Tiani chattering away in the background. As we stood bathed in the green light from the display screen, Jack tapped my visor and indicated we should switch to our private suit-to-suit communication. I pressed the button located in the mini control panel on my sleeve and observed the red icon light up on my HUD display just in time to hear Jack say, "We're just going off-line, you two, we'll be back in about ten minutes, okay?"

"Okay," Tiani and Julian chorused back.

"Finally, we've got some of privacy. I need to clear the air with you, Luke. Where the hell did your comment come from? It's left me bloody gutted."

At first, I couldn't see his face through the visor, but a light came on inside his helmet and he held up his wrist, indicating the button I should press to do the same. In an instant, brightness flooded my face.

"I…" my muscles tensed, as I struggled to answer him. An intense anger bubbled up from somewhere inside and I exploded. "I feel like the three of us are…*were* in a Zarking ménage a trois, Jack." I swallowed, suddenly aware that I was shaking. "Kiera was always going on about the special connection between the two of you. It made me feel threatened and excluded." I stopped to catch my breath. "She didn't discuss you joining Sapioid Inc. with me, she just went ahead and asked you."

I heard Jack's fast intake of breath, as his face registered shock.

"I didn't know that, Luke."

I could hear my own ragged breathing. I needed to calm down. Jack stood watching me, as I took a couple of deep breaths. "Look, I know we're both drowning in emotion because of what's happened. Somehow, it's raked up my past, and brought back stuff I thought I'd laid to rest. I'm ashamed and deeply sorry, Jack." I went to run my fingers through my hair but instead whacked my hand on my helmet. I heard Jack clear his throat, so I kept quiet and waited for him to speak.

"I obviously need to explain a few things, Luke. When I first saw you and Kiera together, I made up my mind to walk away again after everything was over. I'd already done that once. I'd accepted there was no chance of a relationship with her. As her youth counsellor, it would have been unprofessional and unethical, and besides she didn't love me."

"And the connection, Jack?" I said, more tersely than I had intended.

"Yes, Kiera and I do have a special connection. It developed during our counselling sessions. We had a lot in common, plus there were a multitude of intense emotional issues I helped Kiera work through. We developed a deep, enduring understanding of one another." Jack paused, and I nodded in acknowledgement.

"After the trial, Kiera changed my mind when she told me how far the upload program had advanced and what your plans were. I had no idea she hadn't discussed it with you, Luke."

His earnest, open expression convinced me he was telling the truth, so I simply nodded again.

"I jumped at the chance to take my life in a different direction. No matter what I did, I always had a feeling of incompleteness."

"Jack, I…"

Jack held up his hands. "Let me finish, Luke. It's ironic really, working on the upload program wasn't where I found satisfaction and serenity. It was being with you, Kiera, and the kids, Luke. Being part of your family and being included in your world. I love you all dearly—you've given me exactly what I craved."

My insides knotted up, and I could feel my throat tightening. I could see tears shining in Jack's eyes.

"I was never a threat to you, Luke. The only thing I'm guilty of is that I once loved Kiera the way you do. That's well and truly in the past, so can we put this to rest once and for all?" He reached up and touched my shoulder, and I could see the anguish in his face.

"Absolutely, Jack." I reached out and patted his shoulder. "I promise never to mention the subject again."

"And if we find Kiera, please don't mention our conversation."

"Of course not, Jack."

Jack managed a grin before he continued, "Good, I'm glad that's sorted." He flicked off his helmet light. "Right, we had better switch back to general com before we panic Tiani." He pressed his wrist. "We're back, you two."

I pressed my switch just in time to hear Julian say, "Deck twenty-seven S."

"Say again Julian, I didn't catch that," I said.

"We found another person with an FB on deck twenty-seven S."

"What the hell can this mean, Dad?" chimed in Tiani's excited voice. "How can there be so many people with extra stuff? This is so weird."

"Interesting," Jack said, "I hope we don't find too many more because there is an awake protocol I was hoping I didn't have to mention."

"What do you mean?" Julian's voice suddenly sounded strained.

"There are rules about how long we are allowed to remain out of suspension at any one time, once an emergency has been addressed." Jack's tone became serious.

"Why the hell is that?" Tiani responded, sounding abrupt and upset.

"I don't know anything about that, Jack," I said.

"Need-to-know basis. Only the emergency team leaders were briefed on this particular protocol." He had that officious, smug expression of his I found particularly annoying.

"Hey, Uncle Jack, we do need to know so tell us."

Jack sighed. "Apart from the ageing factor, the longer you stay awake the less likely you are to want to go back to sleep. The ship isn't equipped to handle that. Experimental studies have proved psychological problems occur if a couple of people are cooped up together for more than short periods. They begin to become unstable, and for that reason it's not allowed."

"But surely finding Mum *is* an emergency isn't it? Besides, there's four of us and we're all family. We're used to being together." I could hear the strain in Tiani's voice, it wouldn't be too long before she started to cry.

"Since there is no threat to life, or to the ship, there's no real justification for us conducting this search."

"Great Universe, Jack, this may be the only chance we'll have to find her. We won't be able to scan people once everybody's out of hiber-sleep. Having extra chips or whatever is probably not illegal, and since we wouldn't be in an emergency situation, we wouldn't be allowed to scan people without their permission. They're certainly not going to give us that if they're hiding something are they?"

"I'm sorry, Luke, kids, but my original timetable has to stand."

"That's not fair, Uncle Jack." I heard Tiani start to sniffle.

"Life's not fair. That's the way it is. Here's the lift," Jack said tersely, as the fire doors parted, and the lift door slid open in front of us.

"Dad," Julian's tone was angry, "do something."

"I can't. End of discussion." Tiani started to sob, and I listened as Julian tried to calm her down. I swallowed down my feelings and was struggling with my own anger. Jack had been placed in charge, and I had to respect that.

"We are going to suit-to-suit com. We'll check with you in ten minutes." I saw Jack press the isolation switch, and he motioned for me to do the same. I hesitated before I reluctantly pressed my own.

"Why have we gone suit-to-suit, Jack?"

"I didn't want to listen to the two of them. I hated...bloody hell...let's get on with it."

We stepped into the lift, surrounded only by the sound of our breathing.

#

I removed my helmet and took a deep breath; Jack did the same. Since our suits were easy to get in and out of, we shed them and left them lying by the airlock in readiness for our return. As we headed down to module five, I noticed the air held a slight tang I couldn't place. Jack located Peter Cales. To save time, he'd already initiated the reanimation process before we'd started down, so he only needed to check its progress using the module's touch screen.

I wandered down to the living unit and made myself a cup of tea. As I sat, I contemplated the simulated picture window on the opposite wall. This unit had a view of a stormy ocean with white caps that had been whipped up by a fierce gale—and a sky pierced by lightning. The reality was so stunning I could almost hear the thunder. It finally struck me; that puzzling tang in the air—was the smell of salt.

I made Jack some tea and took it out to him. He turned as I approached.

"We're getting there."

I passed him the tea.

"Thanks, K...sorry, Luke," he frowned and took several sips from his cup.

"It's okay, I still freak every time I catch a glimpse of myself. How much longer?" Jack turned back to the screen.

"Forty minutes."

"I'll check with Julian and Tiani while we wait."

Back in the living unit, I sat down at the serenity blue table. I noticed a small panel inset into its edge, on my left. I carefully lifted its lid, not knowing what to expect. Inside, I discovered a mini screen showing a number of icons. One looked suspiciously like a ship. I cautiously tapped, and the tabletop transformed into a translucent display of a huge star chart. Blinking, roughly a third of the way from the right-hand edge, a tiny icon appeared. I realised it represented our ship. Mesmerised, I tapped another icon that appeared to be a blue star. It immediately displayed near the far-left-hand edge of the chart; it had to be the Kalgarin solar system, our destination. My pulse quickened, as I pressed the general com button.

"Julian, Tiani you won't believe this."

"You've found her?" Tiani's voice, full of hope, rang in my ear. Bloody Zark. I should have chosen my words more carefully.

"Not yet, but what I have found is a chart showing the ship's location relative to our destination." I hoped I'd provided enough of a distraction.

"Hey, Dad, that's really something! Is it accessible from the computer? I'd love to see it." I could hear the excitement in Julian's voice. I explained how to activate the display via the panel inset into the table.

"So how far along are we?" Tiani asked.

"About a third."

"So," she said, "we've been asleep for around fifty years…only another hundred to go." The sarcasm in her tone was unmistakable.

At least I'd diverted her focus onto something else "Well, I don't know about you but I don't feel any older." Great Universe, what a tactless comment to make. Julian and Tiani, as sapioids, would never feel physically older ever again. I braced myself for the response.

"How could you possibly know? You're not even in your own body," Tiani shouted in my ear, followed by sniffing sounds. She'd always been oversensitive—she used to drive Kiera insane. She often referred to her as 'my little drama queen'. In truth, Tiani was a lot like me, except perhaps more extreme. Julian, on the other hand, was sensible, quiet and balanced, like Kiera. My mind went blank. Julian came to my rescue.

"We've got some news too. We found another target on deck twenty-seven S, do you want the location now?"

How many more of these things were going to turn up? "No, not yet, let's wait and see what we find here. I'd better check and see what progress Jack's made. I'll get back to you again in ten minutes." Before either of them could reply, I switched back to suit-to-suit com.

I couldn't find an off switch for the table display, so I just flipped the panel lid down. The table immediately became opaque, and the chart vanished. I got up and headed out the door.

Chapter 34

I stood next to Jack and watched the capsule slide forward. The canopy released with a hiss and glided out of sight beneath the left-hand side of the unit. Peter Cales, its occupant, although awake, still appeared out of it. I remembered how I'd felt. It seemed like weeks ago. All the various leads had detached, and I could hear the familiar sound of the soothing female voice I had experienced. The capsule began to tilt upwards. I remembered that feeling, too, as the only time during the revival process that I'd felt afraid.

I went to reach out, but Jack grabbed my hand and put one finger to his lips.

We stood in silence and waited. The straps released, and Peter Cales slid into an upright position. He regarded each of us in turn with frightened eyes.

"It's okay," Jack said, as he reached out and took him by the arm. I followed suit and took his other arm. "We'll take you into the living unit, where you can sit down and get your bearings, Peter," Jack said.

"Are...are we there?" Peter's face took on a slightly bewildered expression.

"No, there's been...a problem," Jack said, glancing across at me, "Nothing to worry about," he added.

"Problem? There's...been something go wrong?" Peter said, as we guided him down the deck towards the living quarters.

"Yes," Jack said, "but not in this section. We'll explain once you've had a drink and you're fully awake."

We wobbled him through the door and sat him down at the table. Jack got him a cup of water, and Peter guzzled it down while we sat next to him. After he finished, he put the cup down and studied us intently.

"Well?" he said, "What exactly is going on?"

"That's what we'd like to know, Peter. Can you explain why you have what appears to be a storage device concealed on your person?" Jack said, holding his gaze and looking serious.

Peter's face flushed. "I don't know what you're talking about, and who the hell are you guys, anyway?"

"I'm Jack Summers, emergency team leader from deck twenty-six P, section seven. I'm in command for the duration of this waking period. No games, Peter, we don't have time. Answer my question, please."

Peter, uncomfortable and flustered now, turned to me and asked, "So who are you?"

"I'm...Kiera Proud. I'm second in charge." I glanced at Jack, he raised his eyebrows quizzically.

"Answer my question," Jack said, more forcefully.

Peter Cales held up both hands, "Okay, okay. The chip contains holographic, audio-visual material of animal surgical techniques. I didn't want to have to go to the trouble of searching the ship's computer for data in an emergency."

"Animal surgical techniques, so what's your designation?" Jack asked.

"I'm a veterinary surgeon."

Jack and I exchanged glances. "We should have checked his file, Jack," I shook my head.

"So where is the chip located?" Jack asked, frowning.

"Why?" There was annoyance in his voice.

"Because we need to access it."

"Why? I've told you what's on it. Are you calling me a liar?" Peter's expression became angry and defensive.

"We need to check. There have been some major security breaches, necessitating the examination of anyone with extra chips. You're the first one on the list. Show me where the chip is located." Jack's face held an expression of authoritative determination. "Once we check that everything is okay, we can put you back to sleep. Let's get on with it. Do I need to remind you I have the authority? "

"Okay, but I'm not happy. The chip's embedded in my wrist." He held out his right hand, palm up, for Jack to examine.

Jack took hold of it and, using his fingers, located the chip. "Okay, Peter. I've brought a portable linkup to connect the chip to the ship's computer so we can see what's on it. I need you come outside and sit down at one of the consoles. Once you've linked, I'll give you instructions on how to bypass your identity spherule to allow the computer to interrogate your chip. Let's go." Jack got to his feet and, taking Peter by one arm, helped him navigate out to the deck and over to the nearest computer console chair.

Peter only grudgingly complied. No one spoke as the headband engaged, and Peter's eyes glazed over.

"Somewhat excessive, don't you think, Jack?" I was getting sick of his smug, dictatorial attitude. This wasn't the Jack I knew. "Was the linking necessary?"

"No, but it will keep him occupied while I check the chip." He attached one end of the lead via a gel patch to Peter's wrist, then connected the other end to a small jack in the side of the headband of the chair opposite Peter. "Okay, I'm going to link and examine the chip. It shouldn't take long. Oh," Jack said, turning to me, "I'll instruct the computer to disconnect him, before I come out. Okay?"

"Yes," I said, a little hesitantly. Great Universe, I hope nothing goes wrong. I watched Jack's headband engage and his expression go blank. I noticed my fingernails were digging into my palms, so I took a deep breath and relaxed my hands. In spite of my efforts, restlessness still compelled me to pace from one end of the deck to the other while keeping a wary eye on both of them. Minutes dragged by like hours, and my pacing became more rapid as my anxiety rose. I saw movement out of the corner of my eye and spotted Peter's headband disengaging. As I hurried over to him, Jack's headband began separating. That sight made me feel better.

"What happened?" Peter Cales asked, once the headband had slid away. He pushed himself out of the chair and stood up.

"I don't know yet," I said, coming to a halt in front of him.

Jack stood up. "Your chip's fine, Peter. Thanks for that. Now," he came around to our side of the console, "let's get you back to sleep." He went to take Peter's arm, but Peter pulled it away.

"I can manage by myself, thank you," he said, tersely. "I'm going to report this when we get to Kalgarin." He stalked off in the direction of his capsule.

"Fine," Jack called after him, "Everything I've done will have been recorded in the ship's computer logs."

We followed Peter to the capsule.

"So, what happens now?" Peter asked.

"I'll reactivate the system. Once it reverts to the horizontal position, you can lie down, and I'll reattach all the leads to your sleep suit. They won't engage until after you're asleep, so you won't feel anything, okay?" Jack pressed various buttons on the small panel embedded in the side of the unit. When he'd finished, the upright sleep unit began to tilt and slide out towards us as it reverted to the horizontal position. We moved out of its way.

Peter turned to Jack, "I haven't done anything illegal, so I don't think your actions were warranted or justified. You will be hearing from my solicitors once we get to our destination. You won't get away with this." He turned away from us and laid down in the unit.

"I'm sorry you feel like that." Jack stepped in and began to re-connect the colour-coded leads to Peter's sleep suit. Peter remained silent during the process but glared directly at me. After Jack had finished, he leant across and pressed a button inside the unit, "It *was* necessary, Peter."

Seconds later, the canopy slid out from under the unit and sealed into place with a thud. We heard a hissing sound, as the capsule began to fill with a colourless gas. We watched as Peter's eyes drooped and finally closed. The capsule slid backwards and slowly glided back into its original position.

"Is that it?"

"Yes," Jack replied, while keeping his eyes on the monitor panel attached to the section.

I stood eyeing him, unsure of what I should do next.

"You go and get suited up, I'll only be a few more minutes here."

I walked down to where we'd left our suits. They lay on the ground like two beheaded corpses, the heads (our two helmets) neatly by their sides. I picked up my suit and began to get into it. I hadn't finished when Jack appeared beside me and began scrambling into his. He grinned, "Well, that went well."

"Oh, absolutely Zarking great! We'll probably have a posse of solicitors waiting in ambush for us when we wake up."

"Probably aren't any. Admin may have decided they'd spend too much time arguing the legalities of everything after we arrived, and nothing would get done. We could locate them all and turn them off," Jack said, looking deadly serious.

My jaw dropped, as I froze and stared in disbelief.

"For God's sake, Luke, I'm joking. Look, I'm well within my rights. There's nothing to worry about." He picked up his helmet.

"You might be, but what about me?" I said, as I did the same.

"You were acting under my authority, so you're protected." He donned his helmet and the seal hissed shut. He gave me the thumbs up signal. I put my helmet on and followed him into the airlock.

I heard him say through my suit com, "Hey kids, we're back. No luck I'm afraid. Just a vet with his precious surgical files. The next FB is one deck up on the port side, is that right?"

"Hey, Uncle Jack, hey Dad. Yes, that's correct, she's in section one." I could hear the disappointment in Julian's voice in spite of his valiant effort to hide it.

"Okay, initiate the pressurisation and wake-up process please, Julian."

"Will do. So, how did it go?" He added.

"Great. Just great. How are you two going?"

"We're okay. Tiani is having a nap."

"Good to hear you, Julian," I said. The fact he was sounding so normal buoyed me up.

"Okay, we'll switch to in-suit com, and check with you when we get there," I heard Jack say. I pressed my button, and my icon turned red in the HUD, just as the airlock door slid closed.

"On to the next one," Jack said, as he pressed the depressurising button.

Chapter 35

Our next victim, Sarah Jane, paramedic, couldn't bear to part with her second cat, Tilda. She had paid to have Tilda's stem cells preserved in a tiny phial and planned to reconstitute her pet once we had settled on a planet in the Kalgarin system. Pets preserved by that particular process were allowed, provided they had had their genes altered to render them infertile. People were restricted to one pet only, per person.

Sarah Jane, embarrassed and apologetic, had already put one cat in storage but couldn't bear to part with the second, so she'd resorted to subterfuge. We found her to be a sweet, gentle lady, and we knew there wouldn't be any complaints about us from her.

We travelled down then across to deck twenty-seven S, where there were two males with FBs. The first, Gerrard Colebatch, bio electrician, behaved in a docile and compliant manner. His FB held two beloved pets, a dog and a cat. He'd been conned into paying an excessive amount for his pets' consciousnesses to be uploaded onto chips. The chips were, of course, blank, and to cover ourselves we had to tell him. He was devastated.

Our second male, Paul Tozer, a robotics expert, turned out to be a handful. Jack and I were forced to restrain him. After tying both his hands and feet together, Jack sedated him. We'd half dragged and half carried the unconscious man to the console chair. When Jack scanned his FB, he found it held the schematics for hundreds of un-patented robotic prototypes. Afterwards, we lugged his tall, heavyset body back to the capsule. By the time we got him back to sleep, we were both nearing exhaustion. At 5:30 p.m., ship time, we'd gone to the living unit to grab something to eat and drink.

"We've only got one left on deck thirty," I managed between mouthfuls of something purported to be a chicken sandwich. With our finds so far proving unfruitful, my hope was evaporating into despair. I found it hard to keep going, especially when talking with Julian and Tiani. They too were sounding tired and despondent, par-ticularly Tiani.

"I did warn you," Jack said, wiping his mouth with his hand. "I thought it would be a Higgs boson chase." He studied his plate. "But you never know, there's still one left."

I didn't answer him. I sat and stared into space, worried sick about how Julian and Tiani would cope when we came up empty-handed.

I let out deep sigh. "I'm exhausted, Jack. I'm finding it an effort just to lift one foot after another," I said, taking a swig from my cup.

"The suits aren't helping." Jack regarded me with tired eyes. "I suggest we grab a couple of hours sleep, prior to moving on to the last one. It's going to be quite a trek. He's right over the other side of the deck relative to where we are now."

"Good idea, but how are we going to limit it to a couple of hours? I feel like I could sleep for a week."

"I'll get the kids to buzz us. There's an emergency alarm they can use to override our suit-to-suit coms. I'll just duck out and get my helmet." Jack got up, dumped his plate in the sink, threw his cup in the recycler and went outside.

I rinsed our plates, dried them with a couple of paper towels and stowed them away in the cupboard under the sink. By the time Jack returned, I'd pulled out the bunks.

"All organised. Tiani sends her love, Julian's asleep. They'll buzz us in two hours." He laid his helmet next to the bunk, grabbed a blanket and pillow from the cupboard and laid down. He pulled the blanket up over his head. "Night, Luke."

I followed suit and went to sleep almost instantly, only to be woken seemingly minutes later by the alarm. I sat up. Jack switched it off from somewhere inside his helmet.

"Okay," Jack said, "let's get moving." He stowed away his bedding, pushed the bunk back into the wall, grabbed his helmet and walked out.

I wanted to pull the blanket over my head, to curl up, and withdraw like a snail inside my shell. I took a deep breath and heaved myself off the bunk on leaden legs. As soon as I stood up, my head began to throb.

After I packed up the bedding, I joined Jack. He'd already suited up and stood waiting. He was talking to Julian or Tiani, so I quickly squirmed into my suit and jammed the helmet into place.

I heard Julian say in a defensive tone, "It was Ti's idea, not mine."

"I'm not happy, Julian. It could have waited until we came back," Jack said, angrily.

"What could have waited?" I asked, wondering what was going on.

"Jack hasn't searched our section, so Tiani went ahead and set it up. Your search had already finished, Jack, so it hasn't interfered with anything. She does know what she's doing." I could hear the tension in Julian's voice.

I tapped Jack's shoulder and he turned to face me. "Why did you miss our section?"

"You'd already checked it, Luke. I didn't think it was necessary." He had flicked on his helmet light to show me his face. I couldn't remember ever seeing him look so furious.

"I quickly checked through the photographs, Jack. You said later that they could have been substituted and they weren't reliable." I realised I'd raised my voice.

"Perhaps I didn't allow enough for your sloppiness, under the circumstances," Jack shouted.

"Uncle Jack—Dad—Please stop," Tiani pleaded. "I've located a person with two FBs in module one, your module. I'm just about to start the revival process." She sounded excited.

"Don't! You don't know enough about it. You wouldn't know what to do if something goes wrong. Wait until we get back." Jack said, struggling to keep his voice moderate.

"But..." Tiani began.

Jack interrupted. "I absolutely forbid it," he roared. "Do you understand, and that goes for both of you?"

"Yes," Tiani said. I knew from the tone, she was choking back tears.

"Julian?" Jack said.

"Yes, Jack. We'll wait, okay?"

"Okay, switching to in-suit com." Jack pointed to my wrist.

I sighed and pressed the button.

"You didn't need to shout at them, Jack." I had flicked my helmet light on so we could both see one another. Jack's face was flushed with anger.

"So, I should have just let Tiani go ahead?" His voice held a terse tone.

"No, of course not, but you know what Tiani's like. And Jack, I don't like to be blamed for your sloppiness. Why can't you just admit you made a mistake for once?" I put my hands on my hips.

"All right," Jack roared, "all right, I made a bloody mistake. There, satisfied now? Your Mr Infallible, Jack, who has to make all the decisions, has to fix everyone else's problems and come up with instant solutions, has made a mistake. I'm sorry, if for once, when I'm bloody exhausted and under pressure, I can't live up to everyone's usual expectations. Perhaps you'd like to takeover, Luke? Perhaps you'd like to try and stay calm while you make some difficult decisions, life-and-death decisions, would you?" He switched off his light, turned away and stomped into the airlock.

I kept quiet, still digesting what Jack had said. I realised that none of us had thought about, or even attempted to understand, the extreme strain and pressure Jack's responsibility had placed upon him. I had forced difficult decisions on to him. Decisions I should have made myself. He was right. Our expectations were unrealistic, and he obviously needed more support than we had given him.

I followed him into the airlock, "Sorry, Jack. Sorry for loading so much on you. You've done an incredible job."

He stood, silent and still with his back to me, his head resting on the wall. He raised his arm up in acknowledgement before letting it drop. I stood and waited patiently. Several minutes passed before he turned and spoke.

"Apology accepted. Now let's get on with it." He turned and pressed the button.

Chapter 36

Jack was right about it being a marathon trek to reach David Kariba, now our second last person with an FB. We trudged for over an hour through endless dark sections to reach the appropriate lift to take us up to section ten on deck thirty S.

David Kariba, GP, had the added qualification of psychiatry. African in descent, his, frizzy, black hair stood out in all directions. It made him look like he'd been struck by lightning. His FB consisted of a chip purported to contain a fragment of his wife's consciousness—salvaged after she'd sustained severe head injuries in a trans-car accident. Doctors had been unable to salvage enough of her consciousness to upload her.

Dr Kariba had never accessed the chip, but he'd found it an incredible comfort to have part of her so near. He told us his heartbreaking story, and I found myself wiping away tears by the time he'd finished. He was adamant he didn't want Jack to tell him what he found on the chip. He preferred the blissful ignorance of imagining that part of his wife's consciousness would be with him forever.

I watched Jack sit him in the chair and go through the familiar process of linking. Exhausted, I sat down on the floor next to Dr Kariba and waited. I must have dozed off because I woke with a start when Jack tapped my shoulder. Dr Kariba, still sitting, remained linked.

I pushed myself up off the floor. "Has something gone wrong?"

"No, everything is fine except..." His face held a look of anguish.

"Except what, what's wrong, Jack?" I reached out and touched his shoulder.

"Dr Kariba's chip—It's blank. The poor devil's been carrying it around inside him all these years, all these lifetimes, thinking it contains part of his wife's consciousness. I'm not sure I can pretend it does. It's all getting too hard."

Jack turned away from me, but I had already seen his tears. I reached out and went to put my arm around his shoulder, but he turned and, flinging both arms around me, held me in a tight embrace. I couldn't do anything but reciprocate, and I could feel him shaking while he wept silently. Awkward, but I guessed in some corner of his mind he still thought of me as Kiera. I held him and patted his back until he stopped.

Without a word he dropped his arms, wiped his face and cleared his throat. He went back to the other side of the console and sat down. I watched as his headband engaged.

About half a minute later, I saw Dr Kariba's headband disengaging. I took a deep breath and steeled myself for some serious lying. I laid my hands on Dr Kariba's shoulders and said, "Well, Dr Kariba, everything's fine." He stared up at me with such sad eyes. I had to look away. Jack got up and, as he came around to join us, managed to light up his face with a brilliant smile.

"There's nothing to worry about, Dr Kariba. So, let's get you back to sleep." He laid his hand gently on Dr Kariba's shoulder.

"Thank you, Jack is it?" Dr Kariba said, smiling.

"Yes, Doctor."

Doctor Kariba turned to me and asked, "And your name is?" He gazed at me with gentle brown eyes.

I cleared my throat. "Kiera, Kiera Proud."

"It's been an honour to meet you, Kiera and Jack. I hope if you are ever in need of medical treatment of any kind, you will do me the honour. I thank you for treating me with respect." He turned to Jack. "Now, it's time for me to sleep and dream pleasant dreams once more. Shall we go?" He indicated with his hand that Jack should go first.

As we proceeded back to his capsule, my thoughts drifted to Kiera. She would have loved this warm and gentle man. He smiled happily as Jack reconnected the various leads to his sleep suit. When Jack had finished, he stepped back and we watched the canopy re-emerge. Just before it clicked shut, Dr Kariba gave a small wave with one hand and smiling said, "Thank you, both. Goodbye for now." The canopy closed, and once Dr Kariba had been put to sleep, the capsule slid back into place.

Jack seemed lost in thought and his face held an expression of sadness.

"Let's get back to our section. Perhaps my hiding in plain sight theory may be right. Finding someone with two FBs sounds promising. Don't lose hope yet, Luke." He patted my shoulder.

Chapter 37

After donning our helmets and checking our air supply, we stepped into the airlock. We switched to general com to let the kids know we were on our way back. Tiani answered the call with a bright and cheerful voice.

After a brief summary of our encounter with Dr Kariba, we switched back to in-suit com for the depressurisation process. Once it completed, Jack pressed the door open button. Nothing happened.

"What the hell?" he muttered, as he pressed the button several more times. The door remained closed. "I'm switching back to general com. Hi Tiani, we have a problem. We've depressurised the airlock, but the external door won't open. You can override it from where you are, but I'll need to navigate you to the ship's schematics.

"Is it in the ship's program list, because I know how to access that?"

"It will be quicker if I guide you through it."

"Okay. Julian's sleeping right now, Uncle Jack. Should I go and wake him up?"

"No, let him sleep, Tiani. You're a smart girl. You can handle it. Now, type 'external airlock doors' and our deck and section number into the search window, it should come up with a list. Found it?"

"Got it," Tiani's voice sounded triumphant.

I registered a twinge of pride in my daughter as I listened to Jack guiding her through to the manual door override. She sounded calm, in control, fast and intuitive.

"It's come up with four choices, do you want me to select 'manual override'?"

"Yes, choose 'open' then 'activate now'."

We both waited. The door still didn't budge.

"Well, that's a no go, Tiani. Go back to the schematic screen. In the right-hand corner at the top there's a red RV icon. Have you found it?"

"Got it."

"Open it. Has it come up with a choice of two?"

"Yes, do you want me to enable the display, for both of you, or just you, Uncle Jack?"

"Both of us."

My HUD display was engulfed by the complex electrical schematics for the door. The various arrays were colour-coded, and my eyes were instantly drawn to a particular circuit, pulsing red.

"Thanks, Tiani. Okay, let's see how we can solve the problem," Jack said.

Tiani remained silent, while Jack and I concentrated on finding a way around the damaged circuit. Exhaustion leached my concentration; I strained just trying to navigate through the electrical schematic. During the next ten minutes Jack and I debated suggestions and batted around strategies while Tiani listened. We came to a conclusion. The only way around the problem was to open the door's control panel and bypass the damaged circuit.

"Jack, why can't we just re-pressurise the section and our air-lock—and go back through to the next section with a lift?"

"Firstly, it takes an hour to depressurise the section, and it can't be interrupted. We're around half way through the process, currently. Secondly, it takes another hour to re-pressurise. Thirdly, the airlock won't open into an area unless the pressure is equal." He frowned in concentration. "It will be a lot quicker to repair the circuit, and besides I'm not comfortable with leaving an unrepaired fault, if I can help it."

"Okay, so what you're saying is, if we can't repair the circuit we're stuck here for around an hour and a half?"

"Yes, so let's get on with it." Jacked turned back to the control panel.

"How are you going to manage a repair without any tools?" I could hear the strain in Tiani's voice.

"We have tools, Tiani," Jack replied. "All the suits are equipped with a tool pack; it's in the right leg pocket." I watched as he unfastened the Velcro flap and removed the pack. He pulled out a small screwdriver and began unscrewing one side of the panel. I followed suit and got to work on the other side. We were soon able to lift the panel clear, exposing the maze of circuits underneath.

"I need spot illumination to make sure I cut the right wires, Luke." He reached into his pocket and passed me his torch.

"Aren't those circuits live, Jack? Won't you need Tiani to isolate the board so you can work on it? "I frowned, it wasn't like Jack to be reckless.

"She can't. But don't worry, our gloves are insulated."

I switched on the torch and shone the beam into the panel.

"Direct the beam a bit lower, Luke. Great. Now, just keep it steady. I need silence because I'm going to talk myself through it, so I don't want any distractions, okay?"

"Understood." It took all my concentration just to hold the beam steady.

"Acknowledged," Tiani said.

In spite of my suit's ventilation system, sweat began to trickle down my neck.

"Okay, I need to pull out the damaged wires. Cut out the damaged sections then reconnect them," Jack muttered to himself.

I could hear his laboured breathing as he reached in to clip the offending wires.

"Zoom schematic—stop. Right, if I just snip this here…"

My hand began to shake. Forced to steady it with my other hand to keep the torch beam constant, I held my breath. A brief, blinding, blue-green flash erupted from the panel. An instant later, my right shoulder slammed into the side wall and pain shot down my arm. My helmet connected with a bang, and my head whipped-lashed sideways, wrenching my neck. I slid to the floor, winded. The airlock's lights had gone out, but almost immediately the emergency lights flickered on, emitting a dull red glow.

"Jack?—Bloody Zark. Jack?" Struggling to breathe, I pushed myself up on all fours. I crunched over the debris scattered on the floor and crawled over to Jack. He'd been flung backwards into the door opposite the panel. He wasn't moving.

"Dad—Uncle Jack—what's happened?" Tiani's anxious voice said.

"Quiet!" I strained, listening for the sound of Jack's breathing. I could hear some sounds; probably Tiani. "I'm switching to in-suit com," I barked. I listened again—nothing but silence. Bloody Zark! What should I do? I've got less than three minutes. If Jack isn't breathing after that, his brain will begin dying. Think. Think and stay calm. I crawled over to where I'd dropped the torch and picked it up. I returned to Jack and, kneeling, shone it on his chest—no movement. I gripped the torch between my teeth and, making a fist with my right hand, thumped his chest hard.

Jack still wasn't breathing. I put my ear to his chest but could hear only an ominous stillness. I placed the heel my left hand on his chest, put my right hand on top, interlaced my fingers, and began pumping vigorously up and down. After thirty I stopped and listened again—still only a chilling silence. I glanced at his opaque face plate. It had been peppered with debris yet appeared to be still intact.

The HUD ghost schematic blanked momentarily and was replaced by a brilliant red text—*'Jack's com out'*. I flipped back to gen com. "Thanks, Tiani." That explained the silence, at least. I shone the torch on his chest again, just in time to see it rise explosively. I gently placed my hands on his shoulders to prevent him from moving until I had checked him for injuries.

I suddenly remembered. Tiani. I had left the gen com on, and could hear her muffled sobs. She'd be frantic, wondering what had happened. "Tiani, Jack's okay."

"What a relief, Dad," Tiani managed in between sniffs. "What are you going to do now?"

"One thing at a time, Tiani. Let me think."

I turned back to Jack. He had switched on his helmet light, but the face plate was so scoured I still couldn't see his face. He raised his arms with his hands outstretched, but I put my hand gently on his shoulder and pressed. He understood, dropped his arms and laid still while I checked for broken bones.

I couldn't see any serious injuries, and nothing appeared broken, so I eased him into a sitting position with his back against the wall. However, I still worried about internal injuries and micro damage to his suit. I gently leant him forward so I could examine his neck and back, which had taken the brunt of his impact. I meticulously checked his air tanks but could see no damage other than a slight dent. I guided him back into an upright position while I examined his legs. Apart from some scorch marks around his chest and shoulders the suit seemed to be intact. A sense of relief rushed over me, and I realised I was shaking.

"Okay," I said, grabbing hold of both his hands, "Let's get you up," forgetting for an instant that he couldn't hear me. I pulled him upright, making sure I didn't let go of his hands because he was now, essentially, blind and dumb. That realisation sent a shudder sliding down my spine. Great Universe. What *were* we going to do next?

"Hi, Dad. Are you both okay? How can I help?"—Julian.

"Julian, good to hear you. We're both a bit shaken, and Jack's helmet has been damaged, so as well is not being able to hear us, he can't see either. Is Tiani okay?"

"I'm okay, now."

"I'm a bit worried about air leaks from Jack's suit. We need to get back to pressurised air, fast. What would you suggest, Julian?"

"I've checked the panel's schematics, and it shows severe damage. Could you verify, please, Dad?" Julian said.

"Okay." I guided Jack over to the far wall housing the wrecked panel and eased him down into a sitting position. I described everything in detail for Julian. When I'd finished, I stood next to Jack in silence as the seconds ticked by. To me, it appeared hopeless.

Chapter 38

Julian finally agreed, the door panel was beyond repair. "Okay, we'll have to go to Plan B. Can I assume Jack's air level is the same as yours, Dad? I can see your readout, but I can't check Jack's because of the com failure."

"Yes, at least I hope so." I was still worrying about hairline cracks in Jack's visor, a slow leak from a minute puncture in his suit or damage to his breathing unit.

I checked my HUD screen; it had reverted to the default display. Julian had turned off the now useless door panel schematic. I had around two hours supply left.

"I can start re-pressurising in ten minutes, Dad. It will only take an hour and ten, so you're still well covered air-wise. Once it's complete, you can come out and change into new, fully gassed suits. After that, it's just a matter of air locking through two sections to the next one with a lift."

He'd made it sound simple. I just hoped everything went to plan. I bent over Jack; still sitting with his back against the wall. I lightly tapped his shoulder. He held his thumb up.

We'd discussed changing our suits before leaving section ten but had decided we had enough of a safety margin to get back to our section.

I think exhaustion had got the better of us. It wasn't just a simple matter of putting on a new suit. Because they were for emergency use, protocol dictated the depleted ones had to be reconnected and set up for re-gassing—so they were ready for the next person to use. In hindsight, I would be feeling a lot more comfortable now if we'd made the effort.

I squatted down and got Jack to bend forward. I methodically checked for damage to his breathing unit, again. Although superficially it appeared intact, it failed to assuage my doubts.

I had kept the gen com on, distracting myself by listening to Julian and Tiani chatting. They sounded so normal. It allayed any doubts about the success of the uploading. They were still very much Julian and Tiani; Julian gently teasing Tiani, and Tiani accepting the bait.

I think I must have drifted off to sleep because I woke with a start to hear Julian say "Dad? Are you okay?" He sounded worried.

"Sorry, I think I just took a little nap." I suddenly realised I had an incredible thirst, and a mouth like parchment.

"The pressurisation is complete, so you can start re-pressurising the airlock."

With a monumental effort, I pushed myself to my feet. My thoughts were clouded, muzzy and slightly confused. The air in my suit had become stifling and breathing it like inhaling thick treacle. The stench of my own stale sweat sent a wave of nausea through me, and the heat in my suit reminded me of being in a sauna. My profuse sweating had caused the inside of my visor to mist up. I staggered over to the undamaged console. For a moment, I couldn't remember what I was supposed to be doing. I concentrated. Pressurise—

pressurise the airlock. I pressed the button. Nothing happened. I pressed again, this time more firmly; still nothing. Great Zarking Universe, not again.

"Julian?" Overcome by dizziness, I slid to the floor.

"Disappointing, but I'm on it. Just give me a few seconds, and I'll see if I can activate it from here."

He sounded so hopeful, but my thoughts spiralled down into despair.

"Okay…Just let me try…Oh…" He swore, muttered something incoherent then trailed off into silence.

My thoughts raced along with my heart. In spite of sitting down, the room began to spin and I thought I was going to faint.

"Dad," Tiani this time, "Julian thinks the explosion must have created a power surge that fried all the internal airlock circuits. It would explain why everything is dead. But don't worry, he has a plan." Her tone of voice was buoyant and full of hope. A monumental effort to fake it, for my sake?

"What?" I croaked. I hadn't meant to snap at her. Right at that moment, a gigantic wave of despair hit me. Is this how it ends? We run out of air in this is Zarking, bloody airlock?

"Dad, I'm on it." Julian was back. "Here's the plan. I'm going to come up the emergency stairs. Once inside, I'll rig the computer to your airlock door panel, bypass the safety mechanism, and then I'll be able to get the door open. Okay?" He sounded so positive.

"Good plan if we had lots of time," I gasped. "I think I've run out of air…The temperature control…It's way too hot…We'll be out of air before you reach us."

I heard Tiani's sharp intake of breath, followed by silence. Julian cleared his throat, "Hey, Dad. Don't panic," his voice, calm— reassuring. "Slow your breathing, you're hyperventilating. Your readout shows you have plenty of air. Your humidity and temperature controls have failed. Stay calm, Dad. I don't need air, so I can reach you in less than ten minutes."

"It...should...work." A wave of pride and relief displaced my despair. Of course! sapioids didn't need air, and Julian could run forever without tiring. How could I have forgotten that?

"I'm on my way now. We're going to have to switch you off, and because I'm not in a suit we're going to have to rely on the ship's mobile communicators. I'll need to give Tiani instructions for the fire doors. She'll let you know when I'm ready to open the airlock door. Love you, Dad." My com went dead; Julian had gone.

Great Universe, please let this work. I crawled back over to Jack. I took his hand and gave it a squeeze, relieved when he squeezed back.

In spite of slowing my breathing, I still had the overwhelming feeling of suffocation. My anxiety spiked yet again when I suddenly noticed moisture condensing on my faceplate. I imagined it trickling into my suit; my suit filling up, and myself drowning in my own sweat. I focused on my HUD display, only to discover my vital signs were missing. Either the system had failed or Julian had turned them off.

I peered around in the eerie, red light, and my heart missed a beat—missed another and another. I panicked, and my heart started beating again—faster and faster. I could see the airlock walls shrinking in on us. Am I imagining it, or am I beginning to hallucinate? What the Zark's going on? I shook my head; the illusion remained. I closed my eyes but struggled to stay calm in the cloying blackness.

To distract myself, I concentrated on Julian; pictured him running up the emergency stairs, pausing only for the fire door to slide open. The stairs were situated just outside the airlock of section one and ten at each end of the ship. These sections opened out into a hangar deck where two shuttles capable of holding 250 passengers were located. They could be used as lifeboats in the event of an emergency, but their main purpose was to transport people to planets once we reached our destination.

When I noticed Jack's slumped body, panic rose in my throat. He wasn't breathing. I hurriedly shone the torch on him. Relief washed over me when I saw his chest rhythmically rising and falling. Just sleeping; I could relax. I began to drift in and out of consciousness. I let go and sank into oblivion.

Chapter 39

"Dad, wake up," the voice shouted in my ear.

I jumped as my eyes snapped open, "I'm awake." I jerked up-right. Where was I? My head swirled, so I laid down again. What had woken me up? "What's going on?"

"Julian's outside the door now. I'll let you know when he's ready to open it."

I knew that voice. Of course—my daughter, Tiani. Julian. Julian's outside the door. We were about to be rescued.

"Okay, I'll wake Jack." I slowly rolled over on to all fours and, ignoring the dizziness, I reached up with one hand and tapped his leg. I still managed to startle him. He jumped and frantically grabbed my hand. I patted his leg again and he relaxed.

"Okay, Dad. Julian's ready to go. He says he thinks you will be safest if you are in one of the corners closest to the doors, so he wants you to move there now, okay?"

"Okay, I'll let you know…when we're ready." I crawled on heavy arms and legs, guided Jack over to the left corner near the door and made him sit with his knees up against his chest. With a bit of trial and error, I got him to embrace his knees and rest his head on them. I gave his hand a reassuring pat, crawled over to the opposite corner, and assumed the same position.

"Ready, Tiani. Tell Julian to be careful. He might get sucked into the airlock…He needs to hang on."

"He said not to worry about him, he'll be okay."

"Okay. Go!" I placed my head on my knees and gripped them tightly with my arms, waiting for the blast of air.

"On the count of three; one, two, three," Tiani counted down, sounding slightly breathless.

I braced. The door whooshed open. A mass of buffeting air slammed me sideways despite all my efforts.

When it stopped, I saw Jack sprawled and unmoving on the floor. Julian shot through the door, scooped me up as though I weighed nothing, and carried me outside. He laid me down and with lightning speed removed my helmet.

"Hey, Dad." He gently patted my face. "Just take slow deep breaths."

He made to start removing my suit, but I flapped him away as I gulped in the cold, sweet air

"Help…Jack…Julian," I croaked, my voice barely audible between gasps.

"Okay, but get out of the suit before it cooks you." He raced back into the airlock and soon emerged carrying Jack. After lying him down, Julian ripped off his helmet. Jack, barely breathing, lay unconscious and unresponsive to Julian slapping his face. His blue-tinged lips were highlighted against his chalky face.

"He needs oxygen," I said, in between breaths. "It's in the…" but Julian had already jumped up. He sprinted into the bathroom. In what seemed like seconds, he reappeared and raced over carrying two small respirator kits. Half in and out my suit, I managed to crawl over to Jack. I lifted his head as Julian knelt down and slipped the mask over Jack's face. He turned on the oxygen. While we waited, Julian peeled the rest of my suit away and fitted the other respirator over my face.

I rolled over on my side and tried a gentle shaking, "Jack, Jack." Still no response.

"Dad, lie down, otherwise you'll pass out. I can deal with it. I'll get him out of the suit so I can check for injuries."

He ripped and peeled Jack's suit and began looking for signs of anything wrong.

"There's nothing obvious apart from massive bruising. I'll get the blood pressure cuff from the medical kit." He dashed back to the bathroom. When he got to the door, he called over to me—just as I was attempting to sit up.

"Stay down, Dad." He darted inside.

I quickly laid down again, because my head swirled and stars peppered my vision. I don't think I could ever remember feeling so tired. All my limbs were stiff, and my whole body had turned to jelly. My sleep suit was drenched, my head pounded, and I had an intense thirst. I couldn't remember the last time Jack, or I, had had food or water.

Julian came back and, kneeling down, wound the pressure cuff around Jack's arm. Before it had had time to inflate, Jack coughed, opened his eyes and fought to get up.

"I'm alright," Jack rasped, coughing again, as he struggled up into a sitting position.

"Stay still, Uncle Jack. I need to check your blood pressure."

Julian and I watched as the blood pressure readout appeared.

"What's the verdict, Julian?" Jack asked.

"It's low, so don't get up." Julian removed the cuff and transferred it to my arm. "Now for yours, Dad." He deliberately turned the machine away from me, so that neither I nor Jack could see the readout.

"Julian," I protested and reached for the machine.

"Stay still!" He gently held my arm in place. The cuff slowly inflated, held, and then relaxed.

"He's become quite bossy, hasn't he?" Jack quipped.

"Yes, he sounds just like you, Jack." I looked at Julian. "Well, what's the readout?"

"It's very low. You've got heat exhaustion bordering on heat stroke, Dad. I'll need to put you on a drip right away to get you rehydrated, fast."

His expression held such concern and resolve, I knew there was no point in arguing. "What about Jack?"

"Uncle Jack's not as dehydrated, so he'll be fine if he drinks a lot in the next couple of hours." He slipped the cuff from my arm and packed up the small machine. "Right. I'll carry you both over to the living quarters, so you can lie down on the bunks. I'll be back in a minute."

Jack and I watched him race across the deck and disappear through the door.

"How are you feeling, Jack?" I hoped like hell he wasn't feeling as bad as I did.

"Like I've been stomped on all over by an elephant. My back's really sore. But not unexpected after being blown up and having an argument with the wall." He managed a weak grin. "What about you, Luke?"

"Well, apart from the headache, nausea, weakness and extreme thirst—I feel great."

Jack laughed but immediately started coughing. He reached up to take his mask off just as Julian reappeared.

"Leave it, Uncle Jack," Julian ordered as he strode over to us.

He bent, slipped one arm under my knees and the other under my arm, picked me up and carried me over to the living unit. After laying me on the bunk, he went back for Jack. He poured us both cups of water. He supported my head, as I drank slowly—savouring the icy, cold, fresh taste. After removing his mask, Jack sat up and guzzled the water down. He gave a resounding burp. We laughed.

Jack watched as Julian expertly set up the drip he'd found in the medical kit.

He checked my temperature—38.5°C. Julian declared it too high, so he rummaged in the fridge and found a cold pack. He wrapped it around the saline pack and stood holding it in place effortlessly.

"I figured cooling the drip, combined with the evaporation from your saturated sleep suit, should be enough to cool you down, Dad." He grinned. "Being able to hold on for ever comes in handy, doesn't it?"

"I'll remember next time I go rock climbing, Julian," Jack said, smiling. "Thanks for coming to our rescue." He frowned. "I'm puzzled. How the hell did you get up here so bloody fast?"

"Up the stairs, Uncle Jack."

"Really? ...Of course, you don't need air." Jack coughed again.

"That's right. I can see there are advantages in being a sapioid. I literally flew up the stairs with no effort at all. I could get used to this," Julian chuckled, looking pleased with himself.

Perhaps I could explain his situation to him now, while he was enjoying his extra powers? What am I thinking? I'm not thinking, and I'm in no condition to have a sensible discussion about life as a machine. It could wait. I was too tired and exhausted, but the subject would have to be broached before Julian was put back to sleep—but not now, I told myself. I wished it was not ever.

We all jumped as a piercing alarm sounded from Julian's chest.

"Bloody hell, it's my communicator," Julian said, scrabbling to remove it from his pocket, "I forgot Tiani. She'll be frantic. He flicked the switch, "Hi Tiani, everything's fine, it all went like clockwork. Sorry, in the excitement I forgot about you," he said, in a relaxed, soothing voice.

"Forgot? I thought you were all dead or something," Tiani shouted back.

I reached across and grabbed the communicator from Julian, "Hi Tiani, we're all okay. Jack's BP is a bit low, and I'm being treated for heat exhaustion. You and Julian have done an amazing job figuring out how to rescue us and executing it so quickly. I'm really proud of you." I heard a sniff. "We have to wait for the drip to run through, and Jack and I will have something to eat before we make our way back, okay?"

Jack, who was sitting up, leaned over and held his hand out. I shoved the communicator towards him.

He took it and said, "I'm starving, so we'll let you know when we're on our way, Ti."

"I'm still furious. Exactly how long will it be before you're back?"

Jack handed the communicator back to Julian.

"Two to three hours. I'm really sorry, Ti, but I had to take care of the medical stuff before I did anything else. We'll see you later." He flicked the switch to off before Tiani had a chance to reply.

"Let's eat," Jack said.

"Seconded," I said.

"Before you stand up, Jack, let's take your blood pressure." Julian wound the cuff around his arm, and we watched it inflate.

"It's okay, Uncle Jack, but stand up slowly." He turned to me. "Stay where you are, Dad," he commanded. "I'll get you to sit up when the food is ready."

Julian helped Jack to organise some food from the synthesiser in the kitchen. He came back with some soup for me, and Jack had what barely passed as a hamburger. Julian got me to sit up slowly and insisted on feeding me the soup himself. I still experienced a little giddiness, but the dreadful nausea had vanished.

In spite of my exhaustion, while he was feeding me I could still see the longing for food in Julian's eyes. I remembered just in time to stop myself from telling him his current body was only temporary, and when he was transferred to his customised one he would be able to eat and drink.

"Did you turn off my HUD display, Julian?" I asked in between sips.

His face took on a slightly sheepish expression, "I wasn't game to tell you, Dad, but after your de-humidifier packed up your suit turned into a sauna. I thought you had enough to contend with. Your suit got up to 38°. If you'd stayed in there much longer you probably would have fried." Julian frowned. "Should I have told you, Dad?"

"No. Julian. You made the right decision. I would have done the same for you." I smiled and patted his arm. His face lit up.

Chapter 40

While we were eating and after a heated discussion, we decided, for Tiani's sake, that Julian would carry us back to our deck. Jack and I would don suits, enabling him to take us down via the stairs. I insisted Julian take Jack first. Julian and I had to unite forces to get him to agree. Julian grinned. I think he was enjoying his new-found power.

He left us partway through our meal to run diagnostics on our damaged suits. He returned looking grim. Jack's suit *had* lost its integrity, and he'd been lucky to survive. Even though my suit remained airtight, the damage to the environmental control module proved too severe to repair, so he'd been forced to place both suits in the recycling chute.

I realised just how close we'd come to losing Jack. It explained his unconsciousness. He'd almost run out of air.

After giving us shots of painkiller, Julian helped Jack and me into new suits. With difficulty, I hoisted Jack into a piggyback position on Julian's shoulders. He refused to be carried in Julian's arms. I watched them enter the airlock that exited onto the shuttle bay. I sat down on the floor, placed my helmet next to me and waited for Julian to return.

He reappeared after about twenty-five minutes. I had no objection to being held in his arms for the journey back to our section.

Tiani hurtled towards us as soon as we emerged and flung herself into my arms, almost knocking me over in her enthusiasm.

"Steady," I said, curling my arms around her and giving her a huge hug. "Ease back a little; you've got a lot more strength now."

"Sorry, Dad," she said, releasing her crushing grip on my ribs. "Is that better?"

"Much better." She beamed up at me.

Jack interrupted us. "First priority—your dad and I need sleep."

Tiani opened her mouth to protest, but Julian leapt in, "Hey, Tiani. Dad and Uncle Jack have been through quite an ordeal, and they're both exhausted. They need rest and a decent sleep, so everything else can wait, okay?"

Tiani didn't look happy, but she nodded and let go of me. She went to embrace Jack, but he held her off. "I think I have some cracked ribs, so no hugs for the moment." He leant forward and kissed her cheek. "That will have to do for now. You two kids have been bloody marvellous," Jack said, glancing across at me.

"I second that," I said, smiling. "We wouldn't be here without the two of you. Thank you. I'm really proud of both of you." I blinked away tears. "Now, let's get some sleep." I hurriedly turned away and made for the living unit, blotting my eyes with my sleeve.

In spite of his tiredness, Jack insisted on taking a shower before sleeping. Unable to raise his arms due to the pain from his ribs, he got me to help him out of his clothes. Our sleep suits were made of a body-hugging, synthetic, self-cleaning, stretchy material. In spite of the zip fastener down the front, it still required some wriggling to get out of it.

I sucked in my breath when I saw the extent and severity of the bruising down Jack's left side and back. Fortunately, his nanocytes were well into repairing the damage. Some of the bruises were already turning yellow. I grabbed the scanner off the wall and took it over to him. His face flushed in embarrassment. It occurred to me it probably felt like he was standing naked in front of Kiera.

"Stand still a minute," I ordered, "I need to do a scan to make sure there aren't any loose ribs or bone chips floating around," or internal injuries, I added silently. He stood patiently, avoiding my eyes, while I lightly ran the scanner over him. He flinched when I moved it down his back. "Sorry, nearly finished."

We both peered at the readout. It showed three simple rib fractures in his back. There were no internal injuries, or bone fragments. The advice—rest for the next twenty-four hours. It would take a week for the bones to be fully healed.

"That's a relief, Jack. The possibility of internal injuries really worried me."

He touched my shoulder. "Thanks, Luke. Can I have my shower now?"

"Yes, go ahead. Will you need help to get dressed?"

"No, I'll wrap myself in the blanket and sleep naked. You can help me when I get up."

"Okay, I'll probably be asleep by the time you get out. I'll have a shower in the morning."

"I'll be quiet. Sleep well." He turned and stepped into the shower cubicle.

"You too," I said, yawning as I went out the door.

#

I slept for around nine hours and woke up ravenous. Jack was still dead to the world. I tiptoed to the food dispenser and got myself something to eat and drink. When I'd finished, I made my way out to the main deck, curious as to what Julian and Tiani were doing.

Julian was seated at the computer terminal and Tiani was standing behind him. "Hi you two. You look busy, what are you doing?"

Tiani turned, "Hi, Dad. You look heaps better." She appeared flustered. The guilty look she'd always got when we'd caught her raiding our biscuit tin as a small child was plastered over her face.

Julian swivelled his chair. "Dad, how are you?" Guilt was written all over his face as well. I wondered just what they'd been up to.

"So?" I stood regarding them both with my hands on my hips.

"We were just looking at the revival protocols," Julian said, trying to look nonchalant. "I mean...hey, we thought it would save time." He suddenly studied his feet.

"Jack's familiar with the process; he doesn't need extra information, as you both well know."

Betrayed by their expressions; they'd obviously been trying to figure out how to activate the program by themselves. "Whatever you are doing, close it down, now." They'd shown such maturity over the past twenty-four hours, but when it came to something like this they were still impatient children.

"I'm awake, finally," Jack said, poking his head around the living unit door. "I need your help, Luke."

After I'd helped Jack get dressed, we confronted Julian and Tiani.

"What's going on?" Jack said, looking from me, to Julian and Tiani and back.

"Nothing." Tiani crossed her arms defensively.

In a flash, Julian turned back to the screen, and pressed a button. He jumped up as the screen blanked. "Hey, Uncle Jack, how are the ribs?" Nice distraction, I thought, but I'd let him get away with it. Obviously, he knew I knew precisely what they'd been up to.

"Mmm," Jack winked at me, and grinned. "Will we wake the two-chipper?"

"Absolutely!" Tiani uncrossed her arms.

"I concur." Julian put on a serious expression. "Hey, I thought you'd never ask," he chuckled.

"So where is he, again?" Jack asked.

"He's in module one, the same one Dad and you were in," Tiani said.

"Let's go." Jack strode over to module one. Once there, he activated its panel. With fingers poised over the keyboard, he turned to Tiani. "What number Ti?"

"Number nine."

Jack raised his eyebrows, "Right next to you, Luke? You did check this section, didn't you?"

"Yes, I already told you that, Jack."

"Sorry, I forgot." He scratched his head.

"Nothing I saw rang alarm bells, and I didn't find anyone I recognised." I became defensive.

Jack, keeping his hands low, held them with both palms up, "Okay, okay—just making sure. Considering your frame of mind at the time, I wouldn't be surprised if you'd missed something."

"You said it was just to distract me," I snapped back.

"What's it matter? Let's just get on with it," Tiani retorted.

"I concur," Julian said, blinking like an old, wise owl and holding his face in a solemn expression.

The tension dissipated as we all laughed.

"Let's get the process underway." Jack turned back to the display. His hands skipped over the keyboard, while command protocols flashed down the screen. We stood in awe, and I wondered how he could move his fingers so rapidly. It was like watching a famous pianist playing at breakneck speed. Minutes passed, and

Jack finally turned and said, "It's underway. There's nothing more we can do for the next hour, and I'm starving."

"Didn't you have anything to eat when you got up?" I said, feeling guilty for my full stomach.

"No, I thought certain people," he skewered Tiani and Julian with his gaze, "would be getting impatient. To avoid being pestered, I thought I'd start the process so I can eat in peace."

Tiani folded her arms and glared. Julian suddenly seemed intent on inspecting his footwear again. I chuckled.

Jack marched off, and we fell in step behind him.

Chapter 41

The four of us stood like expectant parents, as we watched the sleep capsule's canopy disengage and slide away. As the capsule slid silently forward and began to tilt upright, it's occupant's eyes fluttered open. The tall, handsome young man with dark brown eyes fixed his deep, penetrating gaze on me. My heart instantly jolted, and I stiffened. Even though he had altered his appearance, I knew the person staring back at me *was* Logan Williamson.

Rage boiled up in me. Before I had time to think, I'd leapt forward and was about to put had my hands around his throat. "I'll kill you, you murdering bastard."

Just in time, Julian and Tiani, acting in unison with lightning speed, grabbed an arm each and hauled me backwards.

"Think, Luke," Jack said firmly but without raising his voice, "kill him and we'll never find Kiera. Now calm down."

"Dad! Dad! Stop, please." Tiani dragged on my left arm, while Julian kept a vice-like grip on my right.

"For Zark's sake, Dad," Julian said, "you told me there was to be no violence."

"Okay," I said, through gritted teeth, "okay, I..." My mind blanked. Julian and Tiani released my arms, and I stood in a silence broken only by the sound of my heavy breathing. Jack remained calm.

Williamson's face held a mixture of confusion and terror but no hint of recognition. He began to shake as the restraints slipped away, and he slid to a standing position. As the capsule began to retract back into the module, he staggered away from it. I fought to control my anger.

Jack reached out and grabbed his arm to steady him. In a quiet voice, his anger cool and restrained, he asked, "Where's Kiera?"

With terror still in his eyes, and his gaze darting around us all like a cornered mouse, Williamson said, "Keep that psychotic woman away from me. Who are you people, and what exactly is going on?"

"I'm Jack Summers, head of the emergency team for the section. Now answer my question." He grabbed both of Williamson's arms to hold him steady.

"I feel dizzy," Williamson said, in a pleading tone, "Please, I need to sit down."

"Okay." Holding his arm firmly, Jack guided the shaky Williamson towards the living unit. Without a word, the rest of us followed. Williamson, apparently terrified, kept glancing in my direction. After sitting him at the table, Jack got him a cup of water. Williamson's hands were shaking so badly Jack was forced to hold it for him.

"Keep your distance, guys. Let me do the talking."

Julian, Tiani and I sat opposite them on the other side of the table and waited.

When Williamson had finished the water, Jack tried a different tack. "Have you uploaded Kiera's consciousness to one of the two chips you have hidden inside you?"

"What chips and who's Kiera?" His face still oozed fear and bewilderment.

He must've recognised me, although some people took up to half an hour to recover fully from the wake-up process. Either that, or he deserved an Oscar for his performance.

"Look, Williamson," I clenched my fists and stood up. "We know who you are. What exactly did your message mean?" I glared at him. He shrank back as I stepped closer.

"You're not helping, Luke. Sit down." Jack motioned me to sit.

"My name is Gregory Archer. I am not, this...Williamson." He stared directly into my eyes. I could see defiance now, mixed with fear. "Who is Kiera?"

"You know who Kiera is. She's my wife," I shouted, "my dead wife. The person you switched into my body. The person you put my children with in a different section and then sabotaged the section so it would fail catastrophically."

Williamson's jaw dropped, and his face turned pale. He met my eyes. His expression conveyed a mixture of horror, disbelief and something else—sorrow. That shocked me. A niggling doubt surfaced at the back of my mind. What if my own wishful thinking had clouded my judgement? What if I was wrong? What if he wasn't Logan Williamson?

He just stood there, silent, struggling to control his emotions. Seconds passed before he was able to regain his composure. He looked up at me and said softly, "I'm...sorry." Every bone in his body screamed sincerity—his eyes, especially his eyes, his tone and his drooping shoulders.

My heart jolted, and I felt my jaw drop. I couldn't believe what I was hearing. The Williamson I remembered had been clever, manipulative and an expert at maintaining his various masks. Momentary flashes and chinks over time had given him away, but I could see no masks here. Perhaps post-wake-up brain fog explained his puzzling behaviour or...

"What happened to your children?" he asked, quietly in a sympathetic tone.

"You're looking at them."

"But these two are...androids...I mean, sapioids. What happened?" He turned to Jack.

"Module three developed a fault. We had to terminate. I rescued Julian and Tiani, but I couldn't save Kiera. She, along with seventeen other human beings, died." Jack, his expression grim, inspected his hands.

"Having saved them, what possessed you to download them into androids? Why weren't they left on the ship's computer?" Williamson had a controlled, slightly smug, perplexed look on his face. Finally, he'd revealed himself in one of his familiar masks. My doubts evaporated.

"We couldn't leave them on the computer. My anti-virus program, put there to protect the ship from any outside interference while we're in transit, would have deleted them." Jack focused on the table and added, "In hindsight, I wish I'd never thought about it."

"It wasn't your fault, Jack." I tried to sound convincing.

"Wasn't it?" His face held such pain and sorrow it took all my strength not to get up and put my arms around him.

"It's immaterial as to whose fault it was," Williamson said, surveying Julian and Tiani. "But, dear me, now they're trapped. So disappointing for you, Luke, because there won't be any grandchildren, will there?"

Just like flicking a switch, the old Williamson had reappeared. Once again, I found myself drowning in those dark, malevolent eyes. Bloody Zark! Julian!—too late.

"What do you mean, no grandchildren?" Julian stood up abruptly, frozen, motionless, with both arms locked by his side.

"You haven't told him. Well, well," Williamson said, smirking at me with satisfaction.

"Shut the Zark up." I leapt up and stepped towards him. He sat surveying me and his smile widened. "Well well…"

"Luke—don't," Jack warned, "he's baiting you."

"Dad, what the hell does he mean?" Julian's face filled with shock, and his voice dropped to almost a whisper. "You mean I'm stuck in this thing forever?"

No, no, no. This wasn't how he was supposed to find out. Bloody Zark, I should have told him earlier. My mind flooded with regret, guilt, sorrow and grief. I reached out, but he shoved me away. I staggered a few steps backwards before regaining my balance.

"You lied, Dad. You lied to me." His face crumpled with disbelief, disappointment and hurt so intense it sent a stab of physical pain through me; like my insides were being twisted around barbed wire.

"I told you the truth," I said, quietly, "I asked you what you wanted. You told me to go ahead." I ran my fingers through my hair, Kiera's hair.

"When I asked you if it was forever, Dad, you said no."

His eyes held so much accusation, I had to look away. A wave of nausea swamped me. I realised I had had misinterpreted what Julian had said during the link. Perhaps, I had heard what I'd wanted to hear.

"Julian, when you asked me if it was forever, I thought you were asking me if you had to stay in a particular android. When I said no, I meant we would be able to upload you later to a custom android designed to be identical to your biological body. I presumed you realised you would become a sapioid."

Julian shook his head in disbelief. "Did you know about this, Tiani?" He gave her an accusatory look.

"Yes, I knew becoming a sapioid would be permanent." Tiani looked about to cry.

Jack leapt to her defence. "When we realised you'd got the wrong idea, Julian, I told Tiani not to talk about it—that we would tell you when the time was right."

"Except it never was!" Julian spat back.

"I'm so sorry, Julian. It was only later Jack and I discovered you had the wrong idea. I couldn't seem to find the right time to…"As a single tear rolled down his face, I had a bizarre thought. I wondered why they'd bothered giving basic androids the ability to cry. In a microsecond, I snapped back to reality. "I'm so sorry Julian, please…" He turned away, streaked out the door, and a second later we heard the bathroom door slam.

"Julian," Tiani called after him, jumping to her feet.

"Let him go for now, Ti, he'll be all right." Jack stood up, came around the table and patted her arm. She burst into tears. I wrapped my arms around her and patted her back while she sobbed uncontrollably.

"Well, it seems none of you can handle the truth," Williamson smirked. "Such a tragic domestic scene, poor Julian."

Jack whirled, slapped him hard across the face and then winced. "I forgot. We'll deal with you later, Williamson. You might want to think about cooperating by telling us what's on your two chips, because my favourite option is to cut them out." He glanced across at me. "I can think of just the person to do it." He smirked.

"You can't." Williamson stiffened, and the terrified expression returned.

"We can," Jack said, with an air of malice.

"And we will," I added with satisfaction at seeing genuine fear plastered all over Williamson's face.

He opened his mouth to speak, but Jack jumped in, "Not another word or I'll gag you."

Williamson's mouth snapped firmly shut.

#

Jack located a pair of handcuffs and restrained Williamson by securing him to the metal leg of the table. After stuffing a set of earplugs, none too gently, into Williamson's ears, he held up a gag. Williamson, compliant now, had shaken his head. Jack laid it on the table.

Julian still hadn't come out of the bathroom, so we congregated outside the door and Tiani knocked lightly.

"Julian, Julian, please come out." Met with silence, she said, "Dad?"

I shook my head, afraid to speak in case I just made things worse.

Jack sighed. He rapped on the door.

"Julian, you need to come out now. Important issues need to be discussed with regard to Williamson and what we do next. We need your input." For a moment nothing happened, but we heard the lock click and the door swung open. Julian stood staring and immobile in front of us.

I wished I could melt into the floor.

Without waiting to be invited, Jack pushed past him saying, "We need to talk." He pulled out another bench from the wall and motioned for us to sit.

We did.

"Since I'm in charge, I'm responsible for any action we take. So, you three will be just following my orders. Are we clear?"

I didn't like where this was heading. Without hesitating, I decided I couldn't and wouldn't let Jack take the blame for any actions we all agreed on.

"No, Jack. I think we should all share responsibility for any decisions made. Julian, Tiani, do you agree?"

"Absolutely," Tiani said, "we're a team, Uncle Jack."

"Hey, I second that," Julian answered, quietly but firmly.

"That's settled, then," I said.

"Thanks for your support, guys." He looked relieved. "Let's review our options—and hold the questions until I've finished. We have three; option one, we do nothing. We put him back to sleep, put ourselves back to sleep, and deal with it when we reach our destination. Option two; I put him in Virtual to keep him quiet. I access the chips, if I can, to see what's on them. Option three; we wake Dr Kariba, get him to surgically remove the chips, enabling me to access them. What do you think?"

"There is another option you haven't considered, Jack. We could force him to tell us what's on them by some means," I said.

"You mean torture him?" Jack held my gaze and frowned then turned and regarded Julian and Tiani, "How do you two feel about that?"

Tiani jumped in with, "I say we force it out of him."

"You're being too emotional, Ti," Julian said.

"Of course, I'm being emotional; it's our mother we're talking about." She scowled at him.

"As well as the loss of *my* body," I added.

"While I understand how you feel, I can't condone that course of action. We're human beings. We have certain obligations—standards and morals to maintain." He frowned and folded his arms.

"Am I?" Julian asked, his expression poignant, earnest and sorrowful.

"What?" Jack raised his eyebrows. "Still human?"

"Yes. Are Tiani and I still human?" His expression held pain and uncertainty.

"Don't be ridiculous," I said, "you're still the sum total of all your memories, your beliefs and your culture."

We sat there in an uncomfortable silence, until I broke it with, "I have my doubts about Williamson though—he's an animal." But did I really believe that? His recent inexplicable emotional duality raised questions in my mind. Questions I couldn't answer.

"Animal or not, he still has rights, Luke. However, I would support trying a bluff using minimal force. If it doesn't work, we'll have to choose one of the other options, so you might as well make up your minds now. Let's vote on it. Those in favour of option one— we go back to sleep." None of us moved.

"All right, option one is out. How about option two—I try Virtual"

Tiani raised her hand, followed by Julian.

"I'll add my vote too," Jack said, "so, three in favour—Luke?"

"You know my feelings. But out of the three, I'd prefer to wake Dr Kariba."

Julian and Tiani exchanged glances then raised their hands.

"So, you've changed your minds?"

Julian and Tiani nodded simultaneously.

"Traitors." Jack, after giving them an exasperated look, sighed, and with a pained expression said, "Okay, let's try our bluff first. If it doesn't work, I'll go and wake Dr Kariba. Now, who's prepared to play the bad guy?"

"I will," Julian jumped in enthusiastically before I had time to speak.

"How?" Jack cocked his head to one side.

"I'll apply a little arm-twisting."

Julian glanced at me. Was he seeking my approval? I gave him a slight nod, and he acknowledged with a single nod back.

"You'll have to be careful, Julian. Remember you're super strong now."

"I'll remember, Uncle Jack."

Chapter 42

Jack removed the earplugs he had shoved in Williamson's ears to stop him overhearing our conversation. He unlocked the handcuffs, took them off, and motioned to Julian.

Julian stepped in and hauled Williamson upright.

Williamson started to babble, but Jack headed him off with, "Shut up! This is how it works. You will answer questions, but otherwise you will remain silent." Jack's voice held menace, "If I wasn't injured; I would whack you myself. Julian, help me get this bastard over to the terminal. Let's see what's on these chips."

Before Williamson could react, Julian had stepped behind him, grabbed his arm and twisted it up behind his back. For a split-second fear rippled across Williamson's face. He rapidly replaced it with a calm, sneering mask.

"Hey, unlike Uncle Jack, I'm in fine form," Julian said, nonchalantly, pushing him forward with his left hand while keeping Williamson's twisted arm firmly in place with his right.

"How's life as an android?" Williamson smirked.

"Julian, shut him up," Jack said, from behind us. Julian obliged by pulling Williamson's arm further up his back. I had the satisfaction of seeing him grimace in pain.

"Easy," Jack said, "let's get him into the chair."

Williamson began to look genuinely frightened. "No! You can't put me in the chair. Luke? You can't, it will wipe the chips." The colour had drained from his face. This time it was my turn to smile.

"Uncle Jack?" Julian, uncertain, turned to Jack.

Jack leant forward and pressed the button to prevent the headband from engaging. Julian let go of Williamson's arm, and he sagged into the chair, curling up like a frightened child.

Jack stood in front of him, his arms folded. "Out with it."

"You'll damage my chips," he pleaded. "Please don't do this."

"You're lying, Williamson. Chips can't be damaged by going into Virtual. It's standard procedure for checking faults. We've accessed other people's chips without causing any problems, why are yours different?"

"Because..." Williamson, close to breaking down, stared at the floor.

Questions tugged at my mind.

"Yes?" Jack said, angrily.

"He's stalling, Jack." I stepped forward.

Williamson smirked, the confident mask now firmly back in place, and said, "You can't afford to take the risk, can you?"

Julian pushed him forward and, taking hold of his arm, bent it up behind his back again. He whimpered with pain.

"All right...All right...I'll tell you." Julian eased the pressure slightly. "The chips are prototypes, experimental prototypes. They're encrypted and protected by firewalls, but they could be damaged, so please..." His eyes were pleading again.

Jack interrupted, "Stop mucking us around. Tell me now what's on the chips, or I'll let Julian break your arm, and then I'll let him break your other arm. Is that clear?"

"They haven't been put through rigorous testing yet. Outcomes could be," he hesitated, "unpredictable." He still managed to look smug.

"Julian, go ahead."

"All right…All right, they contain my research files, all my patents and designs, many lifetimes of work; I didn't trust the ship's computers, so they're my insurance," a rattled Williamson shouted.

"I'm still not convinced. You wouldn't need two chips; your data would have easily fitted on one, so what's on the other chip?"

"I've already told you, and you're wrong; I couldn't fit all my data on just one chip."

"You're lying," Jack and I said, simultaneously.

Julian didn't wait to be told, he exerted more pressure on Williamson's arm and he screamed.

"Julian! Julian stop it. Stop it all of you," Tiani wailed, screwing up her face.

I was surprised she had lasted this long, even though she had originally been in favour of leaning on him.

"Walk away, Ti," Jack said.

"Uncle Jack, please."

Jack took her arm and pulled her a little way away from us, out of Williamson's line of sight. I watched as he whispered something in her ear, resulting in her trotting off to the bathroom. When he came back, we stood behind Williamson, and I raised my eyebrows. Jack placed a finger on his lips and walked around to face Williamson. "This is your last chance. What's on the chips?"

Williamson's face took on an expression of defiance, and he simply said, "Go to hell."

Julian turned to Jack, but Jack shook his head. Williamson had called our bluff. He had temporarily won.

"Take him back to the living unit, Julian, cuff him and gag him."

Julian hauled Williamson up and frogmarched him away. I walked over to where Jack and Tiani were just emerging from the bathroom.

"Well played, Tiani." I took both of her hands in mine.

"I wasn't..." Tiani trailed off.

"I know, but well done anyway." I gave her a kiss on the cheek. "And I'm glad you couldn't handle it. I would have been upset if you had. Your mum would be proud of you."

She beamed up at me. "Thanks, Dad."

Julian, back from dealing with Williamson, grabbed Jack's arm. "Hey, Uncle Jack. What about I go and get Dr Kariba, using the same route I used to bring you and Dad back here. I know all the protocols now, and I'm sure I can handle it."

I was surprised when Jack said, "Good idea, Julian, but don't carry him. Let him walk down the stairs with you."

"Okay, Uncle Jack. Can you start pressurising deck thirty-five please, Tiani? I'll go and grab the communicator and head off once the pressurisation is complete."

"Can you wait a minute, Julian? Please? Uncle Jack?" Tiani said, using her best wheedling tone.

"Yes, Tiani."

I could tell by his expression he knew what was coming.

"Could I go with Julian, please?"

Jack sighed. "As long as it's all right with your dad."

"It's okay with me, but Julian's in charge, so what he says goes, okay?"

"Yes, Dad." All smiles, she threw her arms round my neck and hugged me. Turning to Jack, but remembering Jack's condition, she leant forward and gently patted his cheek. He suddenly stared at his feet. When he looked up, his face had flushed a brilliant red.

Three quarters of an hour later, with the pressurisation of Dr Kariba's section almost complete, Tiani and Julian were set to go. I lined them up for final instructions outside the airlock that exited our section.

"Please don't tell Dr Kariba anything other than we need his help. Let Jack and me explain the situation when he gets here, okay?"

"Will do, Dad," Julian said, grinning from ear to ear, while Tiani nodded enthusiastically.

"Have you left us one of the communicators?"

"Yes, Dad, on the console," Tiani answered.

"Off you go. And be careful."

Several minutes later, after they had disappeared, Jack said, "In some ways, Luke, they're still kids, but they've taken a huge leap into adulthood in the last few days."

"Gigantic leaps."

"Okay, let's get to work." He sat down at the nearest terminal. "How about fixing us both a cup of tea."

"Right, good idea." I padded off towards the living unit.

"Luke," I turned, "we'd better give Williamson a drink. Can you handle it, or do you want me to do it?"

"No, I can do it. We probably should remove the gag too."

"I think we should shift him to the bathroom, because we don't want him glaring at us while we're explaining to Dr Kariba what we want him to do. And I think we need to give Dr Kariba the right of refusal."

"I agree. I'll go and move Williamson now."

Williamson appeared sullen and white faced. I unlocked the cuffs, pulled him to his feet, and re-cuffed him before guiding him out of the living unit and into the bathroom. I sat him on the bench and unfastened the cuffs. I placed one around his ankle and snapped the other around one of the bench's support legs, leaving his hands free. "I'm going to get you a drink of water."

When I turned around with the cup of water, he was still sitting bolt upright, almost like he was frozen to the spot.

"I'm taking the gag off, and if you keep quiet I'll leave it off." Julian had tied it on loosely, so it came off easily. I handed the cup to Williamson. He took it and guzzled the water down, but there was still defiance in his eyes. When he'd finished, I took the cup, picked up the gag and waved it in front of him. He shook his head. "Okay, but one word, and it goes back on." As I turned to leave, I imagined his eyes focused on my back like a laser gun and had the unsettling feeling that any moment he would fire. After all this time, even restrained, he still had power over me. One part of me wished he was dead.

Chapter 43

"Hey, Dad." Julian emerged from the airlock, followed closely by Tiani and Dr Kariba.

Dr Kariba rushed forward, "My heart is happy to see you again, Kiera." He gently took both my hands in his and shook them. His grip was surprisingly delicate for a man of his size. He let them drop and faced Jack "So you are the father, Jack?"

"Not exactly," Jack's face coloured and he cleared his throat, "I'm their Uncle."

"I…" he looked at each of us in confusion, "I must have mis-heard, my mistake…"

"I think we'd better explain, Jack."

"Over to you, Luke." I watched in amusement as Dr Kariba's eyes went wide.

"Luke? You are the father?"

"It's a long story, Dr Kariba." I glanced at the clock on the wall. "It's 6:05 p.m. It would be a good idea to get back to normal eating and sleeping times, so let's have some tea. We can eat and fill you in at the same time. Are you hungry, Dr Kariba?"

"It is a long time since I have eaten; I would be delighted to share a meal with you. Please, call me Nguma." His face lit with an expectant smile.

"Good thinking, Luke," Jack said, "after you Nguma." He indicated the living unit door.

Julian and Tiani watched as the three of us ate, while I recounted all the events that had led up to our present situation. Jack jumped in when necessary. I was warming more and more to Nguma, as I watched his open, readable face range through disbelief, sadness, horror and finally, outrage. Nothing was hidden from us. I knew he would be a wonderful doctor. His patients could look forward to warmth and understanding along with a high standard of care.

When we'd finished our account, he contemplated us for a moment, "Judging by *your* observations, this Williamson, he is not a man, he is a monster."

"Are you comfortable with removing the chips, Nguma?" I asked.

For the first time since we'd woken him, Nguma's expression became serious, and he frowned.

"You're under no obligation to do what we want, and we'll respect your decision," I added, firmly hoping he wouldn't decline our request.

He reached out and touched my arm, "It is not a problem for me, I am happy to be of service, but," he held up his finger, "I am a great supporter of the Hippocratic oath. I would like to talk to this Logan Williamson myself, to make my own assessment. You are aware are you not, that as well as being a general physician, I am a fully qualified psychiatrist?"

"Yes Nguma," Jack said. "We thought you would probably want to talk to him."

"If he will not speak to me, I cannot do as you ask."

I groaned inwardly.

"We understand," Jack said, with a resigned expression.

I nodded in agreement. Guilt tugged at me—should we have told him about the episode of apparent empathy, even sympathy, Williamson had displayed? It would just add to the confusion. I decided Nguma could make up his own mind.

"I'm glad you agree. I will go and speak with him now, so we may sleep tonight without having to wonder what his answer will be." He stood and disappeared out the door.

"He'll be back in a minute." I rubbed the back of my neck.

"Probably, but you never know," Jack answered.

When Dr Kariba didn't reappear, I filled in time by showing Julian and Tiani how to turn on the table display that showed our ship's location. After we navigated through the menu, we located actual footage of the various planets in the Kalgarin system.

About an hour later, Nguma re-emerged. Although his expression displayed calmness, his usual demeanour had vanished. I turned off the display as he sat down.

"What happened, Nguma?" Jack asked.

"I will need to spend tomorrow morning conducting a series of psychological tests on Gregory." With a troubled expression on his face, he continued, "He is terrified of you all, especially you, Luke. While, under these difficult circumstances I realise there is some justification in you resorting to violence that is not how Gregory has perceived your actions. He is frightened you will harm him further." He paused, to let us digest his words. With a grim expression, he added, "He has asked me for help, and I cannot refuse him."

"Hey, Nguma. I was careful not to injure him," Julian exclaimed, defensively.

"Julian is a gentle person, Nguma," Tiani said, twisting her hair around her finger.

"It was only ever going to be a bluff," Jack added. "He wasn't injured."

"A bluff that didn't come off," I said.

"You may not have harmed him physically, but I am worried about his psychological state. He is extremely distressed, and I am concerned for him." He frowned before continuing, "You are not going to like what I am to tell you next." He paused.

Great Zarking Universe! Anger rose in my throat—not anger at Nguma, but anger at myself for believing enlisting his help would be simple. So, what now? I noticed my fingernails were digging into my palms. With effort, I released the tension and stared at the table waiting for Nguma to continue.

"By asking for help, he has become my client. Unfortunately, anything he reveals to me is entirely confidential. I cannot discuss it with you." Like a bomb exploding, his words hit the table and splintered outwards, spraying us with fragments.

"Bloody hell." Jack stood up. "Bloody hell," he said, again, as he began to pace up and down like a caged tiger.

Julian squirmed in his chair. Tiani's face dropped and crinkled as she tried to stop herself from crying.

"I realise this is distressing news for you all, but I am unable to do otherwise." Nguma appeared distressed.

"So, what do we do now?" I stood up and crossed my arms. "Jack?"

"We have no choice." He turned. "We let Nguma do what he has to."

"I will do my utmost to help you all through this difficult situation. I am very sorry, but I must act in the interests of my client."

Inside my mind, a voice screamed, 'What about Kiera? What about my wife?'

We wore blankets of despondency when we went to bed. Upon Nguma's insistence we grudgingly gave Gregory a pillow and blanket. With an apologetic expression, Nguma asked if we minded him keeping Gregory company as he believed he would find it reassuring. Armed with more pillows and blankets from storage, he left us. I think we wondered just whose side he was now on.

Chapter 44

Awake early, I tiptoed out to the deck to do some stretching and exercise. To my surprise, I found Nguma just standing up from the computer terminal. He beamed at me, and my heart melted.

"You slept well, Luke, I hope?"

Disarmed, I couldn't help smiling back. "Like a log, and you?"

"Surprisingly well, my friend. I have just downloaded a series of tests to Jack's tablet. I will administer them to Gregory after breakfast. He tells me he slept well, apart from a troubling dream."

"Mmm, I'm going to do some exercise to try get rid of some of the stiffness. The others aren't—"

Jack popped out the door trailing Julian and Tiani. "The gang's all here, let's eat. Good morning, Nguma—Luke," Jack said, cheerily.

After breakfast, Nguma took the meal I had fixed using the synthesiser into Gregory. He expected it would take several hours for his tests and a further couple of hours to digest the results. He promised to speak to us when he was finished.

Jack occupied us with a mix of boring tasks—running hardware diagnostics on just about everything in our section. He assigned Julian and Tiani to spacesuits and became terse when they grumbled.

We had agreed to Nguma taking Gregory into the living unit for the duration of the tests. Nguma reappeared about mid-morning.

"May I have a word please, Jack?" His face held a charming and infectious smile.

Jack looked up from his terminal, "Yes, Nguma."

"Gregory has given me permission to access his genetic profile and his mental health files."

"Really," Jack's face held the surprise I registered.

"It would save time if I could view them in Virtual."

"He's given you his code?" Jack's face broadcasted disbelief.

"Yes," Nguma hesitated, "I have gained his trust and he has confided much to me." He eyed Jack.

Jack gestured with his hand to the terminal. "Be my guest."

"Thank you, my friend. It will assist me greatly in my diagnosis." He sat and pressed the headband button.

Jack waited until it was obvious Nguma had connected.

"Right, time for a quick peek, Luke."

Shocked, I stood and stared as he darted over to the other side of Nguma's console and sat down.

"Jack? You're not serious." His headband was already engaging "Jack! You can't," I shouted—too late, he was gone.

Julian and Tiani, hearing my shout, looked up from where they were testing suits. I motioned them to stay where they were. With puzzled looks, they returned to their work.

Paralysed, and with the sound of my own heartbeat thundering in my ears, my mind was inundated with a series of what ifs. If Nguma came out before Jack would he guess what Jack was up to? What if Nguma ran into Jack while they were both inside? Great

Universe—shaking myself loose, I paced around the console. Sweat began to run down my face.

Ten minutes elapsed before I saw Jack's headband disengaging. I rushed over to him. "Are you out of your mind?"

"Actually, yes." He put his fingers to his lips and stood up, grabbed my arm, and pulled me towards the bathroom. Once inside he said, "I've been rooting around in Williamson's, or should I say Gregory's to be more precise, mental history—their combined mental history."

My jaw dropped, and my eyes went wide. "Combined? What the Zark do you mean, Jack?"

"They're one and the same, Luke, but that's strictly between you and me. Not a word to Tiani or Julian."

"You had no right, Jack." I folded my arms and glared at him.

"Desperate times call for desperate measures, Luke."

At that moment, we heard Nguma call our names.

"Not a word, Luke." Jack guided me to the door.

My mind whirled in confusion. On the one hand I desperately wanted to know what he'd found, but on the other I knew it was a gross betrayal of the trust Nguma had given us. My insides knotted, and my head began to throb. I just wanted it all to stop. I followed Jack.

"Aah, there you are. I found myself thinking that you had stepped out for some air." Nguma's eyes twinkled.

I swallowed nervously and made a monumental effort to look normal, whatever that was.

Jack was his usual nonchalant self—calm, laid back and controlled. I envied him.

Nguma cocked his head. "Is anything wrong, Luke?" There was concern in his tone and on his face.

"Just…worried about Kiera…everything."

He reached over and patted my shoulder. "If you would like to talk, Luke, I would be happy to listen."

His face, filled with gentle concern, invited revelations. I almost weakened, but at the moment I couldn't trust myself not to tell all.

"Thanks, Nguma, perhaps another time."

"I would be happy to help you, my friend. I came to tell you that I've finished gathering my facts. I will go and analyse the results now. It will probably take me around an hour, after which I will discuss them with Gregory."

True to his word, about an hour later we saw him escort Gregory back into the bathroom. Great Universe. Now I'm beginning to think of him as Gregory.

Jack took my arm. "Let's talk, I think Nguma will be a while."

After fixing us a cup of tea, Jack sat down to face me.

"Do you want me to tell you what I found, Luke?"

"Will it make any difference?"

"Yes. I really think you need to hear it," Jack said, earnestly.

"Okay," I sighed. I had no idea what he was going to say.

Nguma's head appeared around the door.

"Luke, Gregory would like to speak to you…if you are willing."

"Is that just for his benefit?" It came out in a snarl. I immediately regretted it. "Sorry…" I met his eyes.

They were full of sympathy. "I think you will find, Luke, it will benefit both of you."

I hesitated.

He walked over, placed his hand on my shoulder and asked in a soft voice, "Do you trust me, Luke?"

I choked up. "Yes, Nguma. I trust you. I'll speak to him." I hurriedly wiped my eyes, and stood up.

I followed him into the bathroom, and we sat down on either side of Gregory.

"Luke has agreed to speak with you, Gregory, so please begin." He patted Gregory's hand.

Gregory turned to face me. "What I'm about to tell you, Luke, is for your ears only. I need you to promise me you will not tell anyone else." He appeared calm, relaxed and in control.

A plethora of mixed emotions welled up inside me, a good percentage of which was guilt. Guilt because I knew, Jack knew. I swallowed and nodded.

"I need to hear you say it, Luke."

"I promise."

"I am not the same person you once knew as Logan Williamson. To be brief, Luke, because I wanted so much to be part of this voyage, I underwent extensive genetic modifications. The body you see me in now is a modified clone of Logan, but the genes responsible for his psychopathy have been removed. I thought I had altered my appearance sufficiently that you wouldn't recognise me. I obviously underestimated you, Luke," he paused and glanced at Nguma. He gave a slight nod.

"I did not harm Kiera. I also did not sabotage the unit she and your children were in. I am aware my previous self organised the body swap and the change in the location of Kiera and your children, but I don't know why. My new persona—Gregory—is horrified and mortified by what subsequently happened."

Anger surged up through me and I had to grip the edge of the seat to stop myself from reacting. Through gritted teeth, I said, "I don't believe you."

"Whether you believe me or not, Luke, those are the facts." He turned to Nguma. "Please help me, Nguma." His eyes held a pleading look.

"He is speaking the truth, Luke—at least as far as the genetic modifications in the clone are concerned. Logan was a psychopath,

Gregory is not. He is able to feel sympathy and empathy. He is experiencing difficulty in integrating and suppressing the persona of Logan, and this is something I have promised to help him with after we arrive. I have had experience of this problem before, particularly with psychopaths. The new persona of Gregory will gradually lay down new memories, and over time he will be able to lay the persona of Logan to rest"

I couldn't contain myself any longer. "What about the persona of my wife? What about Kiera? What about the question of my body? What about…"

Nguma abruptly stood, came over to me and placed both hands on my shoulders.

"Be calm, Luke. Be calm."

"I can't. What about the chips? Does he know what's on the chips? Does he know where Kiera is? Why did Logan leave that note?"

"I don't know, Luke. There are some memories the persona of Logan hides from me. I don't know why he left you the note. I don't know what it means or where Kiera is. Please believe me, Luke. I want to help you. I…love…loved Kiera."

There were tears in his eyes. I began to believe him.

"Tell Luke what you feel about the chips, Gregory," Nguma coaxed.

"Although I can't tell you what's on the chips, I have a strong feeling something dreadful will happen if you access them." His face held sincerity and something I never saw in Logan—honesty.

"Are you willing to let Nguma remove the chips so Jack can examine them?"

Gregory's eyes went wide, he clenched his fists and said, "It's happening again Nguma. What do I do?"

"Stay calm, Gregory. Take some slow, deep breaths, as I have shown you." Nguma breathed with Gregory, and before my eyes, over several minutes, he became calm and relaxed.

"Keep breathing, Gregory. I need a brief word with Luke."

He turned and, taking my arm, guided me over to the corner. He didn't give me much choice, holding me in a firm, unrelenting grip.

"Logan's persona surfaces when Gregory is threatened or becomes agitated. It is some sort of defence mechanism. He is conflicted and confused, Luke. For all our sakes, be gentle with him. Can you do that for me?"

I took a deep breath and another before answering him. "I'll try."

He patted my shoulder. "It is enough, my friend." He guided me back to Gregory.

He had regained his composure.

Nguma gently explained to Gregory the importance of finding out exactly what was on the chips. Gregory, finally persuaded, agreed to them being removed. Nguma assured him it was the safest way for Jack to examine them, to determine exactly what they were without causing any damage. Nguma further persuaded him to have a twilight sleep anaesthetic to keep Logan's persona at bay. Gregory agreed.

We left Gregory and went to tell Jack the good news.

"Do you want to do the procedure after lunch or are you too tired?" Jack asked.

"I am not tired; after all, I have been asleep for a long time. I still feel refreshed. I am happy to proceed this afternoon." He regarded us expectantly.

"Excellent. The sooner they're out, the sooner we can find out what's on them."

Jack sounded so confident, but I had doubts. Experience had told me nothing was ever straightforward as far as Williamson was concerned.

After lunch, Nguma disinfected the table and covered it with a sterile surgical sheet. He drew up some anaesthetic into the dispenser and disappeared into the bathroom with Julian. He re-emerged a few minutes later with Julian carrying the prone form of Gregory. Julian carefully laid him down on the table. Jack ran the scanner over him to locate the chips. He found them just beneath the skin underneath Gregory's right arm pit. The small scar was still visible. To be sure, he checked Gregory's identity spherule was where it should be—on the back of his neck just under his skull. It was.

We left the room while the surgery was being done to minimise contamination. Nguma had kitted himself out with one of the disposable surgery kits from the emergency medical supplies. It also contained a basic set of sterilised surgical instruments, swabs etcetera and all the necessary paraphernalia.

Five minutes later, a triumphant Nguma emerged bearing the two bloodied chips in a kidney dish. They were specially coated to prevent immune reactions from the recipient, just as the identity spherules were.

Jack inspected the dish and whistled. "Bloody hell, they're big." He picked up the marble sized spheres, and after carefully rinsing them, dried them with a paper towel. "I'll have to take these down to the lab to access a chip reader. I can look at the internal schematics and find out exactly what I'm dealing with. I may be some time. If it gets late and I'm not back, go to bed and get some sleep. I'll go and suit up now. Julian, could you pressurise the lab please, it's located on deck six." He marched off to the suit storage area.

Nguma, Tiani and I gravitated back to the living unit table, now free of the surgical equipment. Julian had lifted Gregory back into the bathroom. We'd laid him on pillows, covered him with a blanket and had made him as comfortable as possible as one could be on the floor wearing handcuffs. Nguma had advised us to keep him restrained for the time being.

He ducked out to check on Gregory and soon returned. Apparently, he was still dead to the world, and he probably wouldn't wake for another couple of hours. We sat around talking and were soon joined by Julian. We learned Nguma had emigrated from Nigeria as a child and had studied medicine in Canada. He had met his wife, Teresa, when they'd both been attending a course in neuropsychiatry prior to graduating. She had chosen the research path. Nguma had gone into general practice with a side specialty in neuropsychiatry. During his first lifetime, he had become interested in psychopaths, an interest he still pursued. His wife had done extensive research into the condition.

Time flew by. Jack hadn't returned by ten, so we decided to get some sleep. I went out to the deck with Julian to see if there'd been any further progress. He'd been communicating with Jack roughly every hour, apart from the last couple of hours. Jack had found the process so draining he'd decided to grab a couple of hours sleep. He'd only just woken up. The process of examining the chips was proving frustratingly slow and laborious. Because they were unique, he'd decided to use extreme caution to find out as much as possible prior to any interrogation attempts. Julian decided to stay up for another hour.

I was still awake when Julian tiptoed in, grabbed a pillow and laid down on the floor near Tiani. I couldn't relax, my mind kept going around and around wondering what was on the chips. Did one of them really hold Kiera's consciousness? What would we do if it did? Possible consequences spun around my brain, and I found myself becoming increasingly more agitated. In the end, I got up and crept outside to the computer terminal. I sat in the chair and buzzed Jack. The wall clock showed a minute past midnight.

"Julian," he said, irritably, "I told you not to bother me."

"It's not Julian, it's me." I ran my fingers through my hair.

"Luke, I'm doing my best, these things are…" I waited. Jack gave an enormous sigh. "They're so bloody complex. I'm not sure I'm going to be able to find out what's on them without damaging them." I could hear the exhaustion and desperation in his voice.

"What about examining them via Virtual?" I asked, after a long silence.

"After what Williamson said?"

"Look, I'm prepared to take the risk, even if you won't."

A long pause followed. "I…bloody hell, Luke. This is a bloody nightmare."

The strain in his voice tugged at me.

"I'm coming up."

"That's not…" I cut him off because I knew he was going to say not to come. I left a message on the screen for Julian so everyone would know where I'd disappeared to.

Within a couple of minutes, I was in the airlock. When I was half way up in the lift some twenty minutes later, I realised that in my haste I hadn't sighted the floor plan for deck six. I had no idea where the laboratory was located.

We'd all taken a tour of the ship prior to being put in suspension. It had been quick and superficial, and my memory of it was hazy. Lack of sleep was making me stupid, I realised. Great Universe, I hope I am able to raise Jack. The ship's decks were huge, long, complex affairs, and certainly not the place to go wandering about in the dark. I was still berating myself when the lift arrived at deck six and the door opened. An avalanche of light flooded in, and I could see passages heading off in all directions. Julian had obviously turned on all the lights for Jack when he'd come through. He'd left them on, uncertain as to when Jack would come back.

I flicked to gen com, hoping Jack hadn't turned it off.

"Jack! Jack, I'm on deck six, but I haven't a clue where to go." I waited—silence. I tried again.

"You shouldn't have come," Jack said, in an angry tone. "I've a good mind to leave you to wander around." I kept quiet and so did he, but finally, he said, "But I'd worry you'd get yourself into trouble, and I wouldn't be able to concentrate. If you look at your wristband screen you'll see a little FP in the bottom left-hand corner, tap that and the floor plan will come up on your HUD."

I did as I was told, and a schematic spilled into my visor. I noticed a blinking green dot and realised it was indicating where I was. "Use the little keyboard, and tap in C lab. See you shortly." He cut me off.

Feeling chastened, I followed his instructions. Presently, a map with the route to the lab clearly marked popped into view. It appeared close by. I exhaled slowly in an effort to release the tension that had built up. I turned and walked down the appropriate passage. Soon, I was outside the airlock door clearly marked C lab. Once I reached the inside of the lab, I stripped off my suit and gulped in the fresh air. Jack didn't look up from his computer screen until I was standing beside him.

"I'm beginning to think Virtual may be the only way we can find out what's on these things." Jack swivelled his chair, revealing a pale, tired face. "I feel like a novice as far as these things go, Luke. A complete bloody novice." He stood, stretched and rubbed his neck. "Take a look."

I sat and became instantly mesmerised by the schematic of one of the chips. "Are they both the same?" I asked after several minutes of examining the chip from all angles.

"Basically, they are, but one is slightly more complex than the other."

"Okay, hook up the more complex one, and I'll go in and see what I can find." I went to engage the headband button, but Jack stayed my hand.

"It could be extremely risky, Luke. Especially, since we don't know what we're dealing with. How do we know it's not some bloody booby-trap rigged up by Williamson to do a mind wipe or something similar?"

"I'm still prepared to take the risk." I stared up at him, and he released my hand.

"All right." He turned and sat down at another console a little further down the bench while my headband engaged. Presently, Jack's voice came through, "I'm ready, but Luke, be careful. Be prepared for anything, and good luck."

"I'll be careful, Jack, and thanks."

Chapter 46

I went through the linking procedure, including the necessary password to allow me to engage. As I spiralled down—I wondered—will this be the last time I ever do this? Is this a trap set up by Williamson? I pushed the thought away and concentrated. It was too late to panic now. I slowed my breathing and focused on calmness.

I carefully formed the thought.

—Prepare for chip interrogation.

—*Preparing for chip interrogation—please wait.*

I waited. The message repeatedly blinked on the screen. Time dragged. After what seemed like hours, the message changed.

—*Ready for interrogation—Please give instructions.*

—Immerse.

—*Warning—chip does not conform to standard.*

—*This procedure may be dangerous and is not recommended for nonstandard chips.*

"Luke, what the hell are you doing?"

—Immerse.

"No, Luke," Jack screamed in my ear—too late.

A plummeting sensation overwhelmed me. I plunged into a black abyss. Panic set in as the darkness became solid, suffocating and almost overpowering. In the next instant a room materialised around me. Drab curtains covered the windows, and a single naked light bulb swung backwards and forwards from the ceiling. A small boy cowered in one corner while a blonde woman wearing a gaudy floral dress screamed at him.

I had the sense of being physically present, but I knew it was an illusion. I had to be a mere observer, but it was so real. I looked on, mesmerised by the scene. The woman had something in her hand. I tried to move closer, to one side, so I could see what she held. Abruptly, I found myself standing next to her. She was holding a yellow flyswatter which she was using to beat the little boy around the head and neck. I could hear the whack—whack—whack. The boy, aged about three or four, whimpered like a small animal. Anger and pity welled up inside me. I lunged at her arm, but my phantom hand sliced through thin air. I existed only as a powerless ghost.

I focused back on the boy. He cradled something in front of him, trying to protect it. When I strained to see what it was, I was instantly transported to his side. He had his arms firmly wrapped around a small black-and-white kitten. I could just hear its plaintive meowing above all the din.

Move back, I thought—and I did, returning to my original position. Great Universe, what is this? Where is this? Is this someone's memory or a dream? In a flash, I hurtled back into darkness. I began to feel a pulling, stretching sensation, like someone or something trying to tear me apart. It continued on and on, and its intensity increased exponentially. Just when the pain became unbearable and I began to scream, I snapped back into the boy's room.

The scene had changed. The boy was sitting on his bed, moving the limp form of the kitten from one hand to the other. I could see by the angle of its head, by the way it flopped backwards and forwards, that its neck was broken. I wondered what had happened. Instantly, I found myself standing right in front of the boy.

Unexpectedly, he raised his eyes and met mine. My pulse rocketed. Standing before me was Logan Williamson as a child. Paralysed with horror, I just stood—lost in those unmistakable, dark, penetrating eyes. I was inside Logan Williamson's brain. I shrank back, simultaneously assaulted by shock and fear. In a microsecond I was transported to the far corner of the room, before being hurled back into darkness.

I swallowed my panic and tried to think. Perhaps I was creating all this. I experimented. I visualised Williamson as he was currently. Immediately, the ghastly stretching sensation wrenched and tore at all my nerves. It built in intensity, until finally I cried out in pain. The sensation vanished when I materialised in a vaguely familiar room. A youthful Williamson was seated at his desk. He fixed me with a blank stare. When recognition dawned, he began to laugh. It became a maniacal roar. Had I gone insane?

"Well, well, this is a surprise. Frankly, I'm amazed you've got this far." He steepled his hands and gazed up at me. "I'm not sure I like you digging around my brain; slipping in and out of my memories. What did you think of my mother?"

"Was it her that broke the kitten's neck?" I had to know.

"What do you think?" His smile transformed into a sneer.

"I don't know." At the back of my mind, an insistent little voice was saying, 'you shouldn't be doing this, Luke—it's not safe.'

"My mother enjoyed killing things; she broke its neck. She couldn't understand why I wanted to keep the soft, warm, living creature. She never allowed pets; she considered them dirty vermin, much like children really. She rarely touched me and only when she had to. She never touched my father either; I suspect that's why he

304

left. He got tired of begging to be admitted to her bedroom, tired of her constant nagging. He simply packed up and left one night while she was out. She was out, frequently.

When I clung to his coat and pleaded with him to take me with him, he prised my hands away and smacked me full in the face. He told me I was just useless baggage, that he'd never wanted me in the first place, and that I, like her, was unlovable. I was six at the time. Something changed in me that night, like the last piece of a jigsaw clicking into place. I became transformed. I learned to enjoy watching my mother. Gradually, I began to appreciate the sense of power it bought when she let me kill things for her."

I stared at him, sickened and horrified. He started to laugh again, and as it rose to a crescendo a wave of nausea swept over me. The sound vibrated through me with jackhammer intensity and induced the sensation of being shaken apart. I had to get out. I had to get away from Williamson before he killed me.

"Break link," I said. Nothing happened. Abruptly, the laughter ceased. Williamson sat back in his chair and placed his hands behind his head.

"Break link now," I shouted, desperately.

"Get out of my mind," Williamson screamed. "Get out! Get out!

"Jack. Jack help me. Please, help me." Smothering darkness closed over me.

#

Someone was patting my face, but I couldn't open my eyes. Was I just waking up from hiber-sleep? Was that why my eyes wouldn't open?

I heard a voice. Not the soothing voice I remembered from the hiber-pod, it was male. My eyes snapped open, and I stared into Nguma's anxious face.

He placed his hand on my cheek. "At last, Luke, you have come back to us. Let me help you from the chair." He placed both hands under my arms and pulled me up.

Jack rushed forward to help him, "Don't you ever try anything like that again. I thought I'd lost you, you stupid, bloody bastard." He hovered over me, his face grey and drawn.

Even though I had a raging headache and was a little wobbly, I shrugged both of them off. "I'm alright, and I know what's on the chip."

"What?" Jack and Nguma asked, simultaneously.

I had to lean on the bench for support before I could answer. Jack stood expectantly, but my hesitancy proved too much for Nguma.

"Please do tell us, Luke."

"It's Williamson's consciousness; all of it."

"Are you certain," Jack frowned, and rubbed his forehead.

"I'm certain."

"Until I laid eyes on these chips, I would have said it was impossible. Bloody hell, Luke. He's really done it."

"Yes. Now, hook up the other one. I'm praying it's Kiera." I sat back in the chair. Just as I reached for the headband button, Nguma grabbed my wrist and wouldn't let go.

"I forbid it. You are dehydrated, and you need rest, my friend." His face was full of concern.

I gazed up into those soft, brown eyes. "How did I get dehydrated? I wasn't in there for long."

"You were in there for nine hours—nine, bloody hours, Luke." Jack's voice was filled with quiet anger. "Even though Nguma put you on an IV, it was taking such a toll on you we were forced to break the link. That was the easy part; we spent a further three hours trying everything we could think of to wake you up. You will only go in there again over my dead body." Jack glared, exhaustion clearly etched into his face.

"Somebody's got to do it," I said, defiantly, massaging my throbbing forehead.

"You heard me," Jack said. "Let's get back down to our deck. I'm exhausted and starving. I won't take no for an answer. Get moving."

Without another word, Jack took hold of one arm and Nguma the other. They escorted me over to our suits and helped me into mine. After putting on theirs, they propelled me into the airlock. We were soon back on deck twenty-six. Julian and Tiani confronted us the moment we emerged. They both rushed forward, and their anxious, expectant faces said it all. Tiani flung her arms around me, while Julian stood next to us.

"We were so worried, Dad. What on earth possessed you to immerse?" Julian asked.

"I don't know." This was the truth. I really didn't know. In hindsight, I realised how impulsive and reckless I'd been. My rash action could have cost me my sanity.

Tiani released me and stepped back.

Julian wrapped his arms around me and gave me a hug. "Promise you won't do it again, Dad."

I hesitated. "Even if it's your mother?"

"Even if it's Mum." Julian's expression conveyed sad determination.

"Ti?"

"I agree with Julian." She began twisting her hair around her finger.

"Perhaps you'll take notice of your kids, Luke." Jack stalked off, prompting us to follow. No one spoke; we were all lost in our own thoughts. Finding Kiera seemed further away than ever.

Chapter 47

After food, sleep, and a great deal of talking, I tried to persuade Jack to let me interrogate the other chip providing I didn't use the immersion technique. Jack's solution was simple; we would connect the second chip to the computer first, because it was a necessary step in the procedure anyway. Following that, I would link and check it was Kiera. If it was, we could go ahead with our plan to upload her into an android.

I still couldn't fathom why I'd taken such a huge risk by diving into Williamson's chip. It was probably something Kiera would have done; perhaps I could blame her female influence again. The idea of residual memory; fragments left behind when a consciousness was uploaded, was becoming more and more of a certainty in my mind.

Immersing myself in Williamson's chip had not been without consequences. My sleep had been fitful, filled with fragments of Williamson's memories. Memories from many lifetimes all spliced together in a jumble, akin to an abstract painting. In some, I was merely an observer, but in others I actually experienced the memory as if it was my own. It gave me a direct insight into Williamson's thinking and his emotions, or more to the point, lack of emotions. Unable to feel any sort of compassion, he was driven by the need to control others. Because of his intellect, he'd learned at an early age to hide his true self. He'd used charm, backed up by clever manipulation, to persuade people to do his bidding. When that failed, he used his skills to press other people's buttons. He manipulated their vulnerabilities and blackmailed them with skeletons from the past to force them into doing what he wanted.

He was obviously a psychopath, exhibiting all the particular character traits—superficial charm, impulsivity, lack of remorse or shame and the inability to feel empathy. I needed to speak to the man before I went up to examine the other chip.

"Nguma."

He looked up from Jack's tablet. "Yes, my friend."

It was going to be a big ask. I steeled myself. "Is there any way you can bring Williamson's persona out? There are really important gaps Gregory can't fill us in on." I held my breath.

"Let me think for a moment," his face took on a vague faraway look as he gazed into the distance. "I may be able to bring him forth by using hypnosis. But Gregory would have to agree to undergo the process." His face became serious.

"Could you go and ask him, please?"

He stood up. "I will try and persuade him." He paused before going out the door. "It could prove beneficial for him, but I cannot force him."

"No, of course not." I hoped like hell Gregory would agree.

Sometime later, Nguma came back. "Good news, Luke. Gregory has agreed. I've already put him under my spell and have coaxed Logan out."

"There's just one thing I need to ask you, Nguma, and please don't take this the wrong way." I shifted uncomfortably in my chair.

"Yes, Luke. Please, ask away."

"Are you one hundred percent certain Gregory is genuine, and it's not Williamson playing us all for fools?" I held his gaze. His mouth quirked with a slight smile, and his eyes crinkled.

"I have had three lifetimes of dealing with people such as these. I am confident in my own judgement. No one can pull the fleece over my eyes—no one, Luke."

I laughed.

He tilted his head to one side. "Is there anything else?"

"No, Nguma, thank you."

"Let us proceed, my friend." He beckoned with his hand.

I got up and followed him into the bathroom.

When we entered, Logan regarded us with a sullen, defiant silence. We sat down on either side of him. He still didn't speak.

"We had to terminate the lives of eighteen people. My wife, Kiera, was among them. You caused their deaths by sabotaging the unit so it would ultimately fail. Tell me how that is not murder?"

"I did not sabotage the unit." His eyes narrowed.

"I don't believe you. I would like you to explain how Kiera and my two children came to be in module three, when they were supposed to be in module one along with Jack and me." I glared at him and my heart thumped in my ears.

He pulled himself erect and glared back. "If you will remember, Luke, there was a calculated module failure rate for the duration of the voyage. Everyone knew there was a risk, be it a small one, that they wouldn't make it alive to the end of the voyage." He paused; his expression smug and confident. It angered me that I was giving him this power.

"So, you are saying it was a coincidence?" Nguma asked.

"Yes, no one was meant to die." He turned to face me. "I will admit to transferring Kiera into your body and you into Kiera's body,

Luke, but it's quite reversible. It's a simple matter of transferring your consciousnesses to your correct clones once they're ready after we arrive. Of course, it does mean you will lose your spare bonus clone." He gave me a nasty smile.

Nguma leant across and tapped Logan's shoulder. "Tell us why you did this, Logan, so we can make sense of it."

He smiled, and I found my fists tightening as he continued. "It was merely a—" Logan paused, "an indulgence, a small amusement, and revenge for the problems you caused me all those lifetimes ago. I transferred them into a different module so you would see my message. You wouldn't have seen it if Kiera and your children had been with you where they were supposed to be."

In a flash, a clear, compelling memory launched itself into my consciousness. Logan Williamson had, in his own sick way, loved Kiera. Its overwhelming intensity swept over me, along with his aching need to be loved and cared about. His compulsive resoluteness had drowned out his intellectual reasoning. I shook my head and pulled myself back to the present. I found myself flooded with pity for this sad, lonely individual sitting in front of me, justifying actions he was incapable of feeling any guilt about.

I sighed. "If we are to believe you, and I'm not saying we do, tell us what's on the other chip. Is it Kiera consciousness? "

"Only if you guarantee I will not be charged for any of my actions."

He appeared so confident. He was filled with the conviction he had done nothing wrong other than to play a nasty trick, a trick that could be reversed.

"So," Logan said, looking at each of us in turn, "do we have an agreement?"

"But what about the fact you've condemned my children to a future life as non-biological entities, a future devoid of children?"

"Aah, I was right about your strong desire for grandchildren."
He smirked.

My pity vanished, suddenly replaced by murderous thoughts,
thoughts of putting my hands round his throat and squeezing.

"Answer me!" I shouted.

Nguma stood up and came over to my side. He reached over
and gently squeezed my shoulder before sitting next to me.

"I've kept the best until last."

Logan's face was filled with lively animation, and I was wondering what was coming next.

"Do enlighten us, Logan," Nguma said, feeding Logan's ego,
"we are all ears."

Logan, pleased in the realisation that he now held all the cards,
was beginning to enjoy himself. Much to my disgust, he appeared to
be revelling in the sense of power. Power I was giving him.

I gritted my teeth and gripped the bench. It took all my self-
control not to hit him.

"I think you have ascertained by now, my prototypes are rather
special. Let me tell you why." He paused for effect, as obvious en-
joyment spilled over his face. "The chips not only hold a person's
consciousness in entirety, they allow the consciousness to be transferred to a *biological* body." Logan sat contemplating us, waiting for a
reaction.

My mind raced as the implications of what Logan had just said
sank in. If Kiera was on the other chip, she could be uploaded back
into her own body but only if I were to vacate it. For me, it would
mean I would lose my biological form and become an android. For
Kiera's sake I was prepared to make that choice.

"Tell me how this process works," Nguma said, "I am a doctor,
I do not have much understanding of these technical things." He
regarded Logan expectantly.

"It's quite simple, the consciousness must be uploaded directly onto my prototype chip. Because the chip is unique, and enables the storage of the full consciousness, it can, via a self-contained program, be uploaded into a biological entity." Logan was in his element now, pride literally oozing from all his pores.

"I would like to see a demonstration of this process," Nguma said, glancing at me. "We have two of your chips to choose from, and I believe we already know your consciousness is on one of them."

Clever, very clever. I could see where this was heading.

"That is what you found, was it not, Luke?" His smile was triumphant.

"Yes, that's right," I grinned. "Let's see, first we empty your chip onto the computer. We upload your consciousness, from your brain to the empty chip, giving us two copies. Following that, if we transfer it from your chip back into your brain, it will allow us to see if the process works." Logan remained silent and we both stared at him intently, watching for the slightest reaction.

He gathered himself up. "I told you interrogating the chip could damage it. The fact you have already done so has probably made it unstable."

We'd got to him. He glared back at both of us.

"I'm quite prepared to go ahead with the process," I paused, waiting for what I'd said to sink in. "The only thing that will stop me is if you tell me what's on the second chip."

Logan squirmed on the bench, looking at each of us in turn.

"Luke is not making a joke of this. I think it is time for you to tell us or he will go ahead with this procedure. And I will help him." Nguma's expression was seriously convincing.

"All right, all right, you win," Logan shouted. The second chip does hold Kiera's consciousness. Satisfied?" He slumped, and I had the satisfaction of finally seeing him look defeated.

"Thank you, Logan," Nguma said in a quiet voice.

"I'll go and talk to Jack, Nguma. I'll leave you to finish up here." We stood up. "And thanks, Nguma."

I left them both. My intended words had now been tucked firmly back into a corner of my mind, perhaps never to be revisited.

Chapter 48

Over our evening meal we discussed Logan's revelations. It reminded me of family conferences held around our kitchen table at home. During previous lifetimes, Jack had become a permanent fixture. Currently, I knew I wasn't alone in regarding Nguma as a new addition to our family. His warmth, sincerity, sensitivity and intelligence had quickly won us over. He had become a different person to the sad shell Jack and I had seen when we'd first awakened him.

"How do we know he's not lying?" Jack said in between mouthfuls.

"Because he was looking so pleased with himself." I put my fork down on my plate. "With Nguma's encouragement, once Logan began showing off, he got carried away and became careless."

"I was quite deliberate with my questions, and it was plain that his ego got the better of him. After all, that was my plan." Nguma flashed us a roguish grin.

"Nguma's had considerable experience in this area. He's an expert at reading psychopaths. There's no doubt in my mind that Logan was telling us the truth."

"It's what he didn't tell you that I'm worried about," Jack said, frowning.

"What do you mean, Uncle Jack?" Tiani said, looking worried.

"He's quite capable of setting up some sort of trap. Perhaps he anticipated possible discovery and took appropriate precautions." He surveyed us all, his face set in a worried expression.

"I'm prepared to take the risk," I said, "so let's discuss the process, shall we?"

Julian leant over and gently put his hand on my shoulder, "Hey, Dad, are you sure about this?"

I patted his face, "I'm sure, Julian." He let his hand drop and sat back.

"I'm not happy, Luke," Jack replied, frowning as he pushed his plate away. "I think we should vote on it. All those in favour raise hands." Four hands went up simultaneously, while Jack's palms remained firmly planted on the table. "All right, but don't say you weren't warned."

After further discussions as to the logistics of the operation, Jack decided, because of the complexity of the procedure, it would be best if we all went up to the lab so extra help would be available if needed. He also decided it was time to put Gregory back into suspension. His wound had already healed, and there was no point in having him around any longer. It would be a relief not to have to worry about him.

Gregory appeared relieved when Nguma told him we were going to put him back into hiber-sleep. He stayed calm and cooperative, happy even, when Jack began hooking him up in the capsule. When Jack had finished, Nguma stepped over to his side.

"I will be there for you, Gregory, when you next wake up." He took Gregory's hand in his. "It will take time, but I am confident that working together we will be able to lay Logan to rest. After that is done, you will be able to move on. I'm certain that you have a new and happy life to look forward to when we reach our destination."

"Thank you, Nguma. You've already helped me great deal, and I'm sure you're right. Goodbye for now."

"Goodbye, Gregory." Nguma let go of his hand and stepped away.

Gregory turned his head towards me. "I'm sorry, Luke…"

To my surprise, a sudden wave of compassion swept over me and compelled me to say what I'd previously left unsaid. I leant over him, put my hand on his shoulder, and said quietly, "I forgive you."

He looked at me with an expression of utter disbelief, "Why? Why would you do that?"

Jack stepped back from the computer screen. "He's ready."

As I moved away, and with Gregory's eyes still locked on mine, I said, "Because, *you* are not Logan. He was a victim of his genes and his tragic childhood environment. You're free from those influences, Gregory. With Nguma's help you can tread a different path, that's why I can forgive you." His expression of bewilderment transformed into relief, and he mouthed "thank you" as the canopy slid closed. I watched as the sleep-gas hissed into the capsule, and Gregory's eyes closed.

When the capsule began to retract, a huge sense of relief poured through me. I experienced the release of a subtle pressure that, up until that moment, I'd been unaware of. In an instant, my whole being flooded with lightness, a sense of freedom, and something I hadn't experienced for a long time—joy.

"What the hell was that about?" Jack's face took on a puzzled expression.

"I'm not sure," I shook my head. "But…I feel…good. In fact, I feel great."

#

Once Gregory was back in suspension, Jack decided to wait until morning to carry out our mission to rescue Kiera. After we'd seen Gregory off, the intense emotions soon evaporated into exhaustion. I think I was still feeling the effects of my trip down the dark wormhole into Williamson's brain. Feeling emotionally drained, I was happy to delay the process.

We went to bed early. Although I had no trouble getting to sleep, I woke up numerous times during the night—my brain inundated with disturbing, intense memories (or were they just dreams?) of Logan's past.

One, in particular, left unsettling and vivid details emblazoned in mind long after I woke up. It began with Gregory frantically waving at me. I ran to him, and he motioned me forward. I could see his lips moving, but I couldn't hear him. Next, we were in Logan's office, and the man himself was sitting in front of a computer. Gregory pointed at the screen with such an expression of terror that I stepped forward to see what he was looking at. Logan twisted around and began to laugh. It thundered through my brain like the launch of a starship. I woke up soaked in sweat, unable to shake the images or the feeling of terror.

Consequently, the next morning a desperate tiredness pervaded every cell in my body. A revitalising hot shower and some breakfast helped a little. Thank the Universe my role in the day's proceedings only involved verifying it was Kiera's consciousness on Logan's prototype chip. A simple link, after we'd connected her chip to the computer, was all that was required. Afterwards, I would be put to sleep. My consciousness would be uploaded to the computer, leaving Kiera's brain vacant. Tiredness was hardly going to be an issue.

Julian and Tiani had insisted on fixing breakfast for us. When we'd finished, they had gathered the remains and were washing the dishes in the sink. Nguma and I sat contemplating the simulated scene in the view screen opposite our table. I wondered what he was thinking. His eyes had a glazed, faraway look. Perhaps something in the scene reminded him of his dead wife.

Jack stuck his head round the door. "Luke, are you happy to stay behind to turn on the lights etcetera and follow us down later?"

"Yes, okay." His request surprise me, but it was logical. It would take time to set the process up. I wouldn't be needed. We could turn the lights on before we left, but perhaps Jack was giving me time to myself to think about what I was going to do, hoping I would reconsider. I wouldn't. My mind was firmly made up. I was happy to indulge him, because I still couldn't shake my desperate tiredness. Actually, it was rather sweet. Great Universe! Another Kiera thought? Would these remnants stay with me when I became a sapioid?

A little later, I watched them all traipse out and disappear into the airlock. After monitoring their departure, I found myself sitting alone with my thoughts, surrounded only by the quiet hiss of the air-conditioning. So much had happened in such a short time. I sighed and thought about Kiera—my beautiful, loving Kiera. I had thought she was lost forever, and now with Jack's help she would be restored to the body that was rightfully hers. I would become the sapioid. I hoped she'd understand.

We'd had many heated discussions around the subject. As far as she was concerned, androids were the last resort. I knew, unlike me, she would cling to her biological humanity as long as she could. She would be devastated by what had happened to Julian and Tiani. I hoped it wouldn't be too much for her. I found my thoughts drifting. I must have actually dropped off to sleep, because the next thing I became aware of was Jack's voice.

"This is going to take longer than I thought, Luke, so you might as well stay where you are for the time being."

My pulse rate immediately jumped, "Is there a problem?"

"No, I was just a bit optimistic about the length of time it would take. Go and have a nap, but leave the com on. I'll wake you with an alarm when it's time to come down." There was something in his voice, but I decided not to pursue it.

"Okay, I do feel quite tired."

"I'll let you know when we're ready."

"Okay." I yawned and got up from the chair. I padded across to the living unit. After a drink of water, I laid on the bunk. I went out like a light, and the next thing I was aware of was the sound of the alarm. I rolled off the bunk and trotted back to the console outside. I flicked the switch.

"We'll be ready for you by the time you get down here," Jack said, sounding pleased.

"So, connecting her chip has been successful?"

"Yes, once I worked out how to do it. It comes with its own program, Luke. It's gone without a hitch. See you soon." He'd already broken the connection. I switched off the com and went to suit up. After pressing the airlock button, I stood and waited for it to re-pressurise.

I thought about the length of time I'd been asleep and found it hard to believe almost three hours had passed. It had been a deep, seemingly dreamless sleep. I still couldn't shake the feeling that something wasn't quite right. I dredged my brain, trying to pinpoint its origin without success.

With the re-pressurisation process complete, I opened the door and stepped inside. While waiting for the airlock to exhaust the air, my thoughts drifted. When I came back here, I would be a sapioid. Great Universe! Please let it go right.

Chapter 49

The air in the lab held a thick tension, as I finally sat in the chair, and the headband engaged. I had a monumental fight to control the anxiety flooding my brain. It took five minutes of controlled breathing and mental exercises to get myself into a state where I could actually engage and link with the computer.

I went through the preliminaries and finally came to the moment I was both dreading and excitedly anticipating.

—Link to Kiera Susannah Proud.

—*Linking.*

I waited, with my heart in my mouth, watching the screen blink, over and over. Seconds dripped through my brain and pooled like hours. I held my breath. I had to stay calm. I had to focus. Otherwise, I would have to start all over again. The message changed.

—*Warning—requested link uploaded from a non-conforming chip.*

—Link to occupant Kiera Susannah Proud.

—*This procedure may be dangerous and is not recommended for uploads from nonstandard chips.*

I invoked the critical emergency override and repeated my request again, and waited.

—*Linking.*

I sat, suspended in time before I spiralled down into blackness.

—Kiera, it's Luke, I need you to confirm your password with the computer.

Silence. I repeated my request.

—Luke, what's going on? Where are you? I can't see anything. Why can't I see anything?

It was her. There was absolutely no doubt in my mind.

—Yes, it's me, Kiera, you're in suspension. I don't have time to explain, please verify your password with the computer.

—Not until you tell me what's going on.

—I don't have time Kiera, please do as I ask. Your life is at stake.

—What!

—Do as I ask now!

—All right, no need to get terse. Locate password for Kiera Susannah Proud.

—*Password located—please verify.*

—White mouse.

—*Password verified.*

—Thanks, Kiera. See you shortly.

—Break link.

—*Link terminated.*

Everyone had gathered around me, and they were all waiting expectantly.

"It's her… It's her," was all I could manage through my sobs of joy and relief. As I got up from the chair, Tiani launched herself at me. She threw her arms round my neck, crying and laughing at the same time. Julian, ecstatic, punched the air, while Nguma looked on, nodded his head and beamed; only Jack remained impassive.

"Are you sure it's her, Luke?" he asked, with a solemn expression.

"Yes, I'm sure."

"Okay, let's get on with it. Places everyone. Time is ticking." He turned away from us. Something in his eyes unsettled me, something I couldn't fathom. If there'd been more time, I would have spoken to him to try and get to the bottom of it. Whatever *it* was.

#

"I still can't understand why it took you so long," I said to Julian, as he fixed various leads onto my head.

"Hey, what's it matter?" He grinned down at me. "You're here now."

The inexplicable time lag, compounded by everyone appearing too Zarking cheerful, was making me uneasy. Great Universe! Now I'm getting paranoid. Relax, Luke. You're just imagining things. Why shouldn't everybody be cheerful? We're about to resurrect Kiera and return her to *her* body.

"He's ready, Jack," Julian called out, patting my shoulder affectionately. "Have a nice sleep, and come back to us." He paused. "Hey, we'll make a pretty mean trio, Dad." He stepped out of the way for Tiani.

She had tears in her eyes. She leaned over and put both arms around me and kissed me gently on the cheek. "I love you, Dad."

"I love you too, Ti." I turned to Julian, "And you too, Julian. Don't worry—I'll be back." Tears began to trickle out of the corners of my eyes, but I was unable to brush them away, for fear of dislodging some of the electrodes.

"Okay, you two," Jack said, "enough of all this sentimental stuff, man your posts."

I lifted my hand and reluctantly shooed them away, as Jack and Nguma stepped up, one on each side of me.

Jack regarded me with a serious expression and said quietly, "Last chance, Luke, are you sure you want to do this?"

"Yes, Jack. I'm sure." I smiled up at him.

"Okay, over to you, Nguma."

As Jack turned and went back to the console, Nguma took my hand. He expertly inserted the line for the anaesthetic, ready to administer it when Jack gave the go-ahead.

"Put him to sleep, Nguma," Jack called.

"I'm running it in now, Luke," Nguma said, as he momentarily held my gaze, "All will be well, my friend."

Just before I drifted into unconsciousness, my brain flooded with a vivid memory. Logan….Great Universe…the chip…wait, I tried to say, but the words died in my leaden mouth. The last thing I felt and heard was Nguma patting my hand and saying, "All will be well, Luke"

Chapter 50

I heard a voice—someone called my name; I struggled against a heavy lethargy to open my eyes.

"It's okay, Luke, just relax." The voice…soft…loving…Kiera. It was Kiera's voice. Great Universe! It had worked.

"You'll be able to open your eyes in just a minute, Luke." She caressed my face, and held my hand in her tender grip. My eyes fluttered open. Kiera's face, blurry at first, slowly crystallised into clarity, and a tidal wave of joy broke over me. I attempted to sit up. I wanted to wrap my arms around her, to feel her arms around me and her lips on mine; I wanted this perfect moment to last forever.

"Easy, Luke." She slipped her hands under my arms and helped me to sit up. "Easy does it. Just sit for a bit while you stabilise." She wrapped her arms around me and laid her head on my shoulder.

I knew she was fighting back tears. So was I. Julian and Tiani hovered uncertainly nearby waiting their turn.

"Come on, you two."

Tiani still hesitated, looking unsure, but Julian came over to me smiling broadly. Kiera gave me a light kiss on the lips before moving back to let Julian and Tiani in. Nguma appeared from somewhere behind me and patted my back.

"Welcome back, my friend. My spirit soars to see you back with us."

Julian hugged me then stood aside for Tiani. She still appeared reluctant, and I could see that her eyes were red.

"What's wrong, Ti? You two chose my android, so it can't be that bad."

Tiani put her arms around me and gave me a gentle hug. After she let go, she looked sad and upset.

Something was wrong. "Where's Jack?"

I looked around the lab; there was no sign of him anywhere. I slid off the transfer table and stood up, still needing to hold on to it for support. "What's happened?" There was an uncomfortable silence. "For God sake, will someone tell me what's happened?" My elation and joy plummeted, as I waited for Kiera to tell me what dreadful thing had occurred.

She took my arm and led me over to a chair. I sat down, and she pulled another up close and sagged into it. The others moved away to give us some space. Confusion washed over me; nothing could have happened to Jack. He hadn't been directly involved in the transfer process, so how could anything have happened to him? There was something else, something I couldn't isolate. I pushed it to the back of my mind. "Well, Kiera?"

"Oh, Luke. I don't know how to tell you this." There was such sadness in her eyes. She sniffed. "Jack was right, you should have listened." She stared at her hands.

"Right about what?" My stomach tied itself in knots.

"While you were immersed in Williamson's chip, he managed, via you, to link with the computer, and he got to Jack's anti-virus program."

"How is that possible?"

"How is any of this possible? I died, and yet here I am back in my body."

I realised how difficult this must be for her. Her last memory would have been of our final day together prior to being uploaded into our new bodies and put into suspension. I didn't know how much she'd been told. I reached out, took her hand and squeezed it gently. The vivid memory I'd had, just before the anaesthetic took effect, suddenly flashed back into my mind.

"Bloody Zark, I've just remembered, the chip—your chip, it was unstable wasn't it?"

"How could you possibly have known that?" Kiera's eyes went wide.

"It was one of Logan's memories that I came across when I was immersed in his mind. So, what happened?"

"Julian told me my chip was unstable. It corrupted when I was uploaded from it. It's—useless." She placed her other hand over mine.

"Knowing Logan, he would have deliberately set it up so nobody could use it again, but how is Jack involved? I don't understand. Did the anti-virus program cause some problem during the uploads?"

"Something like that."

I twisted around in my chair. It had come from an android, no a sapioid, I corrected myself.

"Who the Zark are you?" I glared at him.

"He doesn't know yet, Kiera?" it said.

I turned back to Kiera. Her eyes were wide with shock and disbelief.

"What the Zark?" she whispered.

Julian, Tiani and Nguma materialised from around the corner. I'd forgotten the lab was L-shaped. The sapioid strode over to us, and for some reason anger rose in my throat.

Nguma hurried forward and put his hand on its shoulder. "I think I, should explain this. It needs to be done gently."

"You won't explain it properly," the sapioid said.

"It's not a matter of it being explained giving every technical detail. It is a matter of it being explained with care and consideration for Luke. Would you not agree?"

"Okay, I'll leave you to it, Nguma." The sapioid turned and disappeared back around the corner followed by Julian and Tiani, leaving the three of us looking from one to the other. Nguma grabbed one of the other chairs and sat down between us. He reached out and gently patted my shoulder.

"Jack has made a great sacrifice for you, Luke. He had an immense guilt that was threatening to devour him, so he has made this decision."

Nguma's face frightened me with its sad seriousness. My insides clenched, as I wondered what he was going to tell me next.

"We did discuss it, and your children were in agreement. Jack understood Kiera's feelings about sapioids. He thought that if you too became one, it would be too great a thing for her to bear. It was too much for him to bear, so that is why he has taken this path." He held my gaze with those gentle brown eyes.

Up until now, I had sat patiently, but suddenly I couldn't stand it any longer. I had to know. "For Zark's sake, will one of you tell me what's happened?"

Kiera had tears in her eyes. "Let me tell him, Nguma."

"Of course, of course you should be the one." He sat back in his chair and placed his hands on his lap.

"Jack has given you his body." She sat and stared, waiting for me to react.

A kaleidoscope of emotions hit me all at once; shock, horror, anger, and relief. No wonder I felt so normal. I was still in a human body. I wasn't a sapioid.

"Great Universe! Great Zarking Universe! Why did you let him do this, Nguma? Why didn't you stop him? This is my fault."

Nguma took hold of my hands. "This is not your fault, my friend. Jack chose to do it for you. It was his choice, there is no reason for you to feel guilty."

"Why? Why did he feel he had to give me his body?"

"He blames himself—that he did not anticipate an attack from within, and that he was unable to save Kiera and therefore your body. It is quite complicated. I will leave him to explain it to you."

I turned to Kiera. "Kiera, why didn't you stop him?"

"He'd gone by the time I woke up, so I didn't get the chance," she said, through tears.

"Oh, Jack," I said. "There's no going back."

"Jack says that is not necessarily the case. I will leave it to him to tell you about it," Nguma said.

I stared at him. "What do you mean?"

"Let us go and ask him, all of us together." Nguma let go my hands and stood up.

Kiera wiped her eyes.

"Look, I'm as surprised and shocked as you, Luke. We all thought we'd lost Jack. Let's go and find out exactly what happened, shall we?" She gave me a weak smile.

My mind whirled as I tried to process the fact that I now inhabited Jack's body. At least it was male. The nebulous something that had been lurking at the back of my mind suddenly became crystal clear—Jack's voice. It had subliminally registered every time I opened my mouth. I had the sudden impulse to howl with laughter. I fought the urge, because I knew if I started I wouldn't be able to stop.

Nguma and Kiera helped me to my feet, and the three of us trooped around the corner. Tiani and Julian were huddled around a computer terminal along with the sapioid that held Jack's consciousness.

Chapter 51

We all sat in a semicircle around the computer terminal while Jack explained what had happened.

"The first thing we did was to dump Williamson's consciousness onto the computer, leaving his chip empty." Jack glanced at Julian. "I couldn't have done it without Julian's help. Julian modified the chip reader to enable us to connect it directly to the computer. It took us an age to get past his firewall."

"Once we'd done that, Dad, we were able to look at the programming to make sure the chip was stable and there weren't any hidden traps," Julian said.

"Wasn't that incredibly risky?" I asked.

"Yes, but I thought it was worth it because of the time factor. Our next step was to upload you, Luke, to Williamson's empty chip. We were then able to transfer Kiera back into her own body. When Kiera's upload was finished, Julian began uploading my consciousness to the computer in preparation for my transfer into the android. After that we uploaded you, Luke, to my body. As a precaution, we'd also loaded a copy of my consciousness onto Kiera's vacant chip, but shortly after that had finished, it began to corrupt. Somehow, I became aware of the problem, and I found I could copy myself onto Williamson's chip, so that's what I did. It was touch and go, but we succeeded."

"So, let me see if I've got this straight. Williamson got into the computer via me when I was connected to his chip. He managed to alter your anti-virus program so it would run progressively faster each time you executed an upload of a consciousness onto the computer or a chip?" I said.

"Yes. Before my uploads, I immersed, and I managed to alter the program's progression just enough to allow our various uploads to complete. In the end we still had ten minutes to spare." Jack's face lit with a pleased expression.

"Great Universe, what if it had all gone wrong, Jack?" I ran my fingers through my hair.

"It didn't go wrong, Luke, so it's all moot."

"So, are you saying your consciousness is now held on Williamson's prototype?" Kiera asked.

"Yes, but there's a discrepancy in the amount of data between my sapioid and Williamson's chip. Williamson's chip contains slightly less, so there may be some small gaps in my memory. We had a look. It contains a lot of information, roughly consistent with the amount I'd expect for my consciousness, so I don't expect any major problems."

"But if my chip was unstable, isn't it the same as Williamson's? How come it didn't corrupt when you emptied it?" Kiera's face was creased with worry.

"His chip isn't the same as yours, Kiera. It has a more elegant and intricate structure. I suspect it was the final prototype he made before leaving Earth. It has a crystalline structure consisting of some unknown material. It's one of the most exquisitely beautiful things I've ever seen." Jack's eyes glazed, and he stared off into the distance.

"Let me see if I have understood what you have been explaining, Jack. It will be possible, when we reach our destination, for Luke to be restored to a freshly grown clone of himself, and you will be able to reclaim your body?" Nguma shook his head in disbelief.

"Yes, at least that's what I hope."

"Hey, it was really touch and go though. We couldn't get Uncle Jack to wake up after we uploaded him into the android. There were no detectable signs of brain activity. When you woke up, Dad, we all thought Uncle Jack was dead."

"I noticed that his eyes were twitching when we came back here to let you talk to Mum," Tiani said.

"Does this mean, my friend, that there may be two of you? That one may be a sapioid and the other a biological human?" Nguma's expression held a mixture of surprise and incredulity.

"Yes, that may be the case," Jack said, looking serious.

"Great Universe! You mean we will have to put up with two of you?"

"*You'll* have to put up with two of me. What about me? Just think of the arguments I'll have with myself," Jack laughed.

"Could be interesting," Kiera chortled.

"Okay, let's tidy up here and get back down below. There's nothing more we can do now. It's time to go back to sleep. We're way over our time limit." He regarded us all, looking serious again.

"What happens to us, Uncle Jack?" Tiani asked, looking anxious.

"I'll strap you and Julian into the bunks in the living unit with the appropriate documentation for when we reach Kalgarin. It's quite simple, I'll switch you off. You'll be switched back on again when we all wake up."

Despite being a sapioid, he regarded us with his business-as-usual face. Jack, the person in charge, was back.

"Who switches you off?" I asked.

"I do. I'll set the timer."

"Hey, sounds like boiling an egg," Julian said, grinning.

"Thanks, I'll remember that." He stood up and we followed suit. We tidied the lab and shut down the computers. Jack carefully placed the prototype that hopefully held all his consciousness, in a small storage box and slipped it into his top pocket. He did a final check around while we waited by the airlock. Kiera, Nguma and I had already suited up but had not yet put our helmets on.

Jack came over and put his hand on Nguma's shoulder. "Nguma, there is a spare capsule in each module, so you have the choice of going back to where you were or staying on deck twenty-six with us. What do you want to do? "

Nguma beamed at us all, "I would very much like to stay with you as long as it does not cause any problems."

"No. As soon as I program you in to our module, your record will be erased from where you were previously, and the computer will make a new record showing where you are now."

"So, it is decided. I will remain with you." He grinned at us.

"Okay, let's get back to our deck," Jack said, pressing the button.

We put our helmets on and filed into the airlock.

#

Once back on our deck, after stowing everything away, Jack went to settle Julian and Tiani onto the bunks. He'd found something suitable to strap them down—to keep them safe during the remainder of the voyage.

Kiera and I sat together in the bathroom, and I gave her a full account of what had transpired while she'd been missing; from when

Jack and I had emerged from suspension to when she'd just woken now. Afterwards, we just sat and held one another while we waited for Jack to finish up. I think we were too tired and overwhelmed to speak. I gently stroked her hair. A couple of hours ago, it had been my hair. Strange and unsettling as that was, even more strange was the fact my current body was only temporary. When I next awoke from hiber-sleep, all going to plan, I would, shortly afterwards, be back in my biological clone. I reflected on how lucky we were to have had spares. That, along with an extra clone cycle, had been one of the perks of the voyage. Back on Earth people could only be cloned twice. After that they have the choice of dying naturally or becoming a sapioid.

Jack stuck his head around the door frame, "Okay, it's good night time."

Kiera and I got up, and we joined Nguma on deck where he had thoughtfully withdrawn to—allowing us some time on our own. We traipsed in to where Julian and Tiani were lying, firmly strapped into the bunks in the living unit.

Nguma took Tiani's hand.

Tiani said, "You're part of our family now, Uncle Nguma. I'm looking forward to seeing you when we wake up." She smiled through tears.

Nguma released Tiani's hand and kissed her forehead. He stepped over to Julian and gently shook his hand. "You have all come to mean so much to me. I will treasure the time we have spent together. I very much look forward to seeing you all again soon. Good night, Tiani, good night, Julian. May your dreams be filled with serenity." He turned and strode out the door.

We said our tearful good nights, even Jack, and we stood and watched as Tiani and Julian, following Jack's instructions, closed their eyes. As Jack switched them off, I struggled to hold back tears.

I hated leaving them there like that, but their faces appeared so peaceful. I squeezed Kiera's hand and she squeezed back, giving me a wistful smile.

Nguma chose to be put back into suspension first. Before he laid down he turned and took Kiera's hand. "You have a special husband, remarkable children, and a truly loyal friend in Jack." He went to kiss Kiera's hand, but she threw her arms around him and hugged him. He turned his attention to me. "My heart will fill with joy when I next meet with you, my friend." He embraced me before turning to Jack. "You have given me my life back, Jack. I can now let go of the memory of my dead wife, of the hopeless idea that she can be brought back to me." He turned and gave me a wistful smile. "Part of me was aware the chip was empty. When you first woke me, I needed to cling to the belief she was there and she would remain with me. I thank you both for letting me hold that belief until I was ready to let it go. I will always remember your great kindness, my friends, and you will remain in my heart forever."

Kiera wiped her eyes.

Jack, embarrassed, studied his feet before he raised his eyes and said, "Thank you, Nguma. Your help and knowledge have been invaluable. You have a firm place in my heart too." He stepped forward and, taking Nguma's hand in both of his own, shook it warmly.

"Sleep well, Uncle Nguma," I said, smiling.

His face radiated bliss and contentment as he laid down in the capsule. He was still smiling and waving as the canopy slid into place.

Jack put Kiera into suspension next. We kissed long and passionately just before Jack pressed the button initiating the canopy's closure. When she'd gone, I turned to Jack, "Well, that's that." I still had conflicting emotions about Jack's sacrifice, but he—on the surface at least—appeared totally calm, seemingly prepared and unfazed by whatever fate held in store for him. I stepped over to him, put my arms around him, and gave him a final hug. To my surprise he hugged me back. "Although I don't entirely approve of what you've done, I do realise what a great sacrifice you've made for Kiera and me."

He let go and stood back. "May have made." He grinned. "Maybe it will be all of you making a sacrifice in the future if you've got to put up with two of me."

"Great Universe! Are you trying to give me nightmares, Jack?"

"Okay, let's get you back to sleep," Jack said, matter-of-factly.

My capsule slid out and I laid down.

Epilogue

Lights blinked out sequentially down the length of deck twenty-six, and the air-conditioning breathed out a final sigh.

'The rest was silence.' William Shakespeare

The End

Glossary

Crawler: the common name for a small ant-sized repair robot correctly known as a robo-critter, specifically designed to carry out repairs in electrical circuitry.

Nano-gen: a regenerative technology consisting of the introduction of specific nano-genocytes into the bloodstream, usually carried out between the ages of fifty to sixty. It regresses the body's biological age by thirty years and allows humans to live three times their previous life spans before having to undergo uploading to either an unimprinted clone or a non-biological android. Uploading into clones is limited to two cycles by law. Once the final cycle is completed, humans have the choice to die or be uploaded into an android.

Zark: a swear word derived from the slang term for an illegal clone in reference to Thomas K Zarkingworth. Jailed for creating illegal human clones in 2040, Zarkingworth subsequently suicided in prison. All of the clones he created failed to survive to adulthood.

About The Author

The discovery of accurate speech recognition software allowed me to begin writing in late 2011. My first story, a piece of flash fiction entitled "What If", was published in the Australian online magazine AntipodeanSF in 2012. I write speculative fiction short stories with an emphasis on science-fiction.

Since my passions are science, nature, animals and all things science sci-fi, my stories reflect these interests.

I live in sunny Western Australia with my family and our cat, Tilda.

"Upload" is my first novel.

Find out more at: <http://christaleyes.com>